W9-CJY-942

The Summer Cottage

Books by Susan Kietzman

THE GOOD LIFE

A CHANGING MARRIAGE

THE SUMMER COTTAGE

EVERY OTHER WEDNESDAY

Published by Kensington Publishing Corporation

The Summer Cottage

Susan Kietzman

KENSINGTON BOOKS
www.kensingtonbooks.com

KENSINGTON BOOKS are published by

Kensington Publishing Corp.
119 West 40th Street
New York, NY 10018

Copyright © 2015 by Susan Kietzman

All rights reserved. No part of this book may be reproduced in any form or by any means without the prior written consent of the Publisher, excepting brief quotes used in reviews.

All Kensington titles, imprints, and distributed lines are available at special quantity discounts for bulk purchases for sales promotion, premiums, fund-raising, educational, or institutional use.

Special book excerpts or customized printings can also be created to fit specific needs. For details, write or phone the office of the Kensington Sales Manager: Attn. Sales Department. Kensington Publishing Corp., 119 West 40th Street, New York, NY 10018. Phone: 1-800-221-2647.

Kensington and the K logo Reg. U.S. Pat. & TM Off.

eISBN-13: 978-1-61773-550-9
eISBN-10: 1-61773-550-7
Kensington Electronic Edition: June 2015

ISBN-13: 978-1-4967-0998-1
ISBN-10: 1-4967-0998-5
First Kensington Trade Paperback Printing: June 2015

10 9 8 7 6

Printed in the United States of America

To my parents, Tyler and Frances, and my brothers,
Tip and David, who all swam to the raft with me.

And to Ted, as always.

ACKNOWLEDGMENTS

I thank my agent, Loretta Weingel-Fidel, for sharing with me her wealth of experience and knowledge. And I thank my editor, John Scognamiglio, for his keen insight.

My family and friends continue to astonish me with their support. Thank you, again and again.

CHAPTER 1

JULY 2003

Helen Street pulled her gray Volvo station wagon off the road and onto the patch of dead grass that had always served as the driveway for her mother's shoreline cottage. As she turned off the car, Helen glanced at her mother, who was buckled into the seat beside her. Claire was asleep, her head in an uncomfortable-looking position against the window, her mouth open but silent. Helen opened the driver's side door, stepped out, and stretched her arms to the sky, breathing in the familiar salted air that confirmed she had arrived. As it always did, the seaside air filled her with an urgent longing to shed her shoes and run across the street to the beach, through the warm sand, and into the cool waters of Long Island Sound. Instead, she walked to the house, fishing the cottage key out of her pocket on the way, and then pulled open the squeaky screen door to unlock the wood door that opened into the kitchen. Met by a musty scent, Helen walked swiftly through the downstairs rooms, opening every window that would. She then climbed the stairs to the narrow hallway leading to the four bedrooms, constructed like the rest of the cottage with vertical pine paneling, darkened by close to a century of sun. Helen tugged at the bedroom window shades, whose quick retreat left her squinting in the sudden brightness. Energized by the light, Helen rushed through the rooms, opening windows and holding them in place with the worn wood props that rested in the sills when not in use. Her father had purchased the dowels at the long-gone hardware store in town, and Helen, at ten, had helped him cut them and then coat them with shellac. Successful in opening fourteen of sixteen windows, Helen dashed down the stairs, as quickly as she had every summer morning of her childhood, and back outside into the sunshine. A quick look at the car revealed that her mother was still asleep, unaware still of the house and the sense of optimism it evoked, or had once evoked, in every member of the Thompson family.

Helen and her three siblings had spent their summers at the cottage that had been in their mother's family for three generations. Claire, at seventy-nine and widowed for five years, had always used the name Gaines, her maiden name, for herself, but everyone at the beach referred to the house as the Thompson cottage, a head nod to those who lived there, to those they knew. Claire was the only one who called it the Gaines cottage, but she did so less and less frequently, as it was never acknowledged, and, obviously, never took.

Helen grabbed the collapsible, aluminum wheelchair from the back of the car and placed it next to the rear passenger door. She pushed and pulled it into shape and then set its brakes. She then gently opened the door that held Claire's heavy head and twig-like body. "Mother," she said quietly. "Mother, we're here."

Claire opened her eyes and blinked several times before speaking. "Where," she said, eyes closed again.

"At the cottage." Helen supported her mother's body with one hand while she opened the door wide with the other. "We're at the cottage."

"I must have dozed off," said Claire, opening her eyes wide, and then, after a moment, wiping the saliva from her chin with the back of her thumb.

"Yes," said Helen, reaching over her mother to unbuckle the seatbelt.

Slowly, together—Claire insisting she do it herself and Helen offering encouragement and balance support—they moved from the passenger seat to the wheelchair. Claire landed with a thud. "I'm so tired of this."

"I know you are," said Helen, pushing her toward the house. "Let's get you settled on the porch. There's a lovely sea breeze."

Once in the kitchen—Helen had run back to the car for her mother's walker—Claire was able to maneuver her way through the dining room and living room and onto the screened-in porch. Helen helped Claire into her favorite spot, an old wicker armchair with faded floral fabric covering the back and seat cushions. Helen then pulled the cracked leather ottoman into place underneath her mother's frail legs. "There," said Helen.

"It is a glorious day," said Claire, breathing heavily from Helen's exertion. "Have you seen the beach yet?"

"No," said Helen. "Perhaps I'll run down before I unload the car."

"Do that," said her mother, closing her eyes. "I'll be fine."

"I'll just be a minute then."

"Take your time, Helen. I'm not going anywhere."

Helen walked outside with the blue and white-checked cotton throw that had spent the winter on the back of the couch and shook the dust from it. She returned to the porch and draped it over her mother's lap. "Are you settled?"

"Yes," said Claire. "Go to the beach."

Helen stepped back outside and eased the screen door shut behind her. She sat on the front steps, removed her running shoes and white ankle socks, and set them down on the slate paving stones at her feet. She walked gingerly across the hot street, along the grassy right-of-way, and down the dozen cement steps to the beach. As a child, she had routinely leaped off the seawall to the sand, a shortcut taught to her by her brother, Thomas. At forty, Helen was content to jump from the second step up from the beach, her feet sinking into the warm sand on impact. Feeling more like a liquid than a solid, the sand filled the gaps between her toes. Helen shielded her eyes from the sun with her hand and looked at the horizon, taking in the familiar islands, rocks, wood pilings, and boats moored in the inlet. The raft bobbed in the distance, waiting for eager swimmers to climb its ladder and sun themselves on its deck, to jump from its diving board. Helen looked down the beach to the left, then to the right. She spun around to check out the houses atop the wall, with their rectangular screened-in porches facing the water. Many were built in the 1920s—the Thompson cottage was one of the first in a neighborhood that had managed to withstand the 1938 hurricane and every other tropical storm that had made its way up the Eastern seaboard since.

The cottages bore the marks of bad weather and of cold, salty winters: peeling paint, rotting window sashes, curved, discolored wood shingles. Sitting on beachfront property, the cottages, if in top condition, would have been worth more than most people could afford. The lots alone would fetch more than a million dollars apiece. But the long-time residents weren't selling, even when offered twice the going rate by New York bankers and Internet entrepreneurs. This was not a tear-down neighborhood like Rocky Point, where the turn-of-the-last-century cottages had been razed and replaced by gleaming glass, shiny steel, and plumbed walls. The cottages at Little Crescent Beach were comfortable cottages, full of sand from the beach and hearty families from New England, who did their own maintenance on their houses and knew their neighbors, breezily lending tools and advice and sharing stories and their favorite warm weather recipes. Many of them had family money that was securely tucked away for retirement or into savings accounts for the children, who were now grown-ups themselves. Their everyday money, the husbands' salaries, had been used over the years on the same things—upgrades to their "city" homes, the houses they lived in ten months of the year, orthodontia, boarding school and college tuition, secondhand cars their offspring had driven to their summer jobs. Whatever was leftover had gone, still went, to the grocery store that had supplied the hamburgers and hotdogs, barbequed chicken, watermelon, marshmallows, and tonic water to the summer community and all its weekend guests for fifty years, and to the drive-in theater that featured family movies every weeknight in July and August.

Helen again faced the water and then strode toward it. She winced as her tender feet moved from the soft sand over the rounded pebbles at the shoreline. She hesitated for just a few seconds before walking into the water right up to her knees. Placing her hands on her hips in a tacit, unconscious display of satisfaction, she closed her eyes. She was back at the cottage with the entire summer ahead of her. And this year, if her mother got her way, Helen's three siblings would be arriving over the next several days for the Fourth of July weekend. Helen had not seen her brother, Thomas, or her sister, Charlotte, since their father's funeral five years before. And her sister, Pammy, while living less than a two-hour drive from Helen's home in the Connecticut hills, had visited just twice in the last year, in spite of knowing how much her company meant to Helen, in spite of recently being told that their mother would not see 2004. Helen talked to Pammy once a week or so on the phone, but Pammy kept the conversation focused on herself and day-to-day light details rather than larger life issues.

When Helen returned to the house, Claire was again asleep. Concerned, but not alarmed, Helen looked at her mother and was struck, almost matter-of-factly as Helen was sometimes, by the thought that Claire was dying. She slept many hours of the day, as well as the night, exhausted by months of treatment and now by months without it. She was as mentally acute, it seemed, as she always had been, although the pain medication she occasionally let Helen talk her into taking on her bad days made her drowsy. She was increasingly resigned to her imminent fate, a clear indication of her level of battle fatigue. Claire, until mid-March, when her straight-talking oncologist told her the chemotherapy had made no difference, had never before given up, on anything.

She had been an Olympic-quality athlete, Claire had, cut in the final round of the selection process for the 1948 American women's swim team. Had she been chosen for the team, she would have swum the 100-meter freestyle and 4 x 100-meter freestyle relay in London that summer with the other top female swimmers in the country. But an ill-timed flu and a bad turn at the 50-meter mark in the qualifying round smashed her dreams. Claire had continued to swim in national meets for the following few years, hopeful that she would qualify for the games in 1952. But by then, the younger swimmers were simply faster and better trained than she was in her late twenties. Had the selection process been made on effort or determination alone, Claire would not only have made the team, but also served as its captain.

Helen gently tucked the blanket around Claire's tiny frame. She then jogged back outside to retrieve their bags and cooler of groceries from the car. After the car was empty, Helen hauled their large cloth duffels upstairs—Claire's to the front room and Helen's to the pink room behind her. Helen returned to the kitchen, where she unpacked the cooler and the brown paper grocery bags that held dinner and breakfast materials. She and her mother would go to town the next morning for more food when they had the final count for the upcoming weekend. After folding the bags, which they reused to line the plastic kitchen garbage bin, and placing them in the cupboard closest to the six-burner stove, Helen walked back out to the porch and picked up a copy of *The New Yorker* magazine from the previous summer. She put her bare feet up on the wicker table and flipped through the pages, waiting for her mother to awaken.

CHAPTER 2

1973

As soon as the bedroom was light, Helen, who had just turned ten, climbed down off the top bunk. She gave her thirteen-year-old sister, Pammy, who slept on the bottom, a nudge. "Wake up," Helen whispered urgently.

Pammy rubbed her eyes and yawned. "What time is it?"

"Who cares?" said Helen, stripping off her pajamas. "The sun's out."

Pammy lifted her head and shoulders off the mattress to look out the window. "Barely, Helen. The sun is barely out. It's dawn."

"Let's go crabbing," said Helen, still naked. She had the body of a recent graduate of fourth grade, nipples flat on her chest, a slightly protruding stomach, hairless underarms and crotch. She crossed the room and reached into their shared bureau for clean underwear, then grabbed yesterday's shirt and shorts from the floor. She was dressed in a flash.

"You're crazy."

"Come on, Pammy. If we go now, the crabs will still be sleeping. We'll get millions of them."

"You go," said Pammy, lowering her head back onto the pillow. "I'll come soon."

Helen put her hands on her nonexistent hips. "You're going back to sleep. I can tell."

"Just for a few minutes. Then I'll meet you at the docks." Pammy flipped onto her back.

"You'll miss all the fun, Pammy."

"I'll have fun later," said Pammy, sleep in her voice.

"Promise you'll come?"

"I promise. I'll meet you at the docks in"—Pammy squinted at her Timex watch—"twenty minutes."

Doubtful but fleetingly satisfied, Helen left the bedroom, tiptoed down the hallway and then descended the stairs, carefully avoiding the fifth one from the top, which creaked. She walked quietly through the living room and onto the screened-in porch. She had her hand on the screen door when she heard her mother, another early riser, call from the kitchen. "Helen, is that you?" Helen didn't answer. She didn't want orange juice. She didn't want cereal. She didn't want to be quizzed about her tennis match with Amanda the day before. Her mother cared who won these friendly, casual games much more than Helen did. Helen hesitated for just a moment, and then she opened the porch door and launched herself out into the day.

"Helen?"

Claire heard the door slam and shook her head. Day after summer day her youngest daughter rose with the birds and bolted out into the world without breakfast or as little as a morning greeting. She was a go-getter, her Helen, with energy and drive that would serve her well in life. Claire took the last sip of coffee from her mug and returned to her grocery list. A moment later, she glanced out the kitchen window to watch Helen, with a plastic cleaning bucket containing crabbing line held tightly in her right hand, run barefoot down the road to the docks.

Helen veered off the road at the Tetreau property, carrying her bucket through the itchy beach grass on her way to the breakwater that protected the docks from storm waves and strong currents. It was low tide, as she already knew, so it would be easy to find the mussels she used as bait. They attached themselves, often in clusters, to the granite rocks that had been hauled out of the now-abandoned quarry in town. Within a minute, Helen had two dozen of them in her bucket. On her way back, Helen waded into the water to find a good smashing rock and to feed the whale. The whale was actually a large rock protruding out of the water. It was split right where a real whale's mouth would be, and Helen routinely fed it, as if it were a living, breathing mammal. On this day, she dumped a half dozen mussels into its mouth, patted its head, and then began her search for the right rock, which, once spotted, she retrieved and put into the bucket alongside the mussels and her line. She ran back to the road and then across the strip of grass that separated it from the first dock. Once she reached the dewy, wide pine planks, Helen slowed to a walk. Her stubbed left big toe, which she had caught on an uneven plank the other day, was still healing. At this leisurely pace Helen was able to listen, for the first time that morning, to the sounds of the shoreline, the water lapping against the dock pilings, the seagulls calling to each other. In her haste to get to her work, to catch as many crabs as she could, she often missed these pleasant reminders of where she was and what she was doing. Helen made a mental note to be more mindful of her surroundings, something her father told them was important to the enjoyment of life. She reached out to touch the pilings with her free hand as she passed them, counting them and the boats and noticing the empty slips that were usually occupied by whalers owned by the Wallaces, Smiths, and Johansons. They were out fishing, the teenage sons with their fathers. Helen had heard and seen them walking down the street past her house when it was still dark, fishing gear in hand, talking in hushed voices that carried up to her bedroom window anyway.

When she reached the end of the dock, Helen lay down on her stomach and peered into the clear water. At first, she saw nothing but a fish head, some green seaweed, and the submerged Coke can she had noticed the day before. But slowly, as her eyes adjusted to the slight ripple on the surface, she could see the crabs on and around the fish head. Some ate voraciously, one bite after another, while others were more cautious, taking a piece of meat and then scurrying off the head and into the relative safety of a nearby clump of eel grass. Prey assessed, Helen transferred the mussels, the smashing rock, and her crabbing line from her bucket to the dock. She gingerly descended the rickety dock ladder to fill her bucket with water. Safely back on the dock, she set the half-filled bucket down, smashed a lone mussel and then pulled away the bits of blue-black shell to expose the orange flesh the crabs adored. Meticulously, she tied the fractured mussel onto the end of her crabbing string, and then dropped it into the water, where it slowly sank to the bottom. Within five seconds, a large fiddler crab was upon it, eating heartily. Ever so gently, Helen inched the mussel and its hungry companion to the surface. In the air and halfway to the confines of Helen's blue plastic prison, the crab suddenly let go of the bait and dropped with a plop back into the water. "Rats!" she said.

Determined to lure that very crab back, to best him as her mother would say, Helen re-baited her line and threw it into the seaweed where her prey had scampered. In an instant, the same crab crept toward the mussel cautiously. Hearing the hum of a distant engine, Helen glanced up and saw a boat rounding the breakwater and approaching the docks. She waved as it slowed down, in observance of the five-mile-per-hour no-wake zone, to glide into a slip at the other dock. She recognized the men, not by name, but she had seen them many times before. They lived up in the Heights, like most of the boat owners at the second dock. Their dock was newer and easily accessible by cars, which the Heights residents parked along a sandy, unpaved section of the road that wound through the Little Crescent Beach community and ended at their dock. They didn't linger, the Heights residents, in Helen's neighborhood. They had their own swimming area, their own dock, their own way of doing things. Many of them lived at the beach throughout the year in neat, well-kept ranch houses, which Helen had observed just once on a long bike ride. When she had asked her older brother, Thomas, about the Heights people when she returned from her ride, he cautioned her to stay away. There were wolves that roamed the wooded areas adjacent to the streets, hungry wolves. And even though Thomas was always kidding around about stuff like that, Helen had never ventured back. From the tracks, when she watched trains, she could see the Heights houses and their occupants, sitting in screened-in porches, gardening, mowing the lawn, doing all the things everyone at her beach did. But mingling with the people who lived on the other side of the tracks was tacitly discouraged. They were winter people, and the Thompsons and their immediate neighbors were summer folk.

Helen looked back down at her bait, which now hosted two crabs, and reached for her bucket. She drew up the line, faster this time, knowing she could lose one, but might keep the other. Out of the water, both crabs continued to snack, seemingly oblivious to their new, drier environment. Helen lowered them into the bucket and gave the line a quick shake, dislodging the crabs from the mussel. Helen watched them as she untied the mussel and tossed it into the bucket. She always gave her guests a meal.

"Hey!" called Pammy, as she walked down the dock an hour later. Helen, in the middle of tying another mussel onto her line, looked up at her sister. "I know," Pammy said as soon as she reached Helen. "I slept longer than twenty minutes. You know me."

"Yes, I do," said Helen, focused on her work. "The snooze queen."

Pammy walked past her sister and peered over the edge of the dock at the fish head. Fish, dead or alive, reminded her of the Johanson brothers, especially Michael, who was seventeen, blond, and at least six feet tall. He talked to her on the beach sometimes and laughed at her jokes. Once, he smacked at a horsefly that had landed on her back, but he missed it. Pammy liked to think that there had been no horsefly, that he simply wanted to touch her back with his big hands that were rough from yard work and tanned from the summer sun. She pretended she was his girlfriend, instead of big-breasted Tammy Jennings, who lived down the street; Tammy had acknowledged Pammy just once in the last two summers, when she needed to know what time it was. Pammy looked down at her own chest, hoping the padding from the training bra made it look like she had something. That spring, she had pleaded with her mother to replace her undershirts with training bras, insisting that all the thirteen-year-olds wore them. *I don't care what other thirteen-year-olds are doing,* her mother had said, warning

Pammy about the pitfalls of peer pressure. But Claire had nonetheless acquiesced and taken Pammy to Bell's Department Store, where they bought a package of three lacy bras, one each in pink, white, and yellow.

"Get the bucket!" shouted Helen. "I got another one!" Pammy brought the bucket to Helen, who lifted the exposed mussel and the small crab that was tearing away at it out of the water. "Slip it underneath, Pammy! I'm going to lose it!" Pammy held the bucket under the crab, which Helen gently shook until it dropped in with the others. Twelve, no thirteen crabs, Pammy counted. She smiled at Helen, who diligently tied another mussel onto her line.

"Keep this up, Helen, and you may get a hundred."

"They're really biting today, Pammy. Do you want some of my string? You can catch them with me. We may need another bucket, though."

"I think I'll just watch you." Pammy sat down on the dock, her back against a piling, and tilted her face toward the sun. She closed her eyes and listened to Helen drop her line back into the water.

"You're not watching, Pammy. You're sleeping again."

"I'm imagining. I'm imagining you're catching a crab right now. Look at your line."

"There's nothing there," said Helen, peering down through the seaweed at her unoccupied mussel.

"Look again, Helen."

"Hey," said Helen, "here comes your boyfriend." Pammy opened her eyes and shielded them from the sun. In the distance, she saw the Johansons' boat, speeding toward the dock. Pammy ran her fingers through her hair, then tucked her shirt into her shorts. "You've got some toothpaste on your cheek," said Helen, teasing her sister.

"I do not."

"I'm so glad I don't like boys yet," said Helen, looking again into the water. "Charlotte says it will happen any day now." Charlotte, their seventeen-year-old sister, knew everything about boys.

"Charlotte's right," said Pammy, retying the loose laces of one of her Keds sneakers.

"It's too much trouble," said Helen, pulling up her line. The large crab that had been circling her bait suddenly snatched it when she wasn't looking. This time, Helen decided to wrap the line around twice.

"It's no trouble," Pammy said, "especially when Tammy Jennings is still in bed asleep. This crabbing idea has its merits, Helen."

The Johansons backed their boat into the slip, then cut the engine. Pammy waved enthusiastically and walked down the dock to meet them. Dr. Johanson, an orthopedic surgeon, said good morning to Pammy, calling her Miss Thompson as he always did because he didn't know her first name, and then, addressing his sons, told them he'd see them back at the house. After he left, Pammy, Michael, and his younger brother William, the boys with three large bluefish in their hands, walked back toward Helen. "Hey, Helen," said Michael. "Catch anything?"

"A few," Helen replied, not looking up from her task.

"Pammy tells me you have thirteen. That's not bad. But if I remember correctly, you had sixteen by this time yesterday."

"That's because Pammy stayed in bed yesterday," said Helen, looking up at her sister and smiling.

"I did not," Pammy retorted. "I got up early and went to the store with Mom."

"Anyway, I had no distractions," said Helen, using a word she had heard her mother use to describe Charlotte's boyfriends.

"It's a wonder I can catch anything then," said Michael, turning to leave. "I've got more distractions than I can handle." At that, Michael and William let out loud, quick laughs. Pammy laughed too, more for encouragement for the boys than as an indication of her comprehension. And then the boys were gone, walking briskly to join their father who was walking along the same road Helen traveled to reach the dock. Poles in hand, the doctor seemed to be in no hurry. As soon as the boys caught up with him, however, he quickened his pace, eager perhaps for the bacon and egg breakfast waiting for them at home. Every morning Mrs. Johanson cooked a tummy-filling breakfast for her men. Plus, she was the prettiest and nicest mother in the neighborhood. Helen had once been invited in for French toast, which Mrs. Johanson made with a real baguette.

When Helen had shared this tip with her mother, Claire had agreed to try it. But she never did, instead favoring the thin slices of white her husband loved with syrup and powdered sugar on Saturday mornings.

Pammy watched the boys go and then sat down next to Helen. She looked down into the water, head in hands, bent elbows on crisscrossed legs. "You got one," she said. "Pull it up."

CHAPTER 3

2003

Helen put the magazine aside when she heard her mother shift in her chair. Claire enjoyed sleeping in the car and in her bed, but recently she did not like to wake up in what she considered to be a strange place, which the other day meant the couch in her own living room, but mostly referred to chairs in medical building waiting areas. And while the cottage that had been the Thompson family summer retreat since before Helen was born was far from strange, it would be vaguely unfamiliar this first visit this year, Helen guessed, due to her mother's exhaustion. Helen switched chairs to be next to her mother. As soon as Claire opened her eyes, blinking in the afternoon sun that filled the porch with the golden light she loved, Helen laid her hand upon her mother's shoulder. Claire looked in the direction of her daughter, the medication she had taken to ease her pain that morning still working its way through her system. "Did you have a nice rest?" Helen asked, knowing the sound of her voice brought her mother back faster.

Claire nodded her head then, mentally grounded, placed her hand on top of her daughter's. "What time is it?"

Helen looked at her watch. "About four."

"Yes," said Claire, sounding pleased with Helen's answer.

"Would you like some tea?"

"I don't think so." Claire was now fully awake and looking past her daughter at the giant maple tree across the street. "I'd like to see the beach."

"Good idea," said Helen, rising from her chair. "Do you want to walk or shall I put you in your chair?"

"The chair, I think. I'm a bit unsteady on my feet."

Helen grabbed the walker that was resting against the wall and positioned it in front of her mother's wicker chair. Claire grabbed on to the handles and slowly lifted herself until she was vertical. Helen, who had her right arm behind her mother's back to stop her from falling, knew better than to touch her. There was so little Claire could do herself. It was a daily discussion: how much she used to be able to do just a few short years ago compared with how little she could do now. And then there were the days that Claire wanted to talk about how strong she had been as a young woman—a couple times a week, it seemed to surface. Helen, who could have told her mother's story probably better than her mother could at this point, routinely listened attentively. Being her caregiver was more tolerable when Claire was in a good mood and chatted joyfully about her accomplishments. It was less so when she was achy and morose. On those days, she was tough on herself. Helen could do little to appease her at these times, Claire's agitation ending only with sleep.

"Let's head to the back door, for your chair, and then we'll go to the beach." Helen walked several steps behind her mother as Claire rolled and pushed her way toward the kitchen; Helen resisted the urge to walk in front, to set a pace her mother could not match. Once they reached the kitchen, it took Helen and Claire a few minutes to transfer from one transportation device inside the house to the other that Helen had placed just outside the back door. Claire sat down heavily. "There," said Helen, to ward off any complaints. "We're all set."

"You're all set," said Claire, looking up at her daughter. "I haven't been all damn set for three damn years."

"Mom," said Helen.

It had been three years and two months since Claire's diagnosis:

Her breast cancer had returned. She'd had a lumpectomy and radiation therapy in 1992 and had been diligent about her follow-up visits, always complying with the requests of her medical team, a word that she found ludicrous in this usage, and the wishes of her husband John, a pediatrician, even though she felt fine. And for eight years she had been fine—until the morning she noticed some bruising on her left breast. And when she inspected it with her fingers, she felt the mass under the skin. A month later, both breasts were gone. Two months after that, bald from chemotherapy and weak from the cancer's progression, she knew she would not recover. Those burdened with the unhappy diagnosis of secondary angiosarcoma had less than a one in five chance of survival. As a swimmer, she'd once considered twenty percent as fairly good odds in the pool. As a sick old woman, she knew better. "What day is it, Helen? Tuesday?"

"Exactly."

"And when is everyone coming?" They were rumbling along the grassy right-of-way now toward the beach. Claire's chair was what she jokingly called an all-terrain vehicle, with large nubby tires that traversed uneven ground almost as easily though certainly less steadily than flat pavement.

"They're coming in stages, Mom," said Helen, trying to be patient with this the fourth or fifth run-through of the weekend itinerary. "Pammy will be here tomorrow, and Charlotte is scheduled to arrive on Thursday afternoon. Thomas, if he does come, will be here on Saturday."

"We don't know if he's coming? I thought you said he was coming, Helen."

"You know Thomas, Mom. He never commits."

"He'll be here," said Claire as Helen stopped the chair several feet from the top of the seawall and set the brakes. "I do, indeed, know Thomas. He'll be here."

Helen nodded. "Do you want to stand?"

"Yes," said Claire. Helen held out her arm, and Claire held on to it as she lifted herself out of the chair. The cancer, which had spread from her breasts into her lungs and then into her bones, made breathing and moving, simply existing, an effort. Her legs, once strong enough to kick her body through the water to the raft in just over a minute, ignored her pleas for support, hanging from her fragile hip bones, as ineffectual as wind chimes on a still day. Helen and Claire both gazed out at the horizon.

"Top ten, I think," said Helen.

"I think so too."

"And it's only the end of June."

Claire smiled at her daughter. "Good old reliable Helen."

"What do you mean by that?"

"You know damn well what I mean," said Claire. "Let's sit on this top step a moment, so I can concentrate on breathing in this salty air. It's good for what ails me."

"So you keep telling me, Mom," said Helen, helping her mother sit and then encircling her shrunken waist with her arm.

They sat for several minutes, neither woman speaking, until Claire said, "It's times like this that I miss him the most."

"Me too."

"He was a good man, your father, a strong man."

"Yes."

"I keep wondering if I should have kept him home that night."

It was an evening they talked about more often than Helen cared to—a recurring, never-ending conversation, like those about Claire's swimming days and her cancer. When the phone rang at two in the morning the night their "city" home neighbor Joellen's daughter, Bethany, went into labor, it had been raining hard for several hours. *You can't go out in this,* Claire said at the time, mindful that her husband had been battling a bad cold for a week. But they had discussed the imminent birth, John and Claire, and agreed that he would go to the hospital, even though he had recently retired, instead of leaving Bethany in the capable hands of his young, taciturn partner. Normally, neither John nor his partner needed to be present in the hospital's birthing room, but Bethany was expecting triplets, the product of fertility drugs she had been taking for two years that had finally resulted in pregnancy. *He won't talk to her the way you would,* Joellen had said to John about his partner the day she knocked on the back door with a loaf of warm banana bread and the request that he preside over the birth of her grandchildren. So, John put on his galoshes that night, his heavy raincoat and hat, and drove to the hospital and helped with the delivery of the three small but healthy children, two girls and a boy. And he was just about home when a traveling salesman, drinking the last of six beers that had been sitting on the seat next to him, drove his rental car through a red light and into the driver's side of John's Jeep, killing him instantly.

"He wanted to deliver Bethany's babies," said Helen. "There's nothing you could have done." The tears that rimmed her eyes each time she had this conversation with her mother reappeared. She dabbed at them with the sleeve of her T-shirt.

Claire took hold of the railing at the side of the steps and slowly stood. "I think about it every time I see those children—although they are darling," she said. "After that night, I never again cared for banana bread."

Back at the house, Helen again settled her mother into the wicker chair on the porch. "How about that tea now?"

"Yes. I'd love some."

Helen busied herself in the kitchen while the water in the kettle boiled. She washed the lettuce for the dinner salad, set the dining room table for two, and peeled the summer squash, her mother's favorite vegetable. When the kettle whistled, Helen poured the hot water into two mugs that held Constant Comment tea bags and dunked the bags several times. She put the mugs on a tray, along with a salad plate of chocolate chip cookies she had made the night before, and walked back out to the porch. Wanting to change topics, to lighten her mother's dark mood, Helen kissed Claire on the forehead. "Well, what's that for?"

"Nothing," said Helen. "It just feels good to be back, doesn't it?"

"Very good," said Claire, taking the bait. "I love it here."

"We all do."

When the phone rang, fracturing the easy silence that had fallen between them, Helen started, spilling tea in her lap. "Rats!" she said, setting the mug down on the cork coaster on the table next to her before walking to the corner of the living room, where the white Princess phone that hung on the wall continued to ring loudly.

It was her husband, Charles, calling from the campground pay phone in the Adirondacks. He and their sons, Todd and Ned, were having a successful fishing trip, and he wanted to know if they could stay another couple days. And, even though he had been hesitant when the boys suggested he leave his cell phone in the locked glove compartment of the car, Charles had not missed the stream of phone calls from his insurance agency. He told his seven employees before he left that this was a real vacation, and that if they had an emergency, they could call his wife who would be able to find him. He had never done that before, and didn't know if he would ever do it again. But he was grateful for the quiet, for the uninterrupted time with his boys. "The boys are getting along so well."

"They always do."

"You know that's not true, and you know what I mean," said Charles. "Maybe there really *is* something to your fresh-air theory." Helen laughed. "How is everything going there?"

"Fine," said Helen, wishing as she had since her teenage years that there was another phone in the house, one she could talk on without everyone within earshot listening in. It was Claire who insisted that the phone be installed in a central location. *It's easier to get to,* she had said, also noting that no one in their family needed to keep secrets. They had not had a phone in the house at all until 1970, when John finally convinced his wife, after a fire in the Heights destroyed three cottages, that emergencies really did happen.

"Have you heard from Thomas?"

"No."

"He'll come, Helen. He's almost as competitive as your mother. There's no way he'll leave the house and the rest of her estate to the three of you—even if he doesn't need the money."

"I agree."

"Is Pammy still coming tomorrow, and Charlotte on Thursday? How about the boys and I show up on Friday, so you girls can have some fun together before our arrival?"

Helen smiled at the phone. "Okay. But you will owe me."

"That I can handle," said Charles. "Add it to my tab."

"Bring us some fish."

"You can count on it," he said. "And Helen? You're a good egg."

"Yeah," she said. "So I've heard. Give the boys my love."

"They send theirs, honey."

"We'll see you Friday then?"

"Yes. And I'm serious about that fish."

"You better be."

"Love you," he said.

"I know you do," said Helen, uncomfortable still to confess her love for Charles in front of her mother.

"Say it," he said, kidding her.

"It," said Helen, hanging up the phone.

"Delayed?" her mother asked, unable to keep up with the gist of the conversation.

"By choice." Helen returned to her seat and picked up her mug. "The fish are biting, and they can't bear to leave."

"That's too bad," said Claire, the corners of her droopy mouth sinking lower.

"I think it's great. Now we can have a slumber party. No boys allowed."

CHAPTER 4

1973

Another session of prolific crabbing behind her, Helen returned her bucket and line to the dirt-floor garage and ran into the cottage to change into her suit. "Hi, parents!" she called on her way up the stairs, as Thomas did when he walked into the house at dinnertime. Claire and John were sitting on the porch, drinking coffee and reading the newspaper, her mother *The New York Times* and her father *The Wall Street Journal.* They both lifted their hands in greeting, but knew better than to attempt conversation with Helen, who was very busy in the morning. Dressed in the floral Speedo her mother had selected for her at Bell's Department Store, she bolted out the door and sprinted to the clothesline. She pulled at her salt-water-stiff beach towel, sending the wood clothespins fastened to its corners flying into the air and onto the damp grass. She then flew across the street and leaped off the seawall onto the sand. Just past nine o'clock, the beach was still deserted, save for the group of young swimmers struggling to backstroke out to the raft. "Keep your heads down!" yelled their instructor, Art, who had taught classes at the beach the last three summers. "You've got to relax. Kick, now, and pull with those arms!"

The flailing, sputtering children, half-submerged at any point in time, slowly wiggled their bodies toward the raft. When Art stopped talking and resumed swimming, some of the stragglers flipped over onto their stomachs and swam freestyle for a few yards in an effort to catch up with the others. No longer a participant in swim classes, Helen was happy to watch from the beach. She had been in Art's class the previous summer, and had graduated, he said, with flying colors. Helen's mother had thrown her into the ocean when she was two, and she had been comfortable in the water since. Her mother told her she wanted Helen to be confident and able if she fell off a boat in deep water, but Helen knew her mother really wanted her to follow in her aquatic footsteps, or, at the very least, to be "the best she could be," Claire's goal for all her children. Helen overheard her mother one day proudly telling her father that Helen could swim circles around most of the kids on the beach.

Helen spread her towel on the sand and lay upon it, letting the sun warm her back and legs. Minutes later, she flipped. Restless and uninterested in sunbathing, Helen got up off her towel and walked down to the water. She walked in up to the middle of her calves, then stopped. It was still a little early for a swim. She waded out onto the hard, damp sand closest to the water and began walking at a slow pace down the beach, with her head down and her eyes focused on the tiny, iridescent stones that lined the shore. Amongst them, the carefully trained beachcomber could find sea glass, the coveted treasure Helen and Pammy collected with a passion.

"Did you find any yet?" It was Pammy, yelling from the top of the cement stairs that led down to the beach.

"Tons!" Helen yelled back.

Pammy skittered down the stairs and jogged the beach to catch up to her sister. "You're a liar, Helen Thompson," said Pammy, stopping next to Helen, breathing hard. "Let me see."

Helen held out her closed fist, turned it over, and opened her fingers. There, in her damp palm were three beer-bottle brown pieces of sea glass, the most plebian variety. "You believed me for a second though, didn't you?"

"Not really. Where did you start?"

"Johansons' steps." Helen was again slowly walking, her gaze downward, searching.

"I call the other direction—Johansons' steps to Tetreaus' steps," Pammy said, arms across her training bra.

"You better start now then," said Helen, "because I'm heading there next."

"But I just called it, Helen."

"Yeah, but you won't do any serious searching today. You know who just came down to the beach."

Pammy glanced back over her shoulder and saw Michael sitting on the bottom step of the cement stairs that led from his waterside cottage to the beach. "Who cares?" Pammy shrugged one shoulder. "He was snotty to me at the docks yesterday. Charlotte told me to ignore him."

"I'll bet you my ice cream truck money that you can't do that."

Pammy hesitated. "What do I have to do to get your quarter?"

"Not talk to him when we pass by."

Pammy bit her lower lip. "Done," she said, holding out her hand for Helen to shake. Their brother Thomas told them that a handshake was the only universally accepted deal sealer.

"Let's go then," said Helen, now walking in the opposite direction. Pammy fell into step beside her, eyes locked to the ground. The only way she was going to win this bet was to avoid eye contact with Michael. If she looked at him, if her brown eyes met his green eyes, she was toast.

"Rats," said Helen. Pammy looked up. "He's going up." Together they watched Michael's tanned torso ascend the steps, cross over the short stretch of grass in front of the house, and disappear into their screened-in porch. Pammy grinned.

"I think I'm going to have a Chocolate Éclair after lunch and a Strawberry Shortcake after dinner."

Helen stopped and pouted. She had made her bed that morning, and last night set the table and dried all the family dinner dishes for that quarter. Her father had carefully extracted it from his pocket after the last pot was put away in the dish pantry and handed it to her with ceremony, commending her effort. *Nice work, Helen,* he had said, adding that her ice cream the following day would taste better because she'd earned it. "That's not fair," she said. "He isn't even here to ignore."

"The bet was to not talk to him when we passed by. You said nothing about his presence."

"It's still not fair."

"Life isn't fair," said Pammy, repeating something their mother often told them. "Get used to it." Helen resumed walking. "Look," said Pammy, knowing what it felt like to lose a quarter because Charlotte routinely tricked Pammy out of hers. Charlotte didn't even need the money, since she had a job or a boyfriend who would pay her way. She did it for sport. "Mom asked me to organize the garage today. I'll let you do it, and you can earn another quarter."

Helen smiled. "Yeah?"

"Yeah."

"Okay, thanks, Pammy."

Together they walked down the beach, quietly searching for more glass that had been shaped and smoothed by the sea. Even though Pammy was three years older than Helen, she rarely made Helen feel like a kid, and hardly ever told her to get lost. Their older sister Charlotte had little time for either of them. Seventeen and consumed with boys, she slept late, often until noon, enervated from the previous night's party or marathon kissing session on the beach. When she finally arose, she simply could not speak to anyone until she'd had a cigarette and a Coke. Knowing the delicacy of her older sister's stomach, Helen, who was often making herself lunch when Charlotte first walked into the kitchen, would offer her older sister a bite of her sandwich, which was either egg or tuna salad, whatever Claire had prepared and stored in the fridge. Charlotte, inured to her sister's antics, would merely sneer and brush Helen off with a flick of her hand, as if coaxing a fruit fly to move on.

"Look," said Pammy, bending down to pick up a flat, royal blue piece. "I haven't seen this color in years." She held it up for Helen's inspection.

"Noxzema jar," said Helen, with authority.

"What?"

"That's what I call that color. Noxzema jar."

"You mean that blue jar of white stuff Charlotte washes her face with?"

"Exactly."

"I think you're right, Helen," said Pammy, holding the glass up to the sun. "In fact, I think there's a little bit of Noxzema still on here."

"Where?" said Helen, moving closer to Pammy.

"Made you look," said Pammy, triumphant.

Helen hesitated for a moment, then tagged her sister. "You're it!" she said, suddenly breaking into a run. Pammy pursued her, but couldn't catch Helen, who was not only faster, but also a master at running through sand. Fifty yards down the beach, Helen slowed to a jog and then collapsed at Shallow End. There, a sandbar stretched from the shore to Pearson's private dock, where the land suddenly dropped off twenty feet, enabling Old Man Pearson to sail his boat almost to his doorstep. A privilege, Helen was told, that was enormously important to him. Helen was only interested in Shallow End at low tide, when she could walk out into the water for what felt like a half mile and not wet the bottom of her bathing suit.

Within a minute, Pammy reached her sister and sat down next to her in the sand. For another minute, they both were silent, Pammy breathing hard still. Then she said, "Do you really think this piece came from a Noxzema jar?" Pammy held the blue glass to the sun for further analysis.

"No," said Helen. "Nobody but Charlotte uses that stuff. That huge, gross jar has been sitting on her bureau since last summer."

"What else is this color?"

"I don't know, Pammy. It's probably some kind of industrial glass?"

"Industrial glass?" asked Pammy, smiling.

"Glass used in industry," said Helen, pedantically.

"You are a dope." Pammy stood and brushed the sand off her legs.

"And you," said Helen, standing, setting her sea glass down in a neat pile on the sand and casually walking toward the water, "have bird poop all over the back of your shorts." Pammy craned her neck over her shoulder and looked down at the seat of her shorts, which was just as pink as when she put them on. "Made you look!" Helen shouted, as she took off into the water. She ran as fast as she could, not slowing until the water, now thigh-deep, pulled at her legs, forcing an end to her sprint. She leaped up one last time then dove under the surface, allowing the water to swallow her whole. The sand scraped against her stomach as she swam along the bottom. When she surfaced, she turned toward shore and saw Pammy, arms akimbo. "Come on!" Helen shouted. "It's not cold!"

"I can't. I don't have my suit on under my poop-stained shorts!"

"Are you naked under those short?" Helen shouted.

"You," Pammy said, laughing, "are disgusting."

"Yes," Helen said. "I can tell you're disgusted."

Helen waded back to the shore, and then the two Thompson girls started a slow walk back to their section of the beach. The Thompson family didn't own that section—no one owned the beach—but it was where they always sat, on their beach towels, in their sand chairs, under their umbrellas. Everyone had a regular spot. The cottagers that lived atop the seawall simply strolled down the steps in front of their houses and planted themselves. Those who lived across the street or down the road from the beach accessed the beach by the set of stairs closest to their houses and then camped out within fifty yards of the bottom step. Everyone knew where everyone else sat, and no one encroached on anyone else's unofficial turf. Summer after summer, this was the case. The only aberration occurred with renters.

They didn't show up very often, the renters, because most people in Helen's Little Crescent Beach neighborhood spent the summer at the shore. They packed up their shorts, T-shirts, and sandals; their bathing suits, towels, and suntan lotion; their perishable food items, and drove their station wagons out of their "city" home driveways on the last day of school and stayed at the beach until Labor Day. Every once in a while, one of the families Helen had known for as long as she could remember took a vacation elsewhere for part of the summer, or their teenagers had jobs or love interests in their hometowns. When this happened, their cottages typically sat vacant, waiting for their return. But occasionally, the cottages were rented or simply given to friends, neighbors, and coworkers. And the newcomers didn't know any of the rules. They carted their inflatable tubes and Styrofoam surfboards to the beach in wagons, their children often riding two-wheelers behind them. And they parked themselves on the sand wherever they found a free section of beach.

The first time Helen encountered a renter, she was taken aback and unsure how to proceed. One of the renter kids had his towel in the exact spot she usually laid her towel. Looking for advice, Helen had run back to the cottage to her parents, who were drinking coffee and reading their newspapers on the porch. "Someone's in our spot," she said.

John looked up first. "Pardon me, Helen?"

"On the beach," Helen said. "Someone is sitting in our spot."

Claire then raised her head and looked at her daughter. "Well, who is it? It is the Callahan cousins? Sometimes when they are visiting they sit wherever they darn well please."

"No one owns the beach, Helen," said John, looking at Claire over his bifocals.

"I don't know who it is," said Helen. "I think it might be renters."

Claire wrinkled her nose. "Tell them to move over."

"You may *not* tell them to move over," said John, gently but firmly as was his manner.

"Put your towel six inches from theirs then," said Claire. "That should send them a message."

"What kind of message are you looking to send, Claire?" John asked his wife. Claire looked back down at the newspaper in her hands. "Find another spot, Helen. There is plenty of room down there, so I know you won't have any trouble securing a portion of sand for your towel and the required ounces of saltwater for your body in which to swim."

Helen crossed her arms over her chest. "I don't like it."

"Who does?" asked Claire from behind the sports section.

"It's just for one day," said John.

"That's right," said Claire, laying the paper down on her outstretched legs. "Tomorrow morning, you're going to beat them to the beach and lay out your towel wherever you please."

Helen looked at her dad. "Can I do that?"

"You can lay your towel anywhere you wish, just like they can lay their towels anywhere they wish."

Helen smiled. "I can definitely beat them to the beach. I'll go down there just as soon as I wake up."

"That's my girl," said Claire, returning to the paper.

When Helen walked out the front door, John turned to Claire. "Do we have to turn absolutely everything into a competition?"

"Life is a competition, dear."

John reached for the front section of the *Times* that Claire had already read and laid on the table between them. "For some of us."

"For all of us."

Chapter 5

2003

Helen set the dining room table, using the delicate white dinner plates with the blue flower border her mother and father had eaten from for the first twenty years of their marriage. It was a popular pattern that many young brides of the day had chosen for their everyday setting. But Claire had grown weary of its simplicity in her middle age, replacing it with mustard-colored china hand painted with wild birds. Helen had told her mother at the time that she was most likely suffering a midlife crisis, but Claire had simply and unemotionally packed her wedding china into cardboard boxes bound for the cottage. Now, again, Claire found comfort in the tradition of the white and blue plates.

Helen took the dishes from the dining room into the kitchen and set them on the counter next to the stove. She fished peas out of the small sauce pan with a slotted spoon and spilled them onto the plates. She used a wood spoon to scoop a small serving of the baked cheese and rice casserole she had removed from the oven before she set the table onto the plate beside the peas. She again opened the oven door and, ignoring the *whoosh* of hot air, stabbed a stuffed chicken breast with a fork. Placing it next to the peas and the rice, Helen began the tedious task of cutting the chicken into tiny, chewable, digestible pieces. This done, Helen put the plate in the refrigerator to cool its contents.

Claire's illness and subsequent treatments had sensitized her mouth, leaving her with intolerance of hot or cold liquids and foods. Her morning coffee, taken black and piping before, now needed three ice cubes to make it palatable. Ice cream had to be left on the counter until its firm, delicious peaks had succumbed to their tropical surroundings and fallen into vague mounds and soupy valleys. Meals, for the most part, had to be prepared ahead of time, so that each and every component was as temperate as the room in which it was served. When this was impractical, Helen simply cooled hot food in the fridge or heated cold foods in the microwave. Resistant to change in general and this one in particular, Helen had fought her mother, refusing at first to give her cool soft-boiled eggs and tepid orange juice. But in the end, Claire won by simply refusing to eat. The futility of arguing with a seventy-nine-year-old hunger strike victim became frightfully obvious very quickly. Helen's refrigerator/microwave trick shortened the process, which seemed to make it more reasonable, understandable even.

Grabbing another plate, Helen repeated the process for herself, save cutting the chicken and cooling it down. Taking a warm biscuit for herself from the toaster oven, Helen grabbed her mother's plate from the fridge and walked both of the plates back into the dining room. After setting the plates down, she lit the candles. Taking a step back from the table to survey her presentation, Helen smiled, knowing how pleased her mother would be with a well-set, attractive table. The flowers Helen had brought from home sat in a water pitcher, helping to compensate for the empty spaces. "Mom?" she called, walking back into the living room, where her mother had chosen to sit after her late afternoon nap. "Dinner's ready."

"Really?" Claire looked up from the magazine she wasn't reading. "We haven't had lunch."

"Sure we did. Tuna sandwiches at home," said Helen. "Your favorite."

Helen helped her mother off the couch and into the dining room, where Claire's eyes grew large. "Helen! What a lovely scene."

Helen patted her mother's shoulder and then sat her at the head of the table, at her end, in the large, cushioned chair paired with her room-temperature chicken. Helen sat on her mother's left. Like dry-land synchronized swimmers, both women put their napkins in their laps, folded their hands, and closed their eyes.

"Dear Lord," Claire began, and then stopped to clear her throat. "Thank You for this day and for the opportunity to live it. Thank You for this lovely food and for my precious daughter who prepared it. Watch over those traveling here, Lord. Give them a safe journey. And bless John. May he rest peacefully with You. Amen."

Claire prayed for her husband at the dinner table every night. She had loved him with a noticeable devotion that made Helen, as a child, feel safe. Claire would often tell Helen that their relationship was spawned from a different time, that she and John, like many of their friends, looked at marriage as a lifelong partnership. Divorce was not an option, as it was nowadays. Claire wrinkled her nose every time she said the word *divorce.* She thought all divorced people were weak, that they simply hadn't tried hard enough, and that included her oldest daughter, Charlotte, who had been divorced twice. This did not mean that she and John had always seen eye to eye, Claire was fond of saying. But whatever problem that arose to separate them was analyzed until its significance diminished, until they were able to talk about it without anger in their voices. Claire had never thought about leaving John, nor he her, a testament, she thought, to their work ethic as much as their affection for one another.

"Amen," said Helen, pulling her thoughts back to the dinner table. Suddenly ravenous, Helen ate quickly. Claire speared a few peas and lifted them with effort to her mouth, where she chewed them meticulously. Again and again, Claire returned to the small, manageable peas, sweet and comforting. When they were gone, she put her fork on her plate, signaling defeat. "Mom," said Helen, eyeing her mother's plate, "have some chicken. It's your favorite. Plus you could use the protein."

"I'm tired of protein."

"Maybe you're tired because you don't get enough protein."

"What about our tuna salad lunch?"

"You've got me there," said Helen. "Just a few bites of chicken."

Claire forked a morsel of chicken into her mouth. "I feel like a child being coaxed to eat."

"If the shoe fits . . ."

Claire smiled. "Fine. If I eat half my chicken, can I have dessert?"

It was Helen's turn to smile. "You'll be pleased with dessert."

"Blueberry pie, right? You said you were going to make blueberry pie."

"For the weekend," said Helen. "I'm going to make two pies for the weekend."

"Then what are we having tonight?"

"Pudding."

"Really? Butterscotch pudding?" Claire asked, shoveling two pieces of chicken into her mouth.

"With a layer of cream on top."

"Helen," said Claire as she chewed, "you are good to me."

"Don't get too excited. It's instant."

"Nothing wrong with instant."

"Now she tells me," said Helen. "If I had known that, I never would have made Aunt Margaret's scalloped potatoes from scratch."

"Good practice for you, Helen," said Claire. "Although I prefer Stouffer's myself."

Helen laughed. "That is the most ridiculous thing I've ever heard come out of your mouth."

"I like to keep you on your toes, Helen."

"I'm always on my toes," said Helen.

"You always have been, dear."

The next afternoon, Pammy arrived. She parked next to her sister's car and immediately opened her trunk. Beside her bright yellow duffel bag lay four loaves of artisan bread, a half dozen bottles of white wine, dinner for three from Pasta Extravaganza, and two Bloomingdale's shopping bags that held presents for everyone. Leaving the duffel and the shopping bags in the car, Pammy loaded everything else into her arms and walked with purpose toward the back door. Guessing the low success rate of opening the screen door without dropping at least one of the wine bottles, Pammy yelled for help. "Helen!"

Thoroughly engaged on the porch by the latest issue of *The New Yorker,* Helen started when she heard her sister's voice and then ran to the back door. Seeing Pammy, with her cumbersome load and a panicked look on her face, Helen couldn't resist asking the obvious. "Can I help you with something?"

"You've got exactly three seconds to open that door to avoid certain death!" Helen laughed and held the door open for Pammy who rushed past her and dumped everything onto the counter. "Phew," she said. "What an ordeal." She tucked the dark brown hair that had fallen out of the clip at the back of her head behind her ears.

Helen gave her sister, three inches taller to match the three years older, a hug and kissed her on the cheek. "You make it an ordeal, sweetheart. I said bring nothing but yourself."

"But you really don't mean that."

"I really do, though. It's everyone else in the world who doesn't mean it."

"Isn't that the truth? Every dinner party I go to in New York is the same. The hostess says don't bring a thing—after you've exhausted yourself making clever suggestions—and then is offended if you don't show up with cute cocktail napkins, a bottle of wine, or a bouquet of fresh flowers. Then you're supposed to say something, like, 'I just couldn't resist,' when you hand her the goods and give her a perfunctory kiss next to her cheek." Pammy pushed the hem of her shirt back into the waistband of her pressed khaki shorts. She liked order in her life. Without it, without everything in its proper place, she felt adrift; the belt that matched her shoes was like a bow line connecting a boat to its mooring. She had not always been this way, not cared as much. It was when she turned forty and had no husband that she decided the dignity in her life would come from the appearance of having it.

"Still jaded, I see, by city life."

"You know," said Pammy, beginning to unload her bags, "I've lived in that city for twenty years, and I don't think I'll ever make it into the social registry."

"You were invited here, weren't you? This is the event of the season."

"And you never change, thank God."

"I'm so glad you're here."

"How's Mom?" asked Pammy, as she put four of the six wine bottles into the cupboard.

"Going downhill quickly," said Helen, "as you already know."

"Is that why she's so pissed off?" Pammy put the pasta, mushroom sauce, and Caesar salad takeout containers in the fridge.

"Pissed off?" Helen folded her arms across her chest.

"Yeah, pissed off." Pammy mimicked Helen's stance. "I mean, she's got to be pretty pissed off at me, Charlotte, and Thomas to order you to call us with her crazy ultimatum. What kind of mother does that—demands that her kids show up at the cottage if they want their share of the inheritance?"

"Maybe a mother who wonders if her kids care about her at all."

"So you agree with her tactics. You think she did the right thing."

"I'm not saying that," said Helen, lowering her arms. "But you need to look at it from her standpoint."

"We've *lived our lives* from her standpoint."

"No." Helen shook her head. "You've lived part of your life from her standpoint. You're an adult, Pammy, and you can now choose how you react to what she says and does. You barely listen anymore when I try to describe her condition to you."

"Well, Dad used to explain it." Pammy opened the fridge again and placed the remaining two bottles of Chardonnay on the bottom shelf.

"Yeah, I know. Since Dad died, I've been flying solo."

"What do you mean by that?" said Pammy on her way back out the kitchen door.

Helen followed her. "You live a hundred miles away, and we see you twice a year. And when we talk on the phone, we talk about you, not Mom. That's what I mean by that."

Pammy grabbed her duffel bag from the back of her car and handed it to Helen. She lifted the shopping bags out of the trunk and then closed it. "Helen, you know how busy I am."

"Yes, I do," said Helen. "I'm busy too—taking care of Mom all by myself."

"Which you seem to enjoy, by the way. And Thomas and I work seventy-hour weeks, and Charlotte lives on the West Coast. What do you expect?"

"You're welcome," said Helen, striding toward the house and letting the screen door close behind her. Helen marched her sister's duffel bag up the stairs, and set it in the pink room she and Pammy would share. Charles had offered to sleep on the pullout in the den and the boys had begged to sleep on air mattresses on the porch, so that Thomas and his family could have the green room with the double bed and other set of bunks. Charlotte and her latest boyfriend could sleep in the queen-size bed in the yellow room. Claire would stay where she always stayed, in the blue, front room she had shared with her husband for forty-six years. When Helen came back down the stairs, Pammy was sitting with their mother on the porch.

"Come join us," said Claire. "Pammy is just catching me up on work." Helen made eye contact with her sister, holding her gaze for a second longer than Pammy.

"We were just talking about my latest account," said Pammy. "I'll be working with a hot, new IT company."

"How long have you been with Paulson and Garvin?" asked Claire.

Pammy looked at the ceiling, counting the years in her head. "For twelve years," she said. "It will be twelve years in September."

"I remember you telling us—was it at Thanksgiving, Helen?—that you thought you'd make vice president soon," said Claire. "I haven't heard whether or not that's come to be."

Pammy looked at Helen before looking at her mother. "No, Mom," she said. "The job was given to Patrick O'Brien."

"And you stayed?" asked Claire, incredulous. "You got passed over, and you stayed?"

"It's a good company, Mom, and I've got a lot of creative freedom."

"I'd start looking around if I were you. They sent a clear message when they promoted that O'Brien fellow instead of you."

Helen jumped up from her seat. "Who'd like some iced tea?"

"Not me," said Claire, hand to belly. "I'm still full from that wonderful chef salad you made for lunch."

"Pammy?" said Helen. "Let's get some tea and head down to the beach. You haven't seen the water yet. Mom, you don't mind if we go for a quick walk, do you?"

"Go right ahead," said Claire, waving them off. "I'll be here when you get back."

As soon as they had their tea in plastic tumblers and were walking across the street to the beach, Helen said, "She doesn't mean it."

"She most certainly does. She means every damn word of it. God, Helen, and you wonder why I don't get to Connecticut more often."

"You've got to ignore it. Whenever she says hurtful stuff like that, you've got to ignore it."

"Easy for you to say, cherished one."

"I get my share of it, too, Pammy. When you spend several hours a day with your aged, ill mother, you get a ration."

"Not that I've ever heard, Saint Helen."

"It's so easy for you to say that, to justify your absence and your lack of concern." They descended the steps to the beach. Pammy walked into the water; Helen followed.

"I *am* concerned, Helen. I'm just not very good at showing it." Pammy looked over at her sister. "And I know you're a good caregiver. Because you are, the rest of us can take a holiday."

"*I* need a holiday."

Pammy smiled. "You got one, sister. Saturday is the Fourth of July!"

Helen laughed. "Work aside. How are you? How is life in that big, bad city?"

"Big and bad."

"But you love it."

"Most of the time, I do," said Pammy, wading out of the water and onto the sand. "But sometimes I wonder what took me there in the first place."

"I believe his name was Harold."

"You have the memory of twin elephants. How did you ever remember Harold?"

"Easy. How can you forget a guy whose mother named him after hearing 'Hark! The Harold Angels Sing' piped into the delivery room of the hospital on Christmas Eve?"

"I'd forgotten that."

"What I forget is who came after Harold—Sam or Anthony?"

"Anthony," said Pammy, leading Helen back up the stairs, back to the house. "What an ass he was. Remember how you had to call him Anthony? If you called him Tony, he wouldn't respond."

"Yes," Helen said. "I do remember. Charlotte called him Tony the entire Labor Day weekend that year."

"Charlotte was always so contrary."

"She still is," said Helen. "You'll be able to see that for yourself tomorrow."

"How about Thomas? Is he coming?"

"I'm not sure, but I'm hopeful. Saturday, I think, if he comes."

"Only you," said Pammy. "Only you could get Thomas to come."

"It's really Mom who got him to come—if he does come."

"And if he does come, will Barb and the kids come with him?"

"Yes."

"She's a peach, isn't she?" Pammy opened the back screen door for her sister.

"Absolutely," said Helen.

"How about Charles and the boys?" Pammy looked at the floor next to the washing machine and dryer for ratty sneakers and wet towels, evidence of her nephews' presence.

"Fishing. They should be here on Friday." Helen hesitated, wondering if she should ask about Pammy's latest companion. Pammy read her mind.

"Mark's not coming. He's really busy at work right now and didn't think he should take the time."

Seeing the injured look on Pammy's face, Helen wrapped her arm around her sister's shoulders. "Then I've got you all to myself," she said. "Let's check in with Mom on the porch."

"You go. I'm going to head upstairs to unpack."

"Put your suit on, so we can sit on the beach."

"See you in ten."

Helen walked back onto the porch, where Claire was napping in her chair, positioned so that the afternoon sun would hit and warm her torso. Out of habit more than necessity, Helen covered her mother's outstretched legs with the ever-ready blue and white blanket and picked up the magazine article she had been reading when Pammy arrived. She had forgotten to tell her mother that Pammy hadn't gotten the job. Had Helen remembered, she could have explained the situation. And the sharp words Claire had spoken would have been directed at her and not at Pammy. There were a number of things Pammy needed to hear, but commentary on her lack of seniority at work was not one of them. And for that, Helen blamed herself.

CHAPTER 6

1973

Helen and Pammy lay on Charlotte's bed, intently watching her apply pink lipstick to her O-shaped mouth. Nonchalant but dead accurate, Charlotte covered her lips with Pink Blossoms, then blotted them once with a tissue. She fished around her capacious floral makeup bag until she found her Thick 'N Rich mascara and Pretty as a Peacock eye shadow. Helen and Pammy knew all the names of the brands and various shades, since, after Charlotte went out for the night, they made themselves up and pranced around her bedroom like the wild turkeys that lived in the woods behind their Stonefield, Connecticut, house. Next, Charlotte extracted the big rollers from her long cinnamon-colored hair. She brushed out the puffy curls that transformed her straight locks into a thick, wavy mane. She smiled at herself in the mirror, then glanced at her sisters, who were still enchanted by the process. "How do I look?" she asked, well aware of the only possible response.

"Great," said Pammy. "Where are you going?"

"A bunch of us are meeting at the duck pond. Rick said he'd take us to The Lantern for a drink."

"How can you get into The Lantern? The sign says you have to be eighteen."

"You and Helen could probably get into The Lantern," said Charlotte, putting on her faded jean jacket. "That old man will take anybody's money." Charlotte opened the third drawer in the small chest that sat atop her bureau and took out a pack of Marlboro cigarettes. She grabbed her blue suede purse from her unmade bed and stuffed the cigarettes into the side pocket. She hesitated, then took the Pink Blossoms lipstick from her makeup bag and dropped it into the pocket next to the Marlboros. She zipped them in. "You two have got to stop using all my stuff," said Charlotte, looking at her sisters. "Give it up or buy your own."

Feigning shock, Pammy looked at Helen. "Have we touched Charlotte's stuff?"

"Never," Helen said solemnly.

"And I'm a virgin," said Charlotte, her back to them, reaching for the doorknob. Pammy giggled and Helen blanched, wondering if she had overheard something she wasn't meant to hear. Charlotte turned and faced them again. "Look. Leave my things alone tonight and tomorrow I'll take you into town, and we can get you your own stuff. How's that sound?"

"I have eighty-three cents," said Pammy. "What will that buy?" Helen, who was saving her fifty cents for the Good Humor truck, said nothing.

"I have some extra money," said Charlotte. "It will be my treat." Pammy and Helen looked at each other. Charlotte wasn't in the habit of treating or buying anything for anyone but herself, even though John Thompson had explained to all of his children that they would feel better about themselves if they were more focused on giving than on receiving. Helen and Pammy convinced themselves that they were too young to understand their dad's philanthropic philosophy, but they were pretty good at playing along and nodding their heads whenever he gave them their allowance. Thomas played along, too, or maybe he actually subscribed to what their father told them. The only one who didn't understand or pretend was Charlotte, who told her sisters the only thing she faked was an orgasm. Charlotte was not only impervious to the needs of others, but she also always demanded something in return for her efforts. Never give something for nothing, she had told her sisters more than once, and expect more than you deserve. So what was this treat all about? "No strings attached," Charlotte said with a smile. She stood next to the door she had just opened and waited for her sisters to recognize the sign that they were no longer welcome in her room.

Pammy and Helen scrambled off their sister's bed and retreated to their bedroom, where they listened as Charlotte walked down the stairs and onto the porch. They then heard a brief interchange of what they knew were questions asked by their parents about where Charlotte was going and with whom, followed by cursory responses. Within a minute, they heard the screen door open and shut; Charlotte was released into the night. When they knew she was out of the house, they scurried back to her room, and together sat down in front of Charlotte's mirror. "Do me first," said Pammy.

"Who do you want to be?"

"Tammy Jennings."

"You were Tammy last night."

"And I want to be Tammy again tonight."

"Then you stuff your own shirt."

"I did last night, didn't I?"

"He's not that great, you know," said Helen, tentatively.

"Who?" asked Pammy, looking at herself in the mirror.

"Michael Johanson, you dope. If he's been with Tammy Jennings this long, he's even dumber than she is."

"Is that possible?" asked Pammy.

Helen laughed, and then said, "Close your eyes." Pammy, now facing her younger sister on the chintz-covered piano bench Charlotte used as a vanity stool, closed her eyes and imagined herself walking hand-in-hand with Michael on the beach under a brilliant full moon. Helen's gentle application of eye shadow made her shiver, just as Michael's soft caresses would. In her mind, she replayed her favorite fantasy. After their walk, Michael would lead her to a secluded place on the beach. He would sit down beside her on the sand and wrap one of his giant arms around her. He would whisper in her ear that he loved her, always had loved her. Tammy, he would say, was unattractive, and the only reason he dated her was pity. Pammy smiled at this thought, knowing, even in her imagination, how ridiculous it was. “What color lipstick?” asked Helen.

“How about that lip gloss. Is there any left?”

“I think Charlotte hid the peach Pot o’ Gloss,” said Helen, rooting through the bag. “But here’s some strawberry.” Charlotte applied gloss to her lips with her pinky, which is how Helen spread it on Pammy’s lower lip. Afterward, Pammy shmushed her lips together, as Charlotte did, to transfer some of the gloss to the top lip. Pammy was pretty good at it. Next, Helen applied bright pink blush. She brushed the powder from the bottom of Pammy’s cheekbone, just above her mouth, up and out, stopping close to the top of Pammy’s ear. This, Charlotte had told them, was the proper way to use blush. Any other method yielded a clown-like, unnatural look. Helen looked at Pammy, her eyes still closed, and saw exactly what she would describe as unnatural. “You’re done, Tammy,” she said.

“Not yet,” said Pammy. “Michael is just about to kiss me.”

“You’re pathetic. Do me.”

“Who do you want to be?” Pammy opened her eyes.

“You,” said Helen, teasing her sister.

“That’s easy.” Pammy put all the makeup back in the bag. “You’re done.”

Helen opened her eyes when she heard someone open the back screen door, located just underneath one of her bedroom windows. She flipped over onto her stomach and waited while Charlotte made her way up the stairs in the dark. Charlotte walked slowly down the hallway, bumping into the wall, Helen guessed, somewhere between Thomas’s still vacant room and their parents’ room. Charlotte then opened the door to the linen closet, but closed it quickly, apparently realizing it wasn’t the bathroom, which Helen figured was her destination. Finding it, Charlotte flipped open the toilet lid and sat down. Helen could hear everything through the thin pine-paneled walls. Her sister groaned. A moment later, a loud stream of urine hit the water in the bowl. After she flushed, Charlotte skipped washing her hands and made her way to her bedroom. Helen scooted off the top bunk, tiptoed down the hall and into Charlotte's bedroom, and shut the door behind her. Leaning against the wall, Charlotte stepped out of her jeans and underwear and then peeled off her shirt, dropping it on the floor. She pulled her bra over her head, balled it up in her hands, and then threw it in the corner. Then in a crouched, animal-like position, she moved toward her bed. Even though, or perhaps because, their mother forbade it, Charlotte slept in the nude. Every Christmas, Claire bought her three daughters flannel nightgowns, and, every Christmas, Charlotte never took hers out of the box. Pammy and Helen had an extensive collection of Charlotte's castoffs that Pammy wore instead of her own, and Helen used for dressing up since they were too big. "Charlotte," Helen whispered.

"Shit! Helen, is that you?"

"Yes."

"You scared the crap out of me."

"Sorry."

"Well, you ought to be."

"Charlotte?"

"What."

"Are you drunk?"

Charlotte laughed. "Absolutely."

"You shouldn't go out with Rick. He's a jerk," said Helen, speaking her mind because her sister was drunk and would not remember their conversation in the morning.

"He buys me drinks, and he's a good lay. What else is there?"

"Love," Helen said immediately. "I think you should wait until you're in love."

"And I think," said Charlotte, rolling over and facing the wall, "you've been spending too much time with Pammy."

"Because she's in love?"

"You know as well as I know that she's in love with Michael Johanson."

"And that's a bad thing?"

"When Tammy Jennings is still around, yeah."

"What's so great about Tammy Jennings?"

"Nothing."

"So why does Michael go out with her?" Helen used the term her sister used for dating someone to show Charlotte that she was terminology savvy. Charlotte, who burped loudly, didn't appear to care.

"Why do you think, Helen? And please don't tell me it's her scintillating conversation."

"Who'd ever think that?" said Helen, sitting down on the floor.

"She is a bit of a moron, that's for sure. Some guys like morons. It makes them feel superior."

"No kidding."

"No kidding."

Helen told Charlotte she would never intentionally hang around with an idiot. "Sometimes you can't help it," said Charlotte. "But whenever I have a choice, I'd certainly rather be with an interesting person, someone with something to say."

"So you don't like hanging around with dopes?" Helen was hoping her sister might acknowledge, in her inebriated condition, that her boyfriend, Rick, was a dope, which would either make her think about breaking up with him or prompt her to explain to Helen further why she continued to spend time with him, drinks and sex aside.

Charlotte didn't answer. It was only when Helen repeated the question that she realized her sister had fallen asleep.

The next morning, Charlotte slept late. Helen had caught fifteen crabs and was feeding stale hotdog rolls to the ducks when Pammy biked up to her, breathless. "She's up," she said. "She said she'll take us." Helen immediately hurled the last roll as far as she could, and then briefly watched as three ducks swam to and then fought over it. "Helen!"

Helen started to run while Pammy pedaled, slowly at first and then gaining momentum and speed. The only chance Pammy had of beating Helen on foot was to be on her bike. And still, often, Helen won. Claire regularly told the neighbors that her youngest daughter would surely be a track star someday because she was as fast as greased lightning. When they got back to the house, Charlotte was standing next to her ten-year-old Chevy Impala, with her keys in her hand. "First stop is Cumberland Farms," Charlotte said, as she started the car. "That idiot Thomas drank the last Coke."

Helen, actually, was the idiot who drank the last Coke, but she decided to keep quiet. Coke was not her favorite soda, but she knew consuming it was the only way to get Charlotte to town. Charlotte's intentions the night before seemed good, but Helen knew the follow-through could be iffy.

After downing the Coke and smoking two cigarettes outside the convenience store, Charlotte drove Helen and Pammy to Seaside Pharmacy. She walked down the magazine aisle, where she picked up the latest copy of *Seventeen* magazine, to the makeup section in the back. "Maybelline is what we want," Charlotte said with authority. "All the top models wear it."

Helen and Pammy ran their fingers over the diminutive plastic cases. Colorful, shimmering rectangles with names like Iris, Plum, and Sea Foam lay in neat rows, promising to transform the most ordinary maiden into a goddess. Old Fart Higgins, the pharmacist, who was preparing prescriptions behind the tall white counter in the back, peered over his bifocals at them. Secretly fearing him, Helen quickly put her hands in the pockets of her shorts. Charlotte, insouciant as always, pulled several cases off the shelf and held them up to her sisters' faces. Picking two, Charlotte laid the others on the shelf and continued down the aisle. Helen picked up the rejected items and put them back in their proper places, then caught up with Charlotte and Pammy, who were looking at lipsticks. Peach, Passion Fruit, Mango, Cherry, Strawberry—Helen longed to unscrew the lids of each Pot o' Gloss and inhale its intoxicating scent. Keenly aware of Mr. Higgins, who had walked the length of his counter to keep an eye on them, Helen quickly selected Cherry and handed it to Charlotte. Pammy, who loved Pot o' Gloss but thought the stick colors were more grown-up, chose Soft Summer Pink, the lipstick shade featured for July.

They crossed the aisle to consider mascaras. Charlotte told Pammy and Helen she would buy just one tube for them to share. "Helen, you're really too young for this anyway," said Charlotte.

"And Pammy, you've got lashes to die for, so you don't need much." Pammy batted her eyelashes at Helen.

After much deliberation, Charlotte chose Lazy Hazelnut, for "that soft, unstudied look," according to the package. Charlotte put all the cosmetics into her basket and walked to the front of the store. She chose three Snickers bars from the rack next to the cash register, and then placed the basket on the counter, signaling the end of the shopping trip. Pammy and Helen looked at each other and smiled. "I've just got to have a cheeseburger," Charlotte said, as soon as they were outside. "Rick says that's the best cure for a hangover."

"What else does Rick say?" Helen asked, wondering what other axioms ruled Rick's simple life. She wanted to say, "Candy is dandy, but liquor is quicker," but she kept mum. Charlotte despised sarcasm coming from others, and she had, after all, just bought the makeup.

"He says a lot of things, grown-up things, not intended for the ears of a ten-year-old."

"I'm thirteen," said Pammy. "You can tell me."

"When you're fourteen, maybe," said Charlotte, walking to the car ahead of them. "He's really very mature, you know."

"I'll bet," said Helen, attempting to be earnest, but sounding caustic. She had never been good at masking her feelings. Her dad had told her when she was very young that honesty was the best policy, and she subsequently tried to lie only when necessary.

They drove down the street and pulled the Impala into the Friendly's parking lot. Charlotte, again a few feet ahead of her sisters, pulled open the heavy glass doors, strode past the "Please Wait to be Seated" sign, and plopped herself down in an unoccupied booth. Pammy and Helen sat opposite her and looked at the ceiling until a waitress brought them menus. They all ordered Big Beef cheeseburgers, French fries, and strawberry Fribbles. "Thank you," said Helen, "for the makeup."

"Yeah," Pammy added. "It's great."

"Well, now that you have your own," said Charlotte, sounding more like their mother than their sister, "you can stay out of my bag."

"Oh, absolutely," said Pammy, exchanging a furtive look with Helen.

"And lunch, obviously, is my treat, too. Unless you've brought your eighty-three cents, Pammy." Pammy shook her head slowly. "Helen?"

"I don't have any money," she said. "I'm just a kid."

Charlotte laughed at that. "You get lunch because you're amusing," she said to Helen. "And Pammy, you get lunch because you've got potential." Pammy couldn't tell if Charlotte was complimenting her or mimicking what their mother always told them. Either way, her older sister was buying her lunch, a modern-day miracle.

When they got back to the cottage, Claire was waiting with her chore list. Thomas, who was working, was excused. But the girls were expected to sweep out the cottage, fold the laundry on Claire's bed, and shuck a dozen ears of corn. "Take whatever task you wish," said Claire. "Whoever is done the fastest—and has done a good job—gets fifty cents." As soon as Claire disappeared back into the house, Charlotte announced that Pammy and Helen would have to do all the chores since she had no use for her mother's pittance and was meeting her friends on the beach.

"I'll sweep the cottage if you fold the laundry and shuck the corn," Helen said to Pammy. Charlotte, who in the summer wore her bikinis like underwear, had already crossed the street.

Two neatly folded and stacked piles of laundry and one sandless cottage later, Pammy and Helen sat on the picnic table with the ears of corn between them. Helen, who was an efficient sweeper, finished before Pammy and told her she'd help with the corn. Claire found them there on her way to the car. "Where's Charlotte?"

Pammy looked at Helen. "She just left," said Helen, deciding this was one of those occasions for a white lie.

"Yup," said Pammy, ripping the husk from the cob. "Just left."

"How many ears have you done?"

Helen said five the same moment Pammy said four.

"Catch up now, Pammy. You don't want Helen to beat you at everything."

* * *

That night, after Charlotte dressed in her black-and-white waitress uniform and left for the dining room of Ye Olde Tavern, Helen and Pammy sat on her piano bench and made each other up with their sister's makeup. The pretty cases Charlotte purchased that afternoon sat undisturbed in the slim, brown paper bag from the pharmacy. What Helen and Pammy didn't know before they left for town that day was that the makeup was not important. It was surprising, therefore, that in a matter of hours, it seemed to lose most of its initial appeal. What they secretly loved most about painting each other's faces, they now knew, was digging through Charlotte's bag and its familiar contents and making themselves look a little bit more like her.

Chapter 7

2003

Pammy, who had changed into red linen shorts and a dry-cleaned, white cotton blouse, walked quietly down the stairs and out onto the porch where Helen was sitting, waiting. "Still asleep?"

"Yes," said Helen in a lowered voice. She stood and stretched her arms over her head. "Let's go sit on the beach."

"Will she worry if she wakes up and we're not here?" Pammy twisted her shoulder-length hair into a bun and clipped it into place. She slipped out of her leather sandals and into the rubber flip flops she brought along for the walk to the beach. As she was applying lip balm, she looked at her mother, dozing in her favorite chair, head back, eyelids closed but fluttering.

Helen followed her sister's gaze. "Her eyelids always do that," she said. "It's a little odd, I know, but it doesn't mean she's waking up. She can sleep for hours in the afternoon. I'll leave her a note." Helen walked into the living room and took a pad of paper and a pen from the desk. She brought them back to the porch and then jotted down their destination in big letters. She ripped the page from the pad and set it down on the table next to her mother's chair, beside Claire's reading glasses and half glass of water. Helen knew that her mother didn't mind being by herself. She just wanted to know when she was.

Crossing the street, Pammy said, "She's gone downhill quickly. She seemed so much more alive at Thanksgiving."

"She loves holidays and the activity they generate, so she was definitely on her game at Thanksgiving. Remember how excited she used to get at Christmastime? She spent days in the kitchen—baking mini sweet bread loaves and Christmas stollen. . . ."

"And how about all the cookies? Sugar cookies with frosting, chocolate dipsy doos, shortbread, real gingerbread men . . ."

"And when she was done with that, she made chili and Sunday night casserole and hummus."

"She was way ahead of the game on hummus," said Pammy, as they traversed the right-of-way. "It's everywhere now."

"Chickpeas were a part of her training diet, weren't they?"

"Legumes of all varieties, if I remember correctly," said Pammy. "She was a protein hound."

"She still is—although she sometimes needs to be reminded." They descended the cement steps and grabbed two of the six beach chairs Helen had brought down from the garage the day before and stacked against the seawall. "She just doesn't have any appetite."

"I'd like to have that problem."

Helen sat down in her chair. "Were we talking about you?"

Pammy laughed, but Helen was serious. This is how it always was when she and her sister got together, either when Helen, missing her sister, drove into New York for dinner or whenever Pammy made it home. Or when they talked on the phone. Helen would try to have a conversation about their mother's condition, about what the oncologist said, about medication and care choices, but this information about their mother was often met with silence or simply dismissed in favor of another topic. Typically that topic was something about what was going on with Pammy. Living the busy life mandated by corporate Manhattan, Pammy rarely seemed to think about Claire, as evidenced by how much she asked Helen about their mother. Except when Pammy was in Claire's company, she was numb to her mother, Helen thought. Claire's disappointment in Pammy as a child—she had not been athletic or scholarly—and her dissatisfaction with Pammy's adult choices had made a permanent mark. *I don't care if you have children or not,* Claire had said to Pammy at Thanksgiving. *But since it's obvious now that you're not going to have a family, you should damn well be running that agency in New York by now*. Helen acknowledged to herself and to Pammy that Claire shouldn't have said what she said. But Pammy also had to learn to let Claire's comments go. Taking the harsh words of an aged, ill, has-been superstar swimmer to heart was not only damaging but also foolish. Because Pammy had never been in a relationship for longer than a couple years, she had never developed the thick skin needed to deflect unpleasantness. When she was home, she reverted back to her childhood, when, in Pammy's memory, she had done little to impress her mother or quiet her criticism. Pammy didn't dwell on missed promotions or other disappointments except when she was quizzed about them by Claire. When Pammy was away from her mother, removed from her judgment, she considered herself successful.

Pammy sometimes talked to Helen about what she called the troubled mother-daughter thing, but she also sometimes pretended it didn't exist. She covered her resentment and anger well, by sending birthday cards and gifts, and with her banter and her armfuls of food and other goodies whenever she came to the house or the cottage. She was not particularly interested in conversation about family or about topics that didn't directly relate to her, her job, or her current boyfriend. On rare occasions, she would ask Helen personal questions, but mostly, with Helen anyway, she talked about herself. Pammy was guilty of misreading Helen's good listening skills as an avid interest in Pammy's work and social life. And Helen, not wanting to emulate Claire, to make the same mistakes, didn't correct her sister.

Nonetheless, Helen did want Pammy to show more interest in her life and in Claire's life. Helen lived ten minutes from the house she and her siblings had all grown up in, and she saw her mother every day. She shopped and cooked for her mother. She did her laundry. She took her to appointments. She kept her company—all of which took several hours out of every twenty-four. And it was okay, this arrangement, because Helen was well-suited to the task. She was generally more concerned with the health and happiness of her family and those around her than she was for her own mental and spiritual fulfillment. This unselfishness, which her husband said came naturally to Helen, was rarely rewarded or praised by her siblings—and that was the problem. Helen didn't mind caring for her mother; she wanted Pammy and Charlotte and Thomas to acknowledge it, thank her for it, and pitch in once in a while.

Pammy dug her bare toes into the sand. "I love it here," she said. "I love the cottage. I love this beach. This is the only place I can relax."

"You say that every year."

"And I mean it, more every year. I never have a minute to myself in the city. And at Mom's house, the memories muddy my head. I can't think clearly there. Here, it's different. Yeah, there's stuff to do, but it's never more complicated or arduous than shucking a dozen ears of corn, often with a drink in my hand. You're so lucky to spend the whole summer here, Helen. I wish I had more time here. You take this place for granted."

"I don't think so, Pammy." Helen, oversensitive to her sister's remark, had often told Pammy that she, too, could be at the cottage for an extended holiday. But no matter what Pammy said—and she talked about loving her time at the cottage every time she was there—Pammy never blocked out more than four or five days. "How's Mark?" asked Helen, suspecting he was less than wonderful or he would be sitting on the beach with them, choosing the topic for its potential sting.

"He's okay. He's got a lot of work to do this weekend."

"On the Fourth of July."

"Yes," said Pammy. "We don't live in a Monday through Friday world anymore, Helen. Mark often works from home, especially on the weekends."

"Seems like he always has a lot of work."

"What's that supposed to mean?" Immediately defensive, Pammy turned in her chair to face Helen.

"What part don't you understand?" said Helen, ready to bring their conversation to a boil.

"No, you don't understand, Helen."

"I think I do."

"No, you don't. You sit back with your husband and two children, your Tudor house and garden club, and throw judgments at the rest of us. Life doesn't come in neat little packages for everyone."

"What does it come in?"

"Huge boxes," answered Pammy, "with stiff, unyielding sides and dark corners. And as soon as I pick myself up from the last knock on the head, someone shakes the box again, pitching me against another wall or into another worthless relationship."

"Is it worthless?"

"What would you call it, Helen? He never has time for me. He lies about what he's doing. When he does want to see me, it's for one thing. And that's about once a week now, since he sees Nancy Fucking Greenberg three times a week. I've become the sympathy lay."

"You have not," said Helen, backing down.

"Don't patronize me, Helen. You know better."

"So why stay?"

"Because once a week is better than nothing."

"No, it's not. Tell him you've met someone else. Better yet, don't tell him anything. Don't call him. Tell him you're busy if he does call."

"It's not that easy."

"It sounds easy," said Helen.

"You're so naïve."

"Maybe."

Pammy looked at the horizon, blinking back tears. She knew she cried too often and hated the implied weakness. "Why does this always happen to me? Where is my prince? Why didn't I see him?"

"New York is a big city," said Helen. "Try another subway."

In spite of her sadness, of her frustration with Helen's seemingly perfect life, Pammy smiled. "You are impossible," she said.

"Hey, you're the one who likes impossible challenges."

"Is that why I'm still with Mark? Because I think I can win him over?"

"That would, indeed, be a challenge."

"I don't know how to give him up," said Pammy. "New York can be such a lonely place."

"Sometimes, you can be lonelier in a relationship than out of one, Pammy. You don't need him."

"I need someone," said Pammy. "I'm no good at being alone."

"Come see me when you feel lonely," said Helen. "Come see Mom."

Pammy closed one eye. "How about I just come to see you?"

"If that's what it takes to get you out to the country more often, we can do that. I'll hide you away in my guest bedroom."

"Be careful what you wish for."

Helen patted her sister on the back. "I don't need to be careful," she said. "The stuff I wish for never happens."

Chapter 8

1973

As soon as the dishes were done, Thomas washing, Helen and Pammy drying, and Charlotte doing what Thomas called fake drying, the Thompson children, as per instructions given the previous evening at the dinner table, walked out the kitchen screen door and into the yard. Claire, who had gone outside as soon as she'd finished her last bite of barbequed chicken, was sitting on the picnic table, legs crossed, one foot marking time. She had already put the plastic orange bases in their places. She had pumped air into the red rubber ball that they would soon be kicking into the air and throwing at one another. Family kickball was mandatory in the Thompson household, even if Claire could insist that Thomas take a night off from work and Charlotte stay around until dark only two or three times a summer. Thomas didn't mind all that much because he worked too many hours each week already. But Charlotte had become increasingly petulant about board or outdoor games of any kind and inured to her mother's pleas for family unity or passive-aggressive attempts at making Charlotte feel guilty about wanting to opt out. John emerged from the garage, where he had been in the process of gluing a lamp that Helen had knocked over the day before in her exuberance in answering the telephone.

It didn't ring often, so when it did, chances were good that the news and the caller were important.

"Everyone ready?" asked Claire, expecting head nods or verbal assent.

Helen was the only one who responded. "You bet!" she said, using one of her father's phrases. If Charlotte had said the same words, the tone and implied meaning would have earned her a reprimand. There was no danger of these mood-dampening utterances occurring, however, since Charlotte was, momentarily, staging a silent protest.

"Who wants to be a captain?" Claire was now up off the table, rubbing her hands together as she sometimes did when she was excited. No one responded, not even John, whom Claire could usually count on to step up if no one else did. "This is uncanny," she said, hands on hips. "I can't believe no one wants to be a captain. In my experience, being captain is a position of honor."

"There is nothing honorable about family kickball," said Charlotte, switching to a verbal protest.

"Let's see you bring some honor to the game, then, by being a captain. Thomas, how about you? Will you be the other captain?"

"Only if I can choose the name of my team." Thomas was smiling, a common practice for him. His white teeth, which he brushed three times a day, were a stunning complement to dark hair worn longer than Claire liked and his tanned skin. Claire, who had to be more and more careful in the sun as she aged, insisted that Thomas looked exactly like her grandfather, a lanky man whose college education was not wasted because he made his living outdoors. John liked to think that Thomas looked a bit like him. But he and Claire were agreed that Thomas, whoever he looked like, was as unassumingly handsome as he was most-of-the-time good.

"Go ahead," said Claire.

"The Poopheads!" he said. "The name of my team is the Poopheads. Now, who wants to be a poop?" Helen shot her arm into the air.

"Honestly, Thomas."

"I'm honest and serious," said Thomas. "Helen, get over here."

"Hey, who says you get to choose first?" asked Charlotte.

"You haven't even named your team yet."

"Okay," said Charlotte. "My team is the Tampons." Claire closed her eyes and shook her head. "Look," said Charlotte, "if you're going to force us to play kickball like a bunch of grammar school kids, the least I can do is try to elevate the game to the high school level." Charlotte looked at her dad, who winked at her. "I choose Dad."

"Well then, I choose Mom," said Thomas. "And, just in case you were wondering, we are going to officially kick your butts."

Pammy was standing by herself while the others chatted. It was obvious, of course, that she was going to be a Tampon, but she was uncertain if she could join the team until she was actually summoned. For a good two minutes, while the houses rules were reviewed and debated, no one acknowledged her. It wasn't until they were all about to take the field that Thomas turned around and called, "Let's go, Miss Pammy. You, Charlotte, and Dad are up first."

The lot they played on was between their cottage and the Hendersons' cottage next door. Jean and Frank Henderson had eight kids, many of whom were out and about every night after dinner. Often, three or four of the younger ones would wander over if they saw the Thompsons in the yard. Charlotte liked it when they joined in, mostly because her mother was less outwardly competitive when outsiders were part of the group. When it was just the Thompson family playing, Claire was relentless in her pursuit of any kind of triumph, whether it be kicking the ball over her husband's head or earning a run. Winning was the best, but it was even better if, in Claire's words, she buried the other team. However, fair play was above everything else, which somewhat tempered Claire's zest for victory. The Hendersons were noticeably absent on this night. Charlotte guessed they had piled into the two family station wagons and headed for the Dairy Queen in town. Or maybe they were on their way to the drive-in theater. Charlotte and her boyfriend, Rick, had gone to see *American Graffiti* the other night, but they had made out through most of it.

"Shall I pitch?" It was a rhetorical question. Claire, ball in hand, was standing where the pitcher would stand.

"Oh heck, why don't you go ahead, Mom," said Thomas. He was standing midway between second and third base. Helen was on pop-fly duty in the outfield. She stood on the Thompson side of the road, as anything that was kicked beyond the road was considered out of bounds and an automatic out. This was one of the rules that Thomas had brought up for review earlier. He thought that a physical specimen such as himself should be able to boot the ball into the stratosphere. Claire disagreed, to which Thomas said he never thought he'd hear her admit that women were weaker, that they couldn't kick the ball past the road. Claire had replied that the rule was in place so that the outfielders wouldn't spend the entire night chasing balls—and dodging dog poop—in the Walshes' yard. Thomas had very reluctantly agreed.

"Who's up?" Claire asked.

"I am," said Pammy, who backed up several feet behind home base, so she could take a run at the ball.

"I wish all you Tampons the best of luck!" shouted Thomas from the field.

Claire rolled the ball toward Pammy, who, still giggling from Thomas's remark, missed it completely with her right foot.

"How many strikes in kickball, Mom?" It was Thomas again.

"None," said Claire. "But we'll give Pammy another go. Pammy, you've got to focus, honey. If you're not focused, you don't have a chance."

Pammy backed up behind home base again. Thomas and Helen moved in. When Pammy did make contact with the side of the ball, it spun toward third base. Thomas had the ball in his hand before Pammy was halfway to first. He took two steps toward his sister and then fired the ball at her moving legs, striking them just before she crossed the base. "You're out!" he shouted.

"I know, Poophead!" Pammy shouted back, circling around toward her teammates.

John gave her a high-five when she approached him. "Nice try, pumpkin. Your brother's got a good arm."

"Yeah, well, it helps if you kick it more than six feet," said Charlotte.

"Sorry," said Pammy, using the word that came out of her mouth most often during family competitions.

When it was the Poopheads' turn to kick, the Tampons had

earned three runs. Charlotte grabbed the ball to pitch just as Pammy was moving toward it. "Got it!" said Charlotte gleefully, snatching it up from the ground.

"You pitched last time," said Pammy.

"That's because you stink."

"I do not stink!"

"Let's take a vote." Charlotte raised her voice and looked at each member of the family. "Raise your hand if you think Pammy stinks."

"That's enough," said John. Pammy was close to tears.

"It may be enough," said Charlotte, "but that doesn't mean it's not true."

"Oh for God's sake, Charlotte, pitch the ball," Claire said. "Pammy, take your place in the infield and ignore your sister."

Ignoring Charlotte was a challenge. Number one, her large and loud personality was hard to disregard. And number two, in this instance, she was right. Pammy did stink. Everyone in the family knew this, including Pammy, in spite of her protestations. And all the Thompsons accepted it, even Charlotte, who teased her sister only when she was especially put out by Claire's mandates. Charlotte's stink message on this particular evening was aimed more at her mother than her sister. Sure, she teased Pammy about all kinds of things—boys, pimples, being flat chested, the usual sister stuff—but she did not kid her often about her gamesmanship. As far as Charlotte could tell, it was genetic, and Pammy didn't have it. It was not her fault. Teasing people about stuff they couldn't change seemed, to Charlotte, both unfair and mean. She knew that her attempt at irritating her mother injured Pammy. So Charlotte stopped, just as quickly and unpredictably as she started.

Claire did not take this viewpoint. She did think that teasing people about things out of their control was cruel, yes. But she didn't think genetics were to blame for Pammy's athletic failings; she thought her middle daughter simply didn't try hard enough. And Claire, who had put all the effort she could muster into swimming for more than ten years, had little tolerance for a daughter who gave up before she'd warmed up. It had been this way with Pammy since she was very little. Claire had tossed her into Long Island Sound when she was two, like she had with Thomas and Charlotte, and Pammy was the first Thompson child to sink. *"Kick!"* Claire had screamed, using the word she had taught Pammy for moving her legs up and down. *"Pump your legs!"* she had called, running after Pammy, who was wobbling down the street on the tiny two-wheeler her older siblings had both learned to ride when they were four years old. Two bloody knees and two scraped elbows later, John had insisted that Pammy be allowed to ride her own bike, with its pink streamers jutting out of the handles, banana seat, and training wheels.

"If you coddle her," Claire said in bed that night, after John had cleaned his daughter's wounds and covered them with plastic bandages, "she will never succeed."

"Claire, she's five," said John, turning out the lamp on the bedside table.

"But then she'll be six, and ten, and fourteen, and, then you'll be telling me that 'she's just fourteen.' "

"I think she'll be riding a two-wheeler at fourteen."

"I know you think it's a big joke," said Claire, rolling on to her side to face her husband. "But she has got to learn about effort and the fact that it's the key factor to success. Sure, some people are born with abilities and inclinations, but those who put in the effort are the ones who rise to the top."

"Not everyone needs to be at the top, Claire." John put his arm over his wife's shoulder.

"Would you rather have her at the bottom?"

"Of course not. But if you push too hard and she still doesn't live up to your expectations, she will feel like she's at the bottom no matter where on the spectrum she sits."

"Fine," said Claire, who could see she was getting nowhere and was tired of the discussion.

But it wasn't fine. And Claire continued to push and coax. It wasn't until several years after Helen was born that Claire eased up on Pammy. This was not because her husband's gentle lectures were finally getting through, or because Pammy finally upped the amount of effort she put into various athletic activities that her mother had encouraged her to try. No, it was because Helen was a natural athlete. And Claire shifted her attention from a daughter who couldn't hit a Wiffle ball with a plank of wood to one who could do it every time. Seeking her mother's shifted attention, Pammy did try harder for a while—and Claire was pleased with her attempts. But Pammy's results were never as good as Helen's, who could ride a two-wheeler before her fourth birthday, who ran faster than everyone in her elementary school, including the boys, who won the town tennis tournament the summer she first picked up a racket.

As soon as darkness descended from the sky and closed in the yard, John called the game. The Poopheads won, even though Thomas had earned a number of outs for his team by booting the ball over the road, just, as he said, so everyone knew he could. Claire picked up the bases, as she always did, and walked them to the garage with her husband, who carried the ball. Helen and Pammy headed for the back door and their mother's homemade brownies in the kitchen. Thomas said his good-byes and then walked down the street to the duck pond to meet his friend Eddie. Charlotte jogged through the cottage and up the stairs to her room, where she touched up her makeup for her date with Rick. She had her period still—thus the name Tampons for her kickball team—so he would have to be content with just feeling her up. Sometimes she liked that better anyway. She had been more interested in *American Graffiti* the other night than in the back seat of Rick's car. She looked at her watch. Maybe they could go to the late show.

Chapter 9

2003

"Did Charles ever treat you like that?" Pammy and Helen were back at the house, sitting on the porch with their bare feet up on the wicker coffee table in front of them. They had talked about Thomas and Charlotte, briefly, and now were back to Pammy and her quest for the right man. Claire, at the other end of the porch, in the preferred sitting area, was still sleeping. The sisters talked in quiet voices.

"I was lucky with Charles." Helen took a sip of water from one of the glasses she had filled in the kitchen and brought to the porch for Pammy and herself.

"Why can't I be lucky? Why am I a forty-three-year-old woman wondering who my next boyfriend will be? I always thought boyfriends would be irrelevant after my twenty-fifth birthday."

"City life is different."

"Helen, there are lots of married people in Manhattan."

"I know. But they must have met elsewhere. I don't think anyone meets and falls in love there."

"Bill and Donna met in the city."

"Exception to the rule. Think of another example." Pammy

hesitated. "See?" said Helen. "What you need is country life. Then you can meet and marry the local doctor or dentist."

"Don't kid me."

"I'm not. Move out of that ignominious city. Leave the entrapments behind and start again."

"You can't start anything at forty-three," said Pammy, wondering if she could.

"I'm going to," Helen said, patting her sister's hand. "I just can't decide between chess and ice hockey."

Pammy laughed. "Let's go into the kitchen," she said, getting up from the couch. "I brought some fabulous stuff from the bad city for dinner."

"Normal or gourmet," said Helen.

"Very normal, very good."

"I'll be there in a moment," said Helen, glancing at her watch. "I'm going to wake Mom. She's been asleep for almost two hours." When Pammy left the porch, Helen stood and walked the several steps to her mother's chair. She watched her for a minute, looking as she sometimes did for clues to her longevity. There were none any different from those of the weeks and months before, from when Claire had decided to stop the chemotherapy treatments so that, as she said, nature could take its course. Her hair was beginning to fill in, curlier than before, and the color had come back to her face. She looked healthier now than she had in the midst of her treatments. But Helen knew better. The cancer had spread, as the doctor had prognosticated, leaving Claire with a life expectancy of weeks, maybe months, instead of years.

It was shortly after this discussion with the doctor that Claire decided a summer family reunion was in order. Well aware of Helen's attempts at getting her siblings together, of the declined holiday invitations to Thanksgiving and Christmas in Stonefield, Claire decided to take control of the situation. What, she wondered, would make them want to reunite? Since family unity didn't seem to be enough, Claire wondered if she could do something that would force them to gather, other than die. Once she had asked herself that question, it wasn't long before she came up with an answer. If they want to be included in my will, Claire told Helen over tea on Mother's Day, if they want a share of this cottage, they will come to the shore for a long weekend over July Fourth. Upon hearing this, Helen didn't talk to her mother for a day and a half. When she did talk, she said, "It's a mean, idle threat."

Claire's eyebrows moved up an inch. "I can assure you it's not a threat, Helen."

"Well, it sure is mean."

"I'll grant you that," said Claire. "But a little bit of meanness, with good intentions behind it, builds character. Life is not all rose gardens and pleasant moments. It can be difficult and disappointing and frustrating and, yes, mean, Helen."

"So if life can be so crappy, why do you need to add to that pile of crap with threats and ultimatums? Is that how you like to be treated?"

"I was treated like that my entire swim career."

"And my question remains: Did you like it?"

"Whether or not I liked it is immaterial. It's effective, Helen. It works."

"I'm not so sure."

"How else are we going to get them to the cottage, Helen? Pammy will come, moaning and groaning about her latest drama, but Charlotte won't, and Thomas won't either. I'm running out of time here, Helen." Helen said nothing. "I can't pussyfoot around."

"Since when have you ever pussyfooted around anything?"

Claire smiled at her daughter. "Work with me, Helen. You don't have to like it; you just have to communicate it. You can blame the whole thing on me. I suspect they'll do that anyway."

So Helen had dutifully called Pammy, Charlotte, and Thomas, and relayed the loaded invitation from their mother. Pammy, who said she was deeply hurt, told Helen she would come, whether or not she was included in the will. Charlotte, who laughed, said she wouldn't miss this final throwdown for all the money in the will. And Thomas said he would see if he could fit it in. When Helen reported back to her mother, with the information that Pammy and Charlotte were definite yeses and that Thomas was a maybe, Claire had clapped her hands. "I love a good competition," she said, grinning.

And here it was; July Fourth was almost upon them, and Pammy, good to her word, had already shown up. Helen gently laid her hand on her mother's cheek. Claire responded by opening one eye. Not looking at Helen she asked, "Who are you?"

Helen bent down so her face was at the same height as her mother's. She looked into Claire's dark brown eyes, the very color and shape of her eyes. "Three guesses, two don't count."

"Ah," said Claire through a two-second smile. "I recognize that voice. Hello, Helen."

"Did you sleep well?"

"I did," said Claire. "Have I been out long?"

Helen again looked at her watch. "About two hours."

"Good Lord." Claire sat up and reached for her glasses. "Where's your sister?"

"In the kitchen."

"Get me my walker," said Claire. "Let's join her." Ten minutes later, they had righted Claire, stood her up, positioned her in front of her walking device, and taken a few deep breaths. Claire watched as Helen folded the blanket that had been covering her. "Fifty years ago, I would have completed my warm-up in the pool in the time it took me to get out of the chair and ready to walk with this stupid thing." Claire, a scowl on her face, rattled the aluminum walker.

"Oh yeah?" Helen said. "Well, fifty years ago, I wasn't even born yet."

"Ha-ha!" Claire laughed. "That's funny, Helen."

They made their way through the living room and dining room and into the kitchen. When they walked in, Pammy didn't see them right away. She was standing at the stove, her back to them, with the radio turned up—big band tunes. Claire started to sway with the beat. "Tommy Dorsey!" she cried out. "I bet you a hundred dollars this is Tommy Dorsey!"

Pammy wheeled around. "It *is* Tommy Dorsey!"

"Since when have you listened to Tommy Dorsey?" Claire's hips were still moving.

"Whenever I feel like it," said Pammy, shrugging one shoulder.

"Lord, he's good," said Claire. "I saw him once—did I ever tell you that?"

Pammy raised her eyebrows at Helen. "I think you did," Helen started. But there was no stopping Claire.

"At the Rainbow Room in New York. It was a wonderful evening. Your father, of course, was there. We went with one of his patients and her husband. Your father had saved her child's life, you see, and her husband, who was in the entertainment business, was able to get us a prime table." Pammy knew what was coming next. "Do you ever get to the Rainbow Room, Pammy? You live right in New York."

"I have been there," Pammy responded. "It's lovely."

"More like swinging!" Claire was now doing her best to snap her arthritic fingers.

Helen loved seeing her mother this animated. This was the woman she remembered from her childhood, the woman who moved from one task or activity to another from just after it was light outside until she eased herself into her reading chair after dinner. She had always been active, full of energy, especially at the cottage. When she wasn't swimming or playing tennis or weeding the garden, she was chatting with neighbors or organizing a kickball game in the cottage side yard. Occasionally, she opted out of her evening reading so she could join Helen at catching fireflies in glass jars. She was a good cook, too, making everything from scratch. The kitchen was a well- and often-used room; it was where Claire was most at home. In the early morning, coffee mug nearby, she made sauces, marinated meat, baked bars, cookies, and pies for her children and husband, her friends, and for those temporarily incapacitated by a sprained ankle or broken wrist. She tidied up after herself along the way, telling the girls that a messy cook was a lazy cook. Claire also did her own housekeeping, even though many families at the beach had someone in once a week to dust, sweep, and change the bed linens. And she was not a complainer, until recently, which Helen found extraordinary. Most people Helen knew griped about their children or their parents or their husbands or their finances, as if they were the only ones dealing with such universal issues. When Helen was young, she thought there was nothing her mother couldn't do. It was the reverse now. So seeing her mother dance, albeit with a walker, was a moment to be celebrated and encouraged.

"Somebody's refreshed from her nap," said Pammy. "You look good, Mom."

"And you," said Claire, wheeling herself over to the stove to see what was cooking, "were never much good at fibbing." Pammy reddened and looked at Helen, who cocked her head. "Charlotte," Claire continued, stirring the pot with the spoon she had taken from Pammy's hand, "now there was a fibber. She wasn't much good at it either, but that didn't stop her from doing it. She'd put on her best innocent countenance and then tell me she needed to go to the library after dinner to work on homework. She didn't realize, until much later, that I knew the librarian, who knew the two of you, but had never laid eyes on Charlotte. She thought I had two daughters."

Helen laughed. "Charlotte never went to the library?"

"Not according to Nellie Potts, who was the director for twenty-five years."

"Wonder where she was all that time," said Helen, anxious to see what her mother knew.

"You know as well as I do," said Claire, turning to look at Pammy and Helen. "Off with whatever boy would have her. Literally."

"Why didn't you stop her?" asked Pammy.

"You can't stop something like that." Claire turned back to the pot on the stove. "Lord knows I tried. Your father tried, too. But if I had told her that she couldn't go to the library, she would have found another way out. Charlotte, as your father and I discovered when she was still very young, has always been determined. You two were more manageable."

"I was the most well-behaved," said Pammy, batting her eyelashes playfully.

"Except when you weren't." Claire turned down the heat under the sauce. "Let's see. You first smoked when you were thirteen years old. You lost your virginity to Michael Johanson your senior year in high school. You first got drunk the night you lost your virginity. And you didn't brush your teeth for two weeks straight when you were six years old, hoping to lose them all and make a bundle from the tooth fairy." Helen laughed, loving their mother's recollections about her childhood. "Oh, I've got tales about you as well." Claire winked at her youngest.

"Me?" Helen said, splayed fingers to chest, feigning surprise.

"You snuck out of the house fourteen times the summer you were ten years old, which put you in competition with Charlotte. You went swimming at night with Thomas, without our permission, half a dozen times that summer. And you went to the tracks with your responsible older brother the very night your dad grounded you for going to the tracks at night."

"What about her virginity?" asked Pammy, egging her mother on.

"I'm not sure she's lost it yet." Claire grinned at Helen.

"Well," said Helen, smiling back. "Somebody *did* have a good nap."

"What is this, Pammy?" asked Claire, returning her attention to the pot.

"It's a mushroom cream sauce, with chive."

"What are we going to do with it?"

"Pour it over ravioli stuffed with lobster."

"Must be big . . ."

"Ravioli, yes, I've heard that one, Helen," said Pammy.

"If you're so smart, Miss Pammy, where's my glass of wine?"

"Coming right up," she said, crossing the kitchen to open the refrigerator. "Mom?"

"Count me in," said Claire. "I'm going to need at least half a glass if I'm going to swallow a whole lobster wrapped in pasta."

"This is the absolute last time," said Pammy, twisting the corkscrew into the bottle, "I bring you two anything more interesting than hot dogs and beans."

"I love hot dogs and beans," said Claire.

Pammy handed her mother a glass of wine with one hand, and feeling oddly affectionate, briefly hugged her with the other.

After dinner, Pammy and Helen washed the dishes. Claire didn't offer to help because she never had. John Thompson had established early on that since Claire planned the menus, then shopped, chopped, mixed, baked, sautéed, and boiled, she was exempt from washing and drying, which he did until the children were old enough to do it reasonably well. So, before Helen and Pammy cleared the table, they helped their mother into her favorite chair on the porch and lifted her legs onto the ottoman. When they left, Claire closed her eyes and listened to the crickets sing to each other. She could never understand why some people found them annoying, closing their windows at night and cranking up their air conditioners, preferring a cold, silent vacuum to summer's natural sleep aid. She and John used to sit and listen almost every night. They would take their regular coffee to the breezy porch and drink two or three cups and never have trouble sleeping. Charlotte had dubbed them Count and Countess because they each had their special chair (Claire was sitting in hers at that very moment), from which they quizzed their children about who was going where and with whom before letting them pass through the front screen door into the fading light. After all the children were out or upstairs for the night, Claire and John would discuss them, turning to one another to find solutions to the everyday problems they faced. How long would they ground Charlotte this time and what should be the parameters of the punishment? She had broken her curfew three nights in a row. Should they give her another half hour? Would it matter? Claire was grateful for John's interest in their children. Other beach fathers played golf or poker on the weekends and during vacations, but John stayed with his family. If he accepted a golf game, it was because Thomas was included.

"More coffee?"

"Yes, John, that would be lovely."

"It's me, Helen."

Claire looked up at the face of her daughter. "I was thinking about how your father and I used to sit here at night, monitoring the actions of all of you with limited success."

"You were fairly on top of things, as I remember."

"You were all pretty good—well, except for Charlotte."

Helen smiled. "She was the original piece of work."

"My guess is she still is," said Claire.

Pammy appeared at the porch entrance, a square hole the size of the two French doors that were fully opened at the end of June and latched to the porch wall until Labor Day. Pammy held the pot of decaf and a small bowl in her hands.

"You read my mind," said Claire, holding up her mug. It was a mug Pammy had given her many years back, when the "I Love New York" advertising campaign was in full swing.

"And you're using my mug." Pammy filled it halfway. Then, tipped in the kitchen by Helen, Pammy took two cubes of ice from the bowl and slid them into her mother's mug. All of them pretended not to notice.

"It's a nice size," said Claire. "Not too big." Pammy poured coffee into the other two mugs Helen had brought to the porch. All three of them drank their coffee black. "Do you still love New York, Pammy?"

"In some ways I do." Pammy took a sip of her coffee and sat back on the wicker couch she and Helen shared. "I like my job, and I like all the options I have during my off-hours."

"You haven't been able to find a man."

Pammy breathed in deeply. "No, Mother, I haven't been able to find a man."

Claire sipped her coffee. "I'm not saying you need one, Pammy. But it's probably about time to stop searching." Tears came to Pammy's eyes. "Oh Lord, I've said the wrong thing."

"What am I supposed to say to that, Mother?" Pammy looked at the faded wool rugs that covered the floor instead of at Claire.

"All I meant, Pammy, is searching in vain is disappointing and depressing. You cannot begin to realize your potential until you stop thinking it can only be reached through someone else."

"I don't think that, Mom."

"When I was swimming," said Claire, as if she hadn't heard Pammy's remark, "I wanted more than anything in the world to be an Olympian. That was my single focus. The regional and national titles I held? Sure, they were nice, but they didn't make me happy. At some point—much later than it should have happened—I realized that I wasn't going to the Olympics. And while I was absolutely crushed, I was also, somehow, liberated." Helen looked at

Pammy, who was now wiping her nose with one of the napkins she had brought to the porch. Claire continued. She had always been undaunted, unmoved by what she deemed unnecessary emotion. If she hesitated, if she corrected herself, it was out of respect for the person emoting rather than any reaction on her part to the tears themselves. "You may very well find someone dear. But I firmly believe that it won't happen, not at your age, until you stop looking."

Helen stood. "I could use something sweet. Pammy, didn't you say you brought something special for dessert?"

"I did," she said, flashing a fake smile. "Macaroons from my favorite bakery."

"I love macaroons," said Claire.

"I know," said Pammy.

"I'll get them," said Helen, leaving the porch. In the living room she called, "In the white bag next to the fridge, right?"

"Yes."

Pammy sipped her coffee, her eyes resting on the bookcase against the house wall that held paperback novels she had read over the years: *Jaws, The Two Mrs. Grenvilles, Bridget Jones's Diary, Jurassic Park.* Missing were the romance novels that Pammy had been reading almost exclusively for the last five or six years, a substitute for a fulfilling relationship. She hid them from her mother, for fear of being teased or reprimanded. But she read them in front of Helen, who asked her to read the best parts aloud. Pammy was already looking forward to the trip into town, to the secondhand bookstore to find something for the beach.

"Pammy." Pammy looked at her mother. "I'm sorry if I've hurt you." While Pammy wasn't ready to accept her mother's apology, she did anyway, by nodding her head. It was a start, Claire saying she was sorry, because Pammy knew how difficult it was for her mother to do so. Claire was adept at what Pammy called the detached apology, meaning she would say something like, "I'm sorry you were hurt by that remark." But the personal apology she just uttered, attaching herself to the deed done, was rare and, therefore, meaningful.

Helen came back with a plate of macaroons and more napkins.

"Delicious," said Claire, biting into the cookie she had taken when Helen presented them to her. "That's the best macaroon I've ever tasted—blue ribbon."

And while Pammy hated her mother's competition-laced language, she gave her a smile. It did, after all, feel good to receive a compliment, even about something she had purchased, from someone whose praise had always been hard to earn.

"Listen to the crickets," said Helen. "They are outdoing themselves tonight."

And the three of them fell silent, each in her own way grateful for singing insects and stilled tongues.

Chapter 10

1973

Pammy and Helen got dressed without turning on the lights. They had laid their darkest-colored shorts and shirts on the chair next to the window before getting into bed in their underwear to wait. They listened, as they often did, to their parents talking quietly as they climbed the stairs for the night. The girls were normally still, focused on Claire's and John's words, waiting for the names Pammy or Helen to spring forth into the hallway ahead of their utterers. But tonight Pammy and Helen were preoccupied with their plans, with their imminent departure into the darkness. They continued to listen, as Claire and John, in their nightclothes finally, got into the bed that had previously belonged to Claire's parents and grandparents, the bed that creaked with their weight as they shifted, settling in. Helen had then stared, assiduously, at her watch with the illuminated dial, for ten minutes before giving the sign: three soft knocks on the bunk bed railing. She quickly descended the ladder and, crossing the room silently, met her sister at the chair. They slipped on their clothes, then tiptoed to the window that opened onto the roof above the outdoor shower and back door. The screen, which they had earlier unlatched, slipped easily off its hinges. Helen handed it to Pammy, who propped it against the bedroom wall, like they had practiced. Helen boosted herself up onto the sill and stuck one leg out onto the roof. She glanced back at Pammy, who gave her the okay sign, then ducked her head under the raised window and out into the sticky night air. Helen lifted out her other leg, then turned around, so her back was against the house and her bare feet were firmly planted on the slanted roof, toes pointing out to the edge, some fifteen inches away and twelve feet off the ground. Like a crab, Helen inched along the roof until she reached the outdoor shower below. She glanced back at Pammy, now on the roof and looking at the dark grass beneath them. As instructed, Pammy closed the window to within an inch of the sill behind her. Her movements were slow, deliberate, fearful.

"Don't look down," Helen whispered.

"Where else am I going to look?"

"At me," said Helen. "Look at me."

"We should have practiced this."

"You can't practice sneaking out of a bedroom window at night. Just follow me."

Slowly, Helen lowered herself onto the top of the shower's standing wall. The house provided two sides to the outdoor shower, a curtain the third, and a white wood wall the fourth. Once atop the wall, Helen grabbed hold of the iron shower rod and swung down, Tarzan style, to the ground. Pammy sat three inches from the window, frozen. "I can't do this," she whispered urgently.

"Then go back inside and go to sleep."

"Helen!"

"What do you want me to say? I did it. So can you."

Pammy shifted her bottom away from the window. She closed her eyes and felt the tar and sand of the shingles grab at her shorts as she dragged herself along the roof. A meticulous laundress, Claire would know Pammy had been up to something. Helen sat down on the grass, then lay back to look at the stars, innumerable and brilliant against the black sky. Thomas was teaching her the constellations. She had found the Big and Little Dippers when she heard the thud. "Ouch!" said Pammy, picking herself up.

"What happened?" asked Helen.

"Some accomplice you turn out to be." Pammy brushed the

grass off her shorts. "I slipped right off the edge of the shower. You didn't tell me it was wet."

"Showers are always wet." Helen smiled at her sister.

"Well, that hurt. I probably broke my ass," said Pammy, looking at Helen for the impact of using a prohibited word. When she got no reaction, she said, "Wait until you get hurt."

"That," said Helen, offering no sympathy either, "never happens."

Helen started walking across the backyard, looking back at the house for signs of her parents; Pammy followed at a distance. Abruptly, Helen stopped, letting Pammy catch up. Holding hands, they ran through the Callahans' yard, which was illuminated by a giant spotlight affixed to the garage, then down the street and around the corner to the docks.

During the day, the docks were a friendly place. Helen, who crabbed at least once daily, knew every plank. She also knew most of the weekend fishermen, who sometimes congregated after their morning ritual, all holding up their biggest fish in an effort to win storytelling rights for the day. If they cleaned their fish there, Helen watched, never disgusted, as fishing, to her, didn't seem like the slaughtering of innocent creatures. All these fishermen ate what they caught, so the fish were food, pure and simple. The young fathers with toddlers in tow arrived at the docks after the fishermen had gone home for breakfast. With sleep still in their eyes and uncombed hair, they smiled at Helen as they ushered their charges across the planks. Harnessed into puffy orange lifejackets, the kids would scamper into the family Boston Whaler and wait for their dad to start the engine. Down the creek, out to the islands, over to Sandy Point, the destination never seemed to matter to the children, teeth chattering from the early morning chill and excitement, as they embarked on another summer adventure.

But at night, the docks lost their warmth and charm. Poorly lit and eerie, they looked like scary movie graveyards, with each wood piling marking the dead down below. The water gently shoved itself against the boats in quick, slapping waves that sounded, at night, like footsteps. Helen glanced behind her. Was someone coming?

Seeing the tiny orange lights in the distance, Helen and Pammy, still holding hands, knew they had found them. Six—no, eight—Helen thought, as she counted again—including Charlotte and Rick—people stood at the end of the first dock, smoking and, Helen guessed, drinking beer. The night just didn't feel right, she had once overheard Rick say to Charlotte on the beach, without a beer in one hand and a babe in the other. Helen could think of at least a hundred reasons why she wouldn't want to be Rick's babe. Number one was that he was gross. He had straight, jet-black hair down to his shoulders that looked greasy. His beard was scruffy, looking more like a failure than a success, and his chest hair, which was always visible because he hardly ever wore a shirt, barely covered the pimples beneath it. Charlotte, she was convinced, had a screw loose to date him.

"Let's try to get closer," said Pammy.

"I think they'll see us. We can wait here until they go to the beach. That shouldn't be too long."

They lay on the grass, tummies down, and watched the cigarette light show. Pammy wished she were older, while Helen twisted blades of grass between her fingers and simply waited. Within minutes, the teenagers cast their butts into the water and walked back down the dock. Charlotte and Rick, holding hands and bottles of beer, strode within twenty yards of Helen and Pammy, who had put their faces into the grass and were praying they would not be discovered. When Charlotte and the others were gone, Helen and Pammy stood and brushed the freshly cut grass from their clothes. "Yuck!" Pammy said, pulling several blades from her lips. "Did you see where they went?"

"They must have gone to the beach. Let's go by the rocks and see if we can come up behind them."

Helen and Pammy climbed down the huge rocks engineered to retain the dirt cliff between the docks and the houses it supported from extinction. At the bottom, they ran along the water's edge until they reached the stone wall that bordered the Tetreaus' property. Backs to the wall, they moved slowly toward the end, where the bathing beach began, and, they hoped, where Charlotte and Rick and their friends could be found. Once there, Helen peeked around the corner and, seeing nothing, waved Pammy on. Staying close to the sea wall, they walked along the beach in silence, hoping they would see more cigarettes or hear voices. Just when Helen was about to give up on the beach and try the duck pond, she heard Rick say "money." She pulled at Pammy's shirt and motioned for her to be quiet. They got down on their hands and knees and crawled along the sand until they reached the side of the steps that led up to the public access, just down the street from the Thompson cottage. Helen held her breath, believing if Rick found them spying on his gang, he might break her wrist by twisting it or pull half her hair out of her head.

Risking discovery and certain injury at the hands of her sister's dopey boyfriend, Helen peered over the steps and saw Charlotte sitting as part of a circle on the other side of the steps. The distinctive smell of marijuana drifted over and hit Helen like a hot, moist breeze. She sat back down and looked at Pammy, who was smiling and holding her nose.

"Who's in with me?" asked Rick. No one answered. "I can't believe this," he said. "It's easy money, and nobody wants any of it."

"I might be persuaded to take some of it," Charlotte said, with a giggle.

"You'll get plenty of it, babe. But I want a man on the job with me. No babes involved. What about you, Dave?"

"I'm not interested in going to jail, man."

"Nobody's going to jail. We wear stockings over our heads. We wear funky clothes from that consignment store in town. We hold our hands in our pockets like we're loaded, and we get all the cash in the drawer. Then we run out of the store and split. Easy money."

Jimmy Stockton, a fifteen-year-old who Helen knew from Charlotte was anxious to fit in with the group and eager to please Rick, asked when Rick was planning to do the job.

"Anytime. We can go tomorrow night. Can you stay out past ten?" Everyone in the circle laughed.

"I can stay out as late as I want," said Jimmy.

"Good," Rick said. "We'll hit it Monday night, at closing time when it will be quiet, then drive back here and split up the money."

"Fifty-fifty?"

"Sixty-forty," Rick answered. "I'm the brains here." Helen let out a giggle. "Who the hell is that?" Rick stood.

"I giggled," said Charlotte. "Or at least I think I did. God, I'm stoned."

Rick sat back down. "None of you breathe a word of this."

"I think it's *breathes,*" said Charlotte. "I think *none* takes a singular verb, which in this case would be breathes."

"What the hell you talking about, woman?" asked Rick.

"My mother was an English teacher—remember? Sometimes she does grammar drills at dinner."

"Your mother is a psycho," said Rick.

"You've got me there."

Everyone in the circle was quiet for a moment. Most of them were, like Charlotte, feeling the effects of the joint they had shared. It was this middle high time that Charlotte liked best. Bookended by thinking everything was hilarious and eating a pint of chocolate chip ice cream, the middle high presented time for reflection. Sometimes Charlotte focused on her split ends or a chipped fingernail, but other times her mind flew into the night sky, landing on a bright star or the moon, pondering the cosmos.

Rick stood. "Well," he said. "I think it's time to call it a night." They all knew what this meant. And they all dutifully stood, said their good-byes, and walked up the cement steps to the street. Some of them would linger there, smoking the last cigarette of the evening, while others, bound by curfews, would head home, already looking forward to the bag of chips in the kitchen cupboard or the leftover spare ribs in the fridge. Charlotte and Rick stayed, as they always did.

"Let's go," whispered Pammy.

"We're done?"

"I don't think you want to see what's coming next." Pammy started to crawl along the beach, back whence they came. Helen followed her, but stopped for a moment to look back at her sister, who was allowing Rick to take off her shirt. Once out of eyesight and earshot, Pammy and Helen stood and ran the rest of the way. They rounded the Tetreaus' seawall, and then jogged along the cement walkway to the road. They slowed their pace, now that Rick and Charlotte had little chance of discovering them, and walked back along the street-lighted road to their cottage. Helen boosted Pammy to the top of the shower wall, where she stepped onto the roof and crept along until she reached the window. When Helen was at the top of the shower wall, a car pulled onto their grassy driveway, its headlights shining on Helen. She froze.

"Well, well, well," said Thomas as he got out of his Ford Pinto. "What do we have here? Helen Thompson, I do believe you've been up to some mischief."

"Shhhh! Mom and Dad are sleeping."

"I'll keep my voice down all right," said Thomas, smiling at his youngest sister, "just as soon as you tell me what I've missed." He walked to the shower and held up his arms. Helen lowered herself down into them. Pammy, thinking that if Thomas did not talk to her directly she was not caught, scooted through their bedroom window that she had just reopened and then sat on the pine floor, stripping off her shirt and shorts, hoping to get back into bed without further discovery.

Helen never minded getting caught by Thomas; in fact, she liked it because it meant she got to spend time with him. Because he was eight years older than Helen, Thomas was often elsewhere—working mostly—but also hanging around other kids his age. When Helen was able to turn his attention toward her, she instantly turned her full attention to him, reveling in every minute they spent in one another's company, every bit of advice offered, every burst of laughter. They never fought, Thomas and Helen, like he and Charlotte did. And Helen thought the difference in their ages might have something to do with this, at least that's what her mother had told her one day. But she also knew that she and Thomas were connected. Other older brothers barely knew their much younger siblings existed. But Thomas had always been a part of Helen's world—doing puzzles with her when she was in kindergarten; drawing with her when, in second grade, she thought she wanted to be an artist; taking her on biking adventures; and, just this past year, occasionally picking her up at school and driving her to Dairy Queen for a dip cone.

"We were spying on Charlotte and dumb old Rick," whispered Helen.

Thomas laughed. "Colossal waste of time, right?" He set Helen down on the grass next to him.

Helen thought about telling her brother about Rick's plan to rob the store, but decided to hold on to the secret rather than release it. She guessed it would never happen. "Yes. Unless you count cigarette smoking as exciting."

"Which I don't," said Thomas.

"Me neither," said Helen. "And it sure makes Mom crazy."

"Ah, well, I suspect that's the real reason Charlotte does it."

"Really?"

"Really," said Thomas, putting his arm around Helen's shoulder. "Let's go in. I'm dying for some ice cream, and I need someone to help me eat it. Know anyone who's interested?" Helen raised her hand. "I knew I could count on you."

Chapter 11

2003

Helen woke early and pulled on the shorts and shirt she had neatly draped over their bedroom chair the night before, all the while looking at Pammy, as if watching her sleep would guarantee its continuance. Once in the hallway, Helen gently shut the bedroom door behind her and then quietly descended the stairs to the kitchen. She drank a small glass of orange juice and then made a half pot of coffee before walking out the back door onto the dewy grass. She crossed the street and walked down the right-of-way to the beach, misty and deserted. She sat on the top cement step, instinctively pulling her knees toward her chest and wrapping her arms around her legs. Resting her head on her knees, she stared out at the calm, flat, inviting water. A minute later, she descended the steps, crossed the sand, and stood at the shoreline, allowing the Sound to touch her naked toes. It was cold, as it always was in the morning in early July; the water was typically chilly until mid-August. This had never stopped the shoreline residents from diving in as soon as the school year ended. Because they all agreed that when they were in the water, moving through it, the Sound was always what they all called refreshing. Before summer officially started, before Helen was at the cottage for two full months, she swam three mornings a week at the Stonefield Community Center. And even though the water was sometimes eighty degrees, it was always shocking diving in. By the end of her second lap however, Helen was completely adjusted, no longer feeling the chill, no longer feeling anything but the movement of the water as she pushed it alongside her body.

Claire had insisted all her children be what she called capable in the water by their fifth birthday. In fact, she had given them what she deemed proper swimming lessons until they went off to school. Then, Helen and her siblings were driven by their mother to organized swimming lessons at the same community center where Helen now swam. And Claire enrolled them in additional lessons every summer at the beach. By the time they were ten years old, the Thompson children were proficient enough for membership on regional swim teams. Helen was the only one of the four who lasted more than a couple years. But, unlike her mother, Helen had grown tired of daily workouts at the pool in her teenage years. She wanted to try other things, the drama club, field hockey. And even though Claire had fought her, telling her she would regret not excelling at something, Helen, with the help of her father, was able to convince her mother that perhaps one Olympic-grade swimmer in the family was enough.

John Thompson allowed his wife to make the decisions affecting the household, but he was always involved in decisions that pertained to the children. He deferred to Claire ninety percent of the time—she was with them much more than he was; she knew them more intimately—but had no trouble telling his wife, gently always, when she was out of line. Because he was usually right, Claire could rarely raise an effective argument against his point of view. And when Helen landed a plum supporting role in the high school's rendition of *How to Succeed in Business Without Really Trying,* Claire told Helen that she could give up swimming, if she wished, and pursue acting. Helen was, Claire told her husband after they had seen the musical several times, far and away, the best actor on the stage.

Gazing down and seeing a perfectly sized flat rock near her left foot, Helen folded herself in half to pick it up. Holding it just so in her right hand, she flicked it and then watched it skip, five, six, seven times before sinking for good. After skipping a few more stones, Helen looked up at the horizon and could see that the islands had started to take shape out of the mist. She turned and walked back through the sand, up the steps, and through the grass. She rinsed the sand and grass blades from her feet with the hose attached to the side of the cottage and then dried them with a hand towel that hung for this purpose over the shower curtain rod. Back in the house, she grabbed her socks, tennis sneakers, and one of Charles's old sweatshirts Helen wore at the cottage from the chair in the kitchen, and put them on to fight the morning dampness. She then retrieved her yellow and blue porcelain mug out of the dishwasher and filled it with hot coffee. She sat on the porch and read her book for an hour before Pammy, stretching and yawning, appeared at the bottom of the stairs in her pajamas, bathrobe, and slippers. "Good morning," said Helen, looking up from her book.

"Mmmmm," Pammy said. "Any coffee?"

"Lots. I just made a fresh pot."

"Can I get you some?"

"You sit," said Helen, getting up from her chair. "I'll get the coffee. You're dangerous with a mug of hot liquid this early in the morning."

Pammy smiled at her sister and sat down on the couch. Shivering, she grabbed the white cotton blanket that was draped over the back and covered herself from her shoulders to her toes. Helen reappeared and handed her the other blue and yellow mug, which Pammy held tightly in both hands for warmth. "Why is it so cold?" she asked. "It's July."

"There is something about mist in the morning that gets under your skin."

Pammy sipped her coffee. "That sounds like an old wives' tale."

"Some old wives are pretty savvy."

"What time is it?" Pammy asked.

"Almost nine," said Helen, looking at her watch.

"Have you been up long?"

"A while."

"What time does Charlotte arrive?"

"Whenever she wants to," said Helen. "You know Charlotte."

"Is she bringing him?" asked Pammy.

"I don't know."

"How old is he again?"

"You and I both know he's twenty-eight."

Pammy looked through the screen to the empty street. The fog was keeping the children at home. Maybe their mothers were making them pancakes. If Pammy had children, she would routinely make them wonderful breakfasts, as a means to start the day pleasantly and as a sign of her affection. She would be a good mother. "What do you do with someone who's twenty years younger than you?"

"What don't you do," said Helen, smiling.

"Maybe that's my problem," said Pammy. "I shouldn't be looking in the business district or in the bars for a boyfriend. I should be down at NYU, sniffing around the student union. What sensible twenty-something wouldn't take me out?"

"She takes him out," said Helen. "From what I can tell over the phone, she pays for everything. He really is a student."

"When's the last time you talked to her? She never calls me."

"She never calls me, either, Pammy. I call her, which I did on Memorial Day weekend and miraculously got through."

"Maybe they've broken up."

"Tell me you're not jealous," said Helen.

"Not really."

"You could have a twenty-eight-year-old boyfriend, too, you know." Helen drained the lukewarm coffee from her mug

"Honestly, I wouldn't even entertain the thought," said Pammy. "And I guess that's what bugs me. That dating a child is fully within her grasp. Our sister cannot be without a man, or boy for that matter, for five minutes."

"She's always been like that," said Helen. "You could be like that, too."

"But I'm not."

"That's why you haven't been through two divorces and are not dating a Generation Xer."

"Well, sometimes I wish I were like that. Sometimes I wish I didn't give a crap about what everyone else thinks and could focus on nothing but what and who makes me happy." Helen said nothing. Pammy was focused so much on her own happiness that it made her unhappy. "After all," Pammy continued, "how can we be happy if we're not intentional about it?"

"I don't know how happy Charlotte is," said Helen.

"At least she's getting laid."

"Anybody can get laid."

"So says the married woman." Pammy raised her mug to Helen.

"Married nothing. If all you're looking for is sex, you can find that on the beach today. That's not what you're after."

"What am I after, Helen?"

"Companionship. Affirmation. Stuff we all want." Helen stood. "And if Charlotte is finding that with her twenty-eight-year-old plaything, then why not?"

"When am I going to find my plaything?"

Helen shrugged and took two steps toward the kitchen, toward more coffee. "When you quit looking?" She looked back at her sister.

"Boy, you really are a chip off the old block."

"Maybe she's right."

Charlotte drove her black BMW rental onto the grass driveway at four thirty that afternoon. Daniel Bammer, who didn't turn twenty-eight until October, sat in the passenger seat. As soon as Charlotte turned off the ignition, he hopped out of the car and opened the trunk. Extracting with alacrity suitcases and fancy paper bags with handles and smart-looking logos, Daniel emptied the spacious trunk within seconds. He set everything down on the lawn to wait for Charlotte's dispatch and then walked back to the car and leaned in the driver's side window, where Charlotte was reapplying pink lipstick. He kissed her on the cheek. She turned to him and kissed his mouth, sliding her tongue along his top teeth. It was at this exact moment, mid-French kiss, that Helen and Pammy walked outside to greet them. "Hey!" Helen said as soon as she saw what was happening, hoping to alert them, maybe to stop them, more for Pammy's sake than for theirs or her own.

Daniel's head flew out of the window so fast he bumped the back of it on the top of the door. Charlotte, cool as ever, wiped the smeared lipstick from her face with her fingers and expertly reapplied it, finishing just as Helen and Pammy reached the car.

"Well, look who's here," said Pammy, as Charlotte stepped out of the driver's seat.

"Look indeed," said Charlotte, giving both her sisters a hug and a kiss on the cheek. She stepped back, holding both of them at arm's length, and Helen could immediately see it was more so they could get a look at her than she at them. She had already undergone an eye lift, lip augmentation, reconstructive nose surgery, as well as the dye and perms jobs on her tresses on a regular basis. Breast enhancement was the next logical step. "What do you think?" she asked, unabashed. "Daniel loves them."

Helen, Pammy, and Charlotte looked at Daniel, who was blushing as he stood next to the car, a foot soldier awaiting orders from his queen. "Hi," he said.

"Pammy, Helen, this is Daniel," said Charlotte, her arm out like a tour guide directing attention to her man.

"We're glad you could come," said Helen, falling into her hostess role.

"Yes," said Pammy, who, struck with Daniel's athletic physique and handsome face, was not aware she had spoken.

"Why don't you go inside, honey," said Charlotte, dismissing him like the child he was. "We're staying in the hideous yellow room with the creaky double bed. You can put our things there." Charlotte was still annoyed by the fact that her mother had rolled yellow paint over the lavender walls of her bedroom when Charlotte no longer spent her summers at the cottage. It was an insult, she told Claire when she found out; it was disrespectful. Claire told her it was no such thing, that the room simply needed painting and lavender was not her favorite color. They had a discussion about it just about every time they spoke, which wasn't often. Charlotte watched Daniel grab half the bags from the lawn and then disappear into the house. She turned her attention back to her sisters. "So," she said, this time joining Pammy and Helen in checking out her chest. "What do you think?"

"They're big." Helen was at a loss for more descriptive words. "You must have bought a new wardrobe."

"Oh no," said Charlotte. "I'm still wearing a size six up top. You'd be amazed how easily these babies tuck into a blouse."

"Yes," said Pammy. "They certainly look nicely tucked in now."

"And they are fabulous in bed. I can't tell you what a difference they make in my attitude about sex. I can't get enough. Most forty-seven-year-old women I know can barely hold on to their husbands, much less a twenty-seven-year-old stud." Charlotte grinned at her sisters and then, spotting a piece of hair on Pammy's shirt, she removed it with her manicured pink nails. "They make me feel young and sexy."

"I thought he was twenty-eight," said Pammy, still focused on Daniel.

"Not yet, dear."

"Okay," said Helen, feeling Pammy's draining confidence, an immediate reaction to Charlotte's mere presence. "Let's head inside, so you can see Mom. I've made some iced tea."

"Iced tea nothing," said Charlotte, striding toward the back door. "It's five o'clock, isn't it?"

Helen and Pammy followed her into the house, where Charlotte continued to walk through the kitchen, the dining room, and halfway across the living room before calling Daniel's name. Immediately, as if he had been waiting at the top of the stairs, he appeared on the landing. "I need a scotch and water, baby. And get my sisters something innocuous. They look like Chardonnay drinkers to me," she said, as Helen and Pammy walked into the room.

"Rarely touch the stuff," said Pammy, remembering why she didn't call her oldest sister, remembering why they hadn't seen each other since their father's funeral five years earlier. "I'll have a scotch, no water, on the rocks."

"I'll have the wine," said Helen to Daniel. "There's an open bottle in the fridge. You'll find beer in there, too, if you're interested."

Charlotte walked onto the porch and then plopped down on the couch in the preferred sitting area and put her small, wedge sandal-shod feet on the wicker coffee table. She took a slender silver case from her white straw bag and carefully extracted a long cigarette, which she expertly placed between her full pink lips and lit within seconds with a sterling silver lighter. Tilting her head toward the ceiling and exhaling into the air above her, Charlotte then dropped her eyes to meet her sisters'. They had followed her to the porch and were sitting in the wicker chairs looking at her, like students watching their teacher. "So," she said. "What's up with you two?"

Before Helen or Pammy could speak, their mother called down from the top of the stairs. "Charlotte? Is that you?"

"Yes, Mother, it is," answered Charlotte, rising from the couch. She inhaled deeply on her cigarette, then gave it to Daniel, who had just returned with their drinks. She glanced at the mirror above the couch and fluffed her already flawless hair with her hands. She turned. Helen guessed she was expecting to see Claire at the bottom of the steps, waiting with outstretched arms. But Claire was still making her way down, gripping the banister. Charlotte looked at Helen, who said, "Do you want help, Mom?"

"No, Helen. I have to do some things for myself."

Charlotte walked to the bottom of the stairs and looked up. There, halfway down, stood Claire Gaines, bent over and looking, Charlotte thought, like fifteen instead of five years had passed since their last gathering. She was wearing a faded denim skirt, a white cotton blouse with a Peter Pan collar, and a jade green cardigan pulled over her shoulders. On her feet were Birkenstocks, sandals she had worn since the 1970s. For just a moment, they stared at each other, as if trying to remember what to say or how to act. Then Charlotte climbed the stairs, stood on the step below her mother, and put her hand on Claire's boney elbow. "I'm not helping," she said. "I'm simply available should you change your mind."

Minutes later, they were all seated on the porch. Daniel, who was still standing, introduced himself to Claire and thanked her for what he called a lovely invitation.

"I'd put it in the command performance category myself," said Charlotte. No one responded.

"I'll just go unpack," said Daniel. "I don't feel settled until my clothes are in a drawer or closet, and I know you all have a lot to catch up on." Charlotte blew a kiss to him as he ascended the stairs and then put her feet back up on the table in front of her. She ran her fingers through her hair and took a sip of her drink.

"He seems like a nice young man," Claire began. Helen and Pammy sat back in their chairs and waited. Claire was not finished. "How old is he, Charlotte?"

"He's twenty-seven, Mother," she said, lighting a cigarette. Daniel had, apparently, extinguished and disposed of her other one.

"There's no smoking in this house," said Claire.

"Really? Why not? We're on a porch."

"Because I can't and never could stand the smell of it. And it's rude to smoke around nonsmokers. When you were fourteen you didn't smoke in the house, so there's no need now that you're forty-seven."

"Why is this ashtray sitting here then?" asked Charlotte, lifting a square-shaped, shallow tiled dish.

"Because you made it in the summer crafts program when you were eight and gave it to me for Mother's Day." Charlotte gave her mother a long look and then put the cigarette out in the ashtray. "Thank you," said Claire. "So, tell me more about Daniel."

"Well," said Charlotte, taking her feet off the table and planting them firmly on the floor, as if she were going to stand, "he's a student, working toward his master's degree in philosophy. I met him at a winery, and we had the best time getting to know one another. That was"—Charlotte looked at the ceiling for a moment—"Christmas time, I guess, so we've been together for about six months. He's a charming person with lovely manners, and I enjoy his company."

"I enjoy the company of men twenty years my junior also, Charlotte, but I wouldn't presume to sleep with them."

Helen and Pammy made eye contact, but said nothing. Charlotte fell back on the couch, as if she had suffered a push to the chest. Recovering quickly, she looked directly and deliberately at Claire, isolating her sisters from the remark custom-made for their mother. "Who or what I fuck is none of your business."

Helen drained the last sip of wine from her glass and stood. "Anyone need another drink?" she asked, holding out her empty glass to show the others that she was not simply looking for an excuse to leave the room.

"I'll have another," said Pammy, getting up. "Mother? Charlotte? Anything for you?"

Charlotte handed her empty glass to Pammy and nodded her head. Claire, who did not have a glass, asked Helen for white wine. Pammy and Helen walked into the kitchen and shut the swinging door behind them. "Unbelievable," said Pammy. "I simply cannot believe what I heard in there. And she's been here, what, fifteen minutes?"

"I don't blame her," said Helen, getting the wine out of the refrigerator. "I might not have used the word *fuck,* but Mother was clearly setting herself up. She knows Charlotte as well as we do. Charlotte has never taken any crap from anybody."

"I would no more say *fuck* to Claire Gaines than do it in front of her," said Pammy, pouring scotch into her glass. "But, I've never had the balls—and now the breasts—of our sister."

"On the other hand," said Helen, filling a glass with wine for her mother, "Charlotte asks for it. I don't think you can show up at a family gathering with a Chippendales dancer as your date and expect silent respect from everyone. That may fly in San Francisco, but it's not going to fly here. Just wait until Thomas arrives."

"When will he be here? Saturday?" asked Pammy, pouring another drink for Charlotte.

"That's the latest." Helen re-corked the bottle and put it back in the fridge. "Ready?"

They walked back onto the porch with the drinks. Charlotte was sitting in the same position on the couch, and Claire had shifted just slightly in the chair. Both women looked through the same screen at the water. It was keenly obvious they had not spoken to each other. Helen gave her mother the wine, then sat in her seat and looked at her sister Charlotte. Charlotte looked back, and Helen raised her eyebrows, as if to say, *Mom's old and tired. Let it go.*

Charlotte had always had a hard time letting it go, letting anything go. As a teenager, she had to get the last word in, always. It didn't matter if she knew she'd be grounded, or if, on occasion as had happened, she'd get a slap across the face. She had no issue stunning relatives, neighbors, authority figures, anyone at all with her sharp wit, her acerbic tongue. In fact, Helen thought, Charlotte had liked putting adults off balance, letting them know that they were not as wise, not as together as they thought. She prided herself on her ability to come back at and from anything, a characteristic she inherited from her mother.

"The traffic was murder today," said Charlotte, surprising everyone in the room with her small talk. "I've got to stop flying into New York."

"Boston's not much better," said Helen, wanting to smooth over the bumpy beginning, the awkwardness. "You could try Providence next time."

"There won't be a next time," said Claire to no one in particular.

CHAPTER 12

1973

Jimmy Stockton sat in the car Rick parked in front of the 7-Eleven on Thistle Street. Rick sat next to him, in the driver's seat, again going over their plan. They had discussed it three or four times that afternoon, and Jimmy had told Rick before going home for dinner how confident he felt about the job. Here, now, Jimmy was losing faith in the plan. He rubbed his sweaty hands on his jeans, but the moment he stopped, the perspiration resurfaced. He wiped them again, with the same unsatisfactory result, then stopped, sensing Rick's disapproval. "You all right, man?"

"Oh yeah," said Jimmy. "I'm cool."

"I don't need no chickenshit robbing this store with me."

"I'm all set." Jimmy decided against correcting Rick's English, as Charlotte would have done had she been in the car. A double negative, she had taught them all that very afternoon, was just like a positive, in this case meaning Rick actually *did* want a chickenshit robbing the store with him. Rick had forbidden Charlotte to join them, an empty mandate since Charlotte told him she had no interest in tagging along. Jimmy could tell that she was smart. Plus she was the prettiest girl on the beach. When she smiled at him, when she paid him any kind of attention whatsoever, Jimmy felt strong enough to knock Rick to the ground, to claim Charlotte as his. Sometimes when Jimmy was in bed at night, if he squeezed his eyes closed tightly, he could picture her with one of her soft hands pressed gently against his chest as they sat in a secluded area of the beach while her other hand probed the fly of his jeans. His penis twitched.

"I'm going in, and I'm going to work fast. There's no time for error here."

"Yes," said Jimmy, pushing Charlotte out of his mind. "We've gone over this."

Rick looked at Jimmy one last time before he opened the door and got out of the car. Jimmy looked at his watch, which read 10:58. Jimmy followed Rick with his eyes to the plate-glass door. The lights inside shone through the glass, casting a pale yellow glow into the darkness outside. Rick walked into that light, and Jimmy caught a quick glimpse of his face; his forehead was beaded with sweat. Jimmy found comfort in this, even though he figured fearful robbers weren't especially adept robbers. Although his mother had always told him that a certain amount of fear or reverence was a good thing. *It makes you know you're alive,* she had said. Jimmy had no doubts about being alive. His heart was thumping against his clean white T-shirt, and the moisture from his hands had traveled to his armpits, forehead, and crotch. He had to urinate, even though Rick had parked the car on the side of the road leaving the beach less than fifteen minutes ago, so they both could pee in the bushes. Jimmy looked at Rick, hoping he would turn around and announce that the whole thing was a joke. He might laugh and say he needed to test Jimmy, to see if Jimmy was cool enough to hang with his gang. He might call it a rite of passage. But as soon as Rick pulled the door handle and disappeared inside, Jimmy knew it was no joke. He moved over to the driver's seat and gripped the steering wheel.

Because he was not inside the store with Rick, Jimmy had no idea what was happening. Every second felt like a minute. Jimmy tried to imagine Rick checking the three aisles for customers. He tried to picture him, in the large felt cowboy hat Rick had purchased at the Bradlees for this purpose—he had decided a mask or stocking on his face would tip the clerk the moment she saw him—confronting the young woman behind the cash register with the unloaded gun he had taken from his father's top bureau drawer. Would the clerk scream, or would she quietly put her hands over her head as Rick had predicted? Jimmy looked at his watch; it was 11:02. As instructed, Jimmy started the car Rick had taught him how to drive over the last couple days. He was just shifting the car into gear when Rick burst out the glass door and ran to the passenger side of the car. He yanked the door open, tossed the bag of money onto the seat between them, and threw himself in afterward. "Go!" he yelled, slamming the door behind him. Jimmy floored the accelerator. The rancid smell of rubber filled the air as Jimmy sped out of the 7-Eleven lot and onto Thistle Street. He slowed his pace, as they had practiced, once they rounded the corner onto Main Street. A mile down Main, he pulled Rick's Oldsmobile behind the Finast food store on Elk Street, parked behind the Dumpsters, and turned off the engine. There, Rick had said, they would wait until the police had come and gone, and then they would drive home. In the huge, empty parking lot, Rick smoked a cigarette and then counted the money.

"Not bad, Jimmy boy," he said, handing Jimmy a stack of tens. "You made yourself two hundred bucks."

"Great," said Jimmy, still reeling from the robbery.

"That chick was so scared in there," Rick said with a laugh. "She had the cash out of the drawer before I finished asking her for it."

"She's no fool," Jimmy said before he could think not to.

"What do you mean by that?"

"I just mean that I would do the same thing. There's no sense getting dead over a few hundred bucks."

"You would give up the money, just like that?"

"Hell yes," said Jimmy. "It's not her money anyway."

"That's gutless, man."

"No, Rick. That's smart."

"Don't talk to me about smart. Who masterminded this robbery?"

"You did, Rick."

"And who just pulled it off without a hitch?"

"You did."

"You're damn right," said Rick, lighting up another cigarette. They sat in silence while Rick smoked. As soon as he chucked the butt out his rolled-down window, he looked at his watch. "Let's go check things out." Just before getting out of the car, Rick removed his hat and stuffed it under the front seat. Money locked in the trunk, they walked through the parking lot until they reached the loading dock on Spruce Street. There, they hopped over the metal guardrails and walked down Spruce until they reached the hardware store. From the alley between the hardware store and the dry cleaners, they could see the 7-Eleven. Two police cars, lights flashing, were parked outside.

"What now?" asked Jimmy.

"We wait," said Rick, leaning against the wall. "We wait."

An hour later, Rick, back in the driver's seat, dropped Jimmy off at his house. Enervated from the robbery, Jimmy walked through the unlocked front door, up the stairs to his room, and plopped down on his bed. He yanked off his sneakers and threw them on the floor. He pulled off his belt and his blue jeans with the ten dollar bills shoved into the back pocket and lay them on the end of the bed. Just when he was thinking about falling asleep, the shaking started, first in his arms and hands and then in his legs. He breathed in and out deeply, trying to calm himself, hoping they wouldn't be caught and that Charlotte would be as impressed with him as she would be with Rick.

Helen and Pammy had just swum in from the raft when Charlotte walked down the cement steps to the beach. She was wearing her old, blue-jean cutoffs and a green and purple tie-dye shirt she had made the previous summer. What Helen and Pammy had not seen before were the diamond stud earrings in her rarely visible ears. Charlotte's long hair, which was usually as much in her face as it was out of it, was today neatly tucked behind her bejeweled lobes. "Where'd you get those earrings?" asked Helen, as she dried herself with her beach towel.

"Rick gave them to me today. Aren't they beautiful?"

"They're gorgeous," said Pammy. "Is it your anniversary or something?"

"No, he's just trying to keep me on his arm," said Charlotte, with a smile. "Steve Johanson asked me out again last week."

"He must make tons of money at the gas station," said Pammy.

"Not really," said Charlotte, looking past Helen to see who was sunbathing on the raft. "He's been saving for a while I guess."

"Either that or he found a quick way to make a lot of money," said Helen, softly.

"What do you mean?" Charlotte twisted her neck to look at her sister.

Helen looked at Pammy, who mouthed the word *no.* "Nothing," said Helen. "I didn't mean anything."

Charlotte gave her sister a quizzical look, then shrugged. "I'm not asking," she said. "No other girl on the beach has these in her ears."

"You're right," said Helen. "I haven't seen earrings like that on anybody except Mrs. Cummings."

"And she's really rich," said Pammy.

"Well, I feel rich today," said Charlotte, walking away from her sisters to talk to Steve Johanson, who had just waved to her from his house atop the sea wall. "See you later."

"I can't believe you said that," whispered Pammy as soon as Charlotte was several yards away.

"Why not?"

"Because I thought we agreed that hearing that stuff was our secret. If we tell, Charlotte will know that we spied on her, and she will be even meaner to us than she already is."

"It *is* our secret," said Helen. "That doesn't mean I can't hint around."

"Charlotte's not stupid."

"She is for dating that stupid jerk Rick."

"Nobody said he bought those earrings with stolen money," said Pammy, tentatively.

"He robbed the store last night and she has the earrings today. What do you think?"

"I'm not thinking," said Pammy, walking toward the steps. "Are you going to take a shower or not?"

"I'm coming," said Helen, climbing the steps behind her sister. "He's such a jerk. Why does Charlotte hang around with him?"

"You heard what she said. He buys her beer and is a good lay."

"That's so gross."

"That's because you're a child."

"Oh yeah, Miss Intercourse?" Pammy made a sour face. "That's right," said Helen. "You're as grossed out as I am."

"Kissing is nice." Pammy and Helen crossed the street to their lawn.

"Sure," said Helen. "If you like to swap spit."

"Ew!" said Pammy. "That's definitely gross."

"See, I told you."

That night, Rick and Jimmy robbed the Cumberland Farms in Oaksdale, and the night after that they hit the convenience store in Franklyn. Helen's father gave a low whistle as he read the newspaper Saturday morning. "Someone's making a killing out there," he said.

"Out where?" asked Helen, her mouth full of corn flakes. She and her dad were the only two at the dining room table. He often kept her company when she had an early breakfast on the weekends. Claire made eggs or pancakes on Saturday and Sunday mornings. But she served them later on in the morning to accommodate Charlotte and Thomas.

"At the convenience stores. Three of them have been robbed in three days. The clerks at the different stores describe the same bandit—a young man in a large cowboy hat with a gun and a boy who drives the getaway car. They've stolen almost two thousand dollars."

"Wonder if they'll get caught," said Helen, looking into her cereal bowl. She wanted to tell her father; she wanted him to stop Rick. But she didn't want Charlotte to hate her.

"Sure they will," said John Thompson. "They're just kids. They'll mess up sooner or later. So, you ready to go fishing?"

"Never been readier," said Helen, getting up and bringing her bowl into the kitchen. "Where are we going today?"

"Let's row down the creek and see what we can find there."

"Okay," said Helen. "I'll get the worms. I got a ton of them last night."

"Great," her dad said. "Let's hope they don't sink the boat."

Helen smiled at her father. They walked out of the house together and into the garage to get the oars, fishing poles, tackle box, seat cushions, life jackets, and worms. John gathered the bulky items in his huge arms while Helen held the cushion straps and tackle box with one hand, and with the other the twisting and turning worms housed in the dirt-filled Maxwell House coffee can her mother cleaned out for her yesterday. Fully equipped, they walked through the wet grass to the street, then down the hill toward the dock. "Why do people rob stores?" Helen asked.

"Because they want money, I guess."

"What if they already have a job?"

"Then I guess they just want more money. Some people like to spend money, so they need lots of it. Now you and I, Helen, like to fish. That's why we need lots of worms."

"Are they afraid they'll get caught?"

"The worms?"

"No, the robbers."

"Well, sure. But it probably feels exciting when they don't. If someone thinks he can get away with something, he'll keep doing it until he gets caught."

"Do they all get caught?"

"Most of them, Helen. Why, do you know any robbers?"

"No sir," said Helen, looking down at the street. "I'm just curious."

"Me too," said John.

Rick and Jimmy lay on the warm rocks at the old granite quarry near the town dump. Their cutoff jeans soaked from swimming stuck to their bodies, cooling them while the hot sun burned their faces and chests. Rick sat up and lit a cigarette, then took a sip of his tepid beer. He pushed his wet hair back on his head with the palm of his hand. "Let's hit Addison tonight," he said.

"What's in Addison?" asked Jimmy, sitting up.

"That Give 'N' Go on Route 215. They'll be giving us the money, and we'll be gone," said Rick, laughing.

"I don't know," said Jimmy, diffident.

"What don't you know about? The Give 'N Go or tonight?" asked Rick, annoyed.

"I don't know about robbing stores."

"What, you aren't getting enough money? All right, I'll give you half. From now on, we're fifty-fifty."

"It's not the money."

"Then what the hell is it?" said Rick, looking directly into Jimmy's eyes.

"I don't like it," said Jimmy, suddenly resolute. "I'm not going to drive anymore."

Rick took a deep drag from his cigarette. "That's too bad, because you're in it now."

"I was in, and now I'm out," said Jimmy, standing up and grabbing his striped towel.

"You little shit," said Rick, spitting at Jimmy's feet. "You stupid little shit. Once you're in, you're never out."

"That may be true for you, but not for me. I haven't spent a nickel of that money."

"And that's exactly why you don't get the chicks," said Rick, leaning back on his elbows.

"Well, I don't want that kind of chick," Jimmy said in his defense. "If you have to buy her, she really isn't yours, is she?"

"Charlotte Thompson loves me."

"Maybe she does," said Jimmy.

"You know she does."

"I'm not here to talk about Charlotte," said Jimmy. "That's your business. I'm just not going to rob stores anymore. You can do what you want."

"You going to rat on me?"

"No," said Jimmy, wrapping his damp towel around his neck and turning to walk away. He'd hitchhike back to the beach.

"What are you going to do with the money?" Rick called after him. Jimmy raised his arms and shoulders in a shrug, and Rick knew, right then, he had lost him.

"Well, shit," he said.

It wasn't until he walked down the first aisle that the Give 'N' Go cashier noticed the cowboy hat in his hand. She had read the articles in the newspaper. A wave of fear overtook her and, for a moment, she was paralyzed. She then thought about the call button underneath the counter. Mr. Lena had shown it to her when he hired her and told her to use it only in extreme emergencies. The button, when pushed, alerted the Addison police. This is not a button, Mr. Lena had said, to use when you get the creeps. This is a button to use when you fear for your life. She reached for it. But before she pushed it, two police cruisers sped into the parking lot. Within seconds three officers were in the store, guns drawn. Rick, who had seen the lights, ran to the back of the store, where he assumed he would find an exit. But when he pushed through the door next to the milk fridge, he found himself in a barely lit stock room instead of outside. Knocking down cardboard packing boxes in his wake, he stumbled toward the far end of the room where he saw an illuminated red exit sign. When he got there, the door beneath it was locked. As Rick turned, panicking about what to do next, the lights went on. "Put the gun down!"

Rick looked into the face of an Addison police officer, who stood with his legs apart, his knees bent, and both arms extended in front of him. His hands encircled a big gun, which was pointed at Rick's chest. Rick stared at him. "Put your hands in the air, son," said the officer, moving closer to Rick, who, suddenly, had never felt so tired. His eyelids began to droop. He shook his head, more to stay awake than in a show of defiance. He momentarily closed his eyes. Before he could open them, the officer was upon him. Locked into handcuffs, Rick was escorted out of the store. He walked past the counter, where the pretty cashier was talking to another Addison police officer. She looked at Rick as he walked past and he smiled, even though he figured she had turned him in.

It was Helen, actually, who had turned him in. Unable to keep the secret any longer, she unburdened her conscience to her father while they were fishing. When he asked her why she hadn't come forward sooner, she told him what Pammy had told her—that Charlotte would never talk to them again if they ratted out her boyfriend or if she knew they had been spying on her.

"I understand that, Helen," said John Thompson. "But someone could have gotten hurt."

"Did he have a gun," asked Helen, "when he was robbing everyone?"

"Yes, he did. At least that's what the papers say."

Helen started to cry. "I'm sorry, Dad."

John leaned forward in the boat and wrapped his arms around his youngest daughter. "I'm glad you told me now, Helen. We'll fix this."

"Can we fix it without Charlotte knowing?"

John patted his daughter's back. "You leave that to me. In the meantime, let's catch a few more fish."

When they returned to the cottage, John Thompson made a call to the local police department. He gave them Rick's name and address and told them what Helen had told him. And then he got a cup of coffee and took his book to the porch. When Charlotte descended the stairs two hours later, he said nothing to her. He didn't know how much she knew, other than what Helen had overheard. Plus Charlotte would deny it. And if he confronted her with Helen's story, he was quite certain that she would, indeed, be vindictive toward her sisters. He would let it go simply because that's exactly what Charlotte would do. He only hoped she would learn from it, from what can happen in bad relationships.

When Rick headed out that night, he had no idea what was coming. He hadn't noticed the unmarked police car following him earlier in the evening, waiting for him to don his cowboy hat and hit another convenience store. When he walked into the Give 'N' Go, they were just thirty seconds behind him.

News of Rick's capture spread quickly. Everyone who could read saw the article in the morning paper and talked of little else on the beach that day. Teenage girls cried. Other fathers lectured their sons and daughters. And Charlotte, who of anyone had the most potential to be devastated by the news, instantly changed gears, as John Thompson predicted. She put the diamond earrings back into their velvet box, which she neatly tucked underneath her underwear in the top drawer of her dresser. And she went waterskiing with Steve Johanson.

Chapter 13

2003

After preening for close to forty minutes, Charlotte looked at her reflection in the bedroom mirror and smiled. Her copper highlighted hair exemplified the casual chic look touted by her hairdresser. Her lipstick and eye shadow suited perfectly the colors in her new bikini, as did her freshly manicured nails, which had three days before been polished and buffed to her preeminent standards. She moved in closer and studied her face. The age lines around her eyes and mouth had smoothed out with her latest Botox injection. As the doctor promised, she looked a lot closer to thirty than fifty. Slipping her beach coverall over her head, Charlotte walked downstairs for breakfast. Hearing the clatter of knives and forks against dishes, Charlotte sashayed into the dining room and stood until all eyes were upon her. "Good morning," she said.

"Good morning," said Daniel. He stood, cleared his plate, which several minutes ago held three fried eggs, four pieces of bacon, two pieces of wheat toast, and a small mountain of hash-browned potatoes, and offered Charlotte his seat.

"I couldn't eat a thing," said Charlotte, hand to empty stomach.

"Your young man made everything," Claire said from her place at the head of the table. "It was all quite delicious, Daniel. Thank you."

Helen took her last sip of coffee from her mug, then took her plate into the kitchen. From there she called, "There's coffee, Charlotte."

"Let me get you some," said Daniel. "You sit out on the porch, and I'll bring it to you."

"Dear boy," said Charlotte. "I'll cherish you forever."

Pammy waited until Charlotte retreated from the room before walking into the kitchen, closing the swinging door behind her, and making a gagging face at Helen. Helen placed her index finger vertically over her lips and moved her eyes, indicating Daniel's presence in the pantry. "Can you find a mug?" asked Helen.

"Oh yes," said Daniel. His attention was directed at the third shelf, chest level for him, where assorted mugs were stored in neat rows. Claire liked matching china, but she allowed mismatched mugs that had made their way to the cottage over the years as gifts or discards from home. Every Thompson had a favorite. And even though Thomas hadn't been to the beach in thirty years, no one used his plain, white, diner-style mug. "I just can't find the blue and green one she likes best."

"It's on the fourth shelf," Helen answered. "Next to the blue and green bowl. Charlotte hides it from the rest of us."

Daniel laughed. "She hides things from me, too. She has a glass with a cow on it that she likes to drink water from. And it moves from the dishwasher to a secret spot that only she knows about—and then surfaces the following morning." Moments later, Daniel appeared with Charlotte's mug in his hand. He poured a touch of skim milk into it, then two packets of Equal, before filling it with steaming black coffee.

"She doesn't take her coffee black anymore?" asked Helen, filling the sink with sudsy water to do the dishes.

"This is her vacation treat."

"Some treat," said Pammy.

"Thank you for breakfast," Helen said to Daniel.

"My pleasure. I love to cook, especially breakfast."

"Surely you don't eat like that every day," said Pammy, in a soft, flirty tone. She moved across the kitchen and stood next to him. His tight-fitting green gym shorts and black tank top allowed

Pammy visual access to what older, skin-tagged and moled men covered and hid. She could almost feel the firm flesh of his muscular arm. She could picture running her hands up underneath his top to his smooth chest.

"No," said Daniel, lightly resting his free hand on Pammy's shoulder. "Just on the weekends." He winked at Helen, then, mug in hand, pushed open the swinging door and walked back into the dining room.

"Jesus, he is built," said Pammy, after the door closed behind him.

"You're just horny," said Helen, pouring Pammy and herself another mug of coffee.

"How can you not be, with Zeus walking around the house half naked?"

"My soft, middle-aged husband and prepubescent sons are arriving tonight," Helen said with a smile.

"Then you've got the rest of the day to fantasize. Maybe Charlotte would loan him to me for an hour."

"Maybe my Todd can take you out tonight. You'll have to drive."

"And you're sounding more and more like Mother."

"And you're sounding more and more like a love-struck teenager."

"Weren't those the days?"

"Yes, they were," said Helen, sipping the coffee she never tired of in the mornings.

"And Charlotte's reliving that."

"Lucky girl."

"Bitch," said Pammy, walking out of the kitchen.

Her mother and sister reading on the cottage porch, and Charlotte and Daniel still in bed, Helen jogged to the beach to set up camp. She dug a hole in the sand and then plunged the sharp tip of the beach umbrella into it. She then used her foot to push the sand back into the hole, where it surrounded the pole. Finally, she covered the sand with a cup or so of ocean water poured from her coffee mug, creating what she called beach cement. Her mother loved looking at the water, but could no longer abide the sun. Last summer she was still able to get in the water. This summer, she would not have the strength to swim. Helen had already suggested an alternative plan. Claire could dress in clothing that would protect her from the sun, from its burn, and read underneath the umbrella. And at the end of the day, Helen could move Claire's chair to the water's edge, so she could submerge her feet. Claire hadn't complained because she knew it was a good offer, the best of a bad situation. Since John's death five years ago, Claire was more amenable to reading on the beach. She had lost interest in conversing with the neighbors she had known since her childhood. John had been the kindness and gentleness in her life, and losing him prematurely had made her bitter. She tried to hide her contempt, but more often than not, it slipped out, bearing close resemblance to an unwarranted acrid remark, so it was better to just say nothing. Her old tennis friends avoided her now, except for Muffin Ferrigan, who occasionally happened by with a small plastic jug of freshly made lemonade. Muffin would sit down beside her old friend, pour two tart glassfuls, and chat about the old days for an hour or two.

Umbrella set, Helen placed her own chair in the direct sunlight, a few feet away. She took off her shirt to reveal the gingham bathing suit she bought last summer, her new favorite. The tiny red and white checks hid the flaws of an aging body. Charles, her husband, told her often she didn't look a day over thirty-five, but the fine lines that were just starting to appear at the corners of her eyes were more honest. Her gray hairs, too numerous now to pluck out, were painstakingly covered every few months with colorful concoctions mixed by the skilled hairdressers at Bernard's. They, too, always told her how youthful she looked, but Helen was rarely taken in by hollow compliments, especially from people at salons who made a good deal of their income from tips.

Still, she swam three times a week throughout the winter, rode her bicycle in the spring and fall, ran occasionally, and played a decent game of tennis. She could still beat Todd, who would be twelve in September and who played a textbook game of tennis, but she feared this summer would be the last. Ned, who was ten, was their natural athlete. He played tennis, but preferred team sports, mostly soccer and lacrosse. Like his mother had been at his age, he was always in motion. The only time he sat still was at the dinner table or in a boat, fishing with his father. They were so different, Todd and Ned. The elder, resolute and determined, walked through life with the confidence of someone twice his age. Ned was more of a wanderer. One minute he would emulate Todd; the next, he'd run around the neighborhood with a pack of friends, no agenda, no clock. Ned had a ready sense of humor, and an innate ability to turn ordinary events into wonderful stories, whereas Todd, circumspect and wise, could consistently put his exact feelings into very few, perfectly chosen words. Helen looked forward to their arrival.

"Hey," called Pammy, as she descended the cement steps. "Cute suit. Is it new?"

"You've seen this. I got it last summer."

"It makes you look very skinny."

"That's because I am very skinny." Helen smiled at her sister.

Pammy grabbed a beach chair from the stack next to the steps and set it in the sand next to Helen. "I've got to get tan in the next fifteen minutes," she said. "Charlotte has been lying in a booth all winter and looks like a goddess."

"A well-endowed goddess to boot."

"Can you believe she actually went through with that? I remember her talking about it, at Dad's funeral of all places, but I thought she was joking, didn't you?"

"Charlotte lives to shock, horrify, and mock. If shoving gelatinous bags into her body will get a reaction, she's up for it. She's also tremendously afraid of aging, as you and I both know. I think they make her feel younger."

"I'd feel younger too if I were dating a twenty-seven-year-old."

"Exactly," said Helen.

"All the envious stares would balance out any potential embarrassment," said Pammy.

"Charlotte doesn't get embarrassed."

Just then, Daniel jogged down the steps in orange fluorescent bathing trunks. He dropped his towel next to Pammy, then bent down and grabbed his ankles. His broad back, taut and rippled, was close enough to Pammy to touch. She reached out and slapped his shoulder. He looked up from his stretching. "Horsefly," she said.

"Oh, well, thank you."

"They've got a mean bite," said Pammy.

"Where's Charlotte?" asked Helen.

"She's still up at the house. She wasn't happy with her bathing suit, so I think she's going to change it. She's got a great-looking pink bikini," said Daniel, grinning.

"No doubt," said Pammy, gazing down at her convex, pink nylon-covered abdomen and then covering it with her hands. "I hope she chooses it for today."

Helen slapped her sister on the wrist. "Horsefly," she said.

"I'm going to take a run," said Daniel. "I'll be back in about forty minutes."

After he left Pammy said, "Why don't you just run back and forth in front of us?"

"And why don't you behave," said Helen. "You can't covet your sister's boyfriend."

"Well, I do."

"Then stop." Pammy sighed and sat back in her chair. She closed her eyes and tilted her face toward the sun. "You don't really want him."

"Says who?" said Pammy, opening her eyes and looking at her sister.

"Says a rational you. He's just a kid."

"An extremely well-built kid."

"Tell me there aren't extremely well-built forty-five-year-olds at that fancy health club you go to. I can see them, hot and sweaty from the squash court, with their jet-black hair slicked back off their angular faces. You walk by, and they turn their heads to watch you. They give each other a wink, then arm wrestle for your hand in marriage."

"That's exactly what happened last week," said Pammy. "And then the book was over." Helen laughed.

* * *

Charlotte tied the last of three strings on her bikini and looked into the mirror again. She turned to the side and checked her stomach, which was as flat as it was when she was seventeen. God, she was glad—if for just this reason alone—she didn't have children. Pregnancy blew out the belly and breastfeeding ruined the breasts. She'd seen the mothers in the park she regularly walked through on her weekly errands. Two, three, four screaming kids running around loose like feral animals. And the babies sucking and tugging at their mothers' breasts, pulling and stretching them until they hung like dead men on a rope, lifeless, useless except for nursing, completely unattractive. Her breasts, on the other hand, were a perfect, thirty-eight DD. When considering the augmentation, she was torn between the two cup sizes. Daniel had convinced her to go larger, telling her most men, him included, found large breasts very sexy. He was right. Every male, young as well as old, from grocery store stock boys to her friends' husbands, ogled her chest. Even the paperboy had a hard time looking at her face when she tipped him.

When she descended the beach steps, Helen and Pammy were talking. Charlotte cleared her throat and waited. They didn't seem to hear her, so she coughed again. Pammy turned around. "Here I am," she said.

"Here you are indeed," said Pammy. "And you've brought your floats."

"You're jealous."

"Envious, I think it is," said Pammy. "Of your chest and your boyfriend."

"Where is my big boy?" Charlotte asked, looking down the beach through her oversized sunglasses. "Has some college girl taken him away?"

"He went for a run," said Helen. "He'll be back in a little while. Pull up a chair."

Charlotte set her chair next to Pammy and gently lowered herself into it. She stretched her thin, muscular legs out in front of her and crossed her ankles. Closing her eyes, she tilted her head toward the sun. Its intense heat relaxed her instantly, bound her caustic tongue. Inhaling deeply through her nose, she then exhaled slowly through her mouth. Minutes later she was asleep.

Daniel arrived at their chairs soon afterward. Sweaty and glistening in the sun, he bent down to kiss Charlotte. "She's asleep," said Helen.

"Like an angel," Daniel said.

"Sort of," said Pammy.

"Anybody want to go for a swim?" Daniel asked.

Pammy jumped out of her chair. "I'm about ready," she said. "Let's go to the raft."

Daniel and Pammy walked slowly toward the water. Pammy stuck her foot in and, coquettishly, pulled it out quickly. She looked back at Helen, who was shaking her head. Pammy shrugged her shoulders and walked in, up to her knees, up to her hips, then dove underneath the surface. Daniel, who had plunged in the second his toes left the dry sand, was treading water several yards out, waiting for Pammy. She swam to him; they laughed about something Helen couldn't hear, then headed for the ancient gray raft in the distance. Helen watched them swim, side by side, until they reached their destination. Pammy climbed the ladder, then sat down next to the diving board. Daniel sat down beside her.

Losing interest in her sister's antics, Helen returned to her magazine. After finishing an article, Helen closed last week's *Time,* lifted herself out of her chair, and ascended the steps. She crossed the road to the house and walked into the porch. "Mother?" Hearing no response, Helen walked through the living room and dining room into the kitchen, which was vacant. She crossed back through the former maid's quarters, on the opposite side of the house from the dining room, which had decades before been transformed into a sitting room that no one used. That weekend, Charles would sleep there on the pullout couch, which Helen had already made up with fresh sheets. Todd and Ned would sleep on the porch in sleeping bags on air mattresses. Even when there were free beds, the boys chose the porch. From the den, Helen walked back into the living room and then up the stairs. "Mother?"

"Here I am," answered Claire, from her room.

Helen poked her head in. "Hi," she said. "How's everything?"

"Things would be just great if I could just get my arm into this sleeve." She was breathing hard from her failed efforts.

"It's tangled," said Helen, untwisting the fabric. "Try putting it in now."

"Wonderful." Claire slipped her left arm into the cotton blouse.

"I should have come sooner," said Helen. "I was reading. I thought you were doing the same on the porch."

"I was, but I needed this long-sleeved blouse and my hat up here. Daniel helped me up the stairs before his run."

"Well, I'll help you down the stairs."

"I'm glad you came along."

Helen kissed her mother on the cheek, a reward for her pleasantness, and then helped her off the bed. Together they made their way slowly down the stairs and onto the porch. "Shall we go to the beach?" asked Helen.

"Let's."

On the raft, Pammy turned her body to face Daniel's. "So," she said, "tell me about you."

"There's not a lot to tell," Daniel answered. "I'm in transition now."

"Transition?"

"Well, yes, I'm a student."

"What are you studying?"

"Philosophy. I'm working on my master's degree."

"And how does someone working on his master's degree afford living in San Francisco?"

"I work part-time at a gym. I used to have a second job, in retail, but Charlotte doesn't want me out every evening or on Saturdays," he said. "I don't make much at the gym, but it seems to pay for what I need. Plus, I get to work out."

"Do you have an apartment?"

Daniel blushed. "I did have an apartment," he said, "with three roommates. Charlotte made me give it up when we began spending a lot of time together. She told me to use the money for something useful, like taking her out to dinner."

"And do you?"

"Take her out to dinner?"

"Do useful things."

"All the time," he said, smiling.

"You obviously work out a lot."

"Every day. Charlotte sometimes works out when I'm there working."

"Really? She didn't lift a finger if she didn't have to when she was younger."

Daniel laughed. "She told me that. It's hard to believe she never exercised and still looks the way she does. She's in great shape."

"For an older woman, right?"

"I wasn't going to say that."

"But you were thinking it, weren't you?"

"Why is everyone so fixated on our age difference?"

"Aren't you? I mean, if Charlotte looks this good at forty-seven, think about what a twenty-five-year-old would look like?"

"Those women are all so immature. They just want to get married."

"Is that so bad?"

"No," Daniel said. "I want to get married too. I just don't want to get married now."

"Charlotte doesn't want to get married?"

"She thinks twice is enough."

"You want children, I take it."

"I love kids. That's the real reason to get married."

"Not for love?"

"You can find love anywhere."

"If you're young and good-looking, yes, you can. If you're middle-aged and average, it's not so easy."

"So, find somebody young and good-looking," said Daniel.

"You're taken." Pammy reached over and removed a small piece of eel grass from Daniel's shoulder.

Daniel laughed and put his hand on Pammy's knee. Pammy put

her hand on top of his, spreading his fingers with hers. She held his hand for several seconds before releasing him, and then stood up. She walked to the edge of the raft and quickly dove in, letting the cool water refresh her, dispel her fantasies. Daniel dove in after her, surfacing next to her. He spit water over her head. Pammy filled her mouth with water to reciprocate. As she puckered her lips, Daniel covered her mouth with his.

Chapter 14

1973

Helen sat at the dinner table and used her fork to play with her peas. She divided them into groups of five, of which she had six, with three extra. Then she put them into groups of eleven so it would come out even. She formed the three groups into circles, making a green snowman on her plate, using a bit of black olive from her salad for a hat and some rice grains for the arms. "Eat your peas," said Claire. "Honestly, Helen."

"After all," said Thomas, forking the last of his peas into his mouth, "there are starving children in Africa."

"That's enough out of you," John Thompson said.

"I propose we pack up Helen's plate, just like it is, and *send* it to Africa. They might get a kick out of that snowman."

"You just earned solo dish duty," John said to Thomas. "As soon as Helen's done."

Charlotte looked at her watch. "Let's go, Helen. Some of us have plans tonight."

"What are your plans?" asked Claire, finishing the final row on her ear of corn. Charlotte glanced at her mother. "Driving to Hall's Homemade for an ice cream float?"

"Something like that," said Charlotte. "And when we're bored to death with that activity, we can do something fun."

"Like what?" asked Claire. "What is your definition of fun?"

"It's hard to say." Charlotte sipped her water. "What I do know is that it's different than yours."

"Different from mine," said Claire. "When the word different is used in comparisons, it's always followed by the word *from*."

Helen took advantage of her mother's shifted attention by spooning a third of her peas into her shorts pocket. Her father routinely checked her balled-up napkin, but he had not yet asked her to empty her pockets. Helen was always the last child to finish her dinner, mostly because she had no appetite for vegetables. She adored mashed potatoes and corn on the cob—she had eaten two ears that very meal—but abhorred string beans, cooked carrots, broccoli, salad with French dressing, and, especially, peas. They not only made her gag, but they also seemed to grow in her mouth as she chewed them. When she was younger and spit them out of her mouth, her mother had made her scoop them back up and try again. And when she protested eating what she called barf, her mother calmly told her that many animals routinely ate regurgitated food. Helen scattered half the remaining peas on her plate and shoved the others in her mouth. "Done," she said through the peas.

"Lift that lettuce, young lady," her father said.

Hesitantly, Helen picked up the large leaf on her plate and revealed a piece of swordfish the size of a small brownie. Before Helen could open her mouth full of peas to bargain with her father, Thomas, who was sitting next to her, speared the fish and put it into his mouth. Everyone watched him as he chewed. "Now you see it," he said, still chewing. "Now you don't."

"She's never going to learn with you around," said Claire.

"Oh, she learns plenty," Thomas said. "She's going to learn all about dish washing tonight, right, Helen?"

"You don't have to help, Helen," said their father. "Only if you choose to."

"I choose to," said Helen, getting up from the table to bring dishes to the kitchen.

Everyone cleared their own dishes from the table except for Claire and John. John earned exemption from most household chores because he, Claire said, made the money that paid for the food on the plates to be cleared; that bought the clothes that needed to be washed, dried, folded, and put away; that secured the car loans for the vehicles that Thomas and Charlotte drove. And John often reminded his children that their mother planned, shopped for, and prepared their meals, so the least the children could do was tidy up. He knew that if Claire washed dishes with the children, she would certainly take control of it, quickly declaring their efforts substandard. The other reason John wanted his children to do the dishes, the primary reason, was that he thought it was good for them. Hard workers, he often told them, are happier people.

Thomas filled the sink with sudsy water, while Helen grabbed a clean dishtowel from the drawer in the pantry. She stood next to him at the sink and watched as he sunk the water glasses into the white foam. Washing them quickly, yet carefully, Thomas placed the dripping glasses upside down in the drying rack, where Helen retrieved them, one at a time, then dried them, and placed them, right side up, on the proper shelf in the pantry. "You are a terrific assistant," said Thomas. "Would you always help me?"

Helen beamed at her older brother. With his wavy brown hair, green eyes and thin, muscular build, Thomas had his pick of girls, especially at the cottage where everyone Pammy's age and older wanted a summer boyfriend. He liked Catherine, the banker's daughter who lived down the street, but she was snotty and superior and would only talk to Thomas when her beau—her word, Thomas said—from college wasn't visiting for the weekend. Thomas had little time for dating, however, because most of the time he worked. He liked girls, but he liked money more. He worked two, sometimes three jobs every summer and banked most of his paychecks. On his occasional days off, he went to the beach, where a number of girls often offered to put tanning lotion on his broad brown back. Pammy, often observing from a nearby towel, would comment to Helen in disgust. Tramps, she would call them,

Thomas's little harem. Helen routinely pointed out that Thomas didn't seem to mind.

When Thomas wasn't working or out with a few guy friends, he sometimes played Monopoly with Helen. He was always the banker and he always won, which made Helen wonder whether one could exist without the other. She usually owned the prestigious Boardwalk and Park Place, but Thomas never landed on them. He always bought the less expensive but better situated St. Charles trio, as well as their orange New York neighbors. Helen couldn't seem to get down that strip without hitting at least one of them. And when he put up houses, the game was almost over. He always owned the railroads as well.

Helen's favorite times with her older brother were not spent lying on the living room rug beside a game board or running around the yard during a post-dinner game of family kickball. What she liked best was swimming to the raft with him after dark, through the black waters of Long Island Sound, terrified of the seaweed and creatures below, but exhilarated by the daring and secret nature of their missions. He favored the hot, thick nights, when the air, full of moisture, refused to move. On appointed nights like this, Helen would wait until her parents were asleep and Thomas was home from delivering pizza. She would lie still, listening for his car, his cutoff engine, the thud of his car door shutting, and the drawn-out squeak from the back screen door being opened slowly. She would listen to him climb the stairs and stop in his room to change into his suit. And then he would walk quietly down the hallway to her open door and tap on the jamb four times. That was their special knock, which occasionally had to be changed so that international spies wouldn't crack their code. Within seconds, Helen would be out of bed. She'd hurry out of her pajamas, revealing her bathing suit underneath. Without a word, she would follow him back down the hall, down the stairs, and out the front door into the night. *Nice night for a swim,* he would say. And it always was.

"Hey," Thomas said that night as they descended the beach steps, "what are the chances we see Charlotte down here making out with one of her bozo boyfriends?"

"Not very good," Helen replied. "She's already in bed."

"Don't tell me she's dumped Steve Johanson already."

"I don't think so," said Helen, hanging the beach towel she had retrieved from the clothesline over the stairway's steel railing. "She's getting her friend."

"Her what?"

"You know."

"Her period, Helen? Is she getting her period?"

"I hate that word."

"Don't you hate calling it a friend more?"

"Good point," said Helen, jumping down onto the cool sand. "From what Charlotte's told me, that name makes no sense anyway."

"Agreed."

They walked down to the water's edge and waded in up to their ankle bones. "It's cold," said Helen, hugging her torso.

"It's delightful," said Thomas, as he strode out into the water until it encircled his waist. He leaped out of the water like a porpoise and then disappeared under the surface. Helen followed him much like a dog obeys a master, without protest, without thought. The dark, dense water surrounded and held her, cooling her instantly. She swam to Thomas, who was treading water several yards away. "You," he said as she drew nearer, "are Secret Agent Ten." Thomas always made up a game on the way to the raft. "And I am Secret Agent Twenty. Our mission tonight is to swim swiftly and silently to our island base camp, which has been infiltrated by Russian scuba divers. We will bomb them using heavy artillery, trying our best to avoid our own structures, until they surrender. We will destroy their encampment."

A good swimmer, like all the Thompsons, Thomas led with his flawless crawl stroke. Arm over arm and face in the water, he moved efficiently and consistently like a machine. Swimming in his wake, Helen chose the breaststroke. Occasionally she dipped her mouth and nose below the surface, but her eyes, alert and ever vigilant, remained above water. Creatures in the murkiness below could strike without warning. If she stayed close to Thomas, she felt safe. She was so busy looking around that she didn't notice Thomas had stopped and ran right into him.

"Hey!" Thomas said. "Watch it, Agent Ten. Do you want to blow our cover?"

"Sorry," said Helen, breathless.

He grinned at her. "You are a little chicken, Helen Thompson."

"Am not."

"Are too."

"Am . . ."

"Shhh! Listen. Did you hear something?"

"No," Helen said, looking around them.

"I could have sworn I heard a kind of whooshing sound, kind of like a shark fin cutting through the water."

"Drop dead, Thomas," said Helen, trying to sound nonchalant even though her heart was pounding.

"Or maybe it was one of those huge eels racing through the grass below. Helen help! He's got my toe! I'm going under!"

"Some spy you make," said Helen, breathing heavily from fear. "The Russians have already seen us and are breaking up camp."

"No, they aren't," said Thomas, backing off. "That's just the night guards ending their shift. This is our only opportunity. Silence, Agent Ten, is the key to our success."

Helen followed him the rest of the way to the raft, another twenty-five yards or so, where she treaded water while he climbed the ladder. On the third rung, he leaned down and whispered. "What are we?"

"Swift and lethal," Helen dutifully replied.

Thomas jumped up onto the raft's surface and launched into an elaborate exercise of karate kicks and punches. "Hi yah!" he yelled. "Eat eel grass, peasant!"

Emulating her brother's actions, Helen threw her feet and hands into the air, striking imaginary adversaries with gusto. Within minutes, all the Russians were dead or close enough. Helen and Thomas met in the middle of the raft and solemnly shook hands before moving on to the bombing phase of their mission. She stepped onto the diving board and walked out to the end over the water. She jumped once, then twice, testing the spring before returning to the raft. A moment later, Helen turned and jogged four steps along the board. Jumping up, she forced all her weight onto the very end of the plank, which sent her flying through the thick air. She pulled her knees up to her chest and held them there. One, two, three, four, five—her body hit the water with a violent boom, sending water up and out in all directions. "The cannonball," said Thomas, already clapping when she rose to the surface, "by Helen Thompson."

"Good?" Helen asked.

"Stupendous," Thomas answered. "The entire Russian infantry has retreated. Come, feast on potatoes and vodka!"

Helen climbed up the ladder and sat opposite her brother. The moon shone down upon them, lighting the surface of the raft as if it were a small stage. Thomas, using the exaggerated motions of a mime actor, handed her imaginary food and beverage, followed by treasure chests of Russian coin, currency, and valuable artifacts. They counted their booty, which amounted to three billion American dollars, stuffed it into their suits, then dove into the water for the swim back to headquarters on the mainland. Again Thomas led and Helen swam close to him. Bravely putting her face down, she rotated her arms in a crawl stroke and pulled herself gracefully through the water. On the way back to the beach, she was not as fearful of the marine life below. The sharks and eels and giant squid, she reasoned, had fallen back to sleep.

When she could touch the bottom, Helen stopped swimming and walked to the beach. Thomas, wrapped in his blue and green-striped towel, handed Helen hers. She bundled up, and stood, shivering, next to her brother. "You cold?" he asked.

"Not really," Helen said, through chattering teeth.

"Let's go up," he said, putting his arm around her shoulders and giving her a side hug. "We'll run a warm shower for just a minute. Nice work, Agent Ten."

CHAPTER 15

2003

"Mom!"

"Hey, Mom!

"Helen, we're home!"

Helen bolted out of her chair on the porch and jogged to the kitchen, where she found Todd carrying two large bass, Ned carrying three medium-sized bass, and Charles holding a can of Diet Coke. "Hi, guys!" she said, hugging all of them one after the other. "How was everything?"

"Great! We caught a ton of fish. Lots of small ones we had to throw back, but look at these," said Ned, lifting high the fish in his hands.

"Ned, I'm thoroughly impressed." She kissed him on the check. "And look at those, Todd. You didn't catch them, did you?" Todd beamed. "They're beautiful," she said, kissing him on the cheek. She kissed her husband on the lips. "And you must have been fishing in the cooler." She took the soda can from his hand and took a sip. "Put the fish on the butcher block, and we'll see what we can do about getting them ready for dinner."

"I did have a good one on the line," said Charles. "But he got away."

"He almost pulled Dad out of the boat," said Ned. "He was huge!"

"What happened?" asked Helen.

"He broke the line," said Todd, laying his catch on the counter. "It was quite extraordinary."

"I couldn't agree more." Helen reached out and tousled Todd's hair. He was just her height now, but Helen guessed he would be six feet in no time.

"Where is everyone?" asked Charles.

"Mom, Charlotte, and Daniel are still at the beach, and Pammy's upstairs showering. That leaves the outside shower for you three," said Helen, holding her nose.

"Are we that bad?" asked Charles, smelling the sleeve of his shirt.

"You're about on par with your catch." Helen smiled at her husband.

"Okay, men," said Charles. "Let's hit the showers."

Minutes later, Pammy walked into the kitchen. "Just look at these fish," Helen said. "They're resplendent."

Pammy looked over her sister's shoulder. "They look pretty ugly to me," she said. "You're not going to clean them, are you?"

"How else are we going to eat them?" said Helen.

"Let the boys do it."

"They're complete wimps when it comes to this stuff."

"How about Charles?"

"King wimp."

"I'll ask Daniel. I'll bet he'd do it."

"What makes you think that?"

"He's good at everything," said Pammy, reaching into the cupboard for a drinking glass. "I'm sure that includes cleaning fish."

"Really?" said Helen. "I don't know anybody who's good at everything. Have you surmised this yourself, or has Daniel been telling you tales?"

"We had a nice chat on the raft," said Pammy, blushing in spite of her efforts not to as she filled her glass at the sink.

"And this is when he told you he could do everything?" Helen chose the sharpest knife from the butcher block on the counter.

"He kissed me, Helen."

Helen dropped the knife and turned to look at her sister. "What do you mean he kissed you?"

"We were squirting water out of our mouths at each other. I had my eyes closed, and he put his mouth over mine."

"What did you do?"

"I swallowed my mouthful of salt water and kissed him back."

"Shit, Pammy!"

"What was I supposed to do?"

"How about asking him if the name Charlotte rings any bells, for starters." Helen bent down to pick the knife up off the floor. She wiped the blade on her shorts.

"It was all very innocent," said Pammy.

"Then why are you blushing?"

"It must be the sun." Pammy put her hands to her cheeks.

"Don't make trouble," Helen warned. "Charlotte will tear you apart. You know that." Pammy shot a quick smile at her sister and then walked out of the room, pushing the swinging door closed behind her. Helen watched her sister go. Then, she raised the knife in her hand and whacked off a fish head.

Charles, looking trim in khaki shorts and a navy blue golf shirt, stacked the charcoal in the grill and doused it with lighter fluid. As soon as he tossed in a match, the mountain of coals exploded into a yellow fireball, forcing a mass of thick, black smoke skyward. He stood back for a moment, took a sip from his scotch and water, and then settled into a webbed lawn chair a few feet from the grill. From there, he could see through the large window into the kitchen, where Helen and Pammy were preparing the salad and the garlic bread. If he turned his head, he could see the lot next to the cottage, where his sons were playing Frisbee with Daniel. Charlotte walked through the kitchen, breezing past her laboring sisters, and came outside, letting the screen door bang behind her. She was dressed in tight white shorts too short for a woman her age and a blue and white-striped shirt that accented her new breasts. *What wouldn't accent them?* thought Charles, as he pried his eyes from her chest to her face. She smiled at him, and he smiled back. He half hoped she was looking for Daniel and would walk by to find him.

"Hi there," she said, sitting on the picnic table under the apple tree.

"Hi," said Charles, raising his drink in a salute to his sister-in-law.

"You guys caught some mean-looking fish."

"Thank you, I think."

Charlotte laughed. She tossed her head back and ran her fingers through her hair. When her head lowered itself back into place, Charles could tell she'd had a drink or two before the one she currently held in her hand. She could walk without tripping and talk without slurring, but he guessed she was on her way to doing both. Charlotte was mercurial enough when she was sober. But when she was drunk, whatever loosely defined barriers that periodically reined in her behavior disappeared altogether. The drink on the table beside her was half full. "So, what do you think of my young man?" she asked, raising the drink to her lips.

"He seems nice, Charlotte. He's awfully good with the boys."

"Yes, I think he'd make a great father. Do you think I'd be a good mother, Charles?"

"Sure, Charlotte," said Charles, rising from his chair. "Hey, listen. I'm going to see how Helen's doing with that fish. Get an update on the Frisbee game for me." Charles walked into the kitchen, where Helen was shredding Parmesan cheese and Pammy was mincing fresh garlic. "She's gone," he said to Helen, who handed him the fish on a platter.

"What was your first clue?" asked Pammy. "Has she told you she's had three scotches, or did she reluctantly confess that she finds you tremendously attractive?"

Charles laughed. "Neither," he said. "She asked me if I thought she'd make a good mother."

Pammy and Helen both stopped what they were doing and looked at him. "You don't think she's pregnant, do you?" Helen asked.

"Would she be on her third scotch if she were?" asked Charles. "And isn't she too old for that?"

"I don't know," said Pammy.

"Really? I thought women talked about their periods whenever they got a chance."

"Maybe they're thinking about adopting," Helen suggested, ignoring her husband's remark.

"I don't think so," said Pammy. "I don't think Daniel's committed to the relationship."

Helen gave her sister a look, and then pushed Charles toward the door. "Find out what she's talking about."

Hoping Charlotte had wandered closer to the Frisbee game, Charles took the fish outside. Charlotte was still sitting on the table. Her drink was gone. "Where were we?" Charles asked, wincing the minute the words escaped his lips.

"We were talking," said Charlotte, "about children. About having children. Did I make a mistake not having children?"

"I don't know, Charlotte. Not having children has afforded you a lot of freedom."

"And a lot of loneliness." Charlotte tossed the remnants of her ice cubes onto the grass.

"Children can't cure loneliness."

"Sure they can. Look at Daniel. He's a child, and I'm sure as hell not lonely when he's around." Charlotte laughed, throwing her head back again. Charles reached over to steady her, but she seemed unaware of his efforts. She stared into her glass, as if newly aware that it was empty. She set it down beside her on the table. "I think Daniel wants children."

"That's natural, don't you think?"

"But I'm too old to give them to him."

Thank God, thought Charles. "Do you really want children, Charlotte? Or do you want to have them for him?"

"I don't know."

"Somehow," said Charles, spreading out the graying charcoal briquettes with tongs, thinking they needed another few minutes before they were ready to cook the fish, "I think if you wanted children, you would have had them by now."

"Is that what you think, Charles?" asked Charlotte, lifting herself off the picnic table and swaying in front of him. "Maybe after four miscarriages I just gave up."

Charles closed his eyes. When he opened them, Charlotte was removing her shoes. He remained silent when she made eye contact with him and then turned away. She zigged and then zagged her way across the lawn to the far end of the lot. His body tingled with this news, and, for another minute, Charles was immobilized. He wondered for just a moment if he already knew about Charlotte's miscarriages, if Helen had told him one night when they whispered to each other in the dark before bed. But he was quickly certain that he and Helen had not discussed this. He was positive, in fact, that Helen hadn't told him, and that perhaps no one but him knew. The next thought that came to his mind was what an ass he had been. He had assumed that Charlotte had chosen not to have children with either of her husbands because she was consumed with herself and her happiness. He and Helen had discussed this very topic a number of times, both speculating that Charlotte's childless condition was voluntary—and selfish.

It was easy to assume that childless couples were selfish. After all, childless couples could do whatever they wanted to do, outside work and other obligations. And they had a lot more money to do those things, since they weren't paying for their children's food, healthcare, clothing, extracurricular activities, cars, insurance, and whatever other expenses surfaced over the years, including the biggest one of all, college. Charles had agreed with Helen that Charlotte had chosen not to have children because she was too busy pleasing herself. But there was something about this theory that bothered Charles. It was almost as if parents wanted other adults to have children so they, too, could experience the associated constraints on their time and finances.

Charles had recently learned that one of the agents in his insurance agency, who had been married for fifteen years and did not have children, had been through artificial insemination and miscarriage half a dozen times in as many years. The agent, Lori Kennedy, had not volunteered this information. Instead, it had come to light through an insurance claim that Charles had to handle because his administrative assistant was away from the office on vacation. It was then that Charles told himself—and Helen when he got home that night—that childless couples were not always what they seemed to be. And that even if they were, even if they chose to be childless, that this was an absolutely legitimate choice. Helen had agreed. Being around Charlotte could challenge anyone's feelings of good will and nonpartisanship, but Charles now, after a two-minute conversation, felt differently about her.

"Oh no, that's not possible," said Claire, returning her napkin to her lap. "She's left-handed!" Everybody roared with laughter, and Claire sat back in her chair, completely satisfied. As a younger woman, she had always known the latest jokes, political or otherwise, and enjoyed making people laugh. But she had been very selective about sharing her sense of humor with her children. Her husband John had a more easy-going relationship with the children, even though he was the disciplinarian. Claire saw herself as the teacher and the coach, education and athletics being directly linked to quality of life. Where would she be now, she wondered more and more as she aged, without her Smith College education, without her athletic training, her personal goals? Her accomplishments, in the classroom as well as in the pool, earned her the adulation and respect of her peers, her elders, of everyone she met. In the 1940s and 1950s, she was a standout. In an era when women were second-class citizens, when men made the important decisions, Claire Gaines followed her own set of rules. She spoke with confidence. Her actions were not second-guessed. She was completely free from the typical conventions placed on young women at the time; she was entirely capable of choosing her life path. And she worked hard at making sure her children would have the same privileges, which meant they had to work hard, too. Life, she was fond of saying, does not reward a loafer.

"Charles, darling, the fish was delightful," said Charlotte, who puckered her lips and kissed the air in front of her.

"Thank you," he said, embarrassed by her public gesture, but pleased with her compliment. She had stopped drinking after her picnic-table confession. For someone prone to excess, Charlotte was increasingly careful with alcohol. After John's memorial service, she had just two glasses of wine at dinner, announcing her switch to water, announcing her intention of going through this event relatively sober. If there was a reason for this, other than an emotional reaction to her father's passing, Charles couldn't figure it out. Helen had insinuated that Charlotte's second husband, Jeremy, was an alcoholic, but Charles had only met him once.

"And you adorable boys," Charlotte said, raising her water glass. "Here's to the fishermen." Everybody raised their glasses, and Todd and Ned blushed. Helen and Pammy stood and started to clear the dishes from the table. Daniel stood, too, and grabbed some plates. "Sit, sweetheart," said Charlotte. "That's women's work."

"You know me," said Daniel, walking into the kitchen. "I just love being where the women are."

Charlotte laughed. "Shall I help?" she called to her sisters.

"Why start now?" Pammy answered. "You'd ruin a forty-seven-year streak."

"Aren't you cute!" called Charlotte.

"You sure are," Daniel whispered in Pammy's ear. She turned from the sink to face him, but he had already returned to the dining room for more dishes. Pammy looked at Helen to see if she had taken in Daniel's remark, but half her body, including her head, was in the fridge, moving things around, making room for leftovers.

After Helen's cheesecake, which everyone applauded, prompting Helen to stand and take a bow, Pammy returned to the kitchen to finish the dishes, and everyone else scattered. The boys went outside to find their summer friends for a game of capture the flag. Charles took Claire to the porch. And Charlotte went out the front screen door, crossed the right of way, and sat on the cement steps that led to the beach for a cigarette. After Helen put away the food, Pammy told her to "do a Charlotte," meaning grab a cup of coffee and sit on the porch while someone else did the work. Pammy wanted to be in the kitchen alone. She wanted Daniel to join her. After a few minutes, he walked in. "Coffee ready?"

"Just about," said Pammy, hands and forearms in the sink full of dishes and soapy water. "You know where the mugs are, right?"

She looked at him expectantly. When he didn't move, she said, "I can get them." She took her hands out of the water and wiped them on her apron.

"Stay right where you are," said Daniel, walking up behind her. He lined his body up with hers and then slowly pressed his front into her back. He wrapped his arms around her shoulders. Pammy felt his callused hands on her upper arms, his stiff penis in his shorts. "I'm horny," he said in her ear.

"Tell me about it." Pammy pressed her ass into him.

Daniel laughed, moving away from Pammy, and retrieved the mugs from the pantry. He filled them with coffee and poured skim milk into a small pitcher. Sliding two packets of sweetener into his front pocket, Daniel headed for the door. Just before he walked back into the dining room, he turned and looked at Pammy, who was still looking at him. He blew her a kiss and then closed the swinging door behind him.

Helen woke in the middle of the night and checked her watch. The illuminated hands pointed to just after three o'clock. She lay in bed, thinking about the day, hoping to drift back to sleep when the creaking started. At first, the noise was low and irregular, as if someone were rolling over in bed. Quickly, the creaking became louder and more rhythmic. Helen knew instantly whence the sound came. "I can't believe they're fucking in there," she said first in her head and then aloud.

"What?" asked Charles. He rolled over to face her, but kept his eyes closed.

She and Charles were in Thomas's room until his arrival. After that, Helen would go back in with Pammy, and Charles would sleep on the couch in the den. They had volunteered to do this, to split up, so that the others could be together, could feel comfortable in their old rooms. "Charlotte and Daniel. They're in there screwing."

Charles opened his eyes and listened. "Yep," he said. "They're definitely screwing."

"And now the moaning."

"Helen."

"Come on, Charles." Helen was whispering. "My sister is forty-seven years old and still acts like a recalcitrant teenager. She has never helped anyone but herself around here, and she continues to get away with it. The same rules never apply to Charlotte."

"She's different, Helen."

"Why is she different? Charlotte has been labeled different or impossible or stubborn since the day she was born, and the rest of us have had to put up with it. I think it's a lot of crap. I'm different. You're different. Everybody can be different, Charles. It's just that some of us work harder at it than others. She's so busy trying to be different, or irreverent, or funny, or sexy, or young, she doesn't know her liposuctioned ass from her elbow."

"Her life hasn't been easy, Helen," said Charles, putting his arms around his wife.

"And whose fault is that? I didn't start sleeping around when I was fifteen. I didn't go from one boyfriend to the next, depending on the car they drove or the presents they produced for me. Those were choices she made. If she couldn't make a scene, she simply wasn't interested."

"Are you envious?"

"Don't start that, Charles."

"Hey, she's been free and easy her whole life, Helen. She lived in Greece when you were home with two young children. She traveled the world, while you stuffed and licked envelopes for the King Street School PTA. She vacations in a sunny place every winter, while you make chicken soup to take to your mother. I can see where envy might creep into the picture."

"I wouldn't trade my boys for a few trips around the world."

"She might," said Charles.

"What do you mean?" Helen's eyes had adjusted to the darkness. She could make out his face, see his eyes.

"Charlotte wanted to have children and she couldn't, Helen."

"How do you know that, Charles?"

"She told me. Remember when I talked to you and Pammy in the kitchen about Charlotte's wanting to have children? When I went back out to cook, I made a flip remark about her choosing not to. She told me she'd had four miscarriages."

"What?"

"Exactly."

"Why didn't she ever tell me?"

"Maybe the perfect sister wouldn't be the first person you'd run to with problems."

"I'm not perfect, Charles."

"You look pretty close in her eyes, honey."

"Crap," said Helen. "I had no idea."

The moans emanating from the room across the hall became louder. Helen listened again and could hear Daniel saying, "Oh baby," again and again, as the creaking bed lightly bumped against the wall. Creak, bang, creak, bang. Oh baby.

Helen reached out for Charles's face. She put her hands on his cheeks and gently drew him to her. She kissed him on the lips. "It's contagious, isn't it?" she said.

"Tell me we're going to have sex in the same house as your mother."

Helen slipped off her pajama bottoms. Claire slept soundly in her room, as did Todd and Ned downstairs. Pammy, down the hall, was wide-awake, listening to the sounds of lovemaking and pretending Daniel was having sex with her.

CHAPTER 16

1973

Thomas dashed down the stairs, through the living room, and into the kitchen. He poured a glass of orange juice and drank it down in three gulps. He grabbed two pieces of bakery bread from the drawer and put them in the toaster. Tucking his shirt in while he waited, Thomas stared at the toaster, willing it to pop up his breakfast. “Thomas,” Claire whispered, as she walked into the kitchen. “Is everything okay?”

“Yes, except I’m late. I just remembered I switched with Alan and have to drive the first delivery truck today. I have to be at the bakery in ten minutes,” he said, buttering his toast.

“Do you want a ride?” Claire tied the belt of her bathrobe.

“I picked my car up last night. It’s running beautifully.” Thomas gave his mother a two-fingered salute. “I’ll see you later,” he said on his way out the back door.

Outside, the blackness startled him. For an instant, day became night, making Thomas believe he was on his way home from work, rather than vice versa. He looked at his watch, which read 4:21 in illuminated numbers. He had just nine minutes to get to the bakery. Warm toast held by his teeth and lips, Thomas reached into the pocket of his jeans and pulled out his keys. He jogged through the wet grass to his green Pinto, which, with the interior light on, was waiting for him. "Shit!" he said.

He sat in the driver's seat and pulled the door closed behind him. The light went off. Thomas put the key into the ignition and turned it. Like an old man with a chest cold, the engine coughed and sputtered. When it died, Thomas tried again and then again. On his fourth attempt, something caught. Thomas pushed the gas pedal to the floor, feeding the engine. A tremendous zoom shattered the early morning quiet, and Thomas backed the car out of its slot and onto the street. Jerking the car into gear, Thomas flew past the house, buckling his seat belt as he drove.

Walter Sloan was waiting in the truck when Thomas arrived at Sloan's Bakery. Thomas checked his watch. It was 4:32. He parked his car and then ran to the truck. "You're late," Mr. Sloan said.

"I know that, sir. I'm sorry."

"Are you ready to go now?"

"Yes, sir. I've never been more ready," said Thomas, smiling.

"Don't get cute with me, Thomas. I need delivery drivers who can be here when I want them here. If you're going to be two minutes late, you might as well be an hour late."

If I had known that, Thomas thought, *I would have slept another forty minutes*. But he said nothing. Walter Sloan was not finished.

"There are plenty of eager young men out there, looking for jobs like this. The pay is good, and the hours are even better." Thomas coughed. "You're here early in the morning and out by lunch time. Nothing to do but lollygag all afternoon. Swimming, tennis, golf, whatever you're in the mood for. That's what I call free time."

"I work another job, Mr. Sloan."

"In the afternoons?"

"Yes. I drive a delivery van three days a week for *The Gazette.*"

"And how long does that take?"

"I deliver about three hundred papers, which takes anywhere from two to three hours. And sometimes, like last night, I deliver pizza."

"Good Lord, boy. Why all the jobs?"

"I like money, Mr. Sloan," said Thomas.

"So do I, Thomas. But you didn't catch me working three jobs when I was eighteen. What do you do with the money?"

"Spend a little, and bank the rest. I'm learning about the stock market, with my dad. When I feel knowledgeable enough, I'll invest. My dad has a great broker in New York. This guy knows the market like the back of his hand."

Mr. Sloan chuckled as he stepped out of the truck. "I'm sure he does, Thomas. Now, get in that truck and deliver my stuff before you get the back of mine."

"Thomas! You're up!" Thomas leaped out of his chair at Village Pizza and walked to the counter. "Take this pizza to 47 Sharon Avenue. You know where that is?"

"Sort of," said Thomas, who had no clue.

"It's in The Flats. Take a left on Cashew; go all the way to the end; take a right on whatever that street is, and Sharon will be on the right. Got that?"

"Absolutely," said Thomas.

He jogged the large pizza out to the car, turned on the radio, perpetually set to his favorite rock station, and pulled out of the parking lot. He had no idea where Cashew Road was, but he did know how to find The Flats. He drove to the railroad tracks and crossed them. The houses, lawns, and driveways were smaller on the other side, and the cars were bigger. Thomas began looking at street signs: Pearl Street, Diamond Avenue, Ruby Court. Surely the developer of these tiny houses had an ironic sense of humor. Thomas drove around for another five minutes, crisscrossing the streets, working his way through the neighborhood. Finally he saw Cashew and followed it to the end. He took a right, and saw Sharon on the right. Number 47 Sharon was a four-room ranch situated between two identical houses. The trio stood so close to each other, they looked like life-size versions of the miniature wood houses on a Monopoly board. This, Thomas thought, was no Marvin Gardens.

Thomas parked the car on the street and checked his watch. He left Village Pizza twenty minutes ago, so he would surely deliver the pizza within the thirty-minute time limit. Mr. Gingerella's promise to his customers—a hot pizza delivered in less than a half hour or receive it free—was seldom broken because the delivery boys paid for late pizzas out of their salary and tips. Thomas walked the pizza to the front door and rang the bell. Within seconds a small child, who Thomas guessed was no more than four, opened the door. "Hi," said Thomas. "I've brought your pizza."

"Terrific," said the girl, opening the door wide. "Come right in."

Thomas, who was six foot, three inches tall, ducked his head and stepped across the threshold. He stood in the living room and smiled at the little girl, who was staring at him. "Is your mom home?"

"She's in the kitchen," she said. "I'll run and see what's taking her."

Seconds later, a petite woman with long dark hair and large brown eyes walked into the room. She smiled at him, revealing perfectly aligned white teeth. "I had the radio on," she said by means of an apology. "I was absorbed in a news story."

"That's okay," said Thomas, blushing due to her beauty. "Your daughter took care of everything."

"So, she's paid you then?" The woman raised her eyebrows at Thomas.

"Well, no . . ."

The woman laughed. "I'm teasing you," she said. "How much do I owe you?"

Thomas looked at his watch. "Nothing, actually," he said, wanting to please her. "I was a little late. This one's on me."

"No," she said, reaching into a side table drawer for her checkbook. "You found us quickly. Sometimes the pizzas don't come until the next day."

It was Thomas's turn to laugh. "It's my pleasure," he said, handing her the pizza. "It's sort of cold. You'll have to heat it."

When she reached under the box to take it from him, her fingers briefly covered his. He slid his hand out from under hers. "Got it?" he asked, again blushing, this time from her touch.

"Yes, and it is still warm."

"Barely," he said.

"Thank you. You're sweet."

"And handsome," said the little girl. "Stay and have some pizza with us."

Now, the woman blushed. "This is Amy," she said, looking at the child. "She's my daughter and my social director. And I'm Anna."

Thomas bent down and shook Amy's hand. "Nice to meet you, Amy. I'm Thomas."

"Can you stay?" she pleaded.

"I'd love to," said Thomas, meaning it. "But I've got more pizzas to deliver."

"Come back again," said Amy.

"I will," said Thomas.

For the next week, Thomas's thoughts returned several times a day to 47 Sharon Avenue, precocious Amy, and her beautiful mother. He pictured himself delivering another pizza and staying with them. They would have a jolly dinner, the three of them, and then Amy would go to bed. Anna would then take Thomas by the hand and lead him to the worn blue and green plaid couch in her paneled living room. She would tell him the story of her husband, who impregnated her and then disappeared. A single tear would roll down her cheek. Thomas would move closer to her, encircle her with his arms, and hold her while she wept. Soon, she would stop crying and begin apologizing for her emotional display. And Thomas, in an effort to quiet her, would kiss her. And, naturally, she would kiss him back.

Thomas had no idea why she, Anna, affected him this way. He'd met her just once, and briefly at that. She was lovely to look at, which accounted for some of his attraction. But there was something else—was it maturity? The high school girls, even the college girls who called themselves women, were certainly immature in comparison to Anna. Anna was a mother, raising a child, apparently on her own if her daughter asked Thomas to stay for pizza. This meant Anna must have a job to provide for her daughter, unlike the girls at the beach. Many of the girls didn't work, relying on their boyfriends or fathers to get them what they needed. The high school girls who did work put in no more than twenty hours a week, usually babysitting, scooping ice cream, or waiting tables. The college girls worked in banks or other air-conditioned occupations, dressing in skirts and low-heeled shoes and, consequently, considering themselves very grown-up. But they were just as unmotivated as the high school girls. No one had any vision for the future, except for Thomas. Anna, after just five minutes, seemed to be more like him than any girl he had ever met.

This very story was playing through his mind when Mr. Gingerella hollered his name. Thomas jumped out of his seat and hurried to the counter. "You with us tonight, Thomas?"

"Very much so, sir."

"Good. Take this pizza to 47 Sharon Avenue. And these grinders to 86 Park Street. You got that?"

"Absolutely!" Thomas was already grinning.

He drove as fast as he could to Park Street, delivered the sandwiches, then headed across town to Amy and her mother. He parked the car and checked his watch. It was eight o'clock. Thomas combed his hair with his fingers and grabbed the pizza from the seat. Anna answered the door this time. "Hi," she said. "Come in."

Thomas walked in. He looked at the couch, where all his amorous inventions had been playing out all week, and looked back at Anna, at a real woman, who was smiling at him. "Where's Amy?" he asked.

"She's in bed. She wanted to stay up for pizza and the movie, but she was exhausted and fell asleep ten minutes ago. She's had a cold this week."

"Will she be sad to miss it?"

"There will definitely be leftovers," Anna said, laughing. "She'll be more sad about missing you actually. She thinks you're very handsome."

"Thank you," said Thomas. "I mean, tell her thank you."

The woman smiled. "I will," she said. An awkward moment passed. "Here, let me take that pizza from you."

Thomas handed it to her and then followed her as she walked into the kitchen. She took her wallet from her purse and handed Thomas some money. "Please tell Amy I say hello," he said.

"Thank you, Thomas. I will."

Thomas started back toward the front door through the living room. He walked to the front door and then turned to face Anna. "Tell your husband to save a piece for Amy."

"Actually, I'm not married."

"Ah," said Thomas. "In that case, there had better be leftovers."

Anna smiled. "Come back again," she said.

"Keep ordering pizza," said Thomas, and he walked out the door.

Santiago, Thomas said to himself the next day as he flipped through the pages of the telephone book: Anna Santiago. He found her name and circled the number in pencil. He reached for the phone, dialed the first three numbers, then hung up. He looked again at the name in the book: Anna Santiago. He reached for the phone again, held the receiver in his hand, and stared down at the number.

"Want me to dial for you?"

Thomas, sweating, looked up and saw Helen standing next to him. "What are you doing here?"

"I live here," said Helen, repeating a phrase she had heard Thomas say to Charlotte when she routinely told him to get lost.

Thomas blew air through his closed lips. "I'm trying to ask this woman I met out on a date."

"Is she really a woman, or is she just a girl?" asked Helen.

"Oh, she's a woman all right. She's got to be in her twenties, and she has a daughter named Amy."

Helen squinted her eyes at her brother. "Is she married, Thomas?"

"No, Helen. She lives in The Flats with Amy. I've delivered pizza there, twice."

"If she's not married, how'd she get her daughter?" Thomas looked directly into Helen's eyes. He opened his mouth to speak, then stopped. "Maybe she's divorced," Helen offered.

"I think that's probably it," said Thomas. "I think she must be divorced."

"What's her number?" asked Helen.

Thomas opened the book to the page marked by his thumb and

read the number to Helen, who picked up the phone. She dialed, held the receiver to her ear, then handed the phone to Thomas. "It's ringing," she said.

Thomas held the phone against his ear and listened—three, four, five rings. He was just about to hang up when he heard a voice on the other end. "Hello, this is Amy speaking."

"Hello Amy, this is Thomas."

"Well, hello, Thomas," said Amy. "Are you bringing us pizza?"

"Not today, Amy. I'm not working tonight."

"That's okay," she said. "My mom's not ordering any. She says we've got to cut back or we'll lose our waistlines."

Thomas chuckled. "Hey," he said. "Is your mom home?"

"Yes," said Amy. "Would you like to speak to her?"

"Very much," said Thomas.

Helen gave him the thumbs-up sign, and Thomas winked at her. He cupped his hand over the phone and asked Helen to get him a Coke in the kitchen. "Please put it in a glass with a ton of ice," he told her.

"Hello?"

Thomas turned his attention back to the phone. "Hello, Anna," he said. "This is Thomas."

"Thomas," she said. "What a nice surprise. How are you?"

"Fine, actually," Thomas said. "I, uh, was thinking . . ."

"Are you working tonight?"

"No."

"Will you come and have dinner with us? Amy would love it," she said.

"That sounds great," said Thomas. "What time?"

"Come about six. We'll have a cookout."

"Can I bring something?" Whenever the Thompson children went to a friend's house for dinner or the night, Claire always sent a dozen cookies, freshly made popcorn, or, at the very least, a bag of chips.

"Just yourself," said Anna.

"I'll see you at six, then."

"Good-bye, Thomas."

Thomas hung up the phone and leaped out of his chair. He jumped around the living room, as if he were on a pogo stick, and then planted his feet firmly on the floor, so he could focus on beating his fists against his chest. He stopped when he saw Helen standing next to him with his Coke in her hand. "How long have you been standing there?" He cocked his head.

"Long enough." Helen laughed.

Thomas laughed back. "Thanks for the Coke."

"She said yes, didn't she?"

"Yes, she did," said Thomas. "I'm going over there tonight for dinner."

"Will her daughter be there?"

"Yes."

"I could come with you," Helen offered, "to babysit."

"You are an angel, Helen. I think we're all set, though."

Helen watched her brother spring up the stairs. Not until after he was gone did she realize she was still holding his Coke. She knew he wouldn't miss it, hadn't really wanted it, but she had been lectured by her mother often enough to know that she couldn't waste it. So she took it to her room and slowly drank it while she braided pink, white, and yellow strands of gimp into a small bracelet for Amy.

CHAPTER 17

2003

In the morning, Helen woke early. Charles slept soundly as she rolled out of bed and quickly dressed. She went downstairs and made coffee and started the recipe for the cinnamon coffeecake her mother had made for them growing up. She had just finished the batter when Pammy, with the puffy eyelids of someone who needed more sleep, walked into the kitchen. "Coffee's ready," said Helen. "Good morning."

"Morning," said Pammy, taking her mug that Helen had set on the counter next to the coffee maker, then pouring coffee into it.

"You think a double batch of Mom's coffeecake is enough?" Helen was looking at the recipe card, written in Claire's handwriting, mentally checking off that she had added all the ingredients.

"Depends on who you're planning on feeding," said Pammy, taking her coffee out of the kitchen and closing the swinging door behind her.

Helen shrugged, added another egg for good luck, and poured the batter into two Bundt pans. She sprinkled the tops, which would become the bottoms, with a generous amount of cinnamon and then dolloped a mixture of melted butter and brown sugar on top of that. She put the pans in the oven and then refilled her mug with coffee and walked out to the porch to join Pammy. "How'd you sleep?"

"How do you think?" Pammy shot back.

Her eyes were bloodshot—from fatigue? From crying? "I wouldn't know, Pammy," said Helen. "That's why I asked. Seems like you could use a little more."

"When I could have used the sleep was in the middle of the night. Yet, everybody decided they had to fuck at three in the morning."

Helen was embarrassed. "I'm sorry if we woke you."

Pammy sighed. "It wasn't you, Helen. You were quiet and discreet—although I must admit I was surprised you had sex with Mom in residence."

"Charles said the same thing."

Pammy sipped her coffee. "It was Charlotte and Daniel, howling like wolves, who kept me up. And how many times can you say 'oh baby' before the other person tells you to shut the hell up."

Helen laughed. "From what I could hear last night, I think Daniel set a new record."

Pammy's sour mood shifted, lightened. It wasn't Helen's fault. "And Charlotte. I haven't heard her grunt and groan like that since she was screwing Rick Jones." When they were kids, Pammy and Helen had routinely spied on Charlotte and Rick. More than once they had caught them "in the act," as Pammy called it. And while most of the time Pammy had been able to shield her younger sister from full exposure to naked limbs and blended torsos, she had not been one hundred percent successful.

"Rick Jones," said Helen. "Whatever happened to him?"

"After he got out of jail for those convenience-store robberies, he went for the big time—banks. Last I heard, he had taken up permanent residency at Somers."

"What a guy," said Helen, shaking her head.

"Charlotte dumped him before the poor kid was fingerprinted. I still wonder how they caught him. There was something in the paper about an anonymous tip." Pammy looked into her sister's eyes.

"No clue," said Helen, who hadn't told anyone about her conversation thirty years before with her father when they were fishing.

Pammy had questioned Helen more than once over the years, but Helen had never confessed to confessing. Pammy moved the spotlight back to Charlotte.

"Can you believe she started dating Steve Johanson that very day? He was good-looking, but his younger brother, Michael, was the original stud."

"He was," said Helen. "I had such a crush on him."

"You did not."

"I did, really. I just never said anything to you because you were wild about him."

"Did you ever tell him?"

"Pammy, I was ten at the time."

"Did he ever marry?" asked Pammy.

"Four times and counting."

"Charlotte should have married him."

"She did, didn't she?"

Pammy laughed. "Hey," she said. "Can I tell you something?"

"Sure," said Helen. She sipped her coffee, which was still hot. Helen warmed her mug with hot water before she poured coffee into it, a trick her mother had taught her when Claire still liked her coffee scalding.

"Daniel's coming on to me."

"You already told me about the kiss."

"What I didn't tell you is what he did to me in the kitchen last night."

"He kissed you again?"

"No, he came up behind me while I was washing dishes and started grinding his pelvis against my ass. He put his arms around me and told me he was horny."

"No wonder he screwed Charlotte for an hour last night."

"What the hell is he doing, Helen?" Pammy set her almost empty mug on the table next to her chair.

"He's toying with you, Pammy. He knows he's attractive and has a body most women drool over, and he knows you think he's adorable. It's called an ego boost."

"Do you think he really wants me, or is he just fooling around?"

"If he wants you, it's for bragging rights only. It's not like he's going to dump his forty-seven-year-old live-in for her forty-three-year-old sister."

"Thank you very much."

"Come on, Pammy."

"Well, maybe he finds me attractive."

"Undoubtedly, Pammy, but he's not going to leave Charlotte, his meal ticket, for you."

"I could pay for his meals."

"Why would you want to? Unless you're interested in working out in the gym all day and screwing all night, I can't see why you'd want him."

"He's interested in philosophy," said Pammy, wincing at the weakness, the neediness of her statement.

"He's a dilettante," said Helen. "He's going to school so he doesn't have to work."

"You really dislike him, don't you?"

"I don't dislike him, Pammy. I don't know him. I just see him for what he is."

"I see some good qualities."

"You're reaching," said Helen, "and you're playing with fire. This isn't high school anymore."

"No," said Pammy. "It's more challenging."

"What about Charlotte? Maybe she really loves him."

"Charlotte loves herself, Helen. She'd find a new roommate within an hour."

"Are you serious about this, Pammy, or are we just talking?"

Pammy hesitated. "I don't know, Helen. Maybe it depends on what Daniel does. If he leaves me alone, I'll leave him alone."

"That's big of you."

"Look, Helen, you're not the lonely one here."

"And you're not the selfish one, either."

"Yeah, Charlotte's got that department covered."

"So let her have it, Pammy. Let her have him."

Seconds later, Daniel walked down the stairs in his tight orange gym shorts and a white T-shirt, cut off to show several inches of flat, muscular stomach between its uneven hem and the waistband of his shorts. Pammy swallowed. "Good morning," he said, bracing himself against the wall to stretch his legs. "Looks like a great day."

"Yes," said Pammy, turning her head and forcing her eyes to look out at the day through the screen.

"How'd you sleep?" asked Helen.

"Like a baby," said Daniel. "There must be something in the air out here." Pammy glanced at Helen. Daniel looked at Pammy and smiled. "I'll be back in about an hour," he said, walking out the front door. Pammy watched his perfect body jog down the road and disappear around the corner.

"So he's got a nice body," said Helen, standing. "So do I." She turned around and shook her bottom at Pammy. Pammy laughed. "You want more coffee?" asked Helen, holding up her mug.

"Absolutely," said Pammy, getting out of her chair and retrieving her mug from the table. "I have a three-cup minimum."

"Doesn't everybody?"

They walked back into the kitchen, where the smell of cinnamon was so thick Helen thought she could taste it. She opened the oven door to look at the coffeecakes, to momentarily immerse herself in their aroma, and then set the timer for another ten minutes. Pammy refilled their mugs. "I'm just tired of being alone," said Pammy, emptying the pot.

"I know that, Pammy."

"But knowing it and living it are completely different."

"I can empathize, Pammy."

"I need more than that, Helen. I need someone to share my life."

"You'll find someone. Daniel isn't that person."

"Even if he leaves Charlotte?"

"Especially if he leaves Charlotte."

CHAPTER 18

1973

Where's Thomas tonight?" asked John Thompson as he sat down at the dinner table and noticed the empty chair.

"Come to think of it, I don't know. Usually he informs me if he is going to miss dinner," said Claire, handing the basket of rolls to Helen to pass to her father. "He did mention something about delivering pizza tonight. Maybe he went in early, took someone else's shift. You know Thomas." Claire speared a green bean with her fork and then pointed it at Helen. "And I don't want to hear one word out of you, dear Helen, about these beans. You are to put six of them on your plate, and you are to eat them without theatrics."

Helen, who had already started plotting the demise of her beans, instantly reddened. It seemed to her that sometimes her mother could read her mind.

"We all know Thomas, seeing as how we're related and all," said Charlotte, slouching in her chair in an attempt to irritate her mother. "He'd deliver pizza to Mars for another buck."

"Sit up, Charlotte."

"He's on a date," said Helen. "Would somebody pass the potatoes?"

"A date?" said Charlotte, sitting up due to interest rather than compliance with her mother's request.

"He took pizza to a woman's house, and she asked him over for dinner." Helen put a heaping scoop of mashed potatoes on her plate and then passed the serving dish to her father.

"A woman?" asked Pammy.

"Yeah," said Helen. "She's got a kid and everything."

John and Claire put their forks down at exactly the same moment and looked at their youngest child. On the receiving end of her parents' penetrating stares, Helen quickly realized she probably should have said nothing. She stuffed a large forkful of potatoes in her mouth, wishing she could, right then, be on that delivery truck to Mars. "Have you met this woman, Helen?" her mother asked.

Helen held up the index finger of her right hand. She swished the potatoes around in her mouth, buying time. Eventually, she had to swallow. "No." Helen reached for her glass of milk. "Thomas told me about her."

"Tell us about her," said John Thompson.

"He said she was really nice."

"Is she married?" asked Claire, who had not yet lifted her fork and was sporting a tight smile, unlike Charlotte, who was genuinely grinning at Helen.

"No," said Helen. "Thomas said she was probably divorced."

Claire and John Thompson exchanged glances.

"How old is she?" said Charlotte.

"Really old," said Helen. "Thomas thinks maybe in her twenties."

John smiled. "What's her name?"

"Anna," Helen said. "Anna something."

Claire didn't say another word about Thomas or Anna until she and John were settled on the porch with their after-dinner coffee. "I don't like this," she said as soon as they sat down. And while they had discussed a number of topics at dinner after their initial conversation about Anna, including the theft of several lobster pots owned by their neighbors, John knew exactly what she was talking about. He didn't like it either. But he trusted his son, who was rarely foolhardy even though he was only eighteen. "What in the world is Thomas thinking, dating an older woman with a child?"

"We don't know what he's thinking," said John. "And we don't really know what's going on. What little information we have is hearsay, so I suggest we wait on forming an opinion, girding our loins, until we have talked to Thomas. Has he said anything to you?"

"No," said Claire. "Now I do remember his mentioning something about not being home for dinner tonight, but I didn't press him on it, John. I was in the middle of a béchamel sauce, and I just assumed he was working."

"I'm not blaming you, Claire. I was simply asking if you had more information."

"No." Claire's coffee sat untouched on the table beside her.

"Okay," said John, taking his first sip. "Let's leave it alone for now, since there is very little we can do at the moment. I will talk to him when he gets home. How was Julie today?" Julie Dasco was one of their neighbors. She had badly broken her leg waterskiing, and, with four young children to take care of, was very pleased to see Claire that afternoon with a bag in each hand—one holding a family-sized lasagna made with white sauce since Julie's youngest didn't like tomatoes, and the other a meatloaf and a quiche Lorraine.

"Are we really going to talk about Julie?"

John sipped his coffee. "Would you prefer to talk about something else?"

Claire looked at her husband, who raised his eyebrows at her. She sat back in her chair and took her first sip of coffee. She audibly exhaled. "Julie was fine. Her mother is coming tomorrow and can stay for a couple weeks to help her with the kids. And Bill is going to take two weeks of vacation time after that, so she'll be covered for a month. After that, she'll be in a walking cast, which will make life a whole lot easier."

"You're good to bring them food, Claire."

Claire waved her hand in the air in front of her. "It's no trouble. I'm in the kitchen anyway."

"Yes, you are," said John, raising his coffee cup to her. "And I don't tell you often enough how much I'm thankful for it. You are a very good cook."

Claire smiled at him, aware of what he was up to, that he was trying to ease her worry about Thomas. She was appreciative of his efforts, of his compliments, and also of his ability to wait out potential problems that more times than not ended up going away on their own. Claire was the fretter of the pair, something she attributed to motherhood. She wanted so much for her children—and when her plans for them went awry, her stomach churned with anxiety.

Thomas sat in Anna's dusted and vacuumed living room while Anna put Amy to bed in her tiny room at the end of the house's single hallway. He sat back on the couch, his stomach full of hamburger, potato salad, green beans, and ice cream. He had grilled the burgers himself, even though Anna told him she and Amy were "cookout queens." And they had come out pretty well, in spite of the fact that Thomas had had just three grilling lessons from his dad. Standing over the grill in Anna's fenced-in backyard, with a long-handled spatula in his hand, had made him fleetingly feel like a husband and father. And this feeling was a pleasant one, in a daydreamy kind of way. He could hear them in Amy's room, which they had recently painted orange at Amy's request. And he pictured them sitting on one of the twin beds, next to the small wood table with two chairs. This was where, Amy explained during the house tour, she worked while her mother studied at their kitchen table. Anna's room, large enough to accommodate a queen-size bed, two bureaus, and two bedside tables, was just across the hall from her daughter's. The entire house—living room, eat-in kitchen, two bedrooms, and one bathroom—reminded Thomas of a house on a TV set. The viewer would see all these rooms, but know there were more. There would be a staircase in the background that would lead to other bedrooms and other bathrooms. But in this case, it wasn't true. What he had seen on the tour Amy proudly led was it. Thomas could hear them so well because the house was so small. Anna was telling her daughter a story about African animals, and then Amy, full of questions, was adding detail along the way. Within minutes, it was quiet. Thomas could see Amy's light go out, and then Anna appeared. Thomas stood, as his father had taught him to do when a woman entered the room. "Are you leaving?" she asked.

"Not yet," said Thomas. "I mean, not unless you want me to."

"I want you to stay."

"Good," he said.

"Can I get you something to drink?"

"Do you want to split another beer?"

"That sounds perfect," said Anna. "I'll be right back."

"You sit," said Thomas. "I'll get it."

Thomas walked into the kitchen and took one of the beers he had brought with him in a brown paper bag out of the refrigerator. It was very cold, just the way Thomas liked it, and, given his level of nervousness, Thomas knew he could kill it in a minute or two. With most girls, Thomas was relaxed. He was smarter than any of them, so it was they who needed the beer to calm down, to converse. They were overeager, the high school girls, and at a loss for interesting topics of conversation. Who really cared who fell down on the mile run in gym class? Anna was so different. She was comfortable around him because she was comfortable with herself. "Hello again," he said, walking back into the living room with the beer in his hand.

"Thank you," she said when he handed her the bottle. She took the first sip.

"Thank *you,*" he said, "for the terrific dinner and even better company. Your Amy is something else."

Anna smiled. "Four going on forty, right?"

"She's a great kid. She reminds me somewhat of my youngest sister, who's quite precocious when she wants to be."

"It must be her father's genes," said Anna. "He was nothing if not gregarious."

"Where is her father?" Thomas asked, now that Anna had mentioned him.

"In Arizona," Anna said, looking down at the beer, which she handed to Thomas before saying, "He left the day before Amy was born."

"I'm sorry." Thomas took a sip. "I shouldn't have asked."

"Yes, you should have. You've got a right to know. We never married—we were intending to get married, but my pregnancy changed that." Thomas took another sip and then handed the bottle back to Anna. Sharing a beer with a girl, with a woman, was almost as intimate to Thomas as kissing her. "He didn't want children," said Anna, explaining. "When I got pregnant, he thought he might be able to do it. But, in the end, he changed his mind."

"Oh," said Thomas.

"We keep each other company, Amy and I. I didn't realize how lonely I was until you delivered pizza that first night. You were so cheerful and kind that I wanted you to stay, even then." Anna looked at him. But it was Thomas's turn to study his lap. His heart, jump-started by her words, was ba-booming in his chest, against his skin and his cotton shirt. He was certain Anna could see it, could read his feelings. His nervousness bound his tongue. He knew he had never been this panicked with other females. He had always been in charge. In parked cars or on front porches at the end of the night, the girls he dated looked at him shyly, desperately wanting and needing to be kissed as a validation of their date. Although he was sitting on a couch six inches from Anna, he could not lift his hand from his lap to touch her. And kissing her seemed out of the question, even though it was suddenly all he could think about.

"Do you go out much, Thomas?" Anna asked, prompting Thomas to lift his eyes, to look at her face. It was framed with shiny black hair that fell just below her shoulders. He could tell she'd had it in a ponytail earlier in the day because it had a ridge along the back where the coated elastic had been. She had taken out the elastic, let her hair fall, for him. Her eyes were almost as dark as her hair, and her mouth, turned up at the corners, perpetually smiling, was coated with inviting pink lipstick.

"Not really," he said. "I have three jobs, which keeps me pretty busy."

"Oh," Anna said. "Amy will be disappointed."

"I mean, I'm busy, but not too busy to see you two. I have a day off once in a while and a couple nights off, too. Most nights I go to bed early because I drive a bakery truck four mornings a week."

"You *are* busy." Anna smiled at him, as if to announce her pleasure with his productivity.

"How about you?" Thomas asked. "Where do you work?"

"I work every weekday from nine to five at Hudson and Lambert."

"The law office?"

"Yes. I'm a secretary."

"Good for you," said Thomas. "What does Amy do?"

"She goes to preschool five mornings a week during the school year, then gets dropped off at my neighbor's house for the afternoon. Mrs. Purdy is almost sixty and has more energy than I do. She watches five or six kids and has a ball. Amy loves her like a grandmother. She stays there all day in the summer, with a few weeks at day camp here and there." Unintentionally, Thomas yawned. "I'm sorry," Anna said. "I've gone on too long."

"No, no," said Thomas. "I've been up since early this morning. Please go on. I could listen to your voice all night." Thomas blushed as soon as he spoke. He was warm and tongue-tied and suddenly wanted to leave before he made a fool of himself.

"You're sweet," said Anna, standing. "It is getting late, though. Let me get your sweater."

She walked into the kitchen, where Thomas's navy blue sweater lay draped over a padded wooden chair. She grabbed it and held it close to her for a few seconds before returning to the living room and handing it to him.

"Thank you," he said, "for the sweater and the dinner. I had a terrific time."

"Come down here," said Anna. Thomas leaned forward and down until his face was just a few inches from hers. "Thank you," she said, putting her hands on his cheeks, "for waking me up."

Thomas kissed her, softly brushing his lips against hers. She wrapped her arms around his shoulders and kissed him back. And then he did something he had never done to anyone but Helen. He lifted Anna off the ground, and held her to him and kissed her again, feeling her energy flow from her mouth into his, and from his mouth into his body, racing like an ocean current until it crashed into his fingertips and pulsated in his toes. Hesitantly, he put her down. He no longer felt awkward and wanted, again, to stay with this woman. She looked up at him. "Come back," she said.

"I will. I'll call you tomorrow." Thomas bent down and kissed her on the cheek. She led him to the front door and opened it for him. Thomas strode out into the night, feeling like he had just completed a test and had known every answer.

When Thomas approached the cottage in his car, he could see that one of the lights inside the porch was still on. He looked hard as he cruised past the house and could see his father sitting in the chair he always sat in, reading a book. It was late, making Thomas instantly wonder what had gone wrong. "Dad?" he said, as soon as he was in the house, walking from the kitchen through the dining room and living room to the porch. John removed his reading glasses and looked at his son. "Everything okay?"

John smiled at him. "Yes. I just thought I'd wait up for you. Sometimes we pass like ships in the night, you and I. Can you sit?" Thomas sat in the chair next to his father, the chair normally occupied by his mother. "How was your evening?"

"It was fine, Dad."

"Helen told us you had a date." And there it was—the reason behind John's late-night reading session. And because his father was a very reasonable man and Thomas trusted him, even though many of his friends barely spoke to their parents, Thomas told his father about his dinner with Anna and Amy, about the circumstances behind her single-parent status. John nodded as he listened, and then said, "She sounds like a lovely young woman."

"She is, Dad."

"You sound serious about her."

"Dad, we just met."

"I understand that. But sometimes, when we meet people who

we think will be a positive influence in our lives, we can get serious quickly."

Thomas hesitated. Did he want to tell his father that he was, indeed, already feeling serious about Anna? "I like her," he said. "That's all for now."

"Well, enjoy her company then," said John, closing his book and setting it on the table between them. Thomas shifted his weight to the front of the chair. "Do remember that you are headed off to college in the fall and that your studies at Princeton will keep you very busy."

"I sure will," said Thomas, springing out of the chair. "I'm going to grab a quick snack before bed."

"You do that, my boy," said John. "Sleep well."

As soon as Helen heard her father close his bedroom door, she descended her bunk-bed ladder, crept down the hallway, and eased her way down the stairs to the living room. She walked quickly through the darkness to the kitchen, which was lit by the light under the stove hood. Thomas was standing next to the fridge, drinking from a half gallon container of milk. "Hi," she said.

Thomas spilled milk down his chin onto his sweater. "Jesus, Helen, you scared me. What are you doing up?"

"I've been waiting for you to come home."

"Because you squealed on me?" Thomas looked at her sternly.

"I'm sorry, Thomas," she began. "It was out of my mouth before I knew what I was saying. Mom and Dad didn't know where you were."

"I told Mom I wouldn't be home for dinner."

"She forgot, Thomas. And then when I mentioned that you were on a date, all eyes were upon me." Helen's eyes were moist. She could feel his disappointment.

Thomas put the milk carton down and bent down to hug his sister. As soon as he said, "It's okay, Helen," she started to cry. "Hey, hey, what's this?"

"Are you in trouble, Thomas?"

Thomas wiped Helen's two tears from her cheeks, gave her another squeeze, and then released her. He stood tall. "No, I'm not in trouble—at least not with Dad. This is okay. What I did tonight was okay. Anna is a single woman my age. She just happens to have a child."

"Why does she have a child, Thomas?"

"Her boyfriend left her. He didn't want children." Thomas turned his attention back to the counter and the milk, which he lifted with one hand. He took another gulp.

"That's sad."

"Yes, it is."

"Anyway, I'm sorry, Thomas. I should have kept my big mouth shut."

"That's okay, Helen. I wouldn't want you to lie about anything anyway."

"You can be mad if you want."

"I'm not mad," said Thomas. "Did Mom make cookies today?"

"Yes," said Helen, feeling forgiven. "They're in the pantry. I'll get them."

After a glass of milk and two peanut butter cookies each, they walked upstairs. Thomas patted the top of Helen's head and said good night. In his room, he took off his clothes, save his boxers, and climbed into bed. A warm breeze blew in the windows, lulling him to sleep. In the morning, he would tell his mother everything she wanted to know. He would tell her about Anna. He would tell her about Amy. He would tell her about Anna's selfish boyfriend. He would be truthful about everything, except his feelings.

He did not see his mother until the following afternoon, after his bakery run and newspaper delivery. When he walked into the kitchen she got right to the point, saying, "I understand you and your father had a conversation when you got in last night."

"Yes," said Thomas, looking in the fridge so he wouldn't have to look at her.

"He assures me that this situation is not serious."

Thomas turned his gaze onto his mother's face. "What situation is that?"

"Thomas, don't play with me," said Claire, hands on hips. "You are at the very beginning of what promises to be a very productive and successful life. Don't let this kind of distraction derail your motivation."

It was fruitless, Thomas knew, to argue with a statement like this. When his mother made up her mind, she rarely changed it. Facts were irrelevant. "Right-O," said Thomas, shifting his attention back to the fridge. "Helen said there was a burger leftover from the other night."

"Bottom shelf, left," said Claire, looking back at the pot of fish chowder on the stovetop. She was satisfied this was a dalliance, this relationship with the woman on the other side of town. And while she didn't want the woman to get hurt, she admitted to herself that she didn't really care—as long as Thomas stayed on track.

Chapter 19

2003

Claire opened her eyes, blinking at the bright sunlight that came streaming through her windows. For a moment, she wasn't sure what day it was, and then decided upon Saturday. It was the weekend, yes, and today was the day Thomas would arrive, and she would have her four children together in the house for the first time in as long as she could remember. Had it really been thirty years? Helen had been in the house all along, and Pammy had come for a short stay every summer. Charlotte, depending on whom she was married to or dating and where in the world she was living, showed up periodically. But Thomas had not been back to the cottage since that summer after his senior year in high school. It had not been intentional, Claire had decided long ago. He had simply been too busy making money to take any time off from whatever job or internship claimed sixty hours of his week. He had rarely taken time off, telling his mother whenever she had invited him to the cottage that he didn't need vacation time. He found it counterproductive, a setback, like school children returning to the classroom after a bookless summer and remembering nothing from their previous year's instruction. It was a well-documented fact, Thomas had told Claire, that teachers spent the first two months of the academic year reteaching what the children had already learned.

Using her arms, Claire propped herself up on her pillows. Now that her eyes had adjusted to the light, she wanted to look out at the water. Still, after all these years, just seeing water quickened her heartbeat. It was all that time in the pool. When she was a competitive swimmer, she had felt more comfortable in the water than out of it. The chlorine—its smell, what it did to her hair and her skin—was so much more than a chemical that kept the water clean. It was to her like the scent of baking bread was to others, a warm, welcome homecoming.

This is what this weekend was, wasn't it—a homecoming? It was a forced event, one that wouldn't have happened without her insistence, her interference, but she felt no remorse for her actions. What homecoming didn't come with a price? Rearranged schedules, travel, inconvenience—every family gathering exacted its costs from its participants. Life was like that, Claire thought, as she shifted her weight upward, so she could sit on her bottom. You got out of it what you put into it. And those unwilling to take risks or to put effort into something lived marginal, lackluster lives. It was this lesson that she had tried to impart to her children. And the physical and emotional distance between her children told her she had been less successful than she thought.

It had worked for her, after all. Her Smith College education and swimming career had opened doors for her that were locked shut for many women her age. By the time she was twenty-six, she had traveled extensively, given press conferences, signed autographs, and—most important—earned the respect of her male peers. She, like many of her classmates, was certainly interested in earning the admiration of men her age. But it was the respect they showed her that put her in a different league altogether. In fact, she was in *their* league, the athletic league, and because she excelled at what they most revered, she was as close to being one of them as women got. The brazen boasting, pursuit of physical excellence, discussions about the secrets of a stellar performance—the men never tired of this banter. As long as she was breaking records in the pool, they never tired of her. She had been an equal at a time when most women were considered little more than Saturday-night dates. Was it wrong for her to want this elevated status for her children?

She had to use the bathroom, but she was hesitant to get out of bed. In bed, she felt whole again, free from the ravages of cancer and its perfunctory, invasive treatments; free from the pain and weakness that challenged her during the daylight hours. In bed, she could fool herself into thinking she was still an athlete, albeit an aged one. She could daydream about swimming to the raft or running around the backyard or tennis court with her children. She could transport herself back to a better time, when the children were under her wing and when John was alive. He had been her measuring tape, allowing her the inches and feet she needed to run the household her way, but pulling her in if she went too far. He had cautioned her about pushing the children—and had intervened a number of times over the years when she had reduced one of their daughters, usually Pammy, to tears. And at the time, she had occasionally thought of him as soft, weak. He was the quiet, introspective type that Claire had always found interesting, but she wondered if her true appreciation for him was in retrospect. She had sometimes thought, earlier in her life, when she was running around at eighty miles an hour, that he wasn't as capable or motivated as she was. As it turned out, he was simply not as competitive.

The urge to urinate finally drove Claire to shift her legs and feet from underneath the thin summer-weight blanket to the floor. "Helen?" she called. When she got no response, she tried again, louder. "Pammy?"

Pammy, who was on the porch drinking coffee, quickly ascended the stairs and walked into her mother's room. "What is it, Mom?"

"Where's Helen?"

"She went for a walk."

"And you didn't go with her, I see."

"I'm tired, Mom. I didn't sleep well last night."

"Well, I'm sorry to hear that," said Claire, who wasn't the least bit sorry. People who didn't sleep well or didn't feel well or had allergies, Claire thought, should keep their problems to themselves.

As her high school coach used to say to the team when they complained about tough practices, *Get over it.*

"Can I help you with something?" asked Pammy. "There's more coffee in the kitchen if you'd like a cup."

"I would very much like a cup." Claire scooted her bottom to the edge of the mattress. "But if I don't get to the bathroom in the next thirty seconds, we're going to have a mess on our hands."

"What can I do?"

"You can either help me up and down the hall, or you can grab my walker from the corner."

"I'll take you," said Pammy, offering her arm.

"This is not a prom date, Pammy," said Claire. "I'm weak, and I'm going to put my full weight—such as it is—on you. Are you ready?" Pammy braced herself. "Here we go." They moved out of the bedroom and down the hallway to the bathroom at what Claire referred to as a snail's pace. "I hate this," she said, when they finally reached the bathroom.

"Hate what?"

Claire's eyebrows shot up. "Hate being completely dependent on others for whatever I need, especially when those others are clueless."

"Hey, I'm trying to help here."

"Get me to the toilet, please," said Claire. "And then close the door on your way out."

Pammy did as instructed. It was after the door was shut and Claire, Pammy guessed, was on the toilet, that Pammy heard the words "thank you."

"I'll be right here if you need me," Pammy called in response.

"Bring my walker downstairs. And when Helen gets back, tell her I'll need her help getting dressed this morning. Nothing seems to be working properly at the moment."

"I can help you."

"If it's all the same to you, I'll have Helen's help. She does this every day and knows the routine. Thank you though."

Pammy went back into her mother's bedroom and grabbed the walker from the near corner. She carried it downstairs, surprised by its light weight, yet seemingly sturdy design. As soon as she set it up on the porch, Helen walked through the front door. "Is Mom up?"

"She's in the bathroom," said Pammy. "She wanted the walker down here."

"Okay," said Helen, removing her front-zip sweatshirt. "Did she say she'd need help down the stairs?"

"She didn't say," said Pammy. "Helen, what is going on here?"

"What do you mean, Pammy?"

"I had no idea she was so weak."

"Well," said Helen, looking at her sister's face, "if you'd read my e-mails, you'd know exactly what was and is going on."

"I have read your e-mails."

"So, you are well aware that the cancer treatments just about killed her and that the effects of those treatments have left her with very diminished physical capacity. She's dying, Pammy. That's why we're all here." Helen turned her back on her sister and walked into the kitchen. Before she had finished her glass of water, Pammy was standing next to her.

"I know she's dying, Helen. I just didn't realize it was happening so quickly."

"Well, it is." Helen finished her water.

"You don't sound very sad about it."

"Oh for God's sake, Pammy, I live with it, with her, every day. I've seen her go from a vibrant physical specimen to what she is now, as close to a corpse as possible without actually being one. I help her out of bed when she needs it. I help her get dressed when she needs it. I help her in the bathroom. I help her in the kitchen. I drive her where she needs to go. I get her food. I prepare her meals. I keep her company." Helen refilled her water glass and chugged it. "So, yes, I'm sad about her condition, as I have been for some time. I'm also sad that you, Charlotte, and Thomas have no idea what either of us is going through."

"You never said . . ."

"Yes, I *have* said. I've explained in e-mails. I've scanned and sent doctors' reports. Have you read anything?"

Pammy had tears in her eyes. "Yes," she said. "I have read everything. But I don't think I really understood—until right now."

"Well, yes, you wouldn't understand," said Helen, "because you haven't visited Mom since Thanksgiving, even though you live two hours away. And a lot has happened since Thanksgiving, Pammy. Again, this is why we're here. Wake up."

Pammy looked at the floor. "I'm sorry, Helen."

"As you should be." Helen walked back out of the kitchen, through the dining room, and into the living room. She climbed the stairs and knocked on the bathroom door. "Mom? Are you okay?"

"Come in here and help me, dear," said Claire. "I can't seem to get up."

Helen walked into the bathroom and closed the door behind her. She helped her mother off the toilet, pulled up her underpants, and helped her into the hallway. Together, they shuffled to Claire's bedroom, where Helen sat Claire down on the bed. Helen then retrieved Claire's favorite linen jumper from the closet, a white T-shirt from the bureau, and her white leather Birkenstock sandals from underneath the bed. "Are you ready?"

Claire raised her arms over her head. "Let's do this. And then we can have some coffee. I've never wanted a cup more than I do right now."

"You and me both," said Helen, lifting the cotton nightgown over her mother's head.

When they finally reached the porch, after a ten-minute walk down the hallway and staircase, Pammy was waiting for them. She had filled their mugs from a fresh pot of coffee, and she had put an assortment of the pastries she'd brought from New York on a china plate, each piece cut in half. She had fluffed the pillow in her mother's chair that supported her back when she was sitting. And she had given her mother's lap blanket a good shake outside.

This was what she was good at, at making people feel comfortable. Back when she and Mark were happy together, Pammy often had dinner guests to her apartment, the apartment he lived in five or six days a week. She would ask guests two weeks in advance, as any more time than that seemed too planned, desperate even. And then as soon as she had the set number—she liked eight around her dining room table—she'd start the preparations. After work, she ironed the table linens, pored through cookbooks, shopped for table accessories. The week of the gathering, she'd start the food preparations. She often made the dessert first, popping unfrosted cakes and other confections into the freezer so they wouldn't get stale. Then she made the sauces and the soups, followed by the sides: the wild rice, the potato pancakes, the mushroom and rice cakes, the sweet corn pudding. And then the appetizers, using whatever seasonal ingredients looked best. Often the main course was a simply prepared piece of red meat, poultry, or fish, which she thought was the perfect complement to her more complicated offerings. Everyone raved about her dinner parties, exclaiming they had never tasted better food and that, as their thank-you e-mails often said, *the company was even better!* But not many of her guests asked her to their apartments and suburban houses. Mark told her this was because no one could cook like she could. How, after all, could they serve her a grilled frozen burger, when she had served them trout with butter and almonds?

As soon as Claire was settled into her chair, she wrapped her hands around the mug Pammy handed her. After her first sip, she sat back and closed her eyes. "I don't know how anyone can start a day without a good cup of coffee. Is this flavored with something?"

"Yes. It's cinnamon raisin—perfect for a weekend morning," said Pammy. "I get it from a specialty shop in the Village. It's just across the street from my office."

Claire had never been especially fond of or impressed by specialty food items. They were taking over her independent grocery store shelves and coolers, these organic, exotic, hard-to-find-until-now produces, grains, and meats. What was better than a good steak, baked potato, and Caesar salad? Sure, she liked to experiment with sauces and soups in the kitchen. And she could bake for hours on a winter afternoon. But all the ingredients in her recipes could have been easily found by her mother or grandmother. "I like Maxwell House myself," she said.

"Really?" said Pammy.

"Really," said Claire. "Ask Helen. She buys and makes my coffee all the time." Claire and Pammy both looked at Helen. Helen gave her mother a look that only the two of them, because they had spent so much time together, would understand. "But this is a nice change. I like it."

"Well, thank you."

Claire again turned to Helen. "How was your walk? What kind of day do we have on tap?"

"A good one, I think, even with this chilly start." Helen stood and draped the blanket Pammy had shaken out and then folded, over her mother's legs.

"Thomas comes today," Claire pointed out.

"Yes," said Helen, still uncertain about whether he would actually arrive.

"Then it will be a good day indeed," said Claire.

Chapter 20

1973

Thomas walked along Main Street feeling refreshed. He had delivered Mr. Sloan's baked goods by nine o'clock. After dropping the truck off, he stopped at the bank for some cash and then drove home for a quick run and swim before showering, shaving, and dressing in khaki pants and a light blue button-down shirt to take Anna out to lunch. She had just an hour, so he wanted to be prompt. He was always on time anyway, arriving at every destination within minutes of his goal. This had not been the case when he was younger and habitually late to everything, from baseball practice, to and from which he rode his bike, to dinner. His father had taken him aside one evening when he was thirteen or fourteen, when he had been thirty minutes late to the table and Claire had refused to serve him, and told him that late people were under the mistaken assumption that their time was more important than everyone else's. And it was the understanding that being late is a discourtesy to others, much more so than the disappointment in eating cold potatoes for dinner, that swayed Thomas. He hadn't been late since.

He had talked with Anna on the phone several times since the cookout, but he had not seen her, and his heart was active in anticipation. His mother had spoken with him again about Anna, reiterating that she was concerned about his future. He could go as far in life as he wanted to go, Claire told him, unless something or someone held him back. *Not that this Anna probably wasn't a very nice young woman. But the mere fact that she had a daughter presented problems. If he stayed with Anna, he would be forever supporting a child he didn't sire.* Thomas assured his mother that he hadn't yet considered marriage after a single date and that he would take her advice to heart. To push back a little, he asked her about all the children who were adopted and supported by fathers who had absolutely nothing to do with their conception. That, she said, was another matter altogether.

After his swim, shower, and shave, Thomas quickly dressed and then drove into town and parked in front of Anna's building. He opened the thick glass door that read HUDSON AND LAMBERT in gold lettering and walked in. Within seconds, his feet were off the tiled floor and onto a plush Oriental carpet that covered more than half the lobby. Straight ahead was a large mahogany desk, occupied by a young dark-haired woman who was not Anna. Thomas checked his watch. He was two minutes early. He approached the desk. "May I help you?"

"I'm looking for Anna Santiago," said Thomas, looking at the woman and then glancing behind her, hoping to see Anna.

"She's getting ready to go out to lunch," she said. "Is there something I could help you with?"

"No," said Thomas. "I'm the one she's getting ready for."

"Oh," the woman said, visibly startled. "I'll go see if I can find her."

Within seconds, Anna appeared from a room in the back, carrying a large stack of paper. Thomas rushed to her. "Let me carry that," he said.

"I can get it, Thomas." She set the pile down on the side of the desk.

"What is all that?"

"Information," said Anna. "That's what everybody around here calls briefs, reports, their children's summer school term papers—information." She pushed her hair back from her face and turned to the other woman. "I've sorted and labeled everything. So if you can just deliver the right stuff to the right people that would be terrific. I know Mr. Lambert wants to get to this as soon as he gets back to the office."

"You got it," said the young woman, who Thomas realized was more of a girl. She was, Anna told him later, Mr. Hudson's daughter, who answered the phone for Anna during the lunch hour.

Anna turned back to face Thomas and smiled. "Take me out of here."

"Gladly," said Thomas. He put his arm around her for just a moment, guiding her toward the front door. When they reached the sidewalk, Anna took his hand in hers.

"What a morning," she said. "I've spent the last hour at the photocopier. I'm just about blinded by the flash of light from that machine."

Thomas held his hand in front of her face. "How many fingers am I holding up?"

"Fourteen!" Anna laughed.

"I'm so happy to see you," he said. "You look terrific."

"Thank you. You look pretty handsome yourself."

Thomas smiled. "I thought we'd go to that restaurant on the water, the Boat Dock. I think we can get in and out in an hour."

"I can stretch it another fifteen minutes or so."

When they reached his car, Thomas opened the passenger side for Anna, like his father had taught him. He walked around to his side and quickly got in. Just as he sat down, Anna leaned over and kissed him on the cheek. "I've missed you," she said.

"Tell me how much," he said, kissing her lips.

"I've thought about you every day," she said, as he kissed her cheeks and forehead. "And I've thought about you every night." She kissed the tip of his nose. "I've dreamed about you kissing me, just like this."

Thomas picked up her hands and kissed her fingers, slowly, individually. He put her hands back in her lap and started the car. "We've got to go now," he said, "or lunch will definitely not happen." Anna laughed. "How's Amy?" he asked, putting the car into gear and pulling out of his parking space.

"She's great. She was so excited I was having lunch with you today. She's quite the matchmaker, you know."

"Really?"

"Oh, yes. She's got us walking down the aisle together by September." Thomas blushed. "I'm just teasing you, Thomas."

"Is it a joke?" he asked, serious suddenly.

"Thomas, you're eighteen, unencumbered, and headed for college, and I'm a twenty-one-year-old single mother. I understand the law of averages."

"You're only twenty-one?" asked Thomas.

"How old did you think I was?" said Anna. "And be careful, young man."

"I just assumed you were older, because of Amy and all."

"I got pregnant when I was sixteen, Thomas. I dropped out of school and set up house. I did get my high school diploma, though, by going to school at night. I'm taking college courses now and hope someday to go to law school."

"Anna Santiago," said Thomas. "Why am I not surprised?"

"Surprised about what?"

"We're cut from the same cloth. We're both work-till-you-drop capitalists."

"You're the capitalist, Thomas. I'm just a realist. If I want the best for Amy, I've got to set an example, and I've got to pay for it."

"Yes, you do, Anna. There are no free lunches."

"Except for today," she said, smiling.

Thomas pulled into the parking lot of the Boat Dock, a shack-like, wood-shingled restaurant with no more than ten tables inside and many more outside on a deck overlooking the river. They chose the table at the far end of the deck and sat down next to each other. When the waitress came, Thomas ordered a beer and Anna asked for a glass of ice water. "So, tell me more about these plans," he said to Anna when the waitress disappeared.

"I've only taken three courses," Anna said. "I'm taking accounting now."

"What are you going to major in?"

"Economics, I think, with whatever courses I'll need or want to prepare for law school."

"You're serious about this, aren't you?"

"Very," she said. "If I do well in my undergraduate studies, which Hudson and Lambert pay for, they will also pay for my graduate work."

"That's generous."

"Yes, it is. I'll have to work for them afterward, though."

"Do you have to promise them that?"

"In a tacit way," Anna said. "If history repeats itself, and I'm told it does, they'll want me to come back for at least four years."

"That seems fair."

"And if the pay is good and the work is interesting, I'll stay."

When the waitress brought the menu, Thomas glanced at it quickly, then ordered two chef salads with blue cheese dressing on the side. Anna smiled at him. "How'd you know I like chef salad?"

"You told me it was your favorite," he said, "the night you had me over for dinner."

"When I wanted you to stay."

"When I wanted to stay," said Thomas, sliding his hand under Anna's hair and massaging her neck.

Anna put her hand on Thomas's thigh and rubbed his leg. The two stared at each other, sipping their drinks until the waitress came. Thomas asked her if she could put the salads in boxes to go. When she came back, Thomas paid her, put the boxes under his arm, and held Anna's hand tightly. He led her, laughing, through the restaurant and out to the street to his car. Thomas put the salads in the back seat, then opened the door for Anna. He ran to his side, hopped in, and started the car and put it into gear. He looked at his watch. They had forty-five minutes. He drove quickly to Anna's house, where they ran to the front door while she grabbed her keys from her purse. Once inside, Thomas picked her up into his arms and kissed her. He put her down and watched as she took off her suit jacket, blouse, and skirt. He moved toward her. "Wait," she said softly. She took off her slip, stockings, and underwear and stood before him naked. "Now come here."

Thomas went to her. She told him to stand still, but he began to shake as she unbuttoned his shirt. He was breathing hard, almost to the point of panting. She took off his shirt and unzipped his pants. She reached in and grabbed his hard penis and held it in her hand. Within seconds, he came. "I'm sorry," he said afterward, unable to look at her.

"It's okay," said Anna. "Come to my room."

There, she took off the rest of his clothes and led him to the bed. She pulled back the covers, and they both got in. They lay next to each other, holding each other, looking at each other. And twenty minutes later, Thomas was no longer sorry and definitely in love.

CHAPTER 21

2003

Charles lifted the platter of steaming scrambled eggs off the table and scooped some onto his plate. He passed the eggs to Charlotte, who made a face at them and passed them to Daniel. He shoveled a large, yellow mass onto his plate, then held the platter for Pammy, who, blushing, took a small serving. Helen made a face at Pammy, helped herself, and then served her mother, who hadn't taken her eyes off the eggs from the minute Daniel set them down in front of Charles. Thank God, Helen thought, she's hungry. Todd and Ned had shuffled past the adults several minutes earlier, dressed in white shirts and shorts and carrying tennis rackets. They'd had cereal and toast and were on their way to a grudge match with the Fischer twins, who'd beaten them in a tie-breaker in the previous summer's Labor Day tournament.

"This is delicious," Claire said after she'd swallowed her first bite. "Who made the eggs?"

"Charlotte," said Pammy. "She's a whiz in the kitchen."

"Look," Charlotte said to Pammy, "not everyone wants to be Martha Stewart."

"Daniel made them, Mom," said Helen.

"You're quite a cook, young man."

"When you live with Charlotte, it's cook or starve."

"I love this," said Charlotte, pushing her chair away from the table. "Everyone's a comedian today."

"Have some more coffee, Charlotte," said Helen.

"I will have some coffee." Charlotte stood. "And I'll take it to the porch."

She disappeared into the kitchen and then reappeared with a filled mug. She walked through the dining room without saying a word, prompting Pammy to shout, "Miss you already!" Charlotte, not looking back, flipped them her middle finger. She had never been a morning person, finding cheerfulness before noon fake and annoying. No one was bright-eyed and bushy-tailed, whatever that meant, until noon at least, no matter what their mother had told them about early risers. People needed time in the morning, to think about their day, to wonder about their night, and scrambled eggs were simply not a part of that process. She sat down on the porch couch and picked up a magazine. Turning the pages, Charlotte stopped at an advertisement for Lucky jeans. Daniel appeared out of the living room and sat down beside her. "You okay?"

"Fine, darling, thank you. I just needed some time alone."

"Do you want me to leave?"

"Stay, you handsome thing. You're the one I most like being alone with." Daniel smiled. "How would I look in these?" said Charlotte, leaning into Daniel's body and showing him the page with the jeans.

"I'd be the lucky one." Charlotte laughed. "You look great in everything, baby," he said.

"How do I look in nothing?" Charlotte was whispering in his ear. "Let's go upstairs."

"I'd love to, honey, but I promised Todd and Ned I'd watch some of their match."

"Run along then," said Charlotte, putting on a pout.

"Baby," said Daniel, "we'll have time later."

"I can hardly wait." She was looking at the magazine again. "Go watch that match."

Pammy walked onto the porch just as Daniel was leaving. She called good-bye, hoping he'd turn around and engage her with meaningful eye contact, but he just waved and walked across the yard in the direction of the tennis courts. Although she wanted to watch him walk, to follow with her eyes his hard, sexy backside until he was out of sight, she sat down and looked at Charlotte. "Feeling any better?"

"I never felt bad," said Charlotte, eyes on the magazine.

"So storming off and telling everyone to fuck themselves is all in a day's work?"

Charlotte gave her sister a bored look. "It's early, Pammy. At nine o'clock in the morning, I'd rather be sleeping than eating chicken embryos."

"The embryos were terrific."

"Fabulous, Pammy. You can't begin to know how happy I am for you."

"Why are you such a bitch?"

"Why does everyone pick on me?"

"Because you ask for it, Charlotte. With your big hair, double scotches, slim cigarettes, and now, enormous chest, you ask for it."

"You're jealous."

"I don't think so. If I won the lottery, breast implants wouldn't be the first thing on my list." Pammy looked out through the screens.

"Daniel adores them," said Charlotte, taking a sip of her coffee. "He says the twenty-five-year-olds at the gym would love to have my body."

"Why are you in competition with twenty-five-year-olds?"

"We all are, dear. If you want a man, Pammy, you need to know your competition."

Pammy looked down at her protruding abdomen. "I can't compete with women in their twenties."

"Then start looking for a man in his sixties."

"That's doesn't seem right."

"It's not," said Charlotte. "But it's reality."

Pammy sipped her coffee. "Is that what you're doing with Daniel—showing other women your age that you've got what it takes to snag a younger man?"

"Essentially, yes."

"What's he doing with you?"

Charlotte finished her coffee before responding. "I make his life easier with what I can provide him. He makes my life better by making me feel younger and attractive. We have a mutually beneficial relationship."

"Sounds pretty superficial to me."

"Says the woman who's not in any relationship at all."

Helen appeared in the doorway. "Am I interrupting something?"

"Not really," said Charlotte. "Pammy was just telling me my relationship with Daniel is superficial."

"Pammy," Helen said in a schoolmarm's pedantic voice, "didn't we agree not to be mean?"

"I'd be mean too," said Charlotte, "if I hadn't been laid in two years."

"Shut up!" said Pammy. "I could buy a whore, too. That's not the kind of so-called loving relationship I want."

"Oh, so Daniel's a whore now? I can't wait to tell him that."

"I didn't mean that," said Pammy, shoving her hands into the pockets of her shorts.

"What kind of relationship do you want, Pammy?" Charlotte lit a cigarette. "Just exactly who are you holding out for?"

"Someone who means something." Pammy's eyes were moist with tears.

"Then you're going to be a shriveled-up, old spinster," said Charlotte, exhaling a stream of smoke into the room. "If you happen to stumble across one the few men on the planet in his forties who is interesting, caring, smart, sensitive, and employed, he's not looking for a woman in her forties, my friend. He wants someone he can shape and control, a younger woman, with toned muscles, even skin, and straight teeth."

"They're not all like that, the men my age," said Pammy, hoping they weren't.

"Sure they are," said Charlotte. "Why the hell do you think you're still single? All the men your age are looking for women in their twenties." Charlotte took a drag of her cigarette. "When you are a forty-year-old woman in this country, you are invisible to most men—unless you're looking for a sixty-year-old partner. I refuse to be irrelevant." She blew the smoke through the side of her mouth at the screen. Done with the conversation, she put her feet up on the wicker coffee table and stared, without purpose, out the window.

"I won't have smoking in this house!" Claire shouted from the dining room.

"Shit!" Charlotte stood, grabbed her pack and silver lighter, and walked out the porch door. "I feel like I'm still fifteen."

"That's because you are," Pammy said to the space Charlotte had just vacated.

Helen patted her sister's hand. "You stay here," she said. "I'll get some more coffee."

Charlotte walked toward the tennis courts with the vague notion that she would watch her nephews play. She finished the cigarette she had lit as soon as she was outside the cottage and lit another one. She was shaking. How dare her mother holler at her like a disobedient teenager? She was forty-seven years old, for Christ's sake, and didn't need anybody telling her she couldn't smoke in the house. At forty-seven, she could do whatever she wanted, without the approval of her mother—except when she was at home, when she was a daughter again.

Halfway down the road, Charlotte stopped walking and sat on the edge of the grass. She had lost her marginal interest in watching the tennis match and was also not interested in seeing Daniel just yet. Pammy's words had stung. Their relationship was, indeed, superficial. She was attracted to his body, and he was attracted to her money. She lay back on the grass and stared up at the sky. In fact, she knew how much he loved her money because he spent it as if it were his own. He shopped for clothing more than she did, and they ate out three or four nights a week—all at her expense. And even though Daniel usually cooked the other nights and bought the groceries, he never looked at prices, coming home with cloth bags filled with the freshest, organic ingredients from the finest grocery stores and farmers' markets. He wanted a car, to drive to his philosophy classes, and, he said, to whisk her away on weekends. But Charlotte had held out because she was secretly afraid that if she bought him one, he would drive out of her life.

And yet, she wondered, would she care if he left? Couldn't she find another gorgeous body and face to replace his? Several men had propositioned her recently: Pete from the coffee shop; Juan, her yoga instructor; George, who owned the dealership where she'd bought her latest Mercedes. But she had playfully rebuffed their advances, mostly because they were married. The clandestine nature of a relationship with a married man was, at first, thrilling. And the sex was always fabulous, since most of the men had long ago lost any physical attraction to their middle-aged, muffin-top-waisted wives. The Sallys and the Pattys and the Joans and the Jennifers were all pretty and often charming—Charlotte ran into these women everywhere she went—but they were far more enthralled with their Range Rovers and their club luncheons than their husbands' penises. What Charlotte needed, she concluded then and there, was a single man closer to her age. Not a flabby, balding CPA, but a trim, tanned, and devilishly handsome executive. She had the looks and the body, the snappy repartee, to entice a man in his fifties, but she knew that time was running out.

"Charlotte?" She looked up at the man calling her name and, for an instant, thought the gods had answered her plea. Standing before her was a muscular middle-aged man with deep blue eyes and blond hair combed back on his head. She blinked in the sunlight. "Are you okay?"

"I'm fine," said Charlotte, starting to get up. The man extended his hand and pulled her off the ground as easily as she had pulled on her shorts that morning.

"You probably don't remember me," he said. "I'm Steve Johanson."

"Oh my God," said Charlotte, "of course I remember you! What are you doing here?"

"I came down this morning. I've got to get some work done this weekend and there are just too many distractions at home."

"Where's home?"

"In the city. I've lived there for about two years now, since my divorce."

"Oh, you're divorced?"

"Yeah, marriage doesn't seem to agree with me."

"Me neither."

"What are *you* doing here? I haven't seen you in years."

"We're here for a reunion, of sorts," said Charlotte, not wanting to go into the details of her mother's illness, of her family issues. "My younger sister Helen organized it and insisted we comply."

"That's Helen for you. I run into her every now and again when we're both here. She still looks like the ten-year-old I remember running around the beach."

Charlotte laughed. "In many ways, she still is."

"All of you are here?"

"Thomas comes today. We'll be a houseful."

"Who's with you?"

"No one, really." Charlotte was unexpectedly embarrassed about Daniel. "I brought a friend."

"Where are you living?"

"San Francisco. For several years now."

"Really? I've got several accounts there, so I'm out that way a few times a year. Can I call you?" Steve asked. "I mean, are you involved with anyone?"

"No one I can't lose for an evening. I'd love to hear from you."

Steve said good-bye and jogged down the road. He looked good, Charlotte decided as she watched him, in his navy blue shorts and white T-shirt. The muscles in his calves moved up and down as he ran. She would go out with him if he called. And if he didn't call, she'd call him.

CHAPTER 22

1973

Thomas lay on his bed, fully awake, even though it was three thirty in the morning. He could not get to sleep, or perhaps he had been asleep and was now awake, but it seemed like he had been staring out the window since he got into bed at midnight. He counted the stars, thinking that doing so, like counting sheep, might lull him to sleep, nature's nocturnal anesthesia. But instead, it frustrated him, and he was frustrated already. He stopped counting at forty-eight and got out of bed. He grabbed a T-shirt from the chair in the corner of his room and pulled it over his head. He retrieved his jeans from the floor and pulled them on over his boxer shorts. Cautiously, quietly, he stepped out into the hallway and headed for the stairs. Maybe he was hungry.

As he walked down the stairs, he heard a noise on the porch. Once on the landing, he heard more noises, barely audible moans. He peeked around the corner and found Charlotte and Steve Johanson making out on the couch. He pulled back, wondering if he could get past the opening to the porch, through the living room and dining room, and into the kitchen without their knowing. Very gently, Thomas stepped down off the landing and into full view of the moving mass of arms and legs on the couch. Nothing. He took another step. Nothing. Confident, he took three more steps.

"Dad?" Charlotte asked, sounding anxious.

Thomas waited a few moments, then took another step. He looked back over his shoulder to see if Charlotte was looking at him and met her gaze. "Hi," he said.

"What are you doing?" she asked, sounding slightly annoyed. Steve, by this time, was standing next to her, tucking his shirt into his jeans and running his fingers through his hair.

"Hey," he said casually to Thomas, as if they were meeting on the street. Thomas said nothing. While he disapproved of his sister's slutty behavior, he disapproved even more of the boys who took advantage of it. "I've got to go," Steve said to Charlotte.

"Yes," she said, still looking at Thomas. Steve left the living room and walked out the porch door, holding it afterward so it wouldn't slam. "So," said Charlotte, "the question stands. What are you doing?"

"I couldn't sleep, Charlotte. So I came down to get something to eat. I live here, too, so I don't need any crap from you."

"I wasn't going to give you any crap," Charlotte said, coolly. "I just didn't know what the hell you were doing up at"—she looked at her watch—"three thirty."

"I'd ask you the same question, but I already know what the hell you were doing."

"I get enough lectures from Mom," said Charlotte, combing her hair with her fingers. "I don't need them from you."

"Well, apparently you haven't been listening." Thomas turned his back on his sister and continued on through the dining room and into the kitchen. She followed him.

"You sleep like the dead, Thomas," she said, closing the swinging door behind them. Thomas turned on the light over the sink and walked to the fridge. He opened the door and looked in, wondering if there were any leftover meatballs. His mother wasn't big on what she considered ethnic food, but meatballs had enough of an American following that Claire made them once in a while. In the summer, they had them in grinder rolls, with potato chips and homemade coleslaw.

"Not tonight." The meatballs were gone. He remembered that he and Helen had finished them off the other night when they came in from swimming.

"Is something bothering you?" asked Charlotte, fixing one of the buttons on her shirt that she had inserted into the wrong hole.

"I don't know," said Thomas, even though he most certainly did. He also knew that Charlotte was not the best choice of people to confide in. She had a penchant for telling her friends' most intimate secrets at the Thompson dinner table, much to the consternation of their father and mother, who, as a rule, avoided unpleasant talk altogether during dinner. She also shared her friends' foibles, Thomas suspected, in the hope that her parents would see that her behavior was not as bad as they thought. She preached that all seventeen-year-old girls got into one kind of trouble or another every now and again. Her parents were inured to her tactics, often asking Pammy to "pass the butter" when Charlotte was looking for an acceptance or at least an acknowledgement of her argument. John and Claire were not above employing their own tactics, especially when they knew that being ignored frustrated Charlotte even more than being grounded.

Thomas took the packages of bologna and American cheese from the cold cut drawer and tossed them onto the counter. He next grabbed the mustard and mayonnaise from the door shelf. "Get some bread, will you, Charlotte?'

She walked into the pantry and grabbed a sliced loaf from the bread box. She was staring to get hungry too. "You have no idea if something's bothering you or not?" she asked, taking four slices from the plastic bag and then resealing it with a twist tie.

Thomas looked at his sister. She was a young woman like Anna. Maybe she could give him some useful advice. Maybe she would be able to tell him what Anna was thinking or what she wanted to hear. "I think I'm in love." There. His secret found air.

"What?" Charlotte stopped spreading mayonnaise on her bread and looked at her brother.

"I'm in . . ." Thomas began.

"No, I heard you," said Charlotte, knife hovering over the bread. Suddenly uncomfortable, Thomas looked down at his feet.

Charlotte finished with the mayonnaise and then put mustard on the other slice. "Why," she asked, reaching for the bologna, "does that keep you up at night?"

"Because I think about her all the time. She's always there." Thomas pointed to his head with his right index finger.

Charlotte ate half a cheese slice and offered the other half to Thomas. "That's kind of sweet, Thomas. I think every girl wishes she'd find somebody who thinks about her all the time, and not because he wants to take off her shorts. Or maybe that's it. Maybe you just want to get her undressed. Are you in love or lust?" Charlotte made her sandwich, cut it down the middle to form two triangles, and then raised one of the halves to her mouth.

"I think I'm in love." Thomas ate the cheese slice and then three bites of his uncut sandwich. He talked while he chewed. "Hell, you're in love all the time; how do you do it?"

"No," said Charlotte, pouring two glasses of milk. "I don't fall in love. I play love games."

"Why?"

"Because you lose control when you fall in love. You do things you don't want to do because you're half out of your mind."

Thomas drank half the glass of milk. "You got that right."

They were silent while they finished their sandwiches. Wiping the breadcrumbs from her mouth with her fingers, Charlotte walked back into the pantry. She emerged seconds later with the ceramic cookie jar, half full of the oatmeal raisin cookies Claire made the day before. Charlotte took it to the other side of the kitchen, where a round wood table, painted blue, stood with its two matching chairs. Thomas refilled their milk glasses and joined his sister. "Who is this girl?" asked Charlotte, sitting and then taking a cookie from the jar and biting into it.

"Anna Santiago. The woman with the daughter."

"You just met her, right?"

"Yes," he said. "I've known her for three weeks."

"Then you're not in love, Thomas. You're in lust."

"You think so?"

"I know so," said Charlotte, taking another bite. "In the beginning of a relationship, I can't get enough of the other person. And then it starts to get old. And before I know it, I'm looking around for something better."

"I don't think I'll find anyone better."

"Trust me, Thomas. You will." Charlotte finished her cookie. She stood, walked over to the sink, and rinsed her hands and then dried them on the dishtowel that hung on the inside of the cupboard door beneath the sink. She turned to look back at her brother. "In the meantime, Thomas, have fun. Summer is not the time to get poetic over a girlfriend."

"Umm," Thomas muttered, trying to decipher Charlotte's words to see if they had any merit. He was unsure about following her advice, or even the possibility of following it. His love for Anna seemed outside of Charlotte's relationship parameters. He questioned whether he could bring it inside.

"Eat another cookie," said Charlotte, "then go back to bed. She's not worth losing sleep over."

"I think she is."

"She must be one in a million then," said Charlotte. Thomas nodded his head. Charlotte leaned back against the sink. "As long as we're confiding in one another, can I tell you something?"

"Yes." Thomas looked at Charlotte, whose face crumbled. He left his seat and stood next to his sister, the sister who was closest to his age but with whom he rarely spoke; the sister who avoided hard work as passionately as he sought it; the sister who routinely disrespected their parents for sport; the sister who ignored their sisters, who ignored everyone who wasn't advancing her perceived needs and desires. He hated everything about her. But the fact that she was his sister and that she was crying mattered to him. Charlotte made a point of keeping her emotions in check.

"I'm pregnant."

The words hit Thomas like the slap of a hand to his face. He wanted to return the slap, to strike his sister for her irresponsible behavior. He inhaled. "Steve's?"

Charlotte looked into his eyes. "No. Rick's."

Fuck, Thomas thought. Fuck him. Fuck her. He waited and then said, "Does he know?"

"No."

"Does anyone know?"

"You do."

"And we're going to keep it that way. Do not tell a soul, Charlotte. Give me a couple days to figure this out. How far along are you?"

"I've missed one period," said Charlotte, "so five or six weeks."

"Give me a couple days." Thomas repeated. "We'll fix this."

Charlotte turned to leave the kitchen. At the door, she turned. "Thank you."

"You can thank me when it's over."

After Charlotte was gone, Thomas took two more cookies from the jar. He wasn't hungry anymore, but he wasn't yet ready to return to his dark bedroom, where he now had two reasons to watch the clock until sunrise.

Thomas wasn't sure where to find a doctor who would perform an abortion on his sister. His father, of course, could have provided him with a name, even done the procedure himself, but this, for obvious reasons, was out of the question. Nor could Thomas seek his mother's counsel. He did not want to go to a public place, so Planned Parenthood was out. And he did not want to talk with Anna about it, even though he was tempted to do so. Anna didn't know Charlotte. And for reasons Thomas couldn't name, he did not want this to be the first thing she knew about his sister. So, as he did with lesser issues or for philosophical discussion, Thomas turned to his best friend at the beach, Eddie Kozlowski. At first glance, Eddie was an unlikely friend for Thomas. He smoked cigarettes. He used the word "fucking" as an adjective in front of just about every other adjective or verb or noun in at least fifty percent of his verbal sentences. And he couldn't swim, which Thomas thought was inexcusable for an eighteen-year-old beachside resident. However, Eddie was loyal and reliable, characteristics that Thomas sought in friendships. Eddie also happened to have an interest in young women who, like Charlotte, might take their pants off for a burger and a beer. And while Thomas disapproved of this behavior in his sister, he was somewhat more tolerant of it in Eddie.

"I need your help," Thomas said to Eddie the next night as they walked the beach streets.

Eddie lit a cigarette. "Mr. Princeton in the fall needs my fucking help?"

"It's about Charlotte."

"Tell me she has a crush on me, and you will just have made my fucking day."

Thomas hesitated a moment, wondering if Eddie was the right person to talk to. "She's pregnant."

Eddie stopped walking. "Not that asshole Steve Johanson."

"Rick Jones. Another asshole."

Eddie took a deep drag. "As well as a prison inmate. What a fucking idiot."

"Anyway," said Thomas, "the fucking idiot got my sister pregnant."

"And I take it," said Eddie, "that she's not interested in keeping Rick's progeny."

"No."

Eddie gave him the name of the doctor who took care of this issue, Eddie's issue with Darlene, last year's girlfriend. The doctor operated a clean abortion clinic just over the state line into Massachusetts, and he accepted cash as payment. It would cost Charlotte two hundred dollars. She would have some pain, cramping Darlene had called it, and bleeding afterward. But the mistake would be corrected; the problem would be solved.

The next day, Thomas called the clinic and made an appointment for the following week, on a Tuesday. He took the day off from work and drove Charlotte to a small town outside Springfield. She didn't say a word, the whole way up, which was unlike her. Charlotte always had something to say, appropriate or otherwise. She could be very witty and was way smarter than she let on, even though she did poorly in school and made abysmal life choices. They listened to the radio instead. He could tell she was scared; she didn't have to admit it. He understood how she felt because he was scared, too. If something went wrong, the two of them would have to live with it. It would be an unpleasant bond between them. And they would have to tell their parents. And that conversation would yield additional unpleasantness in the form of consequences that neither Thomas nor Charlotte would be able to argue against or ignore.

On the way home, she cried quietly as Thomas drove. When he asked her if the procedure hurt, she wouldn't say anything. When he asked her if she was in pain, she closed her eyes. When he asked her if he could do anything, she told him to shut up. "I don't want to talk about this, Thomas, ever. Thank you for taking me. Now let's just go home and never bring Rick's name or this day up again."

Charlotte was okay, so no one but Thomas, and Eddie, needed to know about her abortion. And because she meant it when she said she didn't want talk about it ever again, Thomas, as the years passed, forgot about it. Charlotte, of course, never brought it up.

CHAPTER 23

2003

Thomas checked his watch as he drove his Cadillac onto the grass beside Charlotte's rental. It was exactly noon. It was a ten-hour drive from Ontario, where they lived in a suburb of Toronto that he had left at two that morning. His wife, Barb, hated the idea of getting up and coaxing the children into the car in the middle of the night. But Thomas promised he'd drive until breakfast time, and then, after an hour's nap in the passenger seat when Barb would take over, drive again until they reached the cottage. It was a long trip, and it would be easier on the children, he reasoned, if they slept halfway through it. They were making excellent time, Thomas pointed out over breakfast sandwiches at a rest stop in upstate New York. No one but truckers and the very hardiest of drivers cruised the interstates before dawn. They also made good time because Thomas was very frugal about stopping, as he was about everything else in life. Every three hours was the rule; anything more frequent than that was unnecessary. He viewed pulling into a rest area as an excuse for Barb to buy postcards and for the kids to plead with him for money to buy candy from the ubiquitous vending machines. Yet, at six and four, Sally and Peter were well mannered and rarely complained. They were accustomed to their father's rules and regulations. And they had a disciplined but attentive mother, who often compensated for what might be seen in their young minds as their father's unyielding behavior. Thomas leaned over and kissed his sleeping wife. She awoke immediately. "We're here," he said.

Barb opened her eyes and looked at her husband. "What time is it?"

"Noon," said Thomas, looking at his watch. "Exactly."

"Just as you predicted," she said. "Aren't you clever." She smiled at him and then looked out the car window at the house. "This is beautiful, Thomas."

"Yes," he said, following her gaze. "I'd forgotten how much so."

Thomas gave his wife another quick kiss and then got out of the car and stretched his arms over his head. He breathed in the seaside air he had not inhaled for thirty years. Now that he was here, it was impossible to understand why it had been that long since his last visit. Sure, he had been busy. But too busy for this?

Helen, who was in the kitchen and had heard the car pull in, came out the door and met her brother on the lawn. Thomas wrapped his arms around his sister and lifted her off the ground. "Thomas," she said, studying his face.

"It's so nice to see you. You look terrific," he whispered in her ear.

"You're looking pretty good yourself."

"The place looks good, Helen," said Thomas, looking beyond his sister at the house. "You've kept it up nicely."

"Dad did most of it. You know how handy he was with a hammer and paintbrush."

"I do, indeed. That's the very reason I'm so handy with a hammer and a paintbrush. He did like having an assist."

Helen smiled at him. "Where's the gang?" she asked, peering around his shoulder.

"Gathering their thoughts," said Thomas, turning to look back at the car. Barb, who had emerged from the passenger seat, walked toward Helen as she reinserted small plastic combs into her short, light blond hair, tucking them behind her ears. Helen crossed the rest of the lawn to meet her. "How was the trip?" she asked, giving Barb a hug.

"Great," she said. "Except we all have to use the bathroom immediately."

"There's nothing like a road trip with old one-stop Thomas."

"Two stops since breakfast. He was feeling magnanimous," said Barb, kissing Helen on the cheek.

Helen bent down to talk to Sally, who had unbuckled herself from her seat in the back and climbed out of the car. She was clinging to her mother's leg. "Hello, big girl. I'm your Aunt Helen."

Sally smiled and said a barely audible hello, and then looked over at her brother, who had also disengaged himself from the car and was now holding on to Barb's other thigh. Peter was not inclined at first to talk to people he didn't know, according to Barb's letter. But his initial shyness would wear off quickly. And he was especially excited to meet his older boy cousins. Both Sally and Peter were comfortable with adults, perhaps because Barb and Thomas took them almost everywhere they went, rarely employing babysitters. Helen gave Peter a quick kiss on his forehead before he could back away. "Come inside," she said. "With any luck, the bathrooms are free." She showed her niece and nephew the tiny blue and white half bathroom off the kitchen, and then led Barb to the porch to see Charlotte and Pammy. Claire was in her room resting, and the boys had returned to the tennis court after a swim. After watching Todd and Ned win their first match, Charles and Daniel had gone to the beach with them. Helen guessed her husband was still dozing on the raft, as reported by the boys on their way through the kitchen in their wet suits.

"Thomas and Barb are here," Helen announced in excitement halfway across the living room. She wanted her sisters to get ready, in the next few seconds, to again see their sister-in-law, their relation they had met just twice, at Thomas and Barb's wedding and at John Thompson's funeral. Helen knew Pammy would be polite and warm. It was Charlotte, whose relationship with Thomas had been strained for as long as Helen could remember, who was the unpredictable one. Claire said Thomas and Charlotte never got along because they were so close in age. But Helen knew that Charlotte's being a jerk, Thomas's favorite word for her, also had something to do with it. Helen remembered that they were closer to one another during Thomas's last summer at the beach, the summer of 1973, but she thought they had not had much contact since. When Helen and Barb reached the porch, Pammy was standing, and Charlotte, while sitting, was looking expectantly at the doorway.

"Hello, Barb," said Pammy, stepping forward and hugging her.

"It's so nice to see all of you again," said Barb. "It's been too long."

"Where's your no-good husband?" asked Charlotte.

"Here I am," Thomas said, from the living room.

When he walked into the porch, Pammy hugged him, and then held him back at arm's length to look at him. "You look pretty good for an old guy," she said.

"Older and wiser, Pammy," said Thomas, with a smile. "Your turn will come soon enough, little sister."

"The coming is always the best part." Charlotte was now standing, Helen suspected, to give her brother and Barb an opportunity to look at her chest.

"Are those new?" asked Thomas, looking at her breasts. "Or did I just sleep through your teenage years?"

Pammy, Helen, and Barb laughed at Thomas's joke, while Charlotte quipped, "I *wish* I'd had these babies in my teenage years," she said. "I'd have been the queen of the beach."

"If memory serves," said Thomas, "you *were* the queen of the beach."

"In a good way or a bad way?" asked Pammy.

Both Charlotte and Thomas ignored what they individually perceived as a stupid and rhetorical, respectively, question. "Where's Mom?" asked Thomas instead.

"She's resting," said Helen. "And Charles is down at the beach with Daniel."

"Who's Daniel?"

"Charlotte's boyfriend," said Helen.

"He's twenty-seven," said Pammy, crossing her arms over her chest.

"That," said Thomas, looking at Charlotte, "would explain the breasts."

"Thomas," said Barb, giving her husband a look.

"Don't worry yourself," said Charlotte. "I can take care of myself."

"Amen, sister," said Thomas, nodding his head once.

They were all silent for a moment before Barb said, "I'm just going to run to the bathroom."

"Yes, yes, of course," said Helen. "Run up the stairs, if you'd like. The bathroom is on the left. Don't worry about waking Claire. She sleeps very soundly."

"Where are the children?" Pammy asked Barb as she was leaving the porch.

"Around here somewhere," said Barb. "I'll round them up in a couple minutes."

"Are you hungry?" Helen asked Thomas.

"No." Thomas held his stomach. "Barb packed enough snacks for a cross-country trip."

"Good," said Helen. "We all had a chicken embryo feast this morning, and I'm still full."

"Eggs," Charlotte said, by way of explanation. "They all had eggs and were disappointed I wouldn't participate."

"I thought you ate almost anything for breakfast," Thomas said to Charlotte, giving her a wink. "Eggs, bacon, wedding attendants."

"That was seven years ago," said Charlotte, picking up Thomas's reference to her behavior at his wedding. Drunk, she offered to peel off her leopard-skin dress and dance naked for Thomas's ushers, if they stopped by her room after the reception. What she didn't tell Thomas was that two out of the three of them did.

"Listen," said Thomas, looking at his watch, "as long as Mom's resting, and we've got some time before the next feeding, I'm going to drive to the motel by the state park and unpack. I'll be back before you miss me."

Helen put her hands on her hips. "I thought you were going to stay here. Charles and I are out of your room, and I've already moved my things back in with Pammy."

Thomas held up his hands. "It's easier this way, Helen. We're right down the street, and I think the kids will sleep better in a bed." Helen's disappointment was evident on her face. Thomas walked the three steps to reach her and put his hand on top of her head. "We'll see how it goes."

"How can you get back in that car after ten hours on the road?" asked Pammy.

"Are you kidding?" said Helen, letting it go, teasing Thomas. "He could drive back to Ontario right now, without stopping."

"Who wants to come with me?" asked Thomas. "Do we need anything in town?"

"We've got enough food . . ." Helen started.

". . . to feed an army." Pammy finished.

"We may be at the beach when you get back. I'll see if the kids want anything to eat before we go," said Helen. "Hurry, Thomas. The water is beautiful today."

"Don't go to the raft until I get back. We have been talking about the swim all week. Peter will need his kickboard, but I think Sally can make it the whole way. She takes after her grandmother in the water."

"God, I hope that's the only thing they have in common," said Charlotte.

Sally and Peter walked onto porch just as Thomas was about to leave. He bent down to hug his children. "This," he said to them, "is your Aunt Pammy and your Aunt Charlotte."

"Hello," the children said softly in unison.

"Well, hello," said Pammy, getting down onto her knees. "I'm happy to see you."

The children smiled at her, but said nothing.

"And isn't that a cool shirt you have on, young man," Charlotte said to Peter, who reached over and wrapped his arms around his father's leg.

"You guys stay here with Mommy," he said to Sally and Peter. "I'm going to unload our stuff at the motel. I'll be back soon, okay?"

"That sounds great." Barb had returned from her bathroom break. She stood next to Helen.

Helen put her arm, momentarily, around her sister-in-law. Helen hadn't been sure until they pulled into the driveway that they, that he, would come.

As Charlotte said, it had been almost seven years. Thomas and Barb were married in August of 1996. All the Thompsons attended the Ontario wedding, but no one had seen him or his wife since, aside from at John Thompson's funeral. Thomas was very busy with the self-storage business he had started in upstate New York after working in Manhattan for a decade in investment banking. One of his business connections had a business connection across the border. There was a dearth of self-storage places, it turned out, in southern Ontario, and the market was ripe, in the mid-nineties, for development and quick expansion. It was in Toronto, walking out of the elevator with his new Canadian partner, that Thomas saw Barb McNaughton in the lobby of an office building on King Street. He was immediately attracted to her, not only to her blond hair, blue eyes, and petite, fit body, but also because she smiled at him like she knew him, like they were childhood friends meeting for the first time in many years. They walked out of the building at the same time and hesitated, both of them, on the sidewalk. Thomas introduced himself to her and asked her if she had time for coffee, to which she replied yes. They talked in the coffee shop for two hours and were engaged three months later.

Thomas could still not get over his good fortune. He had dated several women over the years; he was forty when he met Barb. But all of the women fell short in one way or another: Ashley talked too much; Chantel spent too much time in front of the mirror; Marion was sweet but uncoordinated. (Thomas loved to hike on the weekends; Marion could walk like a runway model in heels, but hiking boots made her feet look ugly, Marion had protested, and gave her blisters.) They were all temporarily very engaging, Ashley, Chantel, and Marion. But each woman's peccadilloes eventually worked their way from the back to the front of Thomas's brain, causing him to lose sight of their good qualities and, shortly afterward, leading to the breakup of the relationship. Barb talked just the right amount.

She glanced at herself in the mirror with both the confidence and indifference of someone who knows she's attractive. And she could beat Thomas at tennis. Barb measured up to every one of Thomas's expectations, pushing for good the faded image of Anna Santiago out of his head. This was the most convincing reason Thomas knew he was in love.

The summer after Thomas's first year at Princeton, he did not go to the cottage because he was still not over Anna. She had written him at school a few times his first semester, and he had written back. But then he stopped communicating with her. Writing to her and Amy made him miss her more; he could not, like others were able to do after a breakup, view her as a friend. He immersed himself in his studies, played club baseball, and hung out with the guys on his floor. That summer, he stayed in Stonefield and worked for a landscaping company. He had talked Eddie Kozlowski into spending the summer at the Thompson family home. And together they mowed lawns during the day and drank beer in the evening. Thomas missed his family, but only in the abstract. He was already, at nineteen, pulled in another, more independent direction.

Anna floated in and out of his thoughts over the years, even when he was dating other women. He knew their relationship had come too early. But that didn't stop him from wondering if they could have worked things out. These musings, imaginings stopped, for the most part, when he met Barb.

When he and Barb were first married, they lived in her condominium on Front Street, not far from the Royal York and Union Station, on the tenth floor of a new building that afforded them a generous view of Lake Ontario. Barb, Thomas found out later, after they were involved and moving toward commitment, had enough personal wealth to purchase a small European country, had it been for sale and had she been inclined. She was grateful for the money she had, for what it had provided in her life, but she was also troubled by it. Savvy suitors had broken her heart in their pursuit of her riches. Aggressive charitable organizations and less fortunate relatives and friends hounded her. Once people knew she had money, came from money—a lot of it—their dispositions around her and their assumptions about her changed. Because Thomas had made his own fortune, he was respectful of hers. They discussed money with their financial advisors and rarely with one another.

When Sally was born, they decided to move out to the country, settling into an old, cold farmhouse in Kingsville, where Barb cheerfully traded suits and low heels for jeans and flats and ran the house as effectively and efficiently as she had the nonprofit in her family's name based in the city. She stayed involved in the organization via telephone and laptop, but she left the day-to-day operations to her capable assistant. Thomas had an office in Toronto and traveled frequently, but when he was home, he made time for his family. He often drove in the driveway before dinner, and entertained the children while Barb, an accomplished cook, prepared their meal from organic ingredients grown in their garden in the summer. Somehow she'd manage to coax Sally and Peter into trying everything on their plates. Peter's new favorite vegetable was sautéed kale.

"Do they like peanut butter and jelly?" Helen asked Barb, leading her out of the porch and though the living room.

"Better than anything else. Let me help you."

In the kitchen, Helen got the peanut butter down from the shelf. "The children are adorable. Your pictures don't do them justice."

Barb smiled broadly. "They are so much fun," she said. "We are able to do more and more with them as they are able to take in and understand more and more. The four of us went to the Ontario Science Centre last week, and Sally was able to tell us five fun facts about rain forests while we were standing in one. Peter almost caught a frog."

"I remember when Todd and Ned were that age," said Helen, retrieving the grape jelly from the fridge. "They were into everything—and not always in a good way."

Barb laughed. "Oh yes," she said. "Peter decided to make scrambled eggs like Mommy's one day when I was in the shower, but had more fun standing on the kitchen table and dropping the dozen eggs he'd taken out of the fridge onto the floor. Frankly, I was relieved he hadn't turned on the burners. The children do some cooking with me, but I don't have them frying anything in hot oil just yet." Helen laughed.

Seconds later, Sally and Peter ran into the kitchen, breathless. "Where have you two been?" Barb asked.

"With Aunt Pammy," said Sally. "She showed us a card trick, and she said she'd show us how to float in the water just like a jelly-fish."

"Can we go to the beach now?" asked Peter.

"Let's eat," Barb said. "Then we'll get our suits on."

Helen took their sandwiches and glasses of milk out to the picnic table, where she and Barb sat and talked while the children ate. Afterward, they all got their bathing suits on and ran, holding hands, across the road to the beach.

Thomas unzipped his suitcase and took out a short stack of golf shirts. He laid them carefully in the large drawer at the bottom of the dresser. He changed into a pair of shorts and put the other pair next to the shirts. After hanging his traveling pants in the closet, he put away his boxers, socks, and the pajamas he wore around the children, and closed the drawer with his foot. He took his shaving kit into the bathroom and set it down next to the sink. Glancing at his reflection in the mirror, he wondered if strangers would know he was forty-eight. Not likely, he thought. He jogged six miles every morning and, with Barb preparing his meals, ate healthy foods. He had always been measured, disciplined in his habits, however, including eating and drinking. When he first met Barb, she thought he was several years closer to her age than he actually was. She was ten years younger than he, which never seemed to be a problem for them. Thomas sometimes wondered what they would be like, what their life would be like, when he was seventy and she was sixty. But he didn't dwell on it long. While many in the business world were fond of discussing five-year plans, Thomas knew that a five-day plan was much more likely to meet with success.

Back in the town he hadn't seen in three decades, Thomas's thoughts returned to Anna. Where was she, and what was she was doing? And where was Amy, who would now be grown and living her own life? His buried memories of Anna shot to the surface. He said her name aloud, something he hadn't done since his first year at Princeton. He indulged his thoughts of her now. Did she finish school? Did she go to law school? His heart came alive in his chest. Did she still live here?

He returned to the car to retrieve everyone else's duffel bags, and then quickly unpacked them in the room. Back in the car, he drove through town, scanning the multitude of storefronts that had appeared since his childhood. By rote, he drove to the corner of Main Street and Summer Avenue and found Hudson and Lambert. He parked his car, walked across the street, and pulled open the glass door. Inside, he recognized the Oriental rug immediately, looking older but every bit as luxurious as it had before. He crossed the room to the large desk, where he had waited for Anna before taking her to lunch that day. A large mug of steaming coffee sat next to the computer, in the space previously occupied by Anna's typewriter, as did a stack of memos and manila folders. An open nine-by-twelve mahogany box held Hudson and Lambert stationery. Thomas picked up a sheet; Anna's name did not appear on the masthead. Disappointed, he set the paper back in the box. Had she finished college and law school on schedule, she would have made partner by now. Maybe she never finished.

"May I help you?"

Thomas looked up and saw a middle-aged, efficient-looking woman who was now standing next to the desk. "Yes," said Thomas. "I was looking for someone who used to work here. Her name was Anna Santiago."

"Oh, yes," said the woman, settling into her desk chair. "She did work here. But she's had her own practice for years."

"Really?"

"Yes. Her office is just down the street. She and Erin Setta are tax attorneys."

"Where's their office? I know it's Saturday, but I thought I might just drive by."

"Attorney Santiago usually works on Saturdays. She might be there. It's just down Main—one, two, three lights," the woman said looking into the air as if at a map. "It's on the corner of Main and Plumber."

Walking back to the car, Thomas checked his watch and decided to drive back to the house. Barb would be wondering where he was. Plus, against odds, he was getting hungry; he wanted to swim to the raft with his children; and he needed to see his mother. "That's that," he said aloud. But when he drove his car out onto the road, he turned left instead of right and continued down Main Street. He would just drive past, he told himself. One, two, three lights. He slowed the car down and pulled over to the side of the road. Directly in front of him, maybe fifty feet away, hung Anna's carved wood sign: SANTIAGO AND SETTA. ATTORNEYS AT LAW. He hesitated just a moment before parking the car in front of their office.

CHAPTER 24

1973

Anna and Thomas lay on the couch together, kissing. Amy had gone to bed after Thomas read her three stories, and she was asleep. "Come into my bedroom," said Anna. "I'll shut the door." She took his hand and led him down the short hallway into her pristine room, with its clean, off-white walls and pressed lace curtains. She pulled back the chenille bedspread, a formal invitation. Thomas lifted her into his arms, spun her around, and then sank back onto the bed, pulling her down with him. While he kissed her, he fumbled with her bra. After long seconds, he unhooked it, and then reached under her starched white shirt to feel her soft warm breasts. Anna whispered encouragement in his ear and pulled down the zipper of his pants. Within a minute, she had rolled a condom onto his hard-on, and he was inside her. Together, they gently, noiselessly, moved on the bed.

Thomas knew that he should have been carried away at this very moment, focused on nothing but sensation, but he wasn't. He liked sex well enough, but he didn't like having it with just anyone, with whoever was willing, even really cute girls. If he didn't feel strongly about a girl, he wasn't interested in getting into her pants. His friend, Eddie, thought he "had a fucking screw loose." Eddie had introduced Thomas to a number of girls at the beach who were interested in having sex with a handsome guy, whether or not it led to anything lasting. Thomas just needed sex with the right girl, Eddie reasoned, or enough sex, or something, to get over this obstacle. It hadn't worked. Thomas wanted to be in love with the girl. And, just as important, he wanted her to be in love with him, too. He opened his eyes to look at Anna. She was underneath him, attached to him, but they were not mentally connected. Watching her writhe and arch and grit her teeth disturbed Thomas. He came, but quickly pulled out of her, and then stopped and waited for Anna to open her eyes. When she did, she smiled at him. "I'm sorry," he said.

"Why are you sorry, Thomas?"

"I'm sorry for doubting you."

She half closed her eyes and looked at him, questioning. "What were you doubting?"

"I wasn't sure if you loved me."

Her eyes were wide now. "Or if I was just using you for sex," she said, smiling again.

"Don't kid me." He pushed himself up on his hands, away from their lovemaking act, away from her.

She wrapped her arms around his shoulders and pulled him back down to her. "Thomas, you are wonderful," said Anna. "Every eighteen-year-old male I've ever known cares about one thing: sex. They want to know if they can get it, when they can get it, and whether they can get it on a regular basis. And then there's Thomas who wonders if I truly love him."

"I do love you, Anna."

"And I love you, Thomas."

"Then marry me."

"Thomas?"

"I want to marry you."

"Oh, sweetheart . . ."

"Do you want to marry me?"

"If we were ten years older, yes."

"Why not now?" Thomas backed off the bed and stood next to it. He raised his jeans to his waist, zipped them, and buckled his belt.

Anna left her clothes where they were and sat up, naked, on the bed. "Thomas, you know why. You're about to go to one of the best schools in the country for a college education. The very last thing you want or need is a wife and a stepdaughter to think about and support. And I'm trying to finish my college education. The only way I can do that is by staying here and working for Hudson and Lambert, who pays my tuition. I want to go to law school, Thomas. I'll be here for a long time."

"I can help you pay for those things."

"Thomas, you've got this incredible opportunity to go to school and work on your studies without the distractions of a full-time job or an instant family. You don't want that obligation, to me or anyone else."

"Maybe you just don't want an obligation to me."

"Oh, Thomas." Anna stood and put her arms around his waist. She laid her head against his chest. "I want you more than you'll ever realize."

But Thomas didn't believe her, not just then. He kissed the top of her head. "I've got to go."

"Stay for a little while," Anna said, rubbing his chest with her hand. "We can sit on the couch and talk."

"Somehow I feel like I'm through talking." He was close to crying.

"That's okay, Thomas. It's okay to go." She released him and grabbed her jeans and cotton blouse from the floor. She quickly put them on and then followed him out of the bedroom and into the living room. She thought he would turn and look at her, say good-bye, but he simply walked out the front door, closing it quietly behind him. He started his car and drove off.

Thomas awoke early. His eyes, tired from holding back tears and occasionally releasing them, found the clock on the bureau. It was almost four thirty. He had a bakery run at six, so he didn't have to dress until five thirty. He closed his eyes, to rest them and ease the ache, but he did not sleep. His head hurt from thinking about Anna, as he had all night. She didn't love him. Amy didn't love him.

On his way home from her house, he'd just missed hitting a pickup truck, when his car drifted across the centerline. So lost in thought, so caught up in his emotional response to her denial, he barely missed his mother's car when he pulled into the driveway. Charlotte, who had come home earlier than normal because she'd grown tired of the guy she was using to make Steve Johanson jealous, heard the car and walked from the porch to the kitchen to talk to him. She popped the top off a can of Coke and sat down on the counter to wait. Thomas walked in, saw his sister, and lowered his eyes. "How's Anna?" Charlotte asked.

"Super," said Thomas, looking at the floor.

"What did you guys do tonight?"

"Well, for one thing," said Thomas, looking at Charlotte, "we decided not to get married."

Charlotte's mouth opened involuntarily. "You asked her to marry you?"

"I asked her, and she said no." Charlotte was silent. "She told me if we were ten years older she would marry me."

"She sounds like a smart girl."

"You have a messed-up idea of intelligence, Charlotte."

"I had no idea you were going to do this, Thomas. I don't know what you were thinking. You wanted them to share your dorm room at Princeton?"

"If you think I need a lecture right now, you're seriously mistaken."

"Okay, Thomas, you're right," said Charlotte. She had never seen her brother this way. He was always so sensible, always right. Because she was often just the opposite, they rarely talked. Yet, they had come together for her abortion, and that had brought them, if only temporarily, a bit closer. She sought his advice over that of their parents, especially their mother, who, as far as Charlotte was concerned, lived in a distant universe. She and Thomas were not yet ready, not responsible enough, to be real adults, but they were miles away from Pammy and Helen, who were still children, still believers.

Tired, Thomas sat down on the floor and covered his face with his hands, and the tears that he had battled to overcome all night refused to be damned up any longer. "It's okay to cry, Thomas." Charlotte got down from the counter. She sat down next to him. "Do you want to talk about it?"

"I don't know," said Thomas. "I'm having trouble thinking."

"I'm sorry, Thomas. I'm sorry for what happened."

"Thanks, Charlotte." Thomas talked through his hands.

"Are you going to be okay?"

"I don't know." Thomas lifted his head and looked at his sister. "I don't know what to do. I've never felt this strongly about anyone or anything in my life. I love Anna. We belong together. I can feel that, Charlotte. I felt it the first time I saw her."

"Maybe you will be together."

"I don't think so. She just said no to me."

"She said no to you *now.* Maybe she won't say no later."

"I can't wait until later, Charlotte. I'm going away to school in the fall. I need her to come with me."

"No, you don't, Thomas. You'll burn your way through Princeton all by yourself. After graduation, you can ask Anna again."

"That's a million years away."

"No, it's not." Claire was always telling them how quickly time passed and that they should take advantage of every minute. This was one of only a handful of things about which Charlotte and her mother agreed.

"I need her, Charlotte."

"You want her, Thomas. There's a difference."

Thomas looked at his sister, not quite believing her. "I need her and I want her."

"Go to bed, Thomas," said Charlotte. "You need some sleep now. You can look at all this again in the morning, okay?"

Thomas nodded his head. "I'll come up in a few minutes."

"Do you want me to stay with you?"

"No," he said. "Go on up to bed, Charlotte." He sat on the

floor, listening to Charlotte walk up the stairs. Ten minutes later, he stood, grabbed a glass from the pantry, and poured himself some cold water from the refrigerator. He drank it quickly, even though swallowing was painful. After his second glass, Thomas felt better and decided his sister was right; he needed sleep. As he walked through the living room, heading for the stairs, the phone rang. Thomas picked it up on one ring; he knew who it was. "Thomas, I'm so sorry," she said. Thomas said nothing. "Thomas?"

"I'm here," he said.

"What do you want to do?"

"I think you've made it quite clear what you don't want to do, so maybe you can tell me what *you* want to do," said Thomas, feeling angry for the first time since their talk that evening.

"If you think about it, Thomas, you'll know why I said what I did. I don't want to hold you back any more than you want to keep me back."

"Actually, Anna, holding you back was the last thing on my mind. I was thinking, foolishly I guess, that marrying might bring us both forward."

"And it would in some ways, Thomas. But I've got to finish school. I've got to provide for my daughter, and I want to take care of myself. I want to do this for me."

"That's crystal clear to me, Anna."

"Thomas, I have to be selfish here. I need to follow a plan that will make my life, Amy's life, better. I don't have a choice. I've made decisions, taken actions that have made my life what it is today. And I, alone now, am responsible for what comes next."

"I offered to help you make those decisions, Anna."

"Thomas, you're not in a position right now to help. After college, maybe, yes, maybe you could help then."

"You had me convinced that you loved me." Thomas sank down onto the wooden side chair next to the telephone table.

"I do love you, Thomas. I love who you are, and I love who you are becoming."

"And what did you want to do with that love? Where were we going with this, in your mind?"

"I don't know, Thomas. I was not thinking about our relationship like you were or are. I was having fun. I love being with you, talking to you, laughing with you, kissing you. I have not had a man pay attention to me in a long time. I have been wrapped up in working, studying, and taking care of Amy; I thought I had no time for a relationship. And then you came along, and I was so happy to have you interested in me. I treasured every second I was with you. I didn't think about the future. I was more immersed in the present, I think, than you were."

"The here and now," Thomas said. "If it feels good, do it."

"In many ways, yes. And I'm not going to apologize for that. There's nothing wrong with loving someone and having fun at the same time. You're eighteen years old, Thomas. I didn't think you were going to propose to me."

"What did you think?"

"For the most part, I simply thought about when I was going to see you again."

"You never thought about the fall?"

"Yes," Anna said. "I admit, I thought about the fall—once. And what I thought was you would go away to Princeton and forget about me."

"Well, you were dead wrong, weren't you?"

"You're too young to marry, Thomas. Believe me, I came very close to getting married."

"You loved him, your boyfriend, Amy's father."

"I did love him, Thomas. But I was wrong to quit school. I was frustrated staying at home. If I had been older at the time, I would have thought to finish school before having a family."

"You're quite the thinker now, aren't you, Anna?"

"Thomas . . ."

"But you know what you didn't factor into your little equation? Me, Anna. You didn't stop to think how I might feel. Do you know what it feels like to have your heart ripped apart? This is not a game, Anna. This is real life, and I'm a real person."

"I know that, Thomas."

"I'm not so sure," he said.

"Come see me tomorrow."

"Come see me," said Thomas. He hung up the phone and, again, put his head in his hands. Helen tapped him on the shoulder. He wheeled around to face her.

"You two had a fight," she said, putting her hand on his shoulder.

"We did have a fight, yes. What are you doing up?"

"I heard you talking on the phone and wondered who you were talking to."

"Are Mom and Dad up?"

"Nope. What did you fight about?"

"Everything," said Thomas. "The whole shooting match."

"You broke up?"

"Absolutely and irrevocably."

"Why?"

Thomas ran his fingers through his hair and scratched the back of his head. "She didn't want to marry me."

"How do you know?"

"Because she said no when I asked her, Helen."

"You asked her to marry you?"

"I did."

Helen yawned. "Do Mom and Dad know that?"

"No, and it doesn't matter much now since she said no."

"You're too young to get married anyway, Thomas."

"Why does everyone keep saying that?"

"Because you have to finish college first."

"Who says, Helen?"

"Everybody," said Helen. "Everybody knows that."

"Everybody but me," said Thomas, taking his sister into his arms for a hug. She wrapped her arms tightly around his neck and whispered in his ear.

"I love you, Thomas."

He gave her a squeeze and released her. "Run up to bed now, Helen. It's late."

"You come up too."

"I will. I'm going to sit here another minute or so. I'll be right up."

Helen walked slowly away from her brother. She stepped onto the landing and looked back at him once before climbing the stairs.

Thomas, still sitting in the chair next to the phone, gave her a lazy wave. Helen stopped halfway down the hallway, just outside Thomas's bedroom, and sat down. She had to pee, but Charlotte was in the bathroom, most likely having a cigarette and blowing the smoke out the window. Helen leaned back against the wall and waited, for a vacant bathroom and for Thomas to come upstairs.

Chapter 25

2003

Helen heard loud voices and laughter. She looked through the porch screen and saw Todd and Ned walking down the street. Judging by their buoyant behavior, she guessed her sons had been victorious. "Hey!" she called.

Todd and Ned looked toward the porch, squinting in the midday sun. Seeing his mother, Ned broke into a sprint. He ran up the steps and into the porch, his eyes wide with excitement. "Guess what?" he said, grinning.

"Oh, I think I'd much rather have you tell me," said Helen, smiling back at him.

"We won again!" Ned shouted.

"You are amazing," said Helen. She got out of her chair and hugged her sweaty son.

Charles and Daniel, towels wrapped around their shoulders, had walked up from the beach and were chatting with Todd on the lawn. Seeing them, Ned dashed back outside, letting the screen door close with a bang. He leaped onto his father's back, almost knocking Charles to the ground. "You," said Charles, wrapping his arms around his son's legs and laughing, "are getting way too big for that."

"You're right," said Ned, sliding down Charles's back. "We're big, brave tennis players."

Charles laughed again and then called to Helen, who was still watching from the porch. "I think our days as tennis king and queen are seriously numbered."

"I won't give up my crown without a fight!" Helen called back.

"Anytime," Ned shouted. "We're ready anytime!"

"Yes," Helen said to her younger son. "I can see that you are."

"We're going swimming," Todd announced. "You want to come?"

"Not just yet," said Helen, "I'm waiting for your Uncle Thomas."

"Uncle Thomas is here?" asked Ned.

"In town, yes," said Helen. "He'll be back in a little bit. Go for a swim. We'll all have time to talk later, okay?"

"Okay," said Todd.

"Wait," Helen said. Todd and Ned turned back around to face their mother. "Your cousins Sally and Peter are down on the beach with your Aunt Barb. Talk to them."

"What do they look like?" asked Todd.

"Like a little boy and a little girl. They'll be sitting in our chairs. Your Aunt Barb has blond hair."

"Todd will talk to her," said Ned. "He loves blondes."

"Cut it out." Todd punched Ned's arm.

"Just be nice," said Helen.

"We will," Todd said, giving Ned a shove. As quick and agile as animals in the wild, they bolted around the corner of the cottage, heading for their still-damp suits on the clothesline.

Charles and Daniel walked into the porch "He's really here?" Charles asked. "In the flesh?"

"I know," said Helen. "I'm still in shock myself. It's been thirty years, Charles."

"You haven't seen him in thirty years?" asked Daniel.

"It's been thirty years since he's been here," said Helen.

"Why?"

"It's a long story," said Helen, hands on hips.

"I've got time."

"He fell in love thirty summers ago," Helen explained to

Daniel, "so much in love that he asked the young woman to marry him. She turned him down, as she should have. Thomas was a month shy of leaving for Princeton, and she was in the middle of earning her college degree here. He had a great first year at college but was unable to disassociate the beach from Anna, so he decided not to come back the following summer. The next three summers, he was offered lucrative internships and jobs in the city. After college, he went to business school, and then worked eighty-hour weeks as an investment banker. When he started his own business, he had even less free time."

"He never came back?" Daniel asked.

"Not here, no," said Helen. "When he was still in New York we saw him at my parents' house on several holidays and at his wedding, of course, and when my father died. But we all haven't seen him at all since the funeral five years ago."

"How do you stay connected?" asked Daniel.

"By the telephone," said Helen. "Thomas and I try to talk every month."

"I don't think Charlotte talks to him."

"With any luck," said Helen, turning to walk into the living room, "that will change after this weekend."

"Where is Charlotte?"

"Upstairs taking a nap," said Helen from the dining room. "She said for me to tell you to join her if you'd like."

"I'm too keyed up to sleep," said Daniel, removing his towel from his shoulders and using it on his wet hair. "I'm going for a walk."

"Pammy left about ten minutes ago. She's headed for the state park," said Helen, without thinking. When her brain caught up with her mouth, she said, "There are some really nice trails down by the creek. I can give you quick directions to get there."

"I'll try that another time," said Daniel. "If I hurry, I may be able to catch up with Pammy."

Daniel walked out the porch door and dropped his damp towel on the lawn. He was running by the time he hit the pavement.

"Somehow," said Charles, watching Daniel jog barefoot down the street, "I don't think Charlotte had sleeping in mind."

Daniel saw Pammy just as she was stepping onto the large boardwalk that stretched from one end of the half mile-long state beach to the other. She was wearing store-bought cutoff jean shorts and a white, button-down shirt that she had tied up at her waist. Daniel came up behind her, gently tapping her bottom. She wheeled around, looking angry, ready to lambaste the offending stranger for touching her, then immediately softened when she saw Daniel. He fell into step beside her and took her hand in his. "You look great today, Pammy."

"And you," said Pammy, smiling broadly, "are a troublemaker."

"How can I get into trouble when I simply enjoy the company of a beautiful woman?" he asked, putting on an innocent look.

"By making comments like that. Besides, too many beautiful women spoil the broth."

Daniel laughed. He turned his head to look out at the water. "This beach is packed. Where do all of these people come from?"

"From all over the state. It doesn't get any busier than Fourth of July weekend."

He turned his face, his attention, back to Pammy. "I'd like to get busy with you." Daniel squeezed her hand, prompting a smile from her. "What's up there?" Daniel asked, pointing at the beach grass jutting out of the sand above the boardwalk.

"Walking paths," Pammy said. "Skinny, sandy walkways that wander in and out of the marshland."

"Let's go," said Daniel, pulling her off the boardwalk and up the steep slope to the top of the dune. They ran down the other side and chose the narrow center path to follow. Daniel led, letting go of Pammy's hand, and she walked behind him. "I like this," Daniel said over his shoulder. "It's much more private."

Pammy studied him, his body. His back was broad and well-defined with thick bands of muscle. His arms were also muscular, but not huge like those of the professional wrestlers Pammy had seen on television. His waist was trim and slid with ease into his faded plaid bathing suit. He could easily be a model, thought Pammy, for a catalog featuring hip, expensive clothing for young people, a catalog she would toss into her recycling box a minute after she took it from her mailbox. Pammy watched the muscles move in his legs as he walked. The hot sun bored into the back of her neck, momentarily taking Pammy's attention away from Daniel's physique. She wished she had worn her straw hat. Daniel stopped and turned to face her. "It's hot," said Daniel. "Let's see if we can find some shade."

Around the next corner, Pammy saw the beginning of the state park forest in the distance. Daniel grabbed her hand again and pulled her toward it. Faster and faster they walked until they were running. They ran the last fifty yards and then collapsed under the trees. Sweating and breathing hard, they lay on their backs, looking up at the tall trees that blocked the scorching sun. "Wow," said Daniel, leaning up on one elbow to look down on Pammy. "This feels great. I think I can even feel a slight breeze."

"Don't talk," said Pammy, struggling not to breathe so hard after their short run. "Boy, that feels good."

The wind, gentle and inviting, swept over Pammy's legs, arms, and face. She closed her eyes and let it cool her body, relieve her hot skin. Its touch became firm, human, and Pammy opened her eyes, suddenly realizing Daniel was stroking the inside of her thigh. "Daniel?"

"Relax, baby," Daniel said in a soft, soothing voice. "I'm just giving you a massage, Pammy. There's nobody here but us. Lie back down."

Pammy lowered herself to the sand. She closed her eyes and relaxed her muscles. She concentrated only on Daniel's hand and how he moved it up and down the inside of her leg. She didn't fight it because she wanted him to touch her. He moved closer to her, their legs and arms now touching, and his hand traveled up her leg, over her crotch, to her stomach and under her shirt. She opened her eyes and turned to him. "Lie back, Pammy," he whispered.

"I want to touch you."

"Not yet."

He moved his hands over her breasts, caressing and squeezing them. Bursts of light exploded in Pammy's head. Her entire body tingled at his touch. Daniel kissed her mouth while he unbuttoned her shirt. Pammy arched her back upward in response. She wanted him to suck all of her into his mouth. She moaned in pleasure.

Daniel unsnapped her shorts and pulled them off. He slid her panties down to her knees, then kicked them off with his foot. No longer able to wait, Pammy reached over and untied Daniel's suit. He took it off, allowing her access to his erect penis. It was huge. She ran her hands over it, and then moved them up to his hard chest, the skin she had been fantasizing about touching. She then wrapped her arms around his back. "Now," she whispered urgently. And he was on top of her, pushing into her. As they moved, she talked to him, coaxed him, promising him sex at the house, in the bathroom, in the shower, in her bedroom, in the kitchen in the middle of the night. He cried out, shuddering, then slowed to a stop. He lay on top of Pammy, like a dead man. "Are you all right?" she asked.

"I'm unbelievably all right," said Daniel, pushing himself up by his arms to look at her. "That was fantastic. You're fantastic." He kissed her on the lips. Looking up at him, Pammy thought about Charlotte. "Don't," he said, as if reading her mind. "Don't think about anything." She smiled at him. "I never made any promises," he continued. "We have a very open relationship."

"Have there been others?" asked Pammy, suddenly hurt.

"No," said Daniel. "No one but you."

"And my sister."

"Don't do this, Pammy," said Daniel, sitting next to her and covering his ears with his hands.

"Okay," said Pammy. "Okay, I'll stop. After one more question."

"What's that?"

"Why?" asked Pammy. "Why do this when you're already screwing a woman in her forties whose body makes my body look like it's ready for the old-age home?"

"Your body is beautiful," said Daniel, "and it's real."

She hugged him. He had told her exactly what she wanted to

hear. Even though he might have known that, she didn't care. He satisfied her longings completely. He pulled her off the sand and dressed her. They walked back to the state beach, tightly holding hands like new lovers. When they reached the boardwalk, Daniel kissed her and ran off, leaving her to walk slowly back to the cottage alone.

CHAPTER 26

1973

Thomas took off the red windbreaker that had the words EAT PIZZA stenciled on the back and hung it up on a hook near the counter. He pulled the crumpled dollar bills out of his pocket and counted them, smoothing them so they would fit into his wallet. He had made twenty-six dollars in tips in four hours, which impressed him. They had been busy, as they usually were on Saturday nights, and Thomas was exhausted. "Good night, Mr. G," he said, as he headed for the door.

"Good night, Thomas. I'll see you Tuesday at six, right?"

"Yes, sir."

Outside, the night air was thick with humidity. Thomas reached into the pocket of his pants for his keys while rounding the corner of the restaurant. His car was parked at the very end of the lot—the closer spaces being reserved for customers—under a weak streetlight. Thomas could see someone standing near his car. As soon as he realized it was Anna, he ran the rest of the way. "Are you okay?" he called to her.

"Yes," she said, "and no."

"Where's Amy?" Thomas was standing next to her now.

"She's home," said Anna, "with my neighbor." Convinced neither she nor Amy was in trouble, Thomas remembered he was angry with her. He folded his arms across his chest and waited for her to speak. "Everything's okay," she said. "I came to see you." Thomas stood still. "I know you're upset with me, and I understand that. You don't have to talk to me if you don't want to. I just wanted to see you."

"Why?" Thomas struggled to hold his emotions in check. All the pep talks he had given himself felt hollow, useless.

"Because I miss you," she said, "and I've treated you unfairly. At the very least, I should have been fair with you." Thomas wanted to encircle her tiny waist with his arms, to rest his hands on the small of her back, to tell her he didn't care about fairness because he loved her. But he stood still, except for unfolding his arms. "Perhaps I shouldn't have come."

"No," said Thomas, gentle now. "I'm glad you're here."

Anna walked a step toward him and then stopped. "I'm so sorry. I didn't want to hurt you. I wasn't thinking about anything but being with you. You're right about that."

Thomas looked at her face, studying her. He hadn't seen or talked to her in almost two weeks. She was just as beautiful, more so even, under the streetlight with the quiet blackness of the night framing her face, her clear skin translucent. He quickly realized he had not learned anything in the thirteen days since they broke up. He loved her and felt himself bending toward her, wanting to ask her if she'd changed her mind, if she'd be his wife.

"I think Amy misses you as much as I do," said Anna, breaking down. Thomas went to her. He pulled her against his chest and held her tightly, not caring that she would feel the beating of his heart and know his true feelings. She put her arms around his waist and cried softly into his shirt. "I thought you would call me."

"I wanted to."

"But you didn't."

"I couldn't, Anna. I have to try to forget about you. Calling someone who's broken up with you does not help with the healing process."

"Are you healed, Thomas? Have you forgotten about me?"

"No," he said. "I'm not sure that's possible."

"I'm not sure it's possible for me, either. I'm so mixed up." Thomas leaned down and kissed her softly on the lips. "Don't stop," she said. "I've missed your sweet kisses." And he kissed her again, longer this time, until he could no longer kiss her without touching her. "Come to my house," Anna whispered when he stopped.

"I want to," Thomas said, "more than anything else in the world."

"But you won't."

"No," said Thomas, amazing himself. "Because if I go to your house tonight and make love to you, I will want to stay."

"You can stay," said Anna. "You can stay all night."

"You know what I mean."

"Yes," she said, sighing. "I know what you mean. How can we change things?"

"I could commute to Princeton," Thomas suggested, smiling.

"You're teasing me," said Anna.

"Because we can't change things," said Thomas, "unless you want to change your mind."

"About marrying you."

"About marrying me."

"No," she said. "I was hoping you'd change your mind."

"About?"

"About being with me, having fun with me, using me." It was Anna who was smiling now.

"Your live-for-today plan," said Thomas, serious again, looking into her eyes.

"Yes," she said weakly, already knowing his answer would be no.

"And mid-August—less than a month from now—we shake hands and promise to write?"

"Thomas, you're impossible."

"Impossibly in love, yes," he said. "I can't see you and be with you, knowing that in September I can't have you near me."

"I'm half tempted . . ." Anna began.

"Don't say things you don't mean," said Thomas, guessing her thoughts, putting his fingers lightly over her mouth. "You'll break my heart all over again."

Anna put her hand on the middle of his chest. "I'm sorry I broke your heart," she said. "I want to fix it."

Anna pulled at Thomas's shirt, pulled him down to her. She put her hands on his cheeks and then moved them back into his hair, which she filtered slowly through her fingers. Thomas closed his eyes momentarily and then lifted Anna up off the ground. She wrapped her legs around his waist and her arms around his neck and kissed him. He put her down on the hood of his car. He put his hands down on the hood as well, on both sides of Anna, and moved closer to her until their faces were almost touching. "I've got to go," he said.

"Don't."

"And you've got to go. If Amy wakes, she'll want you and not your neighbor."

"She loves Mary Purdy."

"But not in the night when she wakes. She wants you."

"How do you know?"

"Because that's when I want you most," said Thomas. "When I'm alone in the dark and the distractions of the day don't drag my thoughts away, and I can think about what I need and want, it's always you."

"Thomas, you're too good."

Thomas kissed her once on the lips, then backed away. Slowly Anna eased herself down from the hood. Once on the ground, she looked up at him. "Where's your car?" he asked.

"Around the corner."

"I'll drive you to it," he said, opening the door for her.

She ducked down and sat on the seat, smelling his scent the moment she was in the car. She breathed in deeply, then moved over to be as close to Thomas as she could as he drove. He started the car and put his arm around Anna's neck. They drove the block and a half in silence. When Thomas saw her car, he pulled over next to it and put his car into park. He got out and let Anna out on her side. He then opened the driver-side door to her car, which she never locked, and stood next to it while she slid inside. She looked up at him. "I'm glad you came," he said.

"Why?"

"Because now I know you love me almost as much as I love you." Anna smiled. Thomas closed her door, got back into his car, and looked at her one last time before he drove away.

Anna sat back in her seat and exhaled. "Maybe more," she said.

CHAPTER 27

2003

Thomas pulled open the paneled wood door to Anna's office. Inside, he stepped on a plush Oriental rug, much like the one he just left in the other law office. He smiled. The successful lawyers he knew all had or hired decorators with impeccable taste. Maroon leather chairs sat next to each other in pairs in the expansive foyer. Two, four, six, eight of them—their color exactly matching the red in the rug. Two antique coffee tables held the finance and architecture magazines found in the spacious living rooms of people with money. Tall, lush plants fed by the sunlight streaming in through several skylights shot out of their colorful ceramic pots. Having second thoughts about seeing Anna, Thomas turned and walked back toward the door. He had been gone an hour, and surely Barb would be wondering where he was. Thomas was, had been for most of his life, acutely aware of time. Punctuality was an issue with him. It was a lesson he learned from his father, who was never late. Habitually late people, Thomas had relearned many times over the years, were always ready with excuses when they showed up ten or fifteen minutes after a mutually scheduled meeting time, but no matter what they said happened, they lost points with Thomas. His business partners valued Thomas's time as highly as they valued their own. Barb had been waiting for his return long enough. Just as he reached the door, he heard Anna's voice.

"I thought I heard someone out here," said Anna, looking at Thomas's back. "May I help you with something?" Thomas turned and faced her. The smile on her face faded, and her eyes narrowed. Two, maybe three long seconds passed before the smile returned. She walked to him, put her hands on his arms, and held him for a few moments at arm's length. "Thomas Thompson," she said.

"Hello, Anna," he said, half in love with her as soon as he said her name. She had not changed, aside from a few gray hairs mixed in with their more numerous, darker companions, and crow's feet around her bright eyes. She was trim and looked fit, and Thomas was wondering what it would be like to pick her up, as he had so many years ago outside Village Pizza.

"Thomas . . . I don't know how many years it's been," she said, stepping back and looking into his eyes. "You look almost the same."

Thomas laughed. "Thirty, Anna. I haven't seen or talked to you in thirty years. And you, by the way, look exactly the same." She smiled at him. "And you've been busy. Look at this place."

"I love it here," she said, looking around. "I've worked hard for it."

"So, you obviously made it through college. You probably sailed through law school. You paid your debt to Hudson and Lambert, then practiced law with another reputable firm, I'm guessing, before striking out on your own. My God, Anna, I feel like I've been sleeping for thirty years."

"You've been doing anything but sleeping, Thomas. Your company is doing quite well."

"You've read about my company?"

"Everyone has," said Anna, blushing. "You've changed the way people look at self-storage. Your places are clean, affordable, convenient, accessible, and secure. We all have something to store, at some point in our lives, and your places and your business philosophy have encouraged more of us to do so much more willingly than in the past."

"You've drunk the Kool-Aid."

Anna laughed. "I have, indeed, as has Amy. She's a lawyer, too, but she's also an artist. And she keeps her supplies and her finished pieces in one of your heated units close to her tiny studio."

"I'm flattered," he said. Anna looked into his eyes, wondering, searching. "Tell me about Amy."

"She lives in Vermont with her husband and two children. She's the only lawyer in a very small town, so she does everything from dog bites to divorce. Her husband's a biology professor at the University of Vermont."

Thomas thought for a moment. "She must be thirty-five or so, by now."

"She is. She turns thirty-five in September."

"Does she look the same?"

"She's changed a little, Thomas. Last time you saw her, she was four," said Anna. Thomas laughed. "And you," she said, "you must have some children by now."

"Very young ones," Thomas said. "My daughter, Sally, is six, and Peter is four."

"And your wife?"

"Barb. She's just a few years older than Amy. Isn't that kind of amazing?"

"You married someone my daughter's age. Thomas, I'm feeling old."

"Don't feel old, Anna. I'm a late bloomer. I got so involved in business that I forgot about my personal life. By the time I made time, it had been so long, I was tempted to start at the high school."

Anna laughed. "And to think you had just finished high school when you asked me to marry you."

"Yes." Thomas looked down at the carpet.

"Sometimes I'm sorry I said no," Anna said, again searching his eyes when they returned to her face.

"No, you're not, Anna. You never would have made it this far. You were right. I was impulsive."

"I like impulsive people, Thomas."

"So." Thomas felt warm and slightly off balance. "What about you? You must have married along the way."

"I did," said Anna. "I married a lawyer I met at a convention in

Chicago. I, too, was older. We had three years together and were thinking about having children when he died, just like that, of a heart attack. He was forty-five."

"I'm sorry."

"After that, I decided to stay away from marriage. Losing a husband as well as scaring off the father of my child is plenty."

"Anna . . ."

"My friends call me the Black Widow."

"Nice friends."

"It's okay," said Anna, "really. I still go out on dates and enjoy the company of men my age. I just don't want to commit to anyone."

"That sounds familiar." Thomas's face got hot.

"Thomas, I'm sorry." She put her hands back on his arms. "I'm still so sorry after all these years."

"Don't be, Anna. I'm absolutely fine. I'm great, in fact." As soon as Thomas said he was great, he knew that he really was.

"Well, you *look* great, Thomas."

Thomas checked his watch. "I've got to go," he said. "My family is back at the house, wondering where the hell I am."

Impulsively, Anna wrapped her arms around him. He responded in kind, pulling her closer. "Thomas," she said into his chest.

"It's okay, Anna," he said, releasing her, then bending down to kiss her quickly, just once, on her mouth. He took two steps backwards, looking at her, then turned and walked toward the door.

"Thomas?" she said. He turned again and looked at her. "Thank you."

"For what?"

"For coming today. For acknowledging our past," said Anna. "But mostly for being who you are. I learned a lot from you."

"I learned a bit from you," said Thomas, a slight smile on his face.

"I never forgot you."

"And you can see by my visit today that I'd totally forgotten you."

"Did I make a mistake?" she asked.

Thomas thought for a moment. "No. While I think that we might have made it work, it would have been difficult along the way. You have fulfilled your dream, Anna, which might not have happened from a dorm room at Princeton." Thomas turned and opened the door. "Be well, Anna Santiago, and give my very best to Amy."

Anna looked at the door for a minute after Thomas walked out and knew, without a doubt, that she had made a mistake—one that, unlike those of her clients, she could not rectify.

CHAPTER 28

1973

"You shouldn't smoke, Eddie."

"You're right, Helen," he said, as he lit a match and held it to the end of the Marlboro hanging out of his mouth. He inhaled deeply and the tobacco caught fire, glowing orange and sending up a stream of gray smoke.

"Don't give it another thought, Helen. Eddie has a death wish."

"Oh shut up, Thomas. You are such a fucking killjoy."

"Language check," said Helen.

"No, really," said Thomas, who was so used to hearing Eddie swear that he didn't hear it anymore, "I figure if you increase your intake to, say, two packs a day, you'll check out by the time you're forty."

"What's with you today?" asked Eddie. "Is this another stage in the great Santiago depression?"

"You leave her out of it."

"I wish you'd leave her out of it." Eddie took a deep drag of his cigarette. "You've been a pain in the ass for three weeks now. It's getting old, Thomas. She's just a girl."

"No, she's not, Eddie. She's a beautiful woman who knows what she wants in life and is willing to work for it, unlike all the nitwits on the duck pond wall. What are their ambitions, other than finding a guy to buy the beer?"

"Your previous obsession, Catherine, is in college. I'd call that ambitious."

"She was hardly an obsession. And she's hardly ambitious," said Thomas, "unless you count rich-husband hunting as a life goal."

"Okay," said Helen, who was accustomed to their bickering, "let's talk about something else."

"What time is it, Helen?" asked Eddie. He never wore a watch in the summer, telling everyone how free he felt without one. Thomas told Helen he suspected it was because Eddie didn't want a tan line from the strap on his wrist.

Helen looked at her watch. "Almost four."

"Let's walk down to the bridge," said Thomas.

The three lifted themselves off the sandy bank next to the train tracks. Helen ran down the hill ahead of her escorts, stopping when her feet hit the gravel that surrounded and supported the rails. She looked down the tracks to the signal tower. The lights had not changed. "Still green and yellow," she called. "Nothing's coming."

She stepped up onto the closest rail and held her arms out for balance. Foot in front of foot, she moved slowly along the track, moving her arms up and down like a large bird preparing for flight. Six, seven, eight steps she took before she had to put her right foot down onto a wood tie. She stepped back up and again began her imaginary tightrope walk. She pictured the circus crowd below her, awestruck by her talent. With every breath she took, they took two. Faster and faster their hearts beat, while Helen moved ever so cautiously along the wire. Being a world-class performer, Helen never worked with a net. Below her, some one hundred feet, stood the enormous elephants dressed in their colorful, ethnic circus regalia. Even they watched as she moved closer and closer to the platform at the end of the wire. Just twenty feet away, Helen focused keenly on her destination. Perspiration dotted her forehead, threatening to drip down into her eyes, but she ignored it. Wiping her brow at this stage would be costly. A fan shouted up from the darkness,

Don't look down, Helen! But she did, and then she fell. "Rats!" she said, abandoning the rail for the stability of the wide ties.

Eddie and Thomas, well ahead of her now, sat on the edge of the little bridge that spanned the creek. Their feet dangling down over the water, they reached back for rocks from the track bedding behind them and dropped them, one at a time, into the water below. Helen ran down the middle of the tracks until she reached them. "What are you doing?"

"Trying to hit that can down there," said Eddie. "See it?"

"Yeah," said Helen, peering over the edge. "Let me try."

The tide was on its way out, so the creek water rushed under the narrow railroad bridge like floodwater toward a storm drain. Helen grabbed a handful of rocks and then sat down beside Thomas. She closed her left eye for what she called laser focus and aimed the rock at the can. She let the rock drop, dead-on she thought, but the rock hit the water and was carried three feet from the can. She took another rock from the small pile next to her and then hesitated. "You hear something?"

"Lawnmower," said Thomas.

Helen waited. The low rumbling sound increased. "You sure?" said Helen, looking down the tracks.

"Yeah," said Eddie. "We've been paranoid for five minutes about that stupid lawnmower." Once he was reminded that he was in her presence, he did his best to curtail his bad language. It was a habit he knew he could correct, but *fucking* had become one of his favorite words. It was more descriptive than most people thought.

Helen concentrated again on the can in the water. She aimed, but missed, missed, missed, and missed. "This game stinks," she announced, getting up.

"Well, it's either the game or it's you," said Eddie, teasing her.

"Definitely the game," said Thomas, standing. "Let's walk back."

Back at the sandy bank, they sat and waited. Thomas, who had filled his pockets with gravel along the way, threw the rocks, one by one, back down at the rails. His object, as always, was to hit the top of a rail. Most of the time he missed, even though he had been one of the best players, had the best arm, on his high school baseball team.

"Why can't you hit those rails?" asked Eddie. "You never hit the damn rail."

"It's not easy," said Thomas, throwing another rock.

"Yeah," said Eddie, "so you've said, varsity athlete."

"I've seen him play tons of times, Eddie. He is really good," said Helen, defending her brother.

"Then hit the rail," said Eddie to Thomas. He threw another rock and missed. "Give me one of those rocks." Eddie threw it and missed. He threw another one and missed. Thomas threw another one and missed. Helen, wanting to join the game, held up her hand like a classroom teacher so the boys would hold their fire. Then she ran down the bank for a handful of gravel. Shallow pockets filled, she ran back up the bank and then again sat down between Thomas and Eddie. She emptied her shorts, laying the pile of rocks down beside her, just as she had done at the bridge. She picked up a rock, closed her eyes, and threw it in the direction of the tracks. *Ping!* "You," said Eddie, lighting another cigarette, "are the luckiest girl on earth."

It was Saturday afternoon. Thomas had driven the bakery run that morning and Eddie, who was a bank teller for the summer, didn't work on Saturdays. They had talked about playing golf, but decided against it when Eddie pointed out how crowded the course would be. They were both tired and considering a nap on the beach when Helen happened upon them on the duck pond wall and suggested they all go to the tracks. Sitting in the baking sun near the tracks was not one of Thomas's go-to pastimes, but he knew their mother forbade Helen to go without an escort. So when he had time, and after he told Helen he had better things to do than watch the trains go by, he usually took her. Helen got the feeling that, once there, he actually liked it. And if Eddie wasn't working, he usually tagged along. She knew he liked going to the tracks because he'd told her if he stayed home, his mother would find half a dozen cottage projects to keep him busy. And he hated being busy, he told Helen, unless he was getting paid for it. Away from his mother's to-do list, Eddie enjoyed sitting, sometimes lying, on the bank leading down to the tracks and smoking cigarettes with his eyes closed to the sun's brightness. He often wore jeans and a white T-shirt in his effort to look like James Dean, which Helen, after Eddie explained who James Dean was, thought was almost as cool as Eddie did.

Any cottage to-do list grows faster than it shrinks, so Thomas, especially as the only son, was under the same pressure as Eddie. Even though John Thompson liked to putter around the place, he was busy at his practice five days out of seven. During the week, Claire was insistent that Thomas help when she wanted a screen replaced, a window painted, or any other number of what she called hardware-store jobs done. While she often made Charlotte run into town for a few items at the grocery store, Claire solicited general cottage errands and help from Thomas, who wouldn't, each time she made a request, give her a ten-minute argument about child labor. In reality, Charlotte labored very little. She worked only when she needed the money, which wasn't often since she managed to talk one of the besotted boys on the beach into paying for everything she desired. Still, John Thompson insisted Charlotte do something other than lie on the beach all summer, so she worked as a waitress two or three nights a week and once in a while during the day. Charlotte told her sisters that she had made it quite clear to the owner of the restaurant that her social life came first. For a reason known only to him, the guy hired her anyway and told her he'd call her when he needed the help. All the other waitresses had six or seven shifts per week, while she had just three, Charlotte boasted. Pammy told Helen that Charlotte must have flirted with the owner. She would flirt with anyone, even old men like their dad, to get what she wanted. The only thing that Charlotte and Pammy agreed upon that summer—at all, actually—was that going to the train tracks was for numbskulls.

Antsy, Thomas walked back down the tracks to check the signal tower lights. "Red and green!" he called.

"Really?" said Helen, running down to him.

"What's that mean again?" shouted Eddie from the bank.

"I think one's coming," said Helen.

"Now we're in business," said Thomas. He took some pennies out of his back pocket and gave a few to Helen. They bent down and laid them on the tracks so the train would flatten them. Helen had a bunch of squished coins back at the house in a box on her bureau. Thomas kept one in his pants pocket, mixed in with his other change, for good luck. Helen laid her pennies in a straight line, about two inches apart. Thomas lined his up in pairs. When Helen was done, she looked down the track, one way and then the other. She looked up at the signal tower where the lights still shone green and red. Thomas was laying more pennies on the other tracks, in case the train was traveling west to east instead of east to west.

"Hurry, Thomas," said Helen, scrambling up the bank.

"There's plenty of time," said Thomas, looking up from his task. "I don't hear anything yet." Just as he spoke, he did hear something: a low rumble. He ignored it, telling himself he had several minutes. The signal lights changed well in advance of the train's actual arrival. To be sure, Thomas looked down the tracks and saw nothing. To double-check, he bent down and put his ear to the track.

"I hear something, Thomas!" Helen shouted from the bank. "Leave the rest of the pennies for another time."

"I've got time," said Thomas, even though his gut told him otherwise.

"Don't fuck around!" Eddie shouted. "The train's coming!"

Thomas looked down the tracks again and saw it. About a mile away, it moved along the track quietly and quickly, pulled by its powerful, indestructible-looking engine. The distinctive pinging sound that reverberated from the tracks as the train approached bounced into the air. Helen and Eddie screamed at Thomas to move, but he wasn't listening. He wondered if Anna would be screaming if she were on the bank. He could see her, sitting at her desk at Hudson and Lambert. She was smiling, talking to someone. She was dressed in the light green linen suit he loved, and her dark hair hung softly around her face, falling on her shoulders. He wanted to touch her. He reached out his hands, but he couldn't move.

Something hit him in the chest and he flew backward, up off the track and down to the ground. The train, twenty feet from him, sped past. Something touched his hand, and Thomas rolled away from it. Bewildered, he looked behind him and saw his friend, lying flat on his stomach next to him. Thomas realized he hadn't been hit by the train; he had been shoved out of its path by Eddie, who was lying next to him, saturated with sweat and covered in sandy dirt. "Are you okay?" Thomas asked him, pushing himself up to a sitting position.

"I think so," said Eddie, not moving. His chin was bleeding.

Thomas stood and then reached out a hand to his friend. Eddie took it, and Thomas pulled him up off the ground. Eddie brushed the dirt from his white shirt, but they both could tell its chances of remaining white after the first and second washing, with bleach even, were close to nothing. Helen ran across the tracks to Thomas. She had tears in her eyes. She jumped up onto his waist and threw her arms around his neck. "Thomas, you scared me," she said. "What were you doing?"

"I don't know," said Thomas, hugging her. "I'm sorry." Thomas looked at Eddie. "Thank you," he said. "I'm quite sure you just saved my life."

"Eddie, you're bleeding," said Helen.

Eddie touched his chin with the back of his hand and then, for a moment, studied the blood on his skin. He looked at Helen. "Just a scratch, I think."

"Let's go home," said Helen.

While Helen often shared her adventures at the track at the dinner table, what happened that day became an instant secret. When Claire asked them upon their return about their excursion to the end of the street, Helen and Thomas locked eyes, briefly, before Helen said, "Nothing much." Helen didn't understand what had happened, what had made her sensible, cautious older brother behave in such an erratic manner, but she never asked him. She did wonder, however, if it had something to do, because everything that summer had something to do, with the woman who broke his heart.

Chapter 29

2003

Daniel took Sally, Peter, Todd, and Ned to McDonald's for dinner because the older boys said they couldn't possibly wait until eight o'clock to eat. Sally and Peter were thrilled at the prospect of having a Happy Meal, something their mother allowed only when they were traveling, and of being in the company of their cousins, who had played with them on the beach all afternoon. They were fast friends. The four of them built a two-story sand castle, wrapped in brown seaweed for extra strength and to gross out their enemies. They caught hermit crabs at the sandy end of the beach, and they closely inspected and commented on the twenty-five snails and mussels they pulled off various submerged rocks. Buoyed by their victories on the tennis court, Todd and Ned had twice their usual energy, which made them perfect companions for their younger cousins. When they played Wild West, Peter was never disappointed in Ned's bad guy death throes. With each imaginary wound, he would feign agony, violently twitch, twirl in place, drop to his knees, and then fall facedown onto the sand. And Sally, who loved being in the water, dove off Todd's shoulders three or four dozen times. McDonald's was the next logical step, according to Daniel, who had been watching and occasionally participating in the afternoon's activities.

As soon as they all drove off in Charlotte's rental, Pammy and Barb took off in Pammy's Lexus for the farm in the opposite direction from town for the corn. Helen, normally in the middle of food runs, meal preparation, and general set-up, helped her mother, awake and reading a novel, out of bed and down the stairs to the porch. The pot of tea Helen had made, before she went to check on Claire, sat on the coffee table between them. As soon as Claire was settled in her chair, Helen poured her a mug of tea and held it out to her. "Careful," she said. "It's still a bit hot."

"Set it down on the table, then," said Claire. "I'll have it in a minute."

Helen poured herself a mug and then sat in the chair facing her mother. "You had quite a nap," she said. "Are you hungry? Barb brought cookies."

"I'll wait for dinner, I think. What are we having?"

"Lobster. Charles and Thomas just left to pick them up in town."

Claire smiled. "I can't wait to see him."

Helen laughed. "Me neither. He arrived, left for town, got back from town, swam to the raft, and then went back into town. I had about five minutes with him."

"And what did you learn in that five minutes?" Keen observation is crucial, Claire had told her children, to assessing one's competition, whether in the pool or in life.

Helen shrugged. "He looks good. He looks like the Thomas we saw five years ago, except a little bit grayer." She smiled.

"Is he still speaking Canadian?"

"Meaning what?" asked Helen, who had had this conversation with her mother before. Claire couldn't understand why he lived in Canada, why he didn't want to come back to his own country.

"You know, that *out* and *about* thing they have."

Helen hesitated. Did she want to get into this again? Did she want to bring up the various accents characteristic of various regions in the United States or anywhere else in the world? Claire had been overly proud of America, blind to its deficiencies, since her swimming days. Nothing Helen could say would open her mother's mind about other countries or cultures. Claire simply didn't want to know. "I didn't notice," said Helen.

"I wonder if he still likes lobster. They probably don't get much of it in Ontario."

Again, Helen held her tongue. She could have told her mother that some considered the food in Ontario to be superior to that of many areas in the United States. She'd read, in fact—had the article been in *The Economist*?—that the produce in Canada was better because it was more often local and organic. "I know *you* like lobster."

"Oh, I do indeed," said Claire. "I love lobster."

"Me too," said Helen, sipping her tea.

"I remember the time your father bought two lobsters here, at the very fish market Thomas and Charles are getting our lobsters from today I suspect, and had them packaged up. He hid them in the car and then stuffed them into the outside refrigerator when we got home. That night, after all you kids were in bed and I was terribly sad—I was always melancholy at the end of the summer when we had to leave this house—he brought them out, boiled them, and we had a lovely lobster dinner in the kitchen."

Helen scrunched her eyebrows. "I don't remember that."

"You wouldn't," said Claire. "You were just three or four at the time. The others noticed though—it was hard not to. You know how boiling lobsters can stink up a house for days. They complained, saying lobsters had always been a family meal."

Helen laughed. "I don't remember them ever saying that about other things, pork chops for instance."

"Pork chops *were* a family meal, every Tuesday. Your father loved them, could have eaten them three nights a week."

They were silent for a minute. "We're all here, Mom," said Helen.

"Yes." Claire sipped her tea.

"I wasn't sure Thomas would make it."

"I was."

"Because you'd cut him out of your will if he didn't show up?" Helen knew she was being mean, but, at that very moment, she wanted to be. She thought her mother's insistence that her children all come to the cottage this particular weekend could have been orchestrated without the threat. Hell, Thomas didn't need the money anyway. None of them did, really. It was the cottage that caught their attention. It was the prospect of losing the cottage, even though none of them, save herself, visited on a regular basis, that was most compelling. Even though Thomas hadn't been to the house in thirty years, he had asked about it numerous times during his phone conversations with Helen. Who was doing the maintenance? Were the taxes still rising at an alarming rate? He told Helen that he missed the place and would get back soon. But it hadn't happened, until now.

"You think I was wrong to put out the ultimatum."

"We've had this discussion."

"We seem to be having it again," said Claire, pushing the cotton blanket Helen had laid on her without asking off her lap and onto the floor.

Helen poured more tea into her mug. Claire's mug was still three-quarters full. "Everyone, including Thomas, would have come anyway."

"I had to be sure," said Claire. "But you're right. I think Thomas would have come no matter what. If not to see me, he'd certainly come to see you. He was always very good to you, Helen. He loved you dearly—still does, I would imagine." She sipped her tea. "He wasn't as good to your older sister."

"I think that's because they're closer in age."

"Fiddlesticks," said Claire. "I think it's because she's Charlotte."

"You may have a point there," said Helen.

"Oh, I've got a point all right, a point I've been meaning to make for a while."

Helen shifted in her chair and directed her gaze firmly at her mother. She wasn't sure where their conversation was headed, but its sudden twist interested her. Charlotte's behavior was something her parents had always acknowledged and punished, but never discussed with their other children. "Your older sister," said Claire, "put every gray hair on my head, put the anger in my voice, and put the creak in these old bones. She's exhausted me, mentally and physically, and yet I still fight. I'm not over the anger, even after all these years, at the selfish way she chose—chooses—to live her life." Helen moved from her chair to the chair closer to her mother. She put her hand over Claire's. "Don't patronize me, Helen. I want to talk."

"I know you do."

"I never understood her. I still don't," said Claire. "Walking in here, into our family house, with a teenager for a boyfriend. Growing up, she never listened to me, or your father for that matter. And that broke his heart. He was ashamed of her behavior, and I didn't blame him. But he blamed himself. He searched and searched for something to be proud of, and when he found it, he encouraged it. Lord, he went to every one of her track meets her freshman year in high school, but that wasn't good enough. She quit after one season, started smoking and fooling around with boys."

"You did what you could," said Helen, though she was convinced otherwise.

"I don't know if I did," said Claire. "I pushed her; I pushed all of you. Maybe I pushed her too hard."

Claire had, indeed, pushed too hard. She insisted Charlotte run track when she wanted to take art lessons instead. She pushed Thomas into baseball. He turned out to be very good at it, but Helen knew he felt that he fell short of his mother's goals. Knowing Pammy had little hand-eye coordination, Claire suggested she swim. But knowing she could never come close to performing the way her mother had in the pool, Pammy suggested volleyball instead. She was an average athlete on her best days and had to endure Claire's sitting at her games with a neutral look on her face and her arms crossed across her chest. Helen, by chance and with effort, was the best athlete of the family. And she sometimes wondered if that was why her mother gave her so much of her attention. As a child, Helen hadn't noticed the difference between the way she was treated and the way her siblings were treated. But she had seen it as an adult. She was the favorite—not in her father's eyes, as he was measured and fair and would, if asked, claim that he loved his children differently but equally. Helen was her mother's favorite, for her athletic abilities, for her proximity, for her willingness to act as caregiver, and the others knew it just as Helen did. Claire's favoritism had become even more pronounced after her husband's death—the voice of reason silenced.

Helen was tempted to speak—to point out to her mother the parenting mistakes Claire had made. It wasn't right to have a favorite child, just as it wasn't right to have a least favorite child. Her mother had treated Charlotte differently. In some ways, Helen thought Claire had given up on her oldest daughter—something Claire would never admit to. Charlotte didn't subscribe to Claire's mandate in life, and when Claire couldn't bend her, mold her like she had the others, she turned her back. John Thompson had never given up, but he couldn't do it alone, and he certainly couldn't influence Charlotte's behavior once she'd left the house for college. Like Thomas, Charlotte moved out at eighteen. Helen, the most moldable, pliant of the four, had rarely bucked or protested.

Claire sipped her tea. "I'm having trouble with this," she said. "She gives me pain, Helen. And I'm too old for that. I want to die loving my daughter."

Helen hesitated. Did she want to bring this up now? Did she want to tell her mother that she'd failed at raising her oldest daughter? Would it do anything other than hurt her mother's feelings? "Then do that," said Helen, resolved to keep her opinion to herself. "Let go of your anger. It won't change her, and it only hurts you. Charlotte hurts all of us, Mom, but I think she hurts herself the most."

Claire produced a weak smile for her daughter, and then lowered her head until it touched the back of the chair. She closed her eyes, tired again, even though she had been up just a short while. She was now often asleep more than she was awake during the day. And she looked exhausted.

Minutes later, Charlotte walked down the stairs and onto the porch. "Where's Daniel?" she asked.

"In town," said Helen. "He took all the kids to McDonald's. They were famished."

"Me too," said Charlotte, laying her hand against her flat stomach. "When's dinner?"

"Not for a while. Charles and Thomas went into town to get lobsters, and Pammy and Barb went to get the corn."

"In that case, where can a girl get a drink around here?"

"We'll have one just as soon as they get back," said Claire, who never had a drink before six. "We've got some wonderful hors d'oeuvres—the Brie is on the counter getting to room temperature. It won't be long."

Charlotte looked at her watch. "I'll have one now," she said, walking out of the porch and into the living room, "and another one with all of you when they get back. Helen, are there any unsalted almonds left?" By this time she was in the kitchen, looking for something to eat rather than a response from Helen.

"See? What is that, Helen? Where did I go wrong with her?" asked Claire, unable to let it rest.

"Charlotte chooses her own path."

"Yes, but why is her path so drastically different from yours, or Pammy's, or Thomas's?"

"I don't know."

"I tried to raise her the same way," said Claire, barely hearing Helen's reply. "She fought me from the outset. She became a terrible two at one and never came out of it."

"She's not terrible, Mom."

"She can be, Helen."

"Perhaps she's more misunderstood," Helen offered.

"She's no more misunderstood than the rest of us. She needs more attention than any one person or family can give her. I'm so tired of it all."

"I know you are, Mom," said Helen, getting up from her seat, signaling the end of the conversation, the end of her patience. "You sit here. I'm going to put the cheeses on a platter and fix the vegetable plate. And I will quickly wash the romaine lettuce for the Caesar salad."

"My favorite," said Claire.

"Mine, too."

"Do you need my help?"

"I always need your help," said Helen. "But today I'll manage without it."

Helen bent over to grab the tray holding the teapot and mugs; she lifted it to her waist and then walked out of the room. From her chair, Claire could see her walk through the living room and into the dining room before disappearing around the corner to the kitchen. Instantly lonely, she looked out the porch screens for something, someone other than Charlotte to occupy her thoughts. A young boy on a bicycle peddled furiously down the street, almost running over a cat on its way across. Then, a woman appeared at the top of the beach steps. When she got closer, Claire could see she was carrying a towel, a chair, and a red cloth bag. She wore a straw hat with an enormous brim, which rested on the top of her large circular sunglasses. The young woman looked into the porch as she walked by and then looked away. Claire waved as she always did, even though she had no idea who the woman was. The old guard was moving out, dying, and the new group was moving in, treating the beach as if they had always owned it.

"To Mother," said Thomas, raising his glass of wine at the dinner table. "Without you, we wouldn't be here."

"In more ways than one," said Charlotte.

The others chuckled amiably before clinking their glasses together and then eagerly digging into the bright red lobsters Thomas and Charles had boiled and split open. For a few minutes, no one talked. They were busy cracking shells and pulling out chunks of lobster, then dipping the sweet meat into the communal bowls of melted butter before popping it into their mouths. Helen disassembled her mother's lobster, casting the entire shell into the giant ceramic bowl at the center of the table.

Charlotte looked at Daniel, who smiled at her. She held his eyes with hers, then ran the tip of her tongue around the piece of lobster on her fork. He winked at her, and she back at him. Pammy, who was sitting next to Daniel, saw the exchange, and her spirits sank. Daniel had promised they would go for a walk that night, but now

Pammy doubted him. Charlotte would discourage him from venturing out alone, and she certainly wouldn't allow him to walk with her sister. And then Pammy felt it. Daniel put his hand on her leg and slid it toward her crotch. She reached for her wineglass and held it to her lips. She watched everyone at the table over the rim of the glass while she took a sip. They were all eating; even Charlotte seemed to be absorbed with her lobster, while Daniel was stroking her. Pammy put her wineglass down and picked up her fork. She tried to eat, but couldn't. All she wanted was to jump up from her seat onto Daniel's lap. She wanted to straddle him and let him run his hands all over her.

"Daniel," said Charlotte. They both started. Pammy knocked her wineglass over, which sent Daniel's fork flying through the air. It landed on Charlotte's plate with a loud clatter. Charlotte picked the fork up and handed it, slowly, back to her lover. "How was McDonald's, darling," she said, as if nothing had happened.

"Great," said Daniel, recovering instantly. "The kids had a great time." Pammy sopped up the spilled white wine with her napkin.

"And Daniel treated us," shouted Ned from the living room, where he, Todd, Sally, and Peter were playing Parcheesi. Ned was helping Peter, who was very good at counting but had no concept of strategy. Sally had caught on quickly. She had already set up a blockade that was foiling Todd's attempts at getting one of his pieces home.

"That was nice of you," said Helen to Daniel.

"You can thank me," said Charlotte. "It's my money he's spending, isn't it, dear?" She looked at Daniel.

"Technically, yes," he said.

"Oh, I just love it when you get technical," said Charlotte. "Actually, I'd love you to treat me, even though I'd actually be treating me, to McDonald's sometime. I'm just dying to try one of those Happy Meals to see if it works."

Thomas laughed. "You need a lot more than a cheeseburger and fries, dear sister, to find happiness."

"Daniel," said Charlotte. "A cheeseburger, fries, and Daniel. That's all I need."

Everyone except Pammy erupted with aahs and oohs, making Daniel, Charlotte, and Pammy blush.

"If you really believe that," said Thomas, "you're smarter than you look."

"I'm smarter than most people here realize," Charlotte said, meeting Pammy's eyes.

"You're a genius, Charlotte," said Thomas, tearing a front claw off his lobster. "Don't let anyone tell you differently."

"Why did we have to invite him?" Charlotte asked Helen.

"For Barb and the kids," Helen answered, winking at Thomas. "We wanted to see Barb and the kids."

"That's right," said Charlotte. "I knew there was some explanation."

Thomas raised his glass to his sister Charlotte. "It's nice to see you haven't changed."

"And equally nice to see that you have," she said, raising her glass.

"I love family reunions," said Helen, sentimentally.

"Except when it's our family," said Charlotte.

"Here's to Helen," said Thomas, raising his glass, serious again. "Thank you. Thank you for arranging this event. Thank you for bringing us all here. You are the core of the younger generation of Thompsons. Your energy and enthusiasm inspire us."

"Your speeches embarrass me," said Helen, hiding behind her wineglass.

"I do love you," he said. And the oohs and aahs burst forth again.

"If she asks, just tell her I'm in my room."

"I don't like this, Pammy," said Helen. "Charlotte's no fool."

"Will you do as I've asked?"

"Yes," said Helen. "I'll do it, but that doesn't mean I want to."

"You're an angel." Pammy kissed her sister on the cheek and snuck out the kitchen door into the night.

In the living room, Daniel waited for Charlotte to go to the bathroom. She always went several times between dinner and bed to do any number of tasks, including brushing her teeth, reapplying lipstick, brushing her hair, or gazing at her reflection to see that everything was just so. As soon as she left the room, Daniel stood and stretched. "I think I'll take a walk," he announced, as if delivering a line in a play.

He quickly walked through the porch and out the front door. On his way to the beach, he looked over his shoulder to see if Charlotte had returned. He could see nothing, however, except the lighted windows and the very top of Helen's head. Daniel ran down the cement stairs and looked in both directions. In the distance, he saw a lone figure, standing on the rocks. He waved, and Pammy waved back. Daniel took one last look over his shoulder and saw no one. He darted toward Pammy. When he reached her, he scooped her off her feet and into his arms. "All I can think about is you," he said, kissing her, and then walking her to the far end of the final set of cement steps. They led to a house whose windows were dark and shut tight.

"I know," she said, "because all I can think about is you." He lay her down in the sand, then stood before her. He pulled his shirt over his head and let it drop to the sand.

"Come down here," Pammy said. "I want you."

He unsnapped and unzipped his pants, then pushed them down his legs and kicked them aside.

"Where's Daniel?" said Charlotte, as she walked into the kitchen where Helen was getting more coffee.

"He went for a walk."

"Really?" she said. "He's gone for quite a few walks lately." Helen said nothing. "Where's Pammy?

"She went up," said Helen, concentrating on her coffee mug. "She's got a headache."

"That's too bad," said Charlotte, smiling, triumphant, not sad. "I'll bet she gets a lot of those."

"I wouldn't know," said Helen, walking past her sister toward the dining room.

"Maybe I'll go for a walk, too," said Charlotte to Helen's back. "Maybe I'll bump into him."

"Suit yourself." Helen let the swinging door close behind her.

Charlotte walked out the kitchen door and down the road toward the docks. She passed several walkers on her way and bid them all a good evening, but saw no sign of Daniel. Clearly, his crush on Pammy would have to be defused. Charlotte knew it would take more than sex, which she already gave to him too freely, too often. She would have to buy him something, or take him out to a very expensive dinner, or maybe to the symphony, or to a concert; his favorite band was coming to The Warfield. They could make a full night of it, with burgers and beer beforehand. She had to get him back to San Francisco. But there were temptations there, too, of course. She had been through this with him before, even though they had been together just six months. She had accepted it as being one of the drawbacks of her age. The other woman a couple months back, the object of his crush, had been twenty-four. And Charlotte, at forty-seven, with her wrinkled, lax skin and brittle, overprocessed hair, had been more upset about the younger woman's age than her presence. It was so hard to compete with the young ones. Yet, young men still stared at Charlotte, lusted after her body. In sunglasses, which she wore even on rainy days to hide the creases around her eyes, she could pass for a woman in her mid-thirties. But Pammy was forty-three, for God's sake. What was Daniel doing with her? Charlotte reached the first dock, wondering if she should dump Daniel instead of woo him back. The problem with younger men was just that; they were younger, immature, unpredictable—not like older men, men in their early fifties. And she knew that it wasn't fair to judge Daniel too harshly, as she, too, had entertained thoughts of entertaining other suitors. She fantasized about other men, married men even, with big enough bank accounts to more than satisfy her as well as their families. Charlotte reached the end of the dock and sat down, dangling her legs over the last board. She could actively pursue another relationship and find a replacement within days. She knew that. He knew that.

"Hi, Charlotte."

Startled, Charlotte quickly turned around to see who had spoken. Leaning against a piling was Steve Johanson. "God, you scared me," said Charlotte, standing.

"Come here," he said. "I want to show you something." Charlotte stood in front of Steve. "If you stand right here, you can see the lighthouse on the point." He put his hands on her shoulders and positioned her. In an instant, the light flashed in their direction, and then disappeared as quickly as it had come. "Five seconds," said Steve, still standing behind her. "It comes every five seconds."

"How about you?" asked Charlotte, turning around to face Steve.

"How about what?"

"How fast do you come?" She was inches from his face.

Steve pulled her to him, used his arm to press her body into his. He whispered in her ear. "Like molasses in January."

Charlotte laughed and stepped back. "God, you haven't changed."

"Neither have you," he said. "You were always the sexiest girl on the beach. You still are."

"You're sweet."

"I'm not sweet. I'm serious."

Charlotte stepped close to Steve again. Immediately, he wrapped his arms around her shoulders. "You were always so good with your hands," she said, encircling Steve's waist with her arms.

"I still am."

"Why aren't you using them now?" asked Charlotte, always the coquette.

"Because you haven't been completely honest with me."

"About what?"

"About that boy you've been kissing on the beach."

"Oh that," said Charlotte, putting on a pout. "He's nothing, and he's going to be even less than nothing after the weekend. We're through."

"Really?"

"Girl Scout's honor," said Charlotte, holding up her right hand, with her three middle fingers extended. Claire had been a Girl Scout leader and, consequently, all her girls had been in her troop at one time or another. Charlotte, the girl Claire thought needed the structure of the organization the most, lasted three meetings before quitting. Pammy and Helen weren't all that wild about the Scouts either, and Claire, who occasionally grew tired of orchestrating every waking moment of her children's lives, had eventually backed off.

"Come back to my house then. For a drink."

Charlotte took Steve's hand and started to walk slowly toward the street. At the end of the dock, Steve put his arm around Charlotte, cupping her bottom with his hand. Gently he messaged her cheek, making Charlotte giddy with anticipation. Currents of sensation ran through her body, electricity through wire. Steve barely got her through the back door of his house before she was upon him, unbuttoning his shirt. He broke free from her embrace. "Not here," he whispered. "Follow me." He led her up the stairs and into a large bedroom decorated in a soft gray. As Charlotte stood in the middle of the room, arms by her side, an errant schoolgirl waiting to be punished, Steve drew the curtains and turned on a low-wattage lamp sitting on a table next to the bed. He approached Charlotte, placing his hands on her hips. He kissed her, softly and lovingly, simultaneously freezing and melting Charlotte's insides. She was incapacitated. Time raced backward, sending a hundred images flying through Charlotte's mind. When it stopped, she was seventeen and Steve was telling her how much he loved her. She begged him to tell her again. He drew his head back and looked at her. "I love you," he said. "I always have."

Chapter 30

1973

Pammy hesitated a few seconds before she walked into Joe's Corner Store. She and Helen had walked the mile and a half to the end of Beach Road, then the half mile down Route 56 to get there. They sat on the curb in the parking lot, wondering if they should ask someone to help them, but finally decided to do it themselves. Pammy pulled a penny out of her pocket and flipped it in the air. "Heads," she said, as the coin fell back in her hand. It was tails. "Damn."

"I'll go," said Helen, standing and brushing the sand off the back of her shorts.

"You just won the toss, silly. You wait here. Come into the store only if you see anybody we know. Or if I'm not back in ten minutes."

Helen checked the time on her watch as Pammy walked in through the glass door covered with advertisements for cigarettes, milk, ice cream, and *The New York Times*. When Pammy's eyes had adjusted from the bright sunlight to the fluorescent lighting, she could see that there were three other people in the store: a matronly-looking woman buying milk; an old man studying dusty cans of soup; and a young man perusing car magazines. Pammy walked slowly to the magazine rack and picked up a copy of *Seventeen*. She flipped through it, looking at the pictures of healthy-looking teenage girls in fall clothing until the woman left, toting two half-gallon jugs, and the old man had made his selection and was walking two cans of Campbell's chicken noodle soup to the counter. She glanced up at the kid, who seemed to be immersed in his reading, and then put her magazine down. She walked back down the aisle and stood in line behind the soup-eater. When he left, Pammy took two quarters from her front pocket, one hers and the other Helen's, and the handwritten note; she handed them to the cashier. "What's this?" the wide woman behind the counter asked, unfolding the note. She reached for her glasses and, with one hand, placed them on her ears and nose.

"A note from my mom," said Pammy. She swallowed and then continued, saying, "concerning cigarettes."

"Well, she should be concerned about cigarettes," the cashier said while she glanced at the note that Pammy had so carefully scripted, disguising her handwriting. The cashier blew her nose with an already-used tissue she extracted from the front pocket of her stretch pants, all the while reading the note. She looked at Pammy, and then she read aloud: "Please allow my daughter, Pamela"—Pammy had used her given name, thinking it sounded more formal, would be more convincing, and Helen had agreed—"to purchase one pack of Marlboro cigarettes for me. If I were not in bed with a virus, I would come myself. Signed, Mrs. Doolittle." Pammy beamed. The note sure sounded authentic. The cashier looked up from the folded piece of paper and stared at Pammy. "How old are you?"

"I'm thirteen," said Pammy, beginning to get nervous again.

"And smoking cigarettes?"

"Oh, I've tried them," she said, taking the offensive, "but they're horrible. I coughed for three days. I don't know how my mom does it, with her virus and all."

The cashier nodded her head in consent and pulled, without looking, a pack of Marlboros down from the plastic rack above her head. She slid them over the counter toward Pammy and gave her another loaded look before handing her the change due. "Tell your mom to get better fast," she said. "Children like you, Miss Doolittle, shouldn't be running her cigarette errands."

"I certainly will," said Pammy, on her way out the door. And then, using one of her father's expressions, she said, "I think she's on the mend."

"Happy to hear it," said the clerk, who had already returned to her *True Romance* magazine.

Helen hopped up off the curb as soon as she saw Pammy. She ran over to her and asked if she got the cigarettes. "Play it cool," said Pammy. "I'm not sure that lady in there fell for the story."

Helen sneaked a peek at the store over her sister's shoulder. The woman behind the counter was staring out the window at them. "She's looking at us, Pammy."

"Turn around, for Pete's sake, Helen, and walk with me. Whatever you do, don't run. We'll look really guilty."

Pammy and Helen walked as fast as they could, arms pinned to their sides in an effort to prevent an inadvertent sprint. As soon as they were out of the parking lot, out of the cashier's line of vision, they both bolted, pumping their arms, across Route 56 and onto Beach Road. They didn't stop until they rounded the corner, where they collapsed into the vacant meadow. "What happened?" asked Helen, as soon as she caught her breath.

"The cashier didn't like it." Pammy was breathing hard. "She smelled something phony, but couldn't put her finger on it." She inhaled deeply. "It was the note, I think, that really sold her. That note was a masterpiece."

"What did she say?" Helen was hoping for details.

"She asked me how old I was."

"Did you tell her?"

"Of course I told her, Helen. Being thirteen is not a crime."

"Then what?"

"Then she said stuff like, 'tell you mother to get better soon,' and 'you shouldn't be doing errands like this, Miss Doolittle.' "

"She called you Miss Doolittle?"

"She did," said Pammy. "In Joe's Corner Store, I'm Miss Doolittle from now on."

"I kind of like that," said Helen. "Miss Doolittle. It sounds dignified."

"Let's go," said Pammy. "We've got to get back, then hide these until it gets dark."

When they got back, Thomas, who had just finished mowing the lawn, asked them where they had been.

"To Joe's," said Pammy, matter-of-factly.

"That's a long haul," said Thomas, rolling the grass-plastered mower toward the garage. "I would have given you a ride."

"That's okay. We needed the exercise."

"Since when have you given a monkey's butt about exercise?" said Thomas, smiling at Pammy.

"Since this morning." Pammy walked past her brother and into the house.

"What did you buy?" Thomas asked Helen, who still stood on the grass, trying to anticipate his questions and, like Pammy, think up snappy answers.

"Gum," said Helen. "Strawberry gum."

"I'd love a piece."

"We don't have any," said Helen. "I mean, we chewed it all."

"On the way home?"

"Yep, on the way home."

Thomas took Helen's hand in his sweaty palm and led her to the picnic table. He sat her down and then sat down next to her. "Cigarettes are bad for you, Helen."

"Charlotte smokes them."

"Case in point," said Thomas. "She should quit."

"We don't plan on making it a habit."

"Did you buy them at Joe's, Helen?"

"Yes." Helen wasn't a good liar, especially with Thomas.

"How did you get them?"

"Pammy wrote a note," said Helen, looking at her brother. "It said her mother was sick in bed with a virus and Pammy was getting the cigarettes for her." Thomas laughed. "It worked," said Helen, defiant. "The cashier even called Pammy Miss Doolittle."

"Miss Doolittle?"

"We decided not to use our real name."

"Of course not," said Thomas, still smiling. "When's the big smoke out?"

"Tonight," said Helen. "After Mom and Dad go to bed."

"I'll go with you," said Thomas, getting up. "I'll get Eddie to come. He's a professional. We'll meet at eleven o'clock at the duck pond." Thomas walked in the house and up the stairs to his room. He took off his damp shirt and shorts, then wrapped a towel around his naked body. Before he headed outside to retrieve his swim suit from the clothesline, he stuck his head into Pammy and Helen's room. Pammy was lying on the bottom bunk. "Hello, Miss Doolittle."

Pammy's mouth opened up into an O. Then she said, "Helen."

Thomas held up one hand. "Not to worry, Miss Doo. Your secret is safe with me, until tonight."

Pammy sat up on the bed. "What's happening tonight?"

"Ask the tattletale."

After delivering pizzas and before collapsing into bed, Thomas sometimes met his friends at the duck pond wall. Some smoked cigarettes; others sipped beers stolen from their parents' garage fridges. Talking was the dominant activity, and flirting comprised ninety percent of the talking. He was completely unclear about the rules on touching, and he abhorred the conversation, which seemed contrived as well as stupid. So Thomas was more an observer than a participant. Plus, he still loved Anna. He hadn't seen or talked to her since the night outside the pizza restaurant, but rarely a daylight hour passed that he didn't think about her. He often thought about her at night, too, when he awoke unexpectedly. He tried not to talk about her, mostly because Eddie had told him to stop. Eddie had said he was tired of listening to a hopeless fairy tale, and that Anna was just a girl, a girl who had said no. Thomas had to let her go, Eddie told him. Thomas tried to follow Eddie's advice, which he knew was good advice, but it was hard for him. Whenever he made time to sit on the wall, he made an effort to talk to the girls. But they were babies, and his heart wasn't in it. And they knew that as well as he did.

That night, as part of the game, the boys and girls started the evening in separate camps. Soon enough, an ambassador from the girls' assemblage approached the boys, looking for matches. One of the boys dutifully produced a book from his pocket and handed it to the girl. As the minutes passed, the errands and requests became more and more farcical, until the groups abandoned all pretenses and simply merged. By eleven o'clock that night, fifteen kids were congregated at the spot on the duck pond wall where Pammy and Helen were to meet Thomas. He saw them, from a distance, standing under the giant bushes that lined one side of the right of way. Since they had snuck out of the house, they avoided the streetlight. Realizing it had been foolish to ask his sisters to approach his peers, he elbowed Eddie, who was sitting next to him. "Let's go, Eddie," said Thomas, standing. Eddie, who was talking to Christine, whom he had lately taken to calling his intended, didn't answer. "Eddie," Thomas said again.

Eddie groaned loudly. "I'm coming."

He removed his arm from Christine's shoulders and stood. "Where are you going?" she asked him.

"On a mercy mission," he said. "Say good-bye to my family."

Several in the group laughed, including Thomas, who had taken a few steps in the direction of his sisters. "I know," said Thomas, as soon as they were out of earshot of the group. "I owe you."

"It's okay," said Eddie. "All night, I've been trying to picture Helen smoking."

Pammy and Helen had moved out from under the bushes and into the street. A cool sea breeze blew their hair onto their faces, into their eyes. It was welcome after the heat of the day, the burn of the sun and the sand. They sat down—hardly anyone ever drove around the streets at night—and busied themselves with the shiny pack of cigarettes. Since it was just about smoking time, Pammy decided to remove the cellophane wrap.

"Why do they put that stuff on there, anyway?" Helen asked Pammy, who was bumbling the job.

"I'll be damned if I know," said Pammy in frustration. "Here, you try it." She tossed the pack to her sister. Helen, holding the

Marlboros up to her face, found the pull-tab and unwrapped the box with ease.

"It's just like a pack of gum, Pammy. See?" said Helen, holding up the thin ribbon of plastic.

"So it is," said Pammy, taking the pack back from Helen.

"Evening ladies," said Eddie, standing over them.

Even though they had seen the boys coming, Pammy started when Eddie spoke, dropping the pack she had just opened and spilling the cigarettes onto the pavement. Scrambling to pick them up quickly, as if swiftly completing the task might eradicate its occurrence, Pammy stuffed the cigarettes back into the box.

"Let me hold them for you," said Thomas, holding out his hand. "My pockets are probably bigger than yours." Pammy gave the pack to her brother, looking up at him expectantly. "This way," he said, indicating with his head the road that dead-ended at the woods. Pammy and Helen never ventured into the woods because Thomas had told them stories over the years that involved supernatural happenings there. They had not even been tempted to enter in daylight, in spite of the fact that all Thomas's tales involved people who wandered into the woods after dark. "Eddie knows a place where no one will find us."

They walked in silence, Thomas and Eddie leading and Pammy and Helen walking side by side behind them. At a break in the wood post and wire fence, they turned off the road and onto a dirt path that led into the trees and overgrown, unattended bushes. "Don't we need a flashlight?" asked Pammy, feeling like her stomach had flipped over.

"Eddie knows the way," said Thomas. "Follow in my footsteps."

"Like I can see your footsteps, Thomas." Pammy was trying to be tough, but Helen could tell Pammy was as frightened as she was.

Thomas said nothing until they came to a clearing. The moon shone down into the space, which was outlined by logs and empty cans of Budweiser and Schlitz. He and Eddie sat down and instructed Pammy and Helen to do the same. "Here are the rules," Eddie began. "I don't like to waste cigarettes, and neither should you. So, when you set out to smoke a cigarette, you're going to finish it. I don't want to see either of you taking a few drags, coughing your fucking heads off. . . ."

"I thought you were trying not to swear so much," said Helen.

"And I've been doing pretty good, until just now."

"Shouldn't it be well?" asked Pammy, uncertain herself.

"Don't start that grammar shit with me, Miss Doolittle. Thomas already drives me crazy," said Eddie. "Okay, where were we?"

"Coughing our bleeping heads off," said Thomas, legs stretched out in front of him, ankles crossed.

"Right," said Eddie. "No matter how much you may want to pitch your cigarette, you must hold on to it. We don't need to start any fires tonight. Understood?" Helen nodded her head. Pammy was looking at Helen, newly cheesed at her sister for telling Thomas about the Doolittle thing since he had obviously told Eddie. "Pammy? Pay attention." Pammy shifted her gaze to Eddie. "Next, everybody's going to inhale. This is a chosen activity, not something you were forced into, so we're not going to be crybabies about this. Breathe the smoke into your lungs—it may burn a bit at first—then slowly let it out. You may feel dizzy, or you may feel sick to your stomachs, but you are to continue until the cigarette has been smoked down to the filter." Thomas looked at his sisters, their widening eyes illuminated by the yellow light cast by Eddie's BIC lighter. "Now," Eddie continued, catching the pack Thomas tossed at him, "you've got twenty cigarettes, and I've got"—he removed his pack from his shirt pocket—"six, seven, eight. That's makes twenty-eight. We're going to sit here until they're gone. I'll smoke more than you two because I've been practicing, but you two must pull your weight. I figure you smoke, let's say seven each, you've smoked your share. Any questions before we start?" Eddie stuck a cigarette in his mouth and held the lighter to its end.

"Wait!" Helen said, a little too loudly. Eddie pulled the lighter away from the cigarette and looked at Helen. "I didn't really plan on having seven."

"No?" asked Thomas, feigning surprise. "How many did you want to have?"

"I thought I'd play it by ear," said Helen, using an expression she thought was grown-up. "I thought I'd just try it, but if I didn't like it, I could stop."

"Stop?" asked Thomas. "How are you ever going to learn to smoke if you stop after one, or half of one?"

"She's right," said Pammy, feeling bolder now that Helen had spoken. "We don't want to smoke seven."

Eddie recounted the cigarettes. They all watched him. "How about six then?" he asked.

"No," said Pammy, a quaver in her voice.

"Five?" asked Thomas, persistent.

"No," said Pammy, standing up. "I don't want any."

"Me neither," said Helen, also standing.

They all waited a few moments in silence. Thomas stood. "Let's go, then."

The boys led the way out of the woods. Pammy and Helen followed closely behind. Hearing noises around them, Helen reached for and then held Pammy's hand. Pammy did not pull it away or protest, like she sometimes did if she thought anyone would see them. "Are you mad, Thomas?" asked Pammy, when they reached the street.

"Why would I be mad?"

"Because we didn't smoke," said Helen.

"Actually, I'm glad you didn't smoke."

"You are?" Pammy was incredulous.

"Absolutely."

Pammy looked at Eddie, who was standing next to her. "Look," said Eddie, resting his arm for a moment on the top of Pammy's head, "smoking is a lousy habit. I started when I was your age, Pammy, because I wanted to be cool. I wanted to belong to a group of people who all smoked. And now I'm hooked and can't mow the lawn without coughing and breathing hard. I'm nineteen years old. How sad it that?" Thomas and Helen looked at him, too. "My best advice to you is never start. Live above the temptation."

"You run home now," Thomas said to Helen and Pammy. "It's late."

"Are you coming?" asked Helen.

"I'll be along soon. Can you sneak in okay?"

"No problem," said Pammy. "Helen could sneak into the White House." Thomas and Eddie laughed, and Pammy was pleased.

"Run home now," said Thomas.

Pammy and Helen took off at a jog down the street. Less than a hundred yards from her brother and his friend, Pammy stopped. "I need to rest, Helen," she said, out of breath. Helen slowed down and walked next to her sister. "Well," said Pammy, "that's the last time we get Thomas to help us smoke. I can't believe he wanted us to smoke seven cigarettes. I'll bet Charlotte would only make us try a puff."

"You're going to ask Charlotte?" asked Helen.

"I might."

"Why?"

"I want to try it," said Pammy. "It looks like fun."

"Pammy, if you can't run a hundred yards and you don't smoke, how far will you be able to run if you do?"

Pammy looked at Helen. "Good point," she said.

A minute later, Pammy said she was ready to run again. They jogged the rest of the way home. Thomas and Eddie walked slowly toward the duck pond. They could see the wall and the outline of its nocturnal teenage inhabitants. "Thank you," Thomas said to Eddie. "You were perfect."

"It was your plan, Thomas. It worked like a charm. Hell, it almost worked on me."

"Yeah?"

"Almost," said Eddie, lighting a cigarette. "Maybe I'll quit."

"That would be good."

"I could start tomorrow," Eddie offered tentatively.

"You could start tomorrow."

"Tomorrow it is then," said Eddie, taking another drag.

They walked several more steps in silence before Thomas said, "I'm going to peel off here, Eddie."

"Yeah?"

"I have the early bakery run."

Eddie looked at his watch. "A half hour, Thomas," he said. "Hang out for thirty fucking minutes. I think Cheryl's got a thing for you."

"Too bad I don't have a thing for her."

"Oh, but you do!" Eddie laughed.

"You are disgusting."

Eddie took a drag from his cigarette. "I speak the truth, Thomas. I speak the fucking truth."

"You may speak the truth, but I'm not giving my thing to Cheryl."

"You gotta give it to somebody, Thomas. You gotta give it to somebody other than Anna."

"Not now," Thomas said. "Not yet."

Chapter 31

2003

Claire woke in the night. Like an animal in the jungle, she quickly surveyed her surroundings, getting her bearings. She moved her heavy legs to the side of the bed, and then forced them over the edge. She lifted with effort her upper body to a sitting position, and then sat, resting. Grabbing her walker from the wall beside her, she lifted herself off the bed. Determined, she moved toward her door by placing the walker out in front of her and then carefully shuffling her feet to catch up to it. She opened the door on her first attempt, an anomaly since the knob had been tightened so many times over the years it was perpetually loose. *I must get up in the night more often,* she said to herself. *I'm superhuman*. However, at the end of the hallway loomed the insurmountable obstacle to the fulfillment of her craving for Barb's oatmeal cookies and cold milk: the stairs. She sat on the top landing, defeated.

"Gainzer?" Her grandchildren, at her request, called her the name she had been called by her teammates so many years before.

Claire stared at the boy at the bottom of the stairs. Every body part had betrayed her except her eyes. "Ned, what are you doing up?"

"I heard you, I guess. What are you doing?" Ned and Todd, who were sleeping on the porch on blow-up mattresses (even though they could have slept on the pullout in the den, since Thomas and his family had chosen to stay in the motel, and Helen and Charles were now sleeping in Thomas's room) had just closed their eyes after a marathon game of Risk. Todd had won, as he always did, and Ned had been sulking, giving his brother the silent treatment. Ned was waiting for Todd to launch into a recap of the game, of Todd's strategy, of his reinforced armies, of everything he had done right and Ned had done wrong. It was always this way. Ned hated the game, but played because his brother called him a baby until he did. But tonight the words hadn't come. Todd met Ned's silence with silence. Within minutes, Todd's even breathing told Ned he was asleep. When his grandmother spoke to him, Ned climbed the stairs.

"I'll tell you what I'm doing," said Claire. "I'm wishing I had my old legs back."

"The legs that could kick you to the raft in less than a minute?" asked Ned, repeating the story that his mother had told to him many times since his early childhood.

"Those very legs."

"My legs still work pretty good," he said. "Do you want me to use them to get you something?"

Claire was proud of herself for not correcting her grandson's poor grammar. Instead, she said, "Sit down, Ned." He sat on the step beneath her and looked up into her face expectantly. While it was dark outside, the streetlight shone in through the porch screens and cottage windows, partially illuminating the staircase and Claire's wizened face. "Do you know what I was thinking?"

"No," he said.

"I was thinking how good some of your Aunt Barb's oatmeal cookies and milk would taste about now."

"No kidding?"

"No kidding."

"That is an excellent thought, Gainzer, but we finished off Aunt Barb's cookies after dinner."

"So, we did," said Claire, remembering. "What else do we have? Any more of Aunt Pammy's brownies?"

"Gone," said Ned. "Daniel ate the last one after the cookies were gone."

"Bummer," said Claire, using a word she'd heard her grandsons say.

Ned thought for a moment. "Would chocolate do it?"

"Where did we get the chocolate?"

"Daniel brought it."

"What kind?"

"One of those big yellow boxes, with the map on the inside of the top that tells you what's in each piece."

"Well, that was nice of him," said Claire. "Yes. That might do the trick."

"You wait here," said Ned, stating the obvious. "I'll be back in a flash."

Claire pushed herself back against the wall and rested her head against it. In an instant, Ned was back, holding a two-pound box of Whitman's chocolates. He sat down and handed it to his grandmother, who removed the lid. Not one piece was missing. Each chocolate, some milk and some dark, sat nestled in its own plastic cubby, waiting to be found on the diagram and then devoured by the person who sought a chewy caramel or a nougat center. It was like a treasure hunt in a box. Claire chose a dark oval with vanilla crème inside. "This," she said, biting into it, "is my absolute favorite." She held out the box to him. Ned chose a milk chocolate square. They both chewed for a few moments. "How do you feel about some milk?"

"That's a great idea," said Ned, standing. "I'll be right back." And within minutes he was back, carrying two tall glasses of milk.

"You are a speed demon," said Claire. "No wonder you beat everyone you meet on the tennis court. I need to hear all about your match with the Fischer twins."

As instructed, Ned started with the first serve of the first game and ended with the glorious overhead smash that sent the twins scrambling for the back fence. Claire listened intently, often interrupting to compliment her grandson on his excellent footwork or racket awareness, encouraging him to practice more, to enter tournaments in the town they both lived in, to compete. And in the middle of the night, Ned believed her, believed that he could win his age group, even though he knew his brother, Todd, carried their team, that he was the better player. But Ned could almost believe he was better than his brother—on some days he actually was—when the house was quiet, when the competition was sleeping.

They had several more chocolates each before Claire put her hand to her stomach. "Oh, I think I've had enough."

"Me too." Ned looked down at the box. They had eaten half of the top layer.

"Can you help me up?"

Ned set the box aside, stood, and then put both hands out for his grandmother to hold. Once he had her hands in his, he pulled her up. She was lighter than he expected. He helped turn her around in the hallway and situated her walker. He walked behind her as she made her way to her bedroom. Once she was seated on the bed, she told him she would be able to do the rest by herself. "You've been a big help," she said. "I'm glad you were awake to come to my rescue."

"You don't need anyone to rescue you," he said.

Claire opened her arms to him, and he walked into them for a hug. "Get to sleep now," she said. "Tomorrow is another busy day." Ned turned and left the room. She heard him descend the stairs and then focused her attention on getting back into her bed. She lay back and then lifted her legs, as flexible as two steel rods, onto the bed. She had lost so much of her strength. Her physical therapist told her she was "doing well," but she knew it was a sham. He said that to all the old people, she guessed, who had one day amounted to something, but were now reduced to a series of diminished percentages. The only thing Clare Gaines Thompson was a hundred percent capable of doing was not dying yet. And those days, no matter what Helen said, were coming to an end.

A couple months ago, this realization permeated Claire's outer layer, the layer she worked so hard to maintain. Her oncologist started using the word *weeks* instead of *months,* and Claire had broken down. Helen had dropped her at home and was running a few errands before their lunch together, so Claire thought her tears would go unnoticed. But Helen had returned early, excited about their forthcoming grilled cheeses and tomato soup, and found her mother in a heap on the kitchen floor. "Doing well," Claire was smart enough to know, meant just the opposite. And it was that very day that Claire told Helen to call her siblings and get them to the cottage for the Fourth of July.

Downstairs, Ned slipped into his sleeping bag. It was oddly chilly for a summer night, and he shivered, and then drew the flannel bag up to his neck.

"Where have you been?" Todd rolled over and looked at him.

"With Gainzer. At the top of the stairs."

"Is she okay?"

"I think so. I helped her back to her bedroom. She ate a bunch of chocolates."

"That's good," said Todd.

"Remember when she used to eat peanut butter and jelly sandwiches like nobody's business?"

"Yeah. She made them on that squishy white bread and raced us. She'd have three or four down the hatch, as she used to say, before we finished our first one. I was six," said Todd, "and you were four."

"And she'd tell us crummy jokes and get us laughing so hard we couldn't eat. What's a shark's favorite game?"

"Swallow the leader," Todd said. "What kind of cheese isn't yours?"

"Nacho cheese," said Ned, grinning. "Hey, I told her all about our tennis match with the Fischers."

"What'd she say?"

"She said it sounded like we played like champions and that she was really proud." Todd said nothing. "Todd?" said Ned.

"I think Gainzer is really sick."

"Yeah. Mom told us her cancer came back. But she's doing the chemo again, right? And that worked last time, Mom said."

"I heard Mom telling Dad that Gainzer was not doing chemo anymore."

Ned shifted in his sleeping bag, so he was on his side, facing Todd. "So, that means she's better, right?"

"Does she look better to you?" Ned could see the whites of Todd's eyes, looking at him.

"No," said Ned, flipping onto his back. "But she was wide-awake tonight. Full of energy."

"That's good." Todd rolled over, away from his brother. "Let's go to sleep now."

But Todd stayed awake, thinking about his grandmother. She had taught him to play Go Fish and checkers and Monopoly. She had been the first to see him ride a two-wheeler. And she had told scary, fabulous, ridiculous stories at their dinner table—still did.

"Todd?"

"Yeah?"

"She'll be okay."

"Good night, Ned," said Todd, closing his eyes.

The picture of his grandmother at their dining room table faded from his mind. Soon, nothing was left but a tiny circle of light surrounded by darkness. His grandmother's face filled that circle, and Todd focused on it, willing it to grow, to push back the blackness. But it shrank, and seconds later she was gone.

Helen lay next to Charles on Thomas's bed for a full five minutes after waking up, looking at the full moon through the window over her head, before getting out of bed. She looked back at Charles, who was sleeping soundly. She slipped her bathrobe over her T-shirt and headed for the open door. Charlotte and Pammy liked their bedroom doors closed at night, but Helen usually had hers open, allowing the breeze to circulate around the room and into the hallway. She walked slowly and quietly down the hall to her mother's room and gently opened the door. She went inside and shut the door behind her. "Mother?" she said to the small, lumpy figure on the bed. Claire, cast in the pale yellow glow from the streetlight on the corner, lay still and silent. "Mother?" Helen said again, moving closer to the bed so she could touch her.

"I'm awake," Claire said suddenly. "Come sit with me." Helen sat down on the bed that her grandmother had slept in as a child. It groaned under her weight. "What are you doing up?" Claire rolled over to face her daughter.

"I heard you and Ned talking on the landing."

"I'm sorry we woke you."

"Don't be," said Helen, now looking at her mother's face. "You took the time to sit and talk to him, which means more to him than you may realize."

"I'm glad to hear that," said Claire. "We devoured half of Daniel's chocolates."

"Good for you."

"Your Ned is becoming quite a tennis player, I think," said Claire.

"They both are."

"You've taught them well."

"Too well," said Helen, smiling. "They want to beat Charles and me next. I think they just might."

"You've taught them many good things, Helen. They're wonderful children."

"Most of the time."

"All of the time," said Claire. "And you've taken good care of me."

"It's my pleasure to be with you, Mom."

"Some of the time."

"All of the time," said Helen, putting her hand on her mother's shoulder.

They were silent again, until Claire swallowed. "I've left this house to you," she said.

"I know," said Helen. "But after this weekend, we're changing your will, right?"

"Part of the will, yes," said Claire. "The money will be evened out. But the house belongs to you. You're the one who cares about this old place."

"Mother," said Helen, squeezing her mother's hand, "we don't need to talk about this."

"Yes, we do." Claire was insistent.

"I thought we had an agreement. That if Thomas and Charlotte and Pammy came this weekend that you would leave the house to all of us."

"And we did have an agreement. But I've changed my mind."

"After they all showed up?"

"So I should recognize and reward their greed?" Helen sighed. "And besides, that's not why they showed up anyway, Helen. They came because they know I'm dying. And no matter what I've done to hurt them over the years, I've managed to teach them the importance of saying good-bye. They didn't have that—none of us did—with your father. And I don't think they wanted to miss their chance with me. Plus, you told them, Helen. You told them my time was short."

"Yes."

"That's why they're here. They're here to see me and to see one another. They're here to be with you. They're not here for the house, Helen."

"They'll be hurt, Mom."

Claire shook her head from side to side. "I don't think so. They know what you've done for me—the past year especially—so they should understand. They have been absent from my life, Helen, and you have been present."

"It's easy when you live in the same town."

Claire held up her hand. "Don't start in with that. Caring for me has been anything but easy. And you have done so with nary a complaint. You deserve this house, Helen, and that's the way it's going to be. Your siblings will come to understand my decision, if they don't right away. In the end, you and your family use this house, and they don't. I'm sure if they want to, you'll let them. Nothing will really change. You'll just have to pay the taxes." Helen smiled at her mother. "Don't fret about this, Helen. I think I've made the right decision. I think your father would have agreed with me. And besides, it's all taken care of."

"You take care of things well," said Helen. "You've always taken good care of me."

"You were always easy to take care of," said Claire, as close to tears as Helen had seen her in weeks. "You were always a source of great strength to me. You still are. And this house should be with you. You are the center of this family. You're the reason Thomas, Pammy, and Charlotte are even here."

"They're here for you, Mother," said Helen softly.

"At your request, Helen. Hold them together. Use this cottage as a gathering place and bring them to you and keep them with you. Family is everything. And I know you know that, but I just wanted to have a chance to tell you again before I go."

"You're not going anywhere." Helen swallowed hard.

"We're all going," said Claire, "some of us a little faster than others. I'm not afraid. I'm ready, actually. I miss your father so."

"I miss him, too."

"Well, then I'll tell him you say hello."

Helen smiled. "You do that, Mother."

"Good night, Helen," said Claire. "Sleep tight now."

"You too," said Helen, standing. "I love you."

"Yes, as I do you."

Helen walked out of her mother's room and back into hers. She got into bed and lay close to Charles. Putting her head against his chest, Helen heard his heart beating. Listening to him breathe, she eventually fell asleep.

CHAPTER 32

1973

Claire Gaines pulled off her tan linen shorts and red T-shirt and kicked off her Birkenstock sandals and then slipped on her white tennis skirt and white Lacoste shirt. She checked her watch. It was ten minutes shy of five o'clock. Grabbing her sneakers and white socks, she ran down the stairs and out the kitchen door and onto the lawn. There she found Thomas, Charlotte, and Pammy, the very three people she was to play tennis with, in now fewer than ten minutes, sitting on the picnic table in their wet bathing suits. "Who are you playing with, Mom?" Thomas asked when she sat down with them.

"You," said Claire, pointing her index finger at Thomas, "and you and you." She pointed her finger at Charlotte and then at Pammy. Thomas's response was to stare at his mother, while Charlotte and Pammy exchanged confused glances. "I told you this morning." Claire sat on the picnic table bench and pulled on her socks. "We have the court from five to six thirty, and it's almost five now."

Pammy and Thomas made unpleasant-looking faces, but hopped off the table and went into the house to change. Charlotte didn't budge. "I'm not playing," she said.

"Oh yes, you are." Claire slid her socked feet into her Tretorn sneakers.

"I hate tennis."

"I'll see you on the court in five minutes or you'll be grounded for the rest of the week." Claire stood.

"You're so unfair," Charlotte protested, standing.

"Life isn't fair, Charlotte. The sooner you learn that the better."

Charlotte hesitated for a moment, studying the chipped pink polish on her fingernails. She looked back at her mother. "Where's Helen?"

"She's at Susan's house." Claire tied her laces into double knots.

"Why can she be at a friend's house and I have to play tennis?" Charlotte was stalling now. Claire didn't have, never had, patience with those who stopped progress. Everyone in Claire's world was expected to suck up whatever was bothering them and move forward.

"Get changed, Charlotte. I'll see you on the court in five minutes."

Charlotte walked into the house and up the stairs to her room, her new room. She had talked her parents into letting her paint and decorate the bedroom she had inhabited since early childhood, with its inherited furnishings, sun-streaked curtains, and dusty wool rug. She was tired of living like an eighty-year-old woman, she told Claire and John. She needed to make the space her own. She showed them the shade of lavender she had chosen at the paint store to coat the dark pine-paneled walls and the fabric she would sew into curtains to hang at the windows. After hearing her pitch, Claire and John told her it was okay with them as long as she finished once she started. If chores were an indication of Charlotte's ability to follow-through, they suspected she would paint half the room and then quit, called away by her latest boyfriend for a boat ride or to a party. To Charlotte's credit, she had finished the painting in two days, and had done an admirable job. Claire was pleased to see some domesticity in her oldest daughter. While Claire was much more concerned with her children's sense of independence and competence, she was smart enough to know that most women, at some point in their lives, would have to cook for themselves, cook for a family. Claire considered proficiency in the kitchen a plus rather than a minus, a strength instead of a weakness. Other women complained about being chained to their stoves, but Claire viewed cooking as a competition, another skill she could master and control.

The finishing touch on Charlotte's room was a hand-painted sign that read KNOCK BEFORE YOU ENTER. Thomas blew right past the sign and into her room, mostly to tell her that it looked pretty good. But before he could compliment her, she screamed at him to get out. And then she forbade him to ever again set foot over the threshold without permission. *Oh heartbreak,* Thomas had said from the hallway where he had retreated. *Now I'll have to go to the store to get condoms.* Charlotte called him immature and insensitive. Thomas had said he was plenty sensitive. *For example,* he had said, *I already know you're almost out of tampons and will have to dash to the store soon, as you must be expecting your period any moment.* With that comment, Charlotte slammed the door.

Her wet bathing suit on the floor, Charlotte sat naked on her vanity stool. She peered into the mirror, looking for the courage to tell her mother to stuff it. "Fuck off, Mother," Charlotte said. "I've never liked tennis, and I never will. You can take your dreams of my winning the club championships and flush them down the toilet." Charlotte checked her watch. She had two minutes to get to the tennis court. She pulled on underwear, shorts, and a pink tank top, knowing that her mother would be furious at her for 1) not wearing a bra, and 2) disregarding the white-clothing-only rule imposed by the association that maintained the two clay courts available to beach residents for an annual fee. She grabbed her sneakers and ran out of the house.

"Here she comes," Thomas announced when he saw his sister rounding the corner onto Seaside Avenue, the street that connected the tennis courts and modest clubhouse to the beach and the Sound. He was surprised by the fact that she was jogging.

As soon as Charlotte was in Claire's line of vision, she slowed her pace to a walk. She sat down on the grass next to the tennis court and tied her sneakers, and then pulled her hair back in a ponytail and secured it with a plastic barrette. "I'm playing under protest," she said, standing.

"You live life under protest," said Thomas, sending a forehand flying over the net toward his mother.

"Thank you for coming, Charlotte," said Claire.

"As if I had any choice."

"You want forehand or backhand?" asked Thomas.

"Forehand."

Thomas hit another ball over the next, this time to Pammy, who missed it. "Bad choice. You've got backhand."

"What a gentleman," said Charlotte, walking past Thomas to her relegated position on the court.

"Everybody ready?" asked Claire.

"Are you kidding me, Mother? I just got here," said Charlotte. "How could I possibly be ready?"

"You missed warm-up," said Claire.

"For God's sake," said Charlotte. "Somebody hit me one ball."

Pammy hit a ball crosscourt to Charlotte. She swung tenaciously, sending it flying into the air and back over the net, where it landed way out of bounds.

"Looks like you're extra warmed up," said Thomas, smiling.

"Looks like you're still an asshole," Charlotte whispered to him.

"What was that?" Claire shouted from the other side of the net.

"Strategy," said Charlotte.

"*M* or *W*," Claire called, spinning her Wilson tennis racket in the air.

"S!" Charlotte shouted impetuously.

Claire stopped the spinning racket in her hand and looked at Thomas. "Just ignore her, Mom," Thomas said.

"*M* or *W?*"

"M," Thomas said.

"It's *W,*" said Claire. "We'll serve."

She took a yellow tennis ball out of her pocket and tossed it to Pammy, who stood at the baseline in anticipation. She caught it, dropped it, and then stopped to pick it up and put it into her pocket with the other ball. She looked across the net at Thomas. "First ball in!" she called. "FBI!"

"CIA!" shouted Charlotte in return.

"Why not," Thomas called back, ignoring his partner. Three seconds later, a ball went screaming past his left ear and hit the fence without touching the ground. "The speed's pretty good," Thomas yelled, "but you're going to have to work on placement." Pammy made a face at her brother. She tossed another ball into the air and hit it just as hard as the first. It bounced off Thomas's head. "Check on placement!"

Charlotte laughed.

"Okay," Claire said over her shoulder to Pammy. "That's enough fooling around, Pammy. You can do this. Just put the ball in the box, okay?"

Pammy wound up a third time and pushed the ball gently over the net into the server's box to Thomas's forehand. Thomas cocked his racket back into position, then hit the ball soundly back at her feet. In defense, Pammy staggered backward and used her racket to scoop the ball into the air, after which it landed, miraculously, on the other side of the net.

"I've got it!" Charlotte yelled, moving closer to the net. She waited for the ball to drop. Then, when it sat three feet above her in the air, she swatted it, sending it careening, untouchable, down the middle of the other side of the court.

"Nice shot," said Claire, before turning to strategize with Pammy. "You're going to have to move over just a bit if we're going to have a chance of getting those down-the-middle shots." Pammy dutifully scooted toward the center of the court, even though she was certain her mother would not have been able to return Charlotte's slam either.

"Nice shot, indeed," said Thomas, giving his sister a high five. Before she could stop herself, Charlotte smiled.

Pammy served to her sister's backhand. Charlotte put two hands on the grip of the racket, dropped the head, and then hit the side of the ball, giving it a topspin she hoped would baffle her mother at the net. Claire, looking as fierce as a warrior, held her racket firmly and dinked the ball back over to the other side. Thomas and Charlotte were miles from where it bounced. "Hit it like a man," said Thomas, walking back to the baseline to receive the next serve.

"I did, Thomas," said Claire. "That particular shot is your specialty."

"The Drop-Shot King," said Charlotte on her way to the service line.

"Okay, okay," said Thomas, facing his mother and sisters. "Are we going to chat all day or play tennis?" Pammy served the ball, which against all odds hit the tape, sending the ball sideways instead of back. Thomas didn't even swing.

"Nice serve, Pammy," said Charlotte, walking backward to the baseline.

Thomas looked at her. "You sure that was in?"

"As sure as you are," she said.

Thomas turned and retrieved the ball in the corner of the court and hit it to Pammy. "Good going, Pammy."

Charlotte hit the ball in the net after Pammy's next serve. Then Thomas, still smarting from the ace, launched his next return of serve into the air and over the fence surrounding the court.

"That's game," Pammy called, grinning. She hardly ever won her serve, which was the part of the game that gave her the most trouble. She also missed most of the balls that were hit to her at the net because she was afraid of balls hit directly at her that didn't have time or space to bounce. Her mother told her if she wanted half a chance of hitting balls at the net, she'd have to open her eyes. Claire had further explained to Pammy that a tennis ball is just a ball, not a weapon, and that the sting she felt when she got hit would quickly pass. But Pammy was afraid nonetheless. It was this fear, Claire thought, that prohibited Pammy from competence at tennis and all other sports. At Pammy's tender age, Claire had been fearless. In many ways, at forty-nine, she still was. She signed Pammy up for tennis lessons every summer—and her daughter had improved somewhat—but the instructor couldn't, no one could give Pammy the courage she needed to play the game well.

So Pammy was pleased, as she had conquered, if only temporarily, her reluctance to serve. It was nerves, she guessed, more than faulty technique. Whenever she played with her mother, she got a stomachache. When no one responded to Pammy's announcement, she called out again, "That's game!"

"Yes, Pammy," said Charlotte, "we all know how to keep score."

Thomas returned to the court, having retrieved the ball from outside the fence surrounding it.

"Oh yes," said Thomas, tossing the ball to Charlotte, staring at her. "Some of us know how to score all right." Charlotte flipped up the middle finger of her left hand at her brother.

"You all are something today," said Claire, walking from her side of the net to the other side. "This is supposed to be fun."

"For whom?" asked Charlotte. "I mean, other than you, of course."

"I'm having fun," Pammy said tentatively.

"That's because you just won your serve for the first time ever."

"Enough, Charlotte," said Claire. "You could be having fun, too. In fact, you could be a very good tennis player, Charlotte. There's more to life than boys and cigarettes."

"Says you."

"Believe me," said Claire, putting her hand on her daughter's shoulder, "I'm smarter than I look." Charlotte looked at her mother, unable to retort. Claire dropped her hand and walked beyond Charlotte to the forehand side of the far court. Charlotte looked back, shrugged, and then walked to the other side of the net. She took two balls to the baseline to serve. "I'll take a couple practice serves."

"What is this, Wimbledon? Just start in," said Thomas.

"Fine," said Charlotte, who bounced the ball five times, like she always did, before tossing it several feet into the air. And when she connected, the ball shot over the net, as if it emerged from the mouth of a cannon. By the time Pammy got to the spot where it landed, all she could do was watch it fly past her.

"Jesus," Thomas urgently whispered to his partner. "Give the poor kid a chance."

"She's never going to get better if we lob them to her, Thomas."

"Yeah, and she's never going to get better if she can't hit them either."

On the other side of the net, Pammy was retrieving the ball out of the corner of the court. When she turned around, Thomas could see that her face was red, like it always got when she was angry or frustrated.

Charlotte next served to her mother. Claire returned the ball to Charlotte's backhand. She sent it back over the net to her mother's backhand. Claire blooped it over the net to Thomas, who hit his return gently to Pammy. Pammy sent the ball into the air, and Charlotte slammed it at her mother's feet. *This game,* she said to herself as her mother rubbed the welt on her right ankle, *does have its merits*. Charlotte called over the net, "Sorry, Mom."

"No trouble," said Claire, making eye contact with her oldest daughter across the net.

Thomas looked at his watch. They had been playing for just fifteen minutes, and things were already heating up. Family doubles often meant family trouble, and this match would be no exception.

CHAPTER 33

2003

Helen, Pammy, Charlotte, and Barb sat in beach chairs on the sand. Todd and Ned had taken Sally and Peter to the shallow end of the beach, where the bottom was sandy. There, they could swim without walking through eelgrass and collect hermit crabs and smooth stones. Charles and Thomas were playing golf, and Claire was taking a nap. Daniel, who had gone for a run at the state beach, returned, sweating and smiling. "Hi," he said, sitting down on the sand next to Charlotte and removing his running shoes.

"Hi," said Charlotte, not looking up from the August *Cosmopolitan* that sat open on her lap.

"How was your run?" asked Pammy, sucking in her abdomen.

"Great!" Daniel winked at her. "Who wants to go for a swim?"

"Pammy," said Charlotte at the same time as Pammy said, "Me." Pammy looked at her older sister, who flashed an insincere smile at her. Pammy slowly lifted herself out of her beach chair. She and Daniel walked together to the water's edge, where Daniel hesitated for just a moment before taking three long strides into the water and diving below its surface. Pammy walked in up to her waist and then dunked herself up to her shoulders. She quickly swam the ten yards to Daniel, who was treading water waiting for her. They swam out past the raft to the large rock behind it, and then climbed through the seaweed, chased away the seagulls, and sat down to talk.

"Charlotte knows something," said Pammy, catching her breath.

"She knows we enjoy each other's company," said Daniel.

"You don't think she suspects anything?"

"She hasn't said anything."

Pammy shook her head from side to side, releasing water from her ears. "That means nothing."

"Not necessarily," said Daniel. "She's pretty straightforward with her opinion when she's got one. She comes right out with it."

"Well, she's giving me all sorts of looks," said Pammy, "and I don't like it."

"You made your own bed, Pammy."

"I didn't make it alone."

"No, you didn't." Daniel took her hand and gently squeezed her fingers.

"Do you love her, Daniel?"

"Charlotte?"

"Yes." Pammy focused all of her attention on his eyes, on what they would communicate to her next.

Daniel ran his hand through his hair, pushing it back from his forehead. "As much as one can love Charlotte, yes."

"What does that mean?"

"It means that Charlotte is difficult to love."

"Why?"

"Pammy, she's your sister."

"Yes, but I don't know her very well."

"Exactly," said Daniel, lifting his face to the sun and closing his eyes. "I don't think anyone knows her very well."

"So what about her do you love then?"

"I love the Charlotte who loves a good time and is willing to take chances."

"And that's enough?"

"I don't know," said Daniel, opening his eyes and again looking at Pammy. "I seem to have a deeper understanding with you."

Pammy smiled at him. "Do you love me?"

"I love many of your qualities." Daniel covered her hand with his.

"That's good enough, I guess. It's only been a few days."

"And I especially love your ass." Pammy laughed. "When can we be alone again?" Daniel ran his hand up and down her thigh.

"Maybe tonight," said Pammy. "Maybe we can sneak out tonight."

"I'll think about you all day."

"You do that," said Pammy. The two sat for another minute or so before Pammy stood. "We'd better head in."

Daniel stood next to her, putting his arm around Pammy's waist and pulling her close to him. She put her hands on his chest, in a weak attempt to stop herself from holding him. The rock was a good distance from shore, but not far enough. Pammy could see her sisters on the beach and knew, of course, that they could see her. Daniel released Pammy and dove into the water, breaking the calm surface. Pammy followed him in and then swam next to him in silence. She was resolved to meet him that night, to make love to him, to make him hers. She didn't care about her sister. This relationship meant nothing to Charlotte. Even if it did, she had always been able to recover from a loss as quickly as it had occurred. Charlotte didn't love him, Pammy thought as she swam, at least not the way Pammy did.

On shore, Daniel and Pammy toweled off. Helen looked up from her magazine. "How was your swim?"

"Great," said Daniel. "I love a good swim after a run. That's why the Bay Area is so perfect for me. I can run on the beach and then take a dip right afterward."

"Isn't the water freezing?" asked Helen.

"It's a very quick dip." Daniel grinned.

"Personally, I love a good swim after a good romp," said Charlotte. Daniel laughed. Pammy frowned. "Don't pout, Pammy," she said. "It doesn't become you."

"I wasn't pouting," said Pammy, sitting down in her chair. "I was thinking."

"Share your thoughts with all of us," said Charlotte, putting down her magazine.

"I'd love to hear them," said Daniel, "but I'm going to head to the other end of the beach. I can't believe the size of the sandcastle they've made down there. This one definitely trumps their other creation. Todd and Ned are unbelievable camp counselors."

They watched Daniel run down the beach. "I'm just dying for one of Daniel's back rubs," said Charlotte, looking at Pammy. "I'm as tense as an old virgin."

"Shut up, Charlotte," said Pammy. "You've got an aching back from hauling around those wrecking balls welded to your chest."

"Oh, here we go," said Charlotte. "It's not enough for you to steal my boyfriend, you have to make fun of me too? You're just such a special sister, Pammy." Pammy had no ready response to her sister's accusations and looked at her blankly. "Come on, Pammy. You think I don't know? You think you can sneak around with Daniel, making a horse's ass of yourself, and no one will notice? Maybe Peter and Sally don't know, but they're the only ones."

"Stop it," said Helen, sitting up in her chair. "Just stop it."

"No, I'm not going to stop it, Saint Helen. If sweet Pammy were sleeping with your husband, would you stop it?"

Barb got up from her chair. "I'm going down to the end of the beach to see that sandcastle," she announced.

"Daniel's not your husband," Helen found herself saying before she could stop herself.

"Well, no, he's not, Helen. But you know and I know and Pammy knows that what she did and is doing is wrong. If you can see that and still side with her, then you're not much better than she is."

"I don't really care," said Helen. "I'm sick to death of Daniel. Anyone who bilks one sister for her condominium, car, and ATM card, and seduces another sister at a family reunion weekend is disgusting. The kid's a common swindler, who has both of you thinking he's the last available man on earth." Pammy and Charlotte were silent.

"He's a diversion," Charlotte finally said.

"From what?" asked Helen. "From your miserable, wealthy life? Yes, you've had relationships that haven't worked out and you haven't been able to have children, and I'm sorry for that. I truly am. But dating children won't make up for not having them. Get into a relationship with a good man and adopt a child for God's sake."

"It's not that easy," said Pammy. "You *have* a good man. You don't know what it's like to be without one."

"You're right," said Helen. "I do have a good man, but that doesn't exempt me from empathy."

"It does exempt you from the loneliness of being single." Pammy dug her toes into the sand.

"Then change that, Pammy. Spend more time with your friends. Find a new challenge at work. Donate your time to a charity or something that matters to you. But for God's sake, stop feeling sorry for yourself."

"Aren't you full of advice," said Charlotte, with a smirk. "You should start your own column, Helen dear."

"I'm just getting started," said Helen. Her heart was racing. She knew she should shut her mouth, that she had already gone too far, but she continued, focusing her gaze on her oldest sister. "Stop trying to look like an eighteen-year-old and start acting like the forty-seven-year-old woman you are. You make a spectacle of yourself with your cartoon breasts and string bikinis. Let go of your need to be in the spotlight. Let someone else have a chance. Believe me, you can learn a lot from the backseat."

"Ah, but you've never been in the backseat, have you, Helen?" said Charlotte. "You've always been front row, center."

"I don't know what you mean."

"Sure you do, favored one," said Charlotte.

"That's not true," said Helen, knowing better.

"Of course it's true," said Pammy. "You wonder why I don't come out to see you and the Queen, when all I get is disappointed looks from both of you."

"Helen could have her own travel company," said Charlotte. "Street Guilt Trips." Helen shifted in her beach chair, looked out at the water. "Do you ever get tired of always being right?"

"I'm not always right," said Helen, mildly defiant.

"That's right," said Pammy. "So quit pretending that you are. We'll give you the Medal of Honor, if you'd like, for taking care of

Mom. But you're going to have to admit that it's not that hard, and you enjoy doing it. Plus, you certainly must enjoy Mom's company because you're just like her."

Helen looked at Charlotte. "Bingo," she said. "Nicely worded, Pammy." Helen started to get up from her chair. "Sit down, for God's sake, Helen. This is not the end of the world here. You were giving us a bunch of shit, and we gave some back. That's what sisters do, right?"

Helen sat. "I didn't realize I was such an asshole."

"Most assholes don't," said Pammy.

After a few seconds, Helen laughed out loud. "Okay," she said. "I'm sorry I've been such an asshole."

"And I'm sorry, too, Charlotte," said Pammy, softly. "What I've been doing is inexcusable. I don't know what's wrong with me."

"That's easy," said Charlotte. "You're not getting enough sex." Helen laughed again. "I don't care," Charlotte said. "While you shouldn't have been hitting on my boyfriend in front of me, I don't really care. He's a child, Pammy. He's not for me, and he's not for you. And, if I really loved Daniel I wouldn't have had sex with Steve Johanson last night."

"What?!" Pammy and Helen said together.

"And he's still a good lay."

"You," said Helen, shaking her head, "are the one and only, Charlotte."

"Speaking of one and onlys," Pammy said. "Here he comes."

Charlotte turned her head and saw Steve walking toward them on the sand. Just as she smiled and waved, Pammy and Helen stood and started walking in the opposite direction. "Where are you going?" Charlotte asked.

"To see the sandcastle," said Helen, who winked at her oldest sister.

Charlotte turned her attention back to Steve, who arrived several moments after Pammy and Helen departed. She grinned at him. "We were just talking about you."

* * *

Helen and Pammy continued down the beach. "I'm sorry I've been such a jerk," said Helen.

Pammy put her hand on her younger sister's shoulder. "You're not really a jerk, Helen. Whatever you do, you do with very good intentions."

"Yeah, but you know what they say about good intentions." Pammy shrugged. "So," Helen began again, "what are we going to do about you?"

"I don't know," said Pammy. "I have feelings for him, Helen."

"What kind of feelings? Are you in love with him or with the idea of loving him?"

"What do you mean?"

"I think you think you're in love because Daniel's young and handsome and flatters you with his attention. What I think you're forgetting is that he probably runs through this routine with every woman he meets. Hell, Pammy, he's blown a few kisses at me. He's an operator, Pammy. Charlotte doesn't care because she's an operator, too. She can get what she wants out of a relationship and ignore the rest. You're not like that."

"I don't know what I'm like," said Pammy. "I guess I know Daniel probably comes on to every woman he meets, but I can't help feeling good when he comes on to me. Men don't pay the kind of attention to me that they do to Charlotte."

"You don't demand the attention Charlotte does."

"That doesn't mean I don't want it."

"We all want attention," said Helen. "We all need it."

"Then how can I get it? At forty-three years old, how am I going to get a man's attention, his affection?"

"By being yourself."

"God, you sound like Dad, Helen."

"And he was usually right on the nose."

"I don't know," said Pammy. "I've been myself for forty-three years, and I'm doing it alone."

"It's okay to be alone, Pammy."

"But I don't want to be alone." They walked a few steps without talking.

"You're a good person," said Helen. "You're witty, intelligent, kind—and attractive. Let that come through naturally. Don't hide or force it. And don't look for love, Pammy. It never comes when you're looking."

"I hate that expression."

"That's because it's true, and you don't want to heed it."

"I wish I could take your advice, Helen. It's hard not to look for something you want so much."

"I know that." Helen put her arm around Pammy's waist for just a moment. "Don't look, just for today. Think about other things. And let Daniel go." Pammy's eyes welled with tears, indicating she did know Helen was right, as usual. They stopped, allowing time for Pammy to appear carefree before they approached the others at the sand castle. Standing with her sister on the beach, as Helen had so many times over the years, brought back a memory from 1973, when she was ten and Pammy was thirteen, and they spent part of every day together looking for sea glass. "Do you still make jewelry out of sea glass?"

Pammy blotted her eyes with the cotton T-shirt she had slipped on after the swim. "What made you think of that?"

Helen shrugged. "I haven't heard you talk about it much lately. And I haven't received any of your handiwork as a gift."

"I've been busy, I guess."

"I think you should take it up again," said Helen. "You are very good at it."

"Yeah?" Pammy raised her eyebrows at her sister. "Mom hasn't worn anything I've made her."

"Have you ever seen her in any jewelry except her wedding band?" Pammy had no response because what Helen said was true. "She has every piece you've ever given her wrapped in a white cashmere scarf. Sometimes she takes it out of her top bureau drawer, rolls it out on the bed, and tells me about a particular set of earrings or a necklace or bracelet."

Pammy rocked back. "What?"

"What indeed," said Helen, resuming their walk.

"You never told me this," said Pammy. "Why did you never tell me this?"

"I don't know. I guess because now seemed like a good time."

"Thank you for sharing that, Helen Thompson Street." Pammy hardly ever spoke Helen's married name.

"You are entirely welcome."

Just twenty or so yards from the sand castle, Pammy said, "I'm going to stay until Wednesday, if that's okay."

"I would love your company, Pammy. I always do. Stay as long as you wish."

"And you will see more of me at home. Even perfect people sometimes need help."

CHAPTER 34

1973

When her father had taken the last bite of his steak, finishing his dinner, Helen popped up from her seat at the table and cleared her place. She walked back in from the kitchen and cleared her father's place. She then took the meat platter, the vegetable dish, still holding several green beans, and the square dish with a bit of wild rice in one of the corners into the kitchen. Helen filled the sink with sudsy water and, after scraping the meager leftovers that her mother would find not worthy of saving into the garbage can, slid the dishes beneath the foamy surface. Pammy brought in her plate and glass and put them in the sink, as did Thomas. "Come on, Charlotte," Helen yelled to her sister, still sitting in the dining room.

"I'm not in any hurry to play that stupid game," Charlotte shouted back, glued to her chair.

"Charlotte?" John Thompson said to his daughter.

"Well, I'm not," she said matter-of-factly to her father.

"What you want to do is, right now, immaterial," he said softly to her. "Your younger sister has been waiting for hours to play. She's been very patient. You've no reason to punish her."

Charlotte sighed and reluctantly got up from the table. She lifted her fork from her plate and brought it into the kitchen, where Helen was busily washing dishes. She threw it into the dishwater. "You're a peach," said Helen, lacing with sarcasm the word her mother used to describe people she liked.

"Likewise," said Charlotte, who went back into the dining room for her glass, which she slowly took into the kitchen. When she started back to the dining room, her father met her at the threshold with her plate, spoon, knife, and napkin.

"Here," he said, handing everything to Charlotte. "This should make your next four trips unnecessary."

Thomas was drying the dishes, and Pammy, taking them from him, was putting everything away. Charlotte joined her sister in the pantry, but sat on the metal stool and folded her arms across her chest instead of helping Pammy.

"So, Mom," Thomas yelled into the dining room. "You had all of us except Charlotte, right? She was definitely adopted."

"Very funny, asshole," Charlotte said to her brother.

"Who died and made you queen?" he asked.

"Drop dead," she said.

"No, really," Thomas continued. "What makes you think you can sit on your butt while we work?"

"I'm not feeling well." Charlotte hardly ever vied for sympathy.

"Yeah," he said. "You haven't felt well since the day you were born. And being around you has made us feel even worse." Charlotte started crying and ran out of the kitchen, through the dining room and up the stairs. Claire walked in and asked Thomas for an explanation. "She was sitting smugly in the pantry while the rest of us worked." He held his hands in the air like a politician appealing to his constituents.

"She isn't feeling well," Claire said.

"So I heard," said Thomas.

"Well?"

"Well, what? If she's not feeling well, then she needs to excuse herself from the dinner table and hit the sack. Why sit there holding up your kid sister, then make a scene in the kitchen? Don't you get a wee bit tired of the drama sometimes, Mom?"

"We all can be dramatic, Thomas," said Claire, giving him a studied look.

"Clearly some more than others," he said.

Claire walked back into the dining room and sat next to her husband. "He's got a point, you know," said John.

"Yes, he's got a point."

"What's wrong with her tonight?"

"She's got her period, honey. She's got cramps."

"Would it help if I talked to her, or do you think she'd rather be with you?"

"I'll go," said Claire, getting out of her seat. She walked up the stairs and down the hall to Charlotte's room. She knocked softly on the door.

"Who is it?"

"It's me, honey," said Claire. "Can I come in?"

"Okay," said Charlotte, getting up from her bed to unlatch the door. Hers was the only lock on any door in the Thompson cottage. Claire had balked at its installation, but her husband John prevailed, telling his wife that it was not unreasonable for a young woman to require privacy. Charlotte opened the door, then went back to bed and got under the covers.

"Can I get you anything?" asked Claire, entering. "Hot tea?"

"How about another older brother?"

"Thomas is harmless," said Claire, sitting on the bed next to her daughter. "You take him too seriously."

"He is anything but harmless, Mom. He picks on me constantly and makes my life miserable."

"And how do you treat him?" asked Claire. "And I want you to think before you answer me."

"If he's nasty to me, I'm nasty back."

"You're never nasty first?"

Charlotte hesitated. "Maybe once in a while," she admitted.

"Now we're getting somewhere."

"I've got horrible cramps. Can we talk about this another time?"

"Have you tried sit-ups?"

"Just once," said Charlotte, "when you told me they got rid of cramps."

"And what happened?"

"The cramps got worse."

"Ah," said Claire. "Well, mind over matter. Don't let these cramps ruin your evening."

"Yes, I know. Suck up the pain, right?"

Claire, who had had menstrual cramps when she was a teenager, demurred. "I know you'll feel better in the morning. The first day is always the worst."

Charlotte nodded her head at the gentler side of her mother, a side she rarely saw, but was always tempted to be taken in by. But they were, had been, especially at odds this summer—Charlotte craving independence, and Claire craving control. A heart-to-heart talk at this point would expose Charlotte's vulnerability. "Can you get me that tea?" she said.

"Sure, Charlotte." Claire got up from the bed. "I'll be back in a few minutes." Claire walked out of the room. On her way down the stairs, she wondered whether she and her oldest daughter would ever be close. Claire had been so hopeful when Charlotte was born that she and her daughter would have the kind of relationship Claire once had with her swim teammates—competitive but supportive. Not that Claire wanted to compete against her daughter, no; she wanted to compete *with* her. And for a while, they had spent time with one another, riding bikes, walking in the woods, playing tennis, being physically active. But Charlotte's interests shifted in middle school. Instead of pursuing activities with her mother or younger sisters, she chased boys. And as soon as she actually caught them, they were her entire focus. Pammy, at thirteen, was just starting to show an interest in boys. But Claire could already tell that she would never seek their company in Charlotte's predatory manner. And Helen's athleticism would hold her attention through high school. There would be boyfriends for both Pammy and Helen, but Claire could already tell that they would be a secondary rather than a primary concern.

"How's she feeling?" John asked Claire when she returned to the dining room.

"About the same."

"Let's go outside. Helen's champing at the bit."

"You go," said Claire. "I'm making tea for Charlotte. I'll be out in a minute."

"Okay," said Thomas, as soon as he saw his mother, "here's the deal. The picnic table we're sitting on is base. I'm it. I'm going to sit here and count to thirty, and you're going to scatter and find some kind of temporary hiding place. The object of the game is not to remain hidden, however. The object is to get back to base before I tag you. Any questions?"

"Can we go anywhere?" Helen was jumping up and down an inch or so off the ground.

"In our yard and in the Hendersons' yard next door. That's it. Ready?"

"Ready," Helen said, moving away from the picnic table.

"Go!" Thomas shouted, closing his eyes and beginning to count, "One, two, three, four . . ."

Helen bolted for the Hendersons' garage, which hadn't housed a car in her memory. Instead, bikes, ride-on toys, inflatable rafts and life rings, hammers, boxes of nails, saws, shutters, cast-off furniture, a broken refrigerator—just about anything anybody could ever want or not want—filled the space. Propped against the far wall was an old rowboat. Helen made a cursory check for spider webs and then ducked underneath. She squatted at the back end, just out of view, and listened. Five, maybe ten minutes later, she heard the squeaky garage door open. She held her breath. She could hear Thomas lifting the rafts off the floor, even checking inside the old refrigerator. She never would have hidden in there because Thomas told her it was dangerous. She wondered why he bothered to look for her there. "Helen?" he called.

She stopped herself from automatically answering him by slowly letting out her breath and holding it again. He walked out of the garage, and Helen counted silently to thirty. She then poked her head out of the boat, and, seeing nothing, she slid her body out from behind it. Placing her feet carefully between, next to, and over the yellow metal Tonka trucks and the multicolored plastic pails and shovels, Helen tiptoed away from the boat and closer to the door. She had just sidled up to the shutters when the door opened and Thomas walked in again. Helen squatted and crossed her fingers; she was thankful for the darkening sky that muted the sharp lines of the garage's content. She was also thankful for the dark clothing she had chosen to wear for the game.

"There's no escape, little girl," he said, looking around the garage. "I've got everybody else. And I know you're in here. It's just a matter of time before I get you." Thomas moved toward the workbench in the back, which he checked under before spotting the boat. He smiled as he stepped over a red tricycle to reach it. "It's all over now, Helen," he said, getting down on his knees and ducking his head to look under it.

Now! Helen thought. She popped up from her hiding place. Hearing her, Thomas jerked his head, hitting it on the boat's seat. Helen jumped over the milk crates filled with magazines that blocked her access and then bolted through the door to the unencumbered stretch of grass that separated her from base. Only then did she dare to look back and was instantly horrified to see Thomas, still holding his head, emerging from the garage. She turned her head and focused on the picnic table, some twenty yards away, where her mother, father, and Pammy were cheering her on. "Run, Helen!" Pammy screamed. "He's catching you!"

Helen pumped her arms and pushed her legs as fast as they would go. Thomas's thundering footsteps were right behind her. She reached out her hands to touch the table, which now sat within a few feet of her grasp. Hearing her brother's laughter and thinking she felt his breath, Helen knew she was out of time. Lifting herself off the ground, Helen dove for the top of the table, landing with a thud against her father, who was sitting on the far side. "Safe!" shouted John, cradling his daughter in his arms and kissing her face. "You are amazing, Helen."

Secure with her father, Helen looked at Thomas, who, with his hands on his knees, was breathing hard and sweating. She flashed him a smile, and he smiled back. "Next time," he said, pointing at her. "Next time, you're mine."

"Who's it?" Helen asked.

"I am," said Pammy, dejected.

"Pammy, you've just got to get more creative in your hiding choices," said Claire, instructing. "The shower is too obvious, dear."

"Okay, Mom," said Pammy, more as a means to restart the game than to acknowledge Claire's advice. Pammy quickly closed her eyes and began to count. Everyone raced from the table. Thomas ran behind the Hendersons' house. John ducked behind their own garage, and Claire stooped behind the garbage bins that stood next to the garage. They were both a short distance from base. Helen chose the crabapple tree in their spacious backyard. She adeptly scaled its familiar trunk and was soon sitting on her favorite branch listening for Pammy. Seconds later, she appeared. "I've got you," said Pammy, rounding the corner of the garage and staring at Helen.

"How'd you know where I was?"

"I heard you climbing."

"No way," said Helen. "You peeked."

"I did not," said Pammy, "and now you're it."

"Not until you tag me," sang Helen.

"What do you mean?"

"You've got to touch me, Pammy. You can't just see me."

As Pammy and Helen talked, Thomas ran to base from his hiding spot behind the Henderson's screened-in porch, and yelled his name. Pammy darted back to base, then back to Helen, who was still sitting contentedly on her branch. "I'm coming up," said Pammy, putting her foot on the tree.

"Glad to hear it," said Helen. "There's a first time for everything."

"I've climbed this tree, smarty pants."

"It's kind of tricky," said Helen. "The bark is slippery."

Pammy hoisted herself up onto a low branch and began her ascent. "Not that slippery," said Pammy, even though she was struggling to get a firm grip. Helen smiled at her sister and counted silently. At ten, she quickly slid her body off the branch, which she briefly hung from before dropping to the ground. Picking herself up, she strolled from the tree to base. "Crap," said Pammy, climbing down. She rounded the corner of the garage and saw all of them sitting on the picnic table. "This game stinks," she announced.

"You were absolutely stellar last time," said John, standing. "I'm heading in. You kids play another round. Your mother and I are ready for coffee."

"I've got the late shift," said Thomas, looking at his watch.

"And I'm going upstairs," said Pammy.

"One more game?" asked Helen, still sitting on the table.

"We love you, Helen," said Thomas, "but not that much."

"It was fun," her father called before disappearing into the house.

"You are a champion, Helen," said Claire following John.

Helen sat down on the top of the table and then lay back to look at the stars just beginning to show in the twilight. "Star light," Helen whispered, "star bright, first star I see tonight." She stared at her star, trying to think of an extra-special wish because it was so bright. Suddenly, another light caught her eye. Tracking it, she discovered it was a moving light, a flickering light, an on-and-off-again light. A firefly! Helen jumped up from the table and ran into the kitchen to look for a glass jar, which she immediately found in the pantry, and a screw top, which proved elusive. The tops in the bottom drawer were too big or too small. Helen searched frantically and finally found a plastic lid that fit perfectly. She took a sharp knife from a drawer in the kitchen and then, putting the lid down on the cutting board, poked five, six, seven holes through it.

She dashed back out to the picnic table, holding the jar in one hand and the lid in the other. Looking and listening, as if she could actually hear the fly turn on its light, Helen walked around the yard, paying close attention to the gardens that lined their property. All bugs like gardens, she remembered from school, as she squatted down to examine the daylily leaves. She flipped over a leaf, and a firefly flew out of the azalea bush next to her and into the open yard. Helen flew after it. Closer and closer she came, waiting for the perfect moment. The hapless fly chose a dandelion on which to rest, and Helen pounced. She scooped him up and snapped on the lid. Holding up the jar for inspection, Helen examined her specimen, waiting for the intoxicating flash of light. Racing around the yard, from one plant to another, Helen filled her jar with flies. When Thomas, changed into his pizza garb, walked out the back door, Helen ran to him with her prize. "Look!" she said, holding up the jar for inspection.

"Very impressive," he said. "You must have a dozen in there."

"Fourteen," said Helen, proud.

"Wow."

"Want to help me get some?"

"I'd love to another time, Helen. I've got to get to work."

"Are you delivering pizza tonight?"

"Yes," said Thomas. "Don't wait up for me because I'll be late."

"I always wait up for you."

"And it's silly," said Thomas. "I always come home."

"That's because I always wait up." Thomas smiled at his sister. "Watch this," said Helen.

"Watch what?" Thomas asked.

"I'm going to let them go."

"That's a great idea."

"You think so?"

"If you want them to live, yes. If you want them to die, then keep them in the jar."

"I want them to live," said Helen. "I think they're sad in there."

"I imagine they are."

Helen set the jar back down on the table and took the top off. She stepped back to give the flies room, and watched as they slowly lifted themselves out of the jar and into the sky. "They seem happier now."

"I think they are," said Thomas. "They want to be free."

"It was fun to have them for a little while."

"I'll bet."

"Where will you deliver pizzas tonight?"

"All over," said Thomas. "I'm the only late-shift driver."

"Maybe Anna will order one," Helen said, looking at her brother. Thomas was quiet for a moment and then said, "I don't think so."

"Do you miss her, Thomas?"

"Yes," he said. "I do."

"You don't want to call her?"

"I can't call her, Helen."

"Why can't you call her? If you've been thinking about her, you should call her."

"It's part of the stupid game, Helen. I just can't call her."

"If she called you, would you talk to her?"

"Of course I'd talk to her."

"Then I'm sure she'd talk to you."

"It's different. If I call her, I'm admitting that I miss her. I'm admitting that I still love her."

"Do you, Thomas?"

"Do I what?"

"Do you still love her?"

"Yes," he said. "Part of me will always love her." Thomas picked Helen up and kissed her forehead. "I've got to go. Be good."

"I'm always good," Helen said. "Teach me how to be bad."

"Talk to Charlotte," said Thomas, walking toward his car. "She's the master."

Helen watched him leave and then turned back toward the house. She walked into the kitchen with the jar, washed it out in the sink, and placed it upside down in the drying rack. Her mother insisted her children dry the dishes after a meal, but she was okay with one or two items drip-drying. Helen stashed the perforated plastic lid in the drawer that held the table linens, underneath the blue and white-checked tablecloth her mother spread on the picnic table for holiday celebrations, for the next time.

Walking through the dining room and living room to the porch, she told her parents, who immediately lay their books on their laps when she appeared, all about the fireflies. Claire told Helen that she was a budding scientist who would one day change the world with an important discovery, and John gently laughed and then complimented Helen on her compassion. She then told them, magnanimously she thought, that she was absolutely in for the night. She had no plans to sneak out. They told her they were pleased and then returned their attention to their books. This nightly habit of theirs allowed Claire and John to read a book a week over the course of the summer. Claire read mostly nonfiction so she could learn something, she told her children. But John, who was busy with his medical practice, made time for prolonged reading only during the summer. And he read fiction. A nice change, he said, from the medical journals that inundated his office mailbox.

Helen climbed the stairs and then walked down the hall to the room she shared with Pammy. "Hi," she said, as she opened the door.

"Hi." Pammy was lying on her stomach on the bottom bunk reading.

"What are you doing?"

"Reading," said Pammy.

"What are you reading?" Helen asked, sitting down next to her.

"Bailey's Beach."

"What's it about?"

"It's a romance novel." Pammy did not look up from her book.

"Is it good?"

"The sentence I've just read three times was good." Pammy turned now and looked at her younger sister.

"It sounds dumb."

"Helen, I don't make fun of your books."

"I'm bored. Let's bug Charlotte."

"I don't think she's in the mood to be bugged."

"You never know."

"No, you never know. I always know," said Pammy, returning to her book.

Helen got up from Pammy's bed and walked out of the room, closing the door behind her. She walked the few steps to Charlotte's door and knocked. "Who is it?"

"It's Helen. Can I come in?"

"What for?"

Helen hadn't anticipated that question. "I want to see how you're feeling," she said. Seconds later, Helen heard Charlotte unlatching the door. Helen walked into the lavender room and sat down in the armchair next to the window. Charlotte walked back to her bed and sat down amid her books, magazines, box of Kleenex, and a pad of paper. "Are you feeling better?" asked Helen, looking at her sister.

"Yeah, the cramps are almost gone," said Charlotte. "The Midol makes me want to puke, but it does take care of the lousy cramps. The heating pad is also a must."

"Are they really bad?"

"They can be. Tonight, they were awful." Charlotte lifted her T-shirt, exposing her red and bubbled abdomen. "I had the heating pad on so high that I gave myself blisters."

Helen shuddered. "I never want to get my period."

"I don't blame you for feeling that way."

"But I'll get it, won't I?"

"You will, indeed, Helen."

Helen shifted in the chair. "Well, I'm sorry you've had such a crappy night."

"And I'm sorry about making cracks about your game. You were very patient, and I shouldn't have said anything. I was just feeling lousy." Helen took her sister's willingness to talk as a sign to chat more. Charlotte wasn't normally interested in prolonged conversation with anyone but boys her age or older.

"When do you think I'm going to get mine?" Helen asked.

"When are you going to get your what?"

"My period."

"Oh," said Charlotte, picking up a nail file that had been buried in the blankets. "Well, I got mine when I was fourteen. And I know Pammy's close because she's been insufferable lately. So I would guess around fourteen, give or take a year."

"What's it like?"

"Horrible."

"Do you bleed a lot?"

"Depends," said Charlotte, shaping her thumbnail. "Some days you bleed more than others."

"I don't really understand this whole thing."

"Nobody does. It's all biology."

"Why do we have to bleed anyway?"

"So we can have babies someday."

"That sounds okay."

"Well, sure. When you want to have the babies, everything's

fine." Charlotte was actually glad to have her period, her first since her abortion. She had bled for a week after the procedure, but she hadn't been sure, until she got her period that morning, that everything had been cleaned out of her, that she was no longer pregnant. She'd had sex with Steve Johanson a few times, but she had been adamant about condom use—even though they had previously done it without protection. "And here's the extra crazy thing," said Charlotte, wanting to shake the abortion image from her head. "You continue to have your period until you're really old, like fifty. Who needs a period for forty years when most people have their children in five or six?"

"I don't know," said Helen, who had never before thought much about periods.

"Nobody," said Charlotte, filing her pointer finger. "Trust me." Thomas had advised Helen never to trust Charlotte, but on that particular night, discussing this particular subject, Helen did. Helen watched her sister file the rest of her nails. Charlotte looked up and saw Helen watching. "Come here," she said, patting the bed next to her. Helen got up from her chair and went to Charlotte's bed. Charlotte cleared a place for Helen and told her to sit down and hold out her hands. Charlotte inspected Helen's nails and began filing the rough edges. Mesmerized by her sister's attention and the rhythm of the board going back and forth across her nail, Helen sat quietly and stared at her fingers.

"You should file your nails instead of chopping them off with that barbaric clipper," said Charlotte. "They're very nice."

"My nails?" said Helen, coming out of her trance.

"Yes," said Charlotte. "They're strong, and they have a nice color."

"Thank you," said Helen, as she always did in response to a compliment.

"What color would you like?"

"I thought my color was good," said Helen, confused.

"What color polish, silly."

Helen looked into the green plastic bucket of nail polish. She took them out, one by one, and studied their labels. Purple Passion, Ruby Red, Cool Cocoa, Striking Strawberry, Summer Pink, Pearly Pink. "That would be good for you," said Charlotte, taking the Pearly Pink out of Helen's hand. "It's subtle."

Helen nodded in agreement and held out her nails to her sister. Someone knocked on the door. "What's the password?" asked Charlotte, winking at Helen.

"Sex," Pammy whispered through the keyhole.

"I can't hear you," Charlotte sang.

"Open the door, Charlotte."

"Get the door, will you, Helen?"

Helen popped off the bed and unlocked the door for Pammy, who casually entered the room, then locked the door behind her. "What are you guys doing in here?"

"Talking about woman things," said Charlotte, buffing Helen's nails with a chamois cloth.

"What kind of woman things?" said Pammy, joining them on the bed.

"The monthly woman thing. The chief woman thing."

"Oh."

"Did you get yours yet?" Helen asked Pammy.

"No," she said. "The doctor thinks I will soon, though."

"Honey, you don't need a doctor," said Charlotte, "to know it's right around the corner." Pammy smiled at what she considered friendly banter.

"You want to get it?" asked Helen, incredulous.

"Absolutely. It means I'm a woman," said Pammy, repeating what she'd heard in health class.

"What it means," said Charlotte, painting Helen's thumbnail, "is excruciating pain and general grossness."

"That's not the way I look at it," said Pammy.

"That's because you don't have it," Charlotte said flatly.

"I never want mine." Helen shook her head.

"I thought you wanted babies," said Charlotte.

"Well, yes, I do want the babies. I just don't want the period."

"I don't think anybody can cut you that kind of deal, Helen," said Charlotte. "Sooner or later, it's going to happen." Charlotte finished painting the nails on Helen's left hand and started on the right. Helen held up the finished hand and blew on the opalescent polish to help it dry.

"They look nice," she said to Charlotte, who stopped painting to take a closer look.

"Yes, they do," she said.

"Will you do mine next?" asked Pammy.

"Only if you can tell me that you've kissed Michael."

Pammy reddened. "You know I haven't."

"Why, for God's sake?" asked Charlotte.

"Two words, two breasts. Tammy Jennings."

"He's not a breast man. I have that on good authority," said Charlotte, using the word *authority* to sound official. It was a phrase she'd heard her father say to a neighbor about the weather forecast for the weekend.

"Tell him that," said Pammy. "Everybody's a breast man."

"You have other attributes," said Charlotte. "For starters, you're much cuter than Tammy."

"You think so?"

"Definitely," said Helen, blowing on her nails. "What's attractive about a big nose and stringy orange hair?"

"I love you, Helen," said Pammy.

"I'll do one hand," Charlotte said to Pammy. "And when you kiss Michael, I'll do the other."

"Great," Pammy said with sarcasm.

"Take it or leave it," said Charlotte, putting the emery board, chamois cloth, and tiny nail polish bottles back in her bucket.

"I'll take it," said Pammy. "I'll figure out how to kiss him tomorrow."

"He's kissed me," said Helen, still looking at her nails.

"What are you talking about?" asked Pammy.

"He kissed me last Saturday, after I dove into the water and retrieved his fishing lure for him. He kissed me on the cheek."

"You didn't tell me that," said Pammy.

"You never asked."

"Don't give me that, Helen. For Pete's sake, I wouldn't think to ask you if Michael Johanson kissed you. It's not like asking you how many crabs you've caught."

"No, it's not," Charlotte chimed in, smiling.

"Crap," said Pammy.

"I didn't kiss him back," said Helen, suddenly nervous that Pammy was upset.

"I'm sure it was a little thank-you kiss, Pammy. Very innocent," said Charlotte.

"I haven't had any kiss, innocent or not." Pammy was now sulking.

"Whose fault is that?" asked Charlotte. "Dive for his lures, girl."

Helen laughed. "He loses them all the time."

"Let me have your hand," Charlotte said to Pammy.

"I'd better have the color Helen has," said Pammy. "So it's not that obvious that one hand's painted and the other isn't."

"Good thinking," said Helen.

"No one will notice anything," said Charlotte, filing Pammy's pinky nail. "Especially if you kiss him tomorrow."

"I thought he had to kiss me."

"I'll take either," said Charlotte. "He can kiss you or you can kiss him."

"What about Tammy?"

"I'll distract her," Helen offered. "I'll ask her a dopey question about gimp. Ever since she took over the craft program, she actually acknowledges my presence. I'm the best weaver, and she can talk about lanyards for half an hour."

"And then, while Tammy's occupied, you find Michael," said Charlotte. "Tell him you want to tell him a secret. When he bends down to listen, kiss him on the cheek."

"Then what?" asked Pammy.

"Then smile at him and walk away."

"I can't do that!"

"Boys love to be kissed," said Charlotte. "Believe me, the more girls they can get to kiss them, the happier they are. And who knows, maybe he'll start to wonder what it would be like to kiss you."

Emboldened by this time with her sisters, by their encouragement, Pammy said, "I'll do it. I'll do it tomorrow."

Awakened by the noise from a car engine outside, Helen sat up in bed. She looked out her window and saw her brother walking toward the back door. Helen got out of bed and walked out of her room to wait in the hallway. Helen heard him walk through the kitchen, dining room, and living room, and then up the stairs. She waited until he reached the second-floor landing before calling out to him. "Hey!" she whispered. "You're late tonight."

"We were really busy," Thomas whispered back.

"Did you have fun?"

"If you call delivering sixty-seven pepperoni pizzas to the Real Men's Baseball League banquet fun, yes."

"We had fun, too," said Helen. "Charlotte did my nails."

"No kidding," said Thomas. "Let's see." Helen held her hands out, and her brother walked the rest of the way down the hall to her. "Impressive," he said, the comment more in reference to the fact that Charlotte spent time with her ten-year-old sister than the condition of Helen's nails.

"Thank you. She's feeling much better."

"That's good," said Thomas. "There was only one way to go."

"I'm glad you're home," Helen said. "I never sleep that good until I hear you in the house."

"You realize if Mom heard you say that sentence, she'd correct your grammar."

"Yes," Helen said. "But she's told me that my grammar, on the whole, is pretty decent for a ten-year-old."

"High praise from the English teacher."

"Well, I'm just a kid. I think she cuts me some slack."

Thomas had just said that very phrase to Helen yesterday, about one of his bosses. He smiled at his little sister. "Well, I'm glad you're here to look out for me," he said. "Good night, Helen."

"Sweet dreams," said Helen.

"You too." Thomas walked into his room.

Helen waited until he shut the door behind him and then hesitated just a moment, in case he'd forgotten to tell her something, before walking back into her room and climbing up to the top bunk. The sheets had cooled in her absence. She drew the blanket up around her shoulders and settled in for the night.

CHAPTER 35

2003

While Helen put the top crust on the blueberry pies, Barb set the table, and Charlotte, with a drink in her hand, leaned against the kitchen counter and watched. Outside, Charles made a chimney of charcoal briquettes in the grill, while Thomas and Pammy shucked two dozen ears of corn. Todd and Ned showed Sally and Peter the rudiments of croquet. And Daniel, who was getting the frost treatment from both his lovers, went for a run to clear his mind.

"Remember Anna Santiago?" Thomas asked Pammy.

"Amy's mother, who broke your heart?" asked Pammy, tearing the husk away from the cob.

"If you must put it that way, yes."

Pammy smiled at her brother. "I didn't really mean anything by that," she said. "I just remember how sad you were about her. Helen was so worried about you."

"Was she?"

"Thomas, she lived to be with you when she was little."

"I guess I didn't know that," he said. "God, she was such a great kid."

"She's pretty great now," said Pammy. "If I didn't love her, I'd hate her."

Thomas laughed. "Spoken like a sister."

"She's tired, Thomas." Pammy was serious. "She's taken care of Mom all by herself, and she had needed, has wanted, our help."

Thomas started in on another ear, tearing the husk away from the cob. "I can see that now," he said. "I didn't see it before now. Helen has certainly communicated Mom's condition, but she's so capable. You know Helen. She's does everything well. So, I've taken her caregiving duties, a lot of things I guess, for granted."

"Don't be too hard on yourself. I haven't done much either. I live a lot closer to Mom and Helen than you do, and I haven't been home since Thanksgiving." Pammy took another ear of corn from the bag between them.

"So, I've been thinking," said Thomas, almost as if he hadn't heard her. "That we should make this an annual thing."

"I don't know how much time Mom has left."

Thomas sipped from his bottle of Rolling Rock. "I don't know either. But let's make an effort—the five of us and then the four of us—to bring whomever we are attached to, to the cottage every summer. For a week."

Pammy had a sip of her Chardonnay. "I'd like to think we can make that happen." Thomas, nodding his head, focused for a moment on the ear of corn in his hand, carefully removing every strand of silk. "Tell me about Anna Santiago," said Pammy, emboldened by their conversation, their sudden intimacy.

She and Thomas had not been close growing up. Thomas was too busy for anyone but Helen—and this was only because she demanded his attention. Pammy had wanted her handsome older brother to spend time with her, but she had been too shy to ask for it. And Thomas, being five years older, had not thought about providing it without a prompt. Their relationship wasn't what some referred to as distant or strained. They simply didn't have one, outside of passing each other food at the dinner table or a very short conversation. As adults, the physical distance between them prevented face-to-face opportunities for even conversational connection. But sitting next to him, for the first time since they buried their father, opened the window.

Thomas raised his eyebrows. "I saw her yesterday."

"No kidding?"

"In town." Thomas swatted at a mosquito that had landed on his arm. "She has a law office off Main Street. She's a tax attorney."

"So, she made it after all."

"Who are we discussing?" asked Charles, who, fire finally started, approached the picnic table.

"The bane of Thomas's teenage years," said Pammy.

"She was not," Thomas countered. "She was a woman I fell madly and desperately in love with when I was eighteen. I actually asked her to marry me."

"Ah, the mysterious Anna Santiago," said Charles, shaking the ice in his drink glass, thinking about another finger of scotch.

"You know about this?" Thomas looked at Charles.

"Thomas, I am married to your sister."

Thomas laughed. "So you are."

"Thomas saw her yesterday for the first time in thirty years," said Pammy.

Charles squeezed one more sip out of his drink. "What was that like?"

"It was funny," said Thomas. "On one hand, it was as if time hadn't passed and I was still eighteen. On the other hand, I felt as if I hadn't seen her in the lifetime it's been and had no idea who she was. Perhaps it would have been different if not for the thirty years between conversations."

"Sometimes, I wouldn't mind stepping back thirty years," said Pammy.

"Pammy, you were lost as a thirteen-year-old," said Thomas. "You lived in Charlotte's shadow."

"In some ways, I still do."

"I don't think so," said Charles, who took an ear of corn from the bag and began removing its covering. "I think you're very different."

"Do you?" Pammy asked.

"Yes," said Charles. "Look how far you've gone in your professional life."

"I'm not a vice president."

"Doesn't matter."

"It does to my mother."

"Forget about Mom," said Thomas. "Charles is right. You've made a name for yourself on Madison Avenue."

Pammy looked at Thomas and closed one eye. "How would you know?"

"You'd probably be surprised by what I know."

"Well, thank you," said Pammy.

"Do you ever wonder," Charles asked, "what your life would be like if you had made different choices?"

"All the time," said Pammy.

"Or if Anna did," said Charles, looking at Thomas, "and married you."

"What about *me?* Let's find someone to marry *me,*" said Pammy. "When I was thirteen, it never occurred to me that I wouldn't marry, wouldn't have children. God, I had my whole life ahead of me."

"You've got a lifetime ahead of you now," said Thomas.

"I want to believe that."

"Marriage isn't the solution, Pammy," said Thomas.

"So Helen is always telling me. It sure seems like the solution when you're single."

"You're single," said Charles, "because the right person for you has not come along. Our single friends think they're defective. And one of them is the most delightful guy I know."

"How old is this delightful guy?" asked Pammy. Thomas laughed. "I'm serious," she said.

"Roger?" said Charles, thinking for a moment. "He's about my age."

"Forty-eight," said Pammy.

"Helen's never told you about Roger Shaw?"

"Specifically? No," said Pammy. "She's always bugged me about coming to visit, but she's never mentioned Roger."

"Come visit," said Charles, "and we'll introduce you to Roger."

"He's never been married?"

"He was married for two years, I think. He said he was young and made a mistake. Since then, he's dated several women, but has never felt comfortable with the idea of marrying again."

"And he's normal?" asked Pammy.

"He's got two heads," Charles said, "but he's very nice."

"Oh stop," said Pammy, laughing.

"Stop what?" asked Helen, emerging from the house with a cutting board topped with steaks.

"How come you never told me about Roger?" Pammy asked her sister.

"I did," said Helen, putting the cutting board down on the table. "You had just met the guy before Mark and were not interested in, as you put it, pursuing a country-club golfer."

"Does Roger play golf?" asked Charles.

"No," said Helen. "Pammy was feeling smug that day."

"How silly of me."

"Oh, Thomas," said Helen. "I almost forgot. I saw Anna Santiago today at the grocery store. She said how nice it was to see you again."

"You saw her at the grocery store?"

"Yes, Thomas. It's where we buy food."

"Have you ever seen her before, at the grocery store?"

"Every summer."

"Why didn't you say anything?"

"Because I didn't want to remind you of how sad you were."

"And today you want to remind me?"

"No," said Helen. "Today, she mentioned that she had seen you."

"We were just talking about her," said Thomas.

"What were you saying?"

"How weird it is to see someone you haven't seen in thirty years," said Charles.

"Did you feel strange, Thomas?" asked Helen.

"A bit, yes."

"I think she did, too. I think . . ."

"What?" asked Thomas.

"Nothing."

"For God's sake, Helen."

"I think, in some ways, she regrets not marrying you. I think she knows she couldn't have, way back when, but wonders what it would have been like if you'd met later on."

"She said that?" Thomas asked his sister.

"Nope."

"Then what are you basing this on?"

"Intuition," said Helen, turning around and walking back toward the house.

"God, I hate it when she does that," said Charles. "The trouble is, she's usually right."

Thomas took a sip of his drink and smiled at what his sister had said. Knowing Anna still thought about him pleased him. He had tried so hard to forget her and had been, in the end, unlike in every other aspect of his life, only marginally successful. But it was okay to think about her now. She could become a pleasant memory because Thomas had realized his mistake, and he had moved forward. And because Barb, not Anna, had become the sun in his universe.

Everyone sat while Charlotte cleared the table. When she was done, they all cheered, except Daniel, who sat at the far end, away from her, away from Pammy, with his arms folded across his expansive chest. He hadn't said a word during dinner, but nobody seemed to notice or care. Conversation had buzzed around, through, and past him as if he were nonexistent, which, in Charlotte's and Pammy's eyes, he knew he already was.

Helen suggested pie and coffee on the porch, which everyone agreed was a great idea. Those still at the table pushed back their chairs and stood, straightening their spines, stretching their arms out in front of them after the long sit. The children were in the yard with glass jars in pursuit of fireflies, and Claire, who had been conversational in an auxiliary kind of way, said she'd have her pie in the morning. Helen helped her mother up the stairs and into her room.

"I can do it from here," said Claire, starting in on her shirt buttons.

"Are you sure?" asked Helen. "I'm here."

"I think I can manage."

"Okay," said Helen. "But I'll be back in ten minutes—after everyone has pie and is settled in."

"That sounds like a plan," said Claire.

Helen walked back down the stairs and into the kitchen. Pammy was making a pot of coffee, and Barb was doling out the pie onto china plates. "There's some ice cream in the freezer if anyone wants to do the à la mode thing," said Helen, on her way out the back door to check on the kids. They were in the midst of it. All of them, even Peter, had several fireflies in their jars. "Are you ready for pie?"

"Blueberry pie?" asked Ned.

"Yes," said Helen.

"That's my favorite."

Helen smiled. "I know."

"Can we have it in ten minutes or so?" asked Ned.

"We have a pact to get a dozen specimens each before we let them go into the night," explained Todd.

"Absolutely," said Helen, turning and heading back to the house.

"Don't eat it all!" Ned shouted after her.

Helen gave her son the thumbs-up sign and then walked into the kitchen. Charlotte told her that Pammy and Barb had gone to the porch with the others, and that she'd be in shortly.

"I'll help you," said Helen.

"Go," said Charlotte. "I'm almost done here. Washing dishes is more therapeutic than I ever imagined." Helen laughed. "Yes," said Charlotte, a smile on her face. "I'm kidding. But I am serious about doing it myself. You guys have been doing this for years." Helen raised her eyebrows at her sister. "Don't get your hopes up, Helen. This is not a new me."

Helen walked to the sink and gave her a quick hug. "I'm going to check on Mom," she said. "And then I'll meet you on the porch."

Helen took her piece of pie to the porch and set it on the table next to Charles, who was telling a story about a phone call from a guy who owned sixteen cars and had been in twenty-seven accidents—and had never had insurance. Helen climbed the stairs and walked down the hallway to her mother's room. She found her, in her pajamas, in bed and reading a volume of poetry by Billy Collins.

"Well, look at you," said Helen, sitting on the bed beside her mother.

Claire laid the book on her blanketed lap. "I did it all by myself."

"I'm impressed."

"Me too," said Claire.

Helen laughed. "What can I do for you?"

"Nothing," said Claire. "Go down with the others. I am perfectly content." Helen bent down and kissed her mother's forehead. "And Helen," she said, "leave the door open tonight."

Helen left her mother and walked back down the stairs to the porch. She sat next to her husband on the couch in the preferred seating area and had her first bite of pie. Pammy, who was returning to the porch from the kitchen, handed Helen a mug of hot coffee. Charlotte, pie in hand, was right behind Pammy.

Upstairs Claire closed her eyes and listened to the conversation of her four children again gathered at the cottage, again family. This was what she had wanted, and she smiled at her accomplishment, her victory. She could leave them now, the Thompson children, knowing the distance between them would no longer keep them apart. She could say her good-byes.

"But that's for another day," said Claire aloud, setting the book on the bedside table and turning off the light. "Good night, John."

Chapter 36

1973

Labor Day weekend, which was aptly named in Helen's opinion, always came too quickly. It not only signaled the end of summer and the beginning of a new school year, but it also meant work. It was the weekend the Thompson family, laboring together, cleaned the cottage and did whatever else was necessary to prepare it for more than nine months of dormancy. Thomas and John spent most of their time making small repairs to screens and windows, fixing broken furniture, and touching up the paint wherever it was peeling. Since John kept a running list of tasks, he and Thomas knew exactly what needed to be done and, after a trip to the hardware store in town, got right to it on Saturday morning. Claire, too, kept a list for her daughters, but it was the same every year: dust, vacuum, and sanitize anything that didn't move. Helen always volunteered to clean the bathroom, mostly because she loved the smell of the Comet cleaning powder her mother kept under the kitchen sink. Plus, being the youngest and smallest, she was the only one who could reach behind the tub. Even if Pammy's arm could fit, she was too afraid of spiders to clear out the webbing they had been spinning all summer long. So, she vacuumed. And Charlotte dusted, which she annually declared was unnecessary since they had to dust all over again in the spring. But it was for this very reason that Charlotte liked the dusting job—Claire was often too busy cooking and getting the kitchen in order to thoroughly check Charlotte's handiwork. So Charlotte could skip the hard-to-reach, under-the-bed corners and rarely used shelves in the back of the bedroom closets and focus on what she called the obvious dusting, which simply meant whatever her mother would see if she did choose to monitor Charlotte's progress.

The very best part of Labor Day weekend was the food. Each year, Claire asked her husband and children what they most wanted to eat, and she would prepare it. It was as comforting for her as it was for them, as making delicious meals helped quell the sadness that Claire always felt at this time of year. This summer was especially hard since Thomas would be going off to college in only a week's time. She had put this thought out of her mind for most of the summer, but she could no longer deny it. Instead of openly mourning the loss of his childhood, the end of his time in the daily life of their family, Claire cooked and baked for him. She knew she should talk to him about his feelings about leaving home, but it was a conversation she struggled with initiating. She had no answers for his questions, and her emotions were as close to the surface as they had ever been. She was just as unsettled about this next step as she could tell he was. John had always been the one with the insight and understanding to talk to their children about larger issues in a way that would be beneficial to both parties.

By Sunday late afternoon, everything on Claire's and John's lists was done. With dinner still a couple hours away, Claire suggested they all take a swim, and even Charlotte—who routinely bickered with her mother for sport—agreed, happy to be done and to rid her body of the sweat-soaked T-shirt that was sticking to her back. Bathing suits on and towels in hand, they crossed the road and headed down the right-of-way to the Sound.

"If I didn't know better," Thomas said, "I'd say it looks like Charlotte is sweating."

"And if I didn't know better," Charlotte said, "I'd say that Thomas is not. Another year of watching Dad do all the work?"

Thomas opened his mouth to reply, but John interjected. "You all worked tremendously hard, and I am grateful. The house has never looked better, so we can enjoy our last evening with our consciences as clean as the cottage."

"Bravo!" said Claire. "Who's up for a swim to the raft?"

"If it's a race, no," said Charlotte.

"It's not a race," said John, looking at his wife. "Just a leisurely family swim."

Thomas strode toward the water and then dived under its surface, followed by Helen and Pammy. Charlotte, who had piled her hair on top of her head and secured it with an elastic and several bobby pins, walked into the water and launched herself off the bottom in the direction of her siblings, keeping her head dry. The four Thompson children swam toward the raft, knowing their parents would be along soon. When John swam with his wife, which was just once or twice a summer, she waited for him.

Helen liked swimming with her sisters and brother because Thomas and Charlotte were too busy stroking toward the raft to pick on one another. Plus, swimming in the midst of a group of swimmers lowered what Helen called the Shark Odds. If she swam to the raft by herself, which she did at least three times a week during the summer, then she would be the target for the great white shark that had lost its way and swum into their quiet harbor in search of a snack. But if she swam with others, the shark might choose one of them instead of her to sate its voracious appetite. Thomas knew his youngest sister was unaccountably but most assuredly afraid of sharks and anything else that lurked beneath the surface, but he teased her about it only when the two of them were swimming alone.

When all the Thompsons reached the raft, they climbed the ladder to its surface and then all lay on their backs, allowing the sun to warm their bodies and their heart rates to return to normal. Thomas sat up. "Cannonball contest!" he said.

"Yeah, for you," said Charlotte, eyes closed. "The rest of us have moved past the cannonball stage in our lives."

"What cannonball stage?" said Thomas. "I don't think you even know how to do one."

Charlotte sat up and faced her brother. "Of course I know how to do a cannonball."

Thomas shook his head slowly. "I don't know about anyone else here, but I've never seen you do one. Helen, have you seen Charlotte do a cannonball?"

Helen looked at her brother and then at Charlotte. "I don't think so," she said. "But I'm quite sure she could!"

"I'm not so sure, Helen," said Thomas. "I mean, if she did a cannonball, she'd have to get her hair wet. And then what would Steve Johanson think of that?"

"Shut up, Thomas."

"I can do a cannonball," said Claire, standing.

With raised eyebrows, Thomas watched his mother walk to the diving board, stride down its length, spring off the end, and then draw her knees into her chest and tuck her head before landing in the water on the small of her back, the perfect location for maximum splash. When she surfaced, she was grinning. Thomas clapped and then, looking at Helen, said, "I do believe you come by the cannonball genetically, Helen Thompson."

"Who do you think taught her?" called Claire from the water.

"I was under the mistaken notion that I did," said Thomas. "Well done, Mother."

John Thompson stood next. "And do you know who taught your mother?"

"This is the strangest spectacle I've seen all summer," said Charlotte to Pammy.

John mimicked his wife's movements and landed just as she had, sending a fountain of water into the air.

"Who's next?" asked Thomas.

Pammy stood. "Can I do a can opener?"

"Absolutely." And it was perfectly executed, as was Helen's cannonball afterward. Thomas turned to Charlotte. "What do you say, dry top? Are you in or are you a wimp?"

"I don't have to prove anything to you," she said.

"Wimp would be the answer to that question then."

Charlotte stood, removed the elastic and pins from her hair, and then shook it out. She gave her brother a look and then ran the length of the diving board, springing off the end and into the air, where she completed a forward flip before cannonballing into the water. When she surfaced, everyone was clapping. Thomas, the lone Thompson still on the raft, walked down the board and jumped as hard as he could on the end. He whooped a yell into the air and landed perfectly, creating the highest splash of all. As they all swam back to shore, they talked about cannonball prowess. Thomas announced that the Thompson family could skunk any other family in the neighborhood. And even though John Thompson downplayed competition as much as his wife played it up, he had to agree.

They had lobster that night for dinner, an indulgence, an acknowledgement of their hard work. Everyone was unusually chatty, telling their best and worst moments of the summer and sharing stories that would be most appreciated by and humorous for family members. The children cleared the table after eating Claire's chocolate meringue pie, and then quickly did the dishes. Charlotte had the last date of the summer with Steve Johanson, and Thomas told Eddie that he'd hang with him at the wall after a game of old maid with Helen and Pammy.

Claire and John retreated to the porch, as usual. But Claire did not open her book when she sat down. She turned in her chair and looked at John. "I'm not ready to say good-bye to Thomas."

John took off his reading glasses and looked back at her. "I know. I'm not ready either. But he is."

Claire looked out through the screen at the sunset. "Are you sure?"

"Yes," said John. "He needs to move forward, Claire. We all will move forward too."

"Already I am thinking about next summer, when we will all be back here again as a family. Do you think it will happen? Will Thomas come back?"

John picked up his book. His thoughts drifted to the relationship Thomas had had with the young, divorced woman and her daughter. It had meant, John knew, more to Thomas than he had confided. Whether or not he would come back to the cottage next summer would be determined by how quickly his heart mended. "We'll see," John said.

CHAPTER 37

2004

Helen and Pammy were in the kitchen making potato salad and blueberry pies when Thomas pulled his Cadillac into the driveway. They quickly washed their hands and then rushed out the back door to see him emerging from the car and stretching his arms over his head. Helen looked at her watch. "I can't believe it," she said. "You're late!"

Thomas looked at his watch and smiled at his sister.

"Don't tell us you lingered over your fast-food lunch," said Pammy.

"No," said Thomas, hugging Helen and then Pammy. "The border was brutal this morning."

Barb got out of the car and approached her sisters-in-law. "And by brutal, he means that we had to wait fifteen minutes."

"I wait fifteen minutes for my Starbucks coffee in the morning," said Pammy, hugging Barb.

"How was the trip, really?" said Helen.

"Fine," said Barb. "We are so glad to be here. Sally and Peter have been talking about Todd and Ned for weeks."

"Are they here?" It was Peter, who had hopped out of the car, along with his sister, and was now standing next to his mother.

Helen bent over and hugged them both. "They are indeed," she said. "They told me to tell you that they would be done with their tennis match by four, and that they would love to go swimming right afterward."

With wide eyes, Peter turned to Barb. "Can we?" he said, shaking with excitement. "Can we go to the beach with Todd and Ned?"

"Of course," said Barb. She looked at her watch. "Let's bring our things into the house and unpack. By the time you've used the bathroom and are into your suits, your cousins will be back from the tennis court."

Thomas popped open the trunk and started to unload: duffel bags, plastic containers filled with baked goods, a woven basket filled with sand toys, a canvas bag with sunscreen and beach towels, and a box holding twelve bottles of wine. He then reached into the backseat for his briefcase and laptop.

"Wait a minute," said Helen, spying the computer. "This is supposed to be vacation."

"And it is," said Thomas. "But you can't expect me to stay for a week and not at least occasionally check my e-mail."

There was the confirmation. Helen had been hopeful that Thomas and his family would stay for a full week, but Thomas had not said so, until now. "Okay," she said, smiling at him. "But how about only very early in the morning when the day's activities have yet to begin?"

"Deal."

Helen grabbed a duffel bag and headed toward the cottage. "You and Barb are in your room, of course," she said. "We can talk about the kids later." Helen thought it would be fun if they slept on the porch with Todd and Ned, but she didn't want to say anything in front of Peter and Sally, in case Barb or Thomas had other ideas. Helen was so thrilled that they were staying at the house instead of the motel at the end of the beach road; she didn't want to make assumptions that might cause Thomas and Barb to second-guess their decision.

"Where is everyone?" asked Thomas, walking toward the house with the other three duffel bags in his hands. Pammy followed with the box of wine, while Barb and the kids brought the bags filled with beach accessories to the garage.

"Let's see," said Helen, opening the screen door to the kitchen. "We sent Charles to town for more charcoal. Charlotte is at the beach. And Pammy's friend, Roger, should be arriving any time now."

Thomas held the door with his back for Pammy, and, lifting an eyebrow, said, "Roger?"

Blushing, Pammy walked past her brother. "Yes, Roger."

"Helen and Charles's friend?" Thomas followed them into the kitchen.

"The very one," said Helen.

"Nice," said Thomas, nodding his head in approval. "Tell me about him."

Pammy set the wine down on the counter. "I went to Helen's for Christmas, and Helen had, conveniently, invited him. And we've been going back and forth ever since. He's a good man, Thomas. He's good to me."

"I can see that," said Thomas, bending down to kiss his sister on the cheek. "You're positively glowing."

"Ha!" said Helen. "See? I told you everyone can tell you're in love."

Thomas started toward the dining room. "And Charlotte?" he called.

"Alone," said Helen.

"Save that thought," he said. "I'll be down in a minute." At the top of the stairs, Thomas put the duffel bags in his room and then walked the several feet of hallway that separated him from his mother and father's room. Thomas could tell by the shoes on the floor and the magazines on the bedside table that Helen and Charles were sleeping there. He also noted the framed photograph of Claire and John Thompson, taken some thirty years ago at the picnic table when they were young and healthy, sitting on the bureau beside Helen's toiletries bag. He walked to it, studied it for a moment, and then picked it up.

Claire had passed away the previous October, peacefully, Helen said, in her sleep. Helen had known, the moment she let herself into the house the next morning. It was quiet, she told her brother and sisters on the phone later that day—the kind of quiet that fills the air before a freak storm or a car accident, a silence that portends dramatic change.

And Helen had wept tears of acknowledgment and sadness as she sat on the bed and looked at the woman who had taught her to be confident and strong, the wife of the man who had modeled compassion and wisdom. Thomas and his family, Pammy, and Charlotte had arrived in town the next day, to help Helen with funeral arrangements and to bury Claire's ashes next to John's. It was then that Thomas knew he would go to the cottage the next summer.

Thomas set the picture back down on the bureau and breathed in deeply, in an effort to extend the connection with his mother and to check his emotions. He turned around and found Helen standing in the hallway. He took a step toward her and wrapped his arms around her. "I haven't thought about her as much as I should," he said.

"You will this week," said Helen. "She's everywhere here."

Thomas held his sister at arm's length. "How are you doing?"

She looked up at him. "I miss her, Thomas. I spent part of every day of my life for the last few years with her. I still catch myself reaching for the phone to call her. Here, especially, it's hard to believe she's gone."

Thomas hugged Helen again. "You were good to her, Helen." He rested his head on top of hers.

"She was good to me."

"She was better than we all gave her credit for. It's amazing that it can take half a lifetime to recognize what's right in front of you."

"I'm so glad you're here, Thomas. I miss you, too."

"Not anymore," said Thomas, leading her into the hallway, transitioning to banter. "You'll see so much of me this week that you'll get sick of the sight of me."

"Not a chance."

When Todd and Ned got back from the tennis court, victorious again, and Charles got back from town, they all went to the beach to find Charlotte. Helen had forgotten to tell Thomas about Charlotte's chest, which was the first thing he remarked on when he saw her. "Wait," he said, approaching her chair. "Are we missing something?"

Charlotte stood and shook her head at Thomas. "That's what I love about you, Thomas," she said. "You always get right to the point." They hugged, as did Barb and Charlotte. "We are, indeed, missing something."

"What about that sand castle?" Barb asked her children.

Given permission, Sally and Peter, followed by Todd and Ned, each carrying one handle of the bag of toys, took off for the shallow end of the beach. Barb, Pammy, Helen, and Charles, then sat down in the beach chairs that Helen had set up that morning. Thomas sat next to Charlotte and looked at her expectantly. "Well?" he said.

"I got rid of them," Charlotte said. "I asked the same surgeon who put them in to take them out."

"Why?"

"You liked them?"

"No," he said. "But I thought you did."

"Yeah, well, I thought I did too. But I actually got tired of people—in the end women mostly—looking at my chest." Thomas laughed. "If you have a huge chest and you let the world see it," Charlotte said, "the only kind of guy you are going to attract is the kind of guy who likes a huge chest. And that kind of guy, from my experience, doesn't have a whole lot of other things going on. Great in the sack; not so great at meaningful conversation."

"So you're into meaningful conversation now?"

"I *live* for meaningful conversation," said Charlotte, laughing. "And seriously? All the women hated me for it."

"We hated her for it, didn't we, Pammy?" said Helen.

"Totally. But I did like her boyfriend." The three sisters all laughed at Pammy's reference to Daniel Bammer, who Charlotte hadn't thought about since she had broken up with him last summer.

"I think you look wonderful," said Barb, leaning forward in her chair to look at her sister-in-law.

"Well, thank you," said Charlotte. "I feel a lot better, too. God, they were heavy."

"What does Steve think?" asked Pammy, airing a question she might not have asked if she and Charlotte were alone.

"Are we talking about Steve Johanson?" asked Thomas. "Tell me you are dating Steve Johanson."

"I *see* Steve Johanson when he comes to California. And I will probably *see* him here this weekend. It's not a big deal," said Charlotte.

"Do you have meaningful conversation?" asked Thomas, grinning.

"Afterward," said Charlotte, smiling back at her brother, "yes."

Charles stood. "Who wants to go to the raft?"

"I do," said Barb, popping up from her chair. "Anyone else want to join us?"

"You go ahead," said Thomas. "The four of us will meet you out there."

As soon as Charles and Barb started their swim, Helen turned to her siblings and said, "Thank you for coming."

"Of course we're here," said Pammy. "Mom would be pleased."

"And God knows how we lived to please Mom," said Charlotte.

"Yeah, you especially," said Thomas, laughing.

"I did give her a hard time."

"That," said Helen, "is the understatement of the week."

"Hey, somebody had to give her a hard time. She gave us a hard enough time. Tell me you've all forgotten her antics."

"But weren't they done, at least some of the time, with good intentions?" said Helen.

"Clearly you, Helen, have forgotten," said Charlotte.

"Maybe Charlotte," said Thomas, "it's time for you to forget too."

Charlotte cocked her head. "Touché, big brother."

Helen couldn't remember the last time she had to put all three leaves in the dining room table. There were twelve of them altogether, counting Roger Shaw, Helen and Charles's friend and Pammy's new love interest, and Steve Johanson, who had arrived at his family cottage a day sooner than Charlotte expected and was very available for dinner with the Thompson family. They all gathered on the Thompson porch for cocktails and kid-friendly hors d'oeuvres, which thrilled Peter and Sally, who had never had French onion dip out of a package and potato chips or ginger ale mixed with cherry juice.

At the dinner table, Thomas sat at one end, in John's seat, and Helen sat at the other end, in Claire's seat. Before them sat the blue and white plates Claire had been so fond of, and various platters and bowls filled with spare ribs, barbequed chicken, potato salad, coleslaw, and baked beans. After they had said grace and before they started eating, Thomas stood and cleared his throat. "Life is filled with irony," he said, "and it is ironic that the two people who would most enjoy this feast, this gathering, are not here with us. However, they would not want us to be sad on this occasion, to mark their absence from our lives with woeful faces and downcast eyes—even though we all miss them, even those who sometimes aren't so sure," said Thomas, making eye contact with Charlotte. "Because John and Claire Thompson made their mark on us. And while the process wasn't always pleasant, it was usually instructional."

Charlotte chuckled, the only one who instantly realized that Thomas's comment was meant to be humorous as well as serious. "Oh yes," she said. "Mom was a teacher to the very end."

Thomas raised his glass to Charlotte and then lowered it. "Looking back, as we tend to do in the present, I understand more about parenting, about expectations, about yearnings, about love than I ever did. I think this is not just because I'm older. I think it's also because I experienced all these things growing up in this cottage. This is where you—Helen and Pammy and Charlotte—and I learned our life lessons, whether we appreciated them or not. And John and Claire Thompson certainly knew how to live life. Their legacy sits around this table—charged with carrying on in the brave and honorable ways that were laid out for us so many years ago." He lifted his glass again. "To John and Claire, our parents, our mentors, and our most fervent supporters. Tonight we honor you and, for the rest of our lives, we walk the path that you started, clearing it for those who follow us."

Pammy burst into tears. Charlotte, who was sitting next to her, wrapped her arm around her sister's shoulders.

"Well said, Thomas," said Helen. "Thank you all for coming to this place that floats in and out of our lives, but is never far from our minds. We are missing our mother and father tonight, but, with everyone here, I feel complete." Helen made eye contact with each one of her siblings and then lifted her fork. "Let's eat."

After dinner, Todd and Ned washed the dishes, assisted by Sally and Peter. And then everyone, even Charlotte, went out into the yard for a twilight game of hide-and-seek.

A READING GROUP GUIDE

THE SUMMER COTTAGE

Susan Kietzman

About This Guide

The suggested questions are included
to enhance your group's
reading of Susan Kietzman's
The Summer Cottage!

DISCUSSION QUESTIONS

1. When Helen arrives at the cottage, she can't wait to get to the beach. What does the beach mean to her?

2. Claire spent a good part of her early years competing in the water. How does her swim career affect her life afterward, outside of the pool?

3. Helen and Pammy are close as ten and thirteen-year-olds. What happens to their relationship as they become adults? Charlotte is not particularly close with either of her sisters. Is she close to anyone?

4. John Thompson and Claire Gaines are as seemingly different as winter from summer. What brings them together and how does their common interest affect their relationship?

5. Because Helen lives close to her parents, she falls into the role of Claire's caregiver after John dies. She is a good caregiver, but does she like it? Do we always like what we're good at?

6. Helen thinks she has effectively communicated Claire's medical issues to her siblings. Why have they not offered more help?

7. Why is Charlotte attracted to Rick Jones? What is her view of Daniel Bammer? Other men?

8. Helen sneaks out of the cottage at night several times the summer she is ten years old. Do Claire and John know this? And if they do, why do they allow it to continue?

9. Of all the men available to Pammy, she chooses her sister's boyfriend. What is Pammy's motivation in pursuing Daniel?

10. Why does Thomas fall so hard for Anna Santiago?

11. John Thompson is measured, the voice of reason in the Thompson family. What is Claire to her children? And what does she want them to learn from competition?

12. What do we learn about each Thompson from the Labor Day cannonball contest?

Three women, each facing an empty nest, come together to cheer and challenge one another in this insightful, poignant new novel from acclaimed author Susan Kietzman.

For years, Ellie, Alice, and Joan enjoyed a casual friendship while volunteering at their children's Connecticut high school. Now, with those children grown and gone to college, a local tragedy brings the three into contact again. But what begins as a catch-up lunch soon moves beyond small talk to the struggles of this next stage of life.

Joan Howard has spent twenty years of marriage doing what's expected of Howard women: shopping, dressing well, and keeping a beautiful home. Unfulfilled, her boredom and emptiness eventually find a secret outlet at the local casino. Meanwhile, Ellie's efforts to expand her accounting business lead to a new friendship that clashes with her family's traditional worldview. And Alice, feeling increasingly distant from her husband, and alienated from her once fit body, takes up running again. But a terrifying ordeal shatters her confidence and spurs a decision that will affect all three women in different ways.

Over the course of an eventful year, Ellie, Alice, and Joan will meet every other Wednesday to talk, plan—and find the freedom, and the courage, to redefine themselves.

Please turn the page for an exciting sneak peek of Susan Kietzman's newest novel

EVERY OTHER WEDNESDAY

coming soon wherever print and e-books are sold!

CHAPTER 1

The calendar on the mustard colored wall of her kitchen confirmed what Alice Stone already knew; it had been two months since her youngest daughter left for college, and Alice was still baking cookies as if Linda were still at home. Every week, she baked two or three dozen, even though her husband, Dave, was running more and eating less, and even though Linda had long ago told her mother that teenage girls didn't eat cookies. It was a habit, this baking, that Alice had initiated when her three girls were young and looking for a snack when they got home from school. And it kept Alice busy for a couple hours, from the mixing of the ingredients she kept stocked in her cupboards to the baking of the dough. Baking cookies was a productive way to pass time, Alice had convinced herself, better than sitting on the couch and flipping through a magazine. And being productive at home was a good enough reason to be at home, to not get a job.

In some ways, Alice did want to work. Having a job would give her something to do, a new purpose in life, now that her girls were out of the house. And on some days, she longed for something to fill and challenge her brain, not to mention the extra money that Dave mentioned regularly. He certainly wanted her to work, so she could help with the "incredible expense of putting three kids through college"—although Hilary had just graduated and Cathy had been out of school for three years—something Alice was well aware of since she paid the bills. But, in terms of getting a job, she knew a lot more about what she didn't want to do than what she wanted to do. She didn't want to work at Fast Pace, the running store she and Dave had opened twenty-eight years ago when they had moved back to Connecticut, and when she was running as many miles in a week as Dave. And she didn't want to perform menial labor, though she had to admit that what she had been doing as a stay-at-home mom, the grocery shopping, meal preparation, driving kids to lessons and school events, and running errands all fit squarely into that category. Working women liked to show their empathy by praising the honorable profession of mothers dressed in sweats instead of suits, by comparing the skill sets of the cookie baking, tantrum thwarting, coupon clipping moms to those of the team building, forward thinking, solution oriented corporate ladder climbers, but women at home knew better. If they were paid for what they did, it would be minimum wage. This had been okay with Alice, because, in addition to performing banal tasks, she had been caring for her girls. But if she tried to join the workforce now, she would be qualified for and have nothing but boring, inconsequential labor to define her days.

Dave told her this was crazy talk; she could do any number of things. She was a college graduate, with a degree in psychology that could be useful in many professions, including, he had said over the years, helping runners find the right gear for their style and activity level. But lately, since they had been talking about Alice working again, Dave hadn't encouraged her to join the team at Fast Pace. Perhaps he, like the rest of the working world, knew that someone who had been out of touch for as long as Alice had been making cookies would have trouble transitioning into the frenzied, twenty-four-hour, global, competitive employment arena.

The timer buzzed, and Alice pulled a sheet of peanut butter cookies out of the oven.

The sole thing Alice liked about the idea of returning to Fast Pace was the incentive it would give her to start running again. She exercised four or five days a week at the YMCA in town, but she hadn't run hard in several years and knew how painful it would be to push her fifty-five-year-old legs to move, as they once had, at a seven-minute-mile pace. She'd have to start at a ten- or eleven-minute mile. She might even have to settle for a twelve-minute mile if she wanted to run more than three. And at that speed, she might as well join the mall walkers. Alice shook her head at the thought.

Alice's body was still thin and toned; she went to the Y to work out more than to socialize. At five foot, five inches, she weighed one hundred and twenty-five pounds, which was what she had weighed in college. She could pull off wearing clothes meant for younger women, though she admitted to herself that she chose the popular, ubiquitous, oversized tops just as much to hide the loose skin around her abdomen as she did to be current. And she kept her blond hair long, down to the middle of her back, which helped her feel youthful and relevant. But looking like a runner and being a runner had nothing in common. And if Alice were going to actually be a runner again, she would have to train like she had in college. Would Dave run with her?

The clock in the hallway struck the hour, and Alice reached for the remote control to the Bose sound system that sat on top of the fridge. NPR was good company in the morning, giving Alice the news she needed to feel informed and the human interest stories that expanded her perspective. Her mind wandered during the news about the Middle East. Alice wanted to care more about events there, but her doing something that would matter to the Afghans, Syrians, Iraqis, or Somalians would look like what, exactly? She was making a mental list of her errands for the day when her thought process stopped. ". . . Shooting at William Chester High School in Southwood, Connecticut, this morning." Alice grabbed the remote and rapidly pushed the up arrow button to increase the volume. ". . . Two confirmed dead in an apparent murder-suicide. Police have indicated that the shooting appears to have been targeted rather than random and that the students at William Chester are not in immediate danger. Still, school officials have canceled classes for the remainder of the day and are in the process of sending students home. The names of the deceased are being held until family members can be notified."

The timer buzzed, and Alice, her head heavy with the weight of the news, moved to the oven. She set the sheet of hot cookies on the countertop and then picked up her phone to text Linda. Less than six months ago, William Chester had been Linda's school—and Hilary's and Cathy's before that. Less than six months ago, Linda would have been in the hallways where this shooting occurred.

Did u hear about the shooting at Chester?

OMG—yes! Emmanuel Sanchez is dead! James Shulz shot him and shot himself!

James Shulz?

From drama—the sound tech. Never talked to anybody. Had a huge crush on Nanette Benoit. Emmanuel's girlfriend

Oh no!

I gotta go—too much going on right now. I'll call later

Alice put her phone down and reached for the spatula. She removed the cookies from the sheet, all the while trying to picture James Shulz in her head. Nothing came. She had no memory of him, even though Linda had been involved in the drama club since her freshman year. Alice did, however, clearly remember Emmanuel Sanchez, a star football player and scholar who had been in the newspaper just last week, smiling in a photo with a caption about recruitment offers he had received from prestigious colleges all over the country. Alice pulled a chair out from the kitchen table and sat for the first time that morning. She picked up her phone again and called Dave. He rarely answered his cell phone when he was at work, but she wanted to hear his voice.

CHAPTER 2

Joan Howard sat in an upholstered chair in the corner of her family room, her slippered feet on the matching ottoman, reading the newspaper. This was how she typically started her weekdays, or rather, how she had started them for a couple months now. She and her husband, Stephen, had moved Liz, the younger of their two daughters, into her college dorm in August, and Joan's mornings had been different, had been like this, ever since. She and Stephen had talked about what it would look like to live in a vacated nest, but they had stayed away from how it would actually feel. Their older daughter, Cassie, had been gone from the house for seven years now, graduating from college and settling into a communications job in Boston and into a rent controlled apartment with her boyfriend. Her departure from the house had been less disruptive for Joan, who still had Liz at home to nurture and protect. But now that Liz was gone, so was Joan's focus, as well as any possible reason for Joan to be sitting in a chair at eight in the morning with a cup of coffee on a nearby coaster. But here she was, skimming the headlines and glancing at the muted local news on the television instead of sipping from a travel mug on her way to another meaningful day at a fulfilling job.

Joan put the newspaper aside and got up out of the chair. She walked her cup to the kitchen, where she filled it for the third time, aware now of the slight buzz behind her eyes and at the base of her skull, thankful for chemical stimulation. She looked out the window over her kitchen sink to the deck and, beyond that, to the yard. The newspaper indicated it would be sunny and warm again today; perhaps she could rake some leaves before her two o'clock meeting of the Southwood Cancer Society. The SCS was one of several organizations Joan belonged to—but even though she still believed in the mission, the intention to do good, she had lately been restless, with her desire to attend meetings and events waning. Was this, too, a result of Liz's departure?

Joan looked at her watch. It was 8:20 a.m. Liz, if she were still living at home instead of at college, would be sitting in her first period class at William Chester High School. And Joan, wearing yoga pants that never made it to a studio, might be making Liz's bed or doing her laundry. Stephen had admonished Joan for "prolonging this dependency," and Joan understood his point. But she liked taking care of the little things for her daughters when they were home while she increasingly let them manage the big things. It beat exercising.

Joan had never been a particularly athletic person, finding skinny people's attraction to sweating, heavy breathing, and routine exhaustion mysterious. She liked to say that life was hard enough without the added misery of exercise. The only thing she liked about exercise was the soft clothing that most mornings tightly blanketed her body. She was only fifteen or so pounds overweight, according to her doctor, but felt larger due to today's continued cultural worship of slim, wrinkle-free women. At fifty-two, Joan had a limited number of options for eradicating the wrinkles around her eyes, but she could certainly lose weight. She dieted, along with, it seemed, every other member of her gender over the age of thirteen, but she was not particularly dedicated, and therefore not particularly successful. She liked fruits and vegetables well enough, but she liked meat and cheese and bread better. And even though her mother-in-law, Sandi, had passed along her best dieting secrets to Joan over the course of Joan's thirty-year marriage to Stephen, Joan liked to eat. Plus, Southwood needed a few chubby women to balance out the troops of fit baby boomers who jogged on the streets and lifted weights at the Y.

This was not to say Joan didn't have style. She dressed beautifully, with an especially good eye for color and accessories. Everything she wore complemented her black, chin-length bob, deep blue eyes, and smooth, blemish free skin, and she was often told how good she looked. Because she dressed so well, people didn't notice right away that she was slightly overweight. Only occasionally would someone inclined to say such things tell her that she carried her weight well. Was that a compliment?

It didn't matter. Stephen liked the way she looked. He was like her, in that he didn't exercise regularly. He went on what Joan called fitness kicks, as she did. But wherever they took place—in the pool at the Y, on a bike around town, along Southwood's running trails—these resolutions didn't last long. Stephen found his energy at the office, and Joan had always been able to recharge through her kids, and, to be honest (in spite of how it sounded), through her weekly manicures at Brenda's. But her battery had been depleted since Liz had left the house, and Joan knew that she needed more than a closet full of clothes and polished nails to move forward in life.

Joan finished reading the first section of the paper and dropped it to the floor. As she unfolded the regional section, she glanced up at the television and saw the words SHOOTING AT WILLIAM CHESTER HIGH SCHOOL in a banner at the bottom of the screen. She reached for the remote and turned on the volume. A Channel 10 news team reporter was standing in front of the main entrance, talking with a student. "No one really knew James," the student said. "He was quiet. He kept to himself. But until today, I would never have thought of him as a violent person, as someone who would take the life of another student."

"And tell us about that other student," the reporter prompted.

"Emmanuel? It's hard to know where to start. He was the star of our football team; everybody knows that. But he was a lot more than that, you know? He was a really nice guy who talked to everybody. He could have been really stuck up because he was such a talented athlete and a smart guy. But he was nice to everybody."

The young man's eyes started to fill with water. He blinked several times in an unsuccessful effort to clear them. The reporter put her hand on his shoulder.

"Thank you," she said. "Thank you for talking to us at this very difficult time."

"It's okay," said the student as he turned away from the reporter and walked out of the camera shot.

"To sum up what we know already, James Shulz, a senior here at William Chester High School, shot and killed fellow student, Emmanuel Sanchez, a Southwood scholar and gifted football player, and then turned the gun on himself. The police have indicated they think this was a premeditated, isolated incident and that the other members of the student body here at the high school are not in immediate danger. Principal Sean Greeley has canceled classes for the remainder of the day, and the students were instructed to go home. As you can see behind me, the buses are pulling out of the main parking lot, transporting the students home to their families. Stay tuned for additional coverage as details become available."

Joan pushed the mute button on the remote and sat back in the chair. She remembered James Shulz as the student had described him, a shy, very quiet kid. But she also remembered his incredible technical abilities. Liz had been very involved with the drama department and had talked about James. Like many of the department participants, Liz hadn't known his last name, but she did know he was the one who routinely coaxed clear and consistent voices and music from aging microphones and an outdated audio system. He was the one who made everyone sound better than they actually did. All of the dramathletes, the moniker the head of the department had given her charges in an attempt at boosting their social status as well as enticing the booster club to contribute more money to her program, respected James. But none of them hung out with him between productions. He was exactly what so often is said about someone who does what he did—a loner.

The phone rang; it was Liz. When Joan answered the call, all she could hear on the other end was her daughter sobbing.

CHAPTER 3

This same morning, Ellie Fagen was sitting at her kitchen table, with her laptop open in front of her and a short stack of spreadsheets to the left of the computer. Today was the day to do something to rev up her bookkeeping business. Today was the day to find a new client. Today was the day to start making enough money so her husband, Chris, would stop talking about her getting another job—a real job is what he meant but didn't say, a job that would handsomely supplement his gym teacher's salary, a job that would help defray the cost of sending their younger son, Tim, to NYU. Ellie had been saying this to herself, giving herself a pep talk just about every day since Tim had packed all his belongings into his grandmother's hand-me-down Passat wagon and driven into New York City to start his freshman year in college, two months ago. In fact, if she were going to be honest about it, Ellie had been talking to herself about this very topic since her older son, Brandon, had driven himself and all his stuff eleven hundred miles from Connecticut to Northern Michigan University two years ago.

She knew why she was, as Chris said, dragging her feet. And she was resolved to work on this troublesome aspect of her personality—this tendency to think and talk about what she wanted in life, only to do nothing about it, zero follow-up. And while it was natural to talk about change rather than take the soul stretching steps to accomplish it, Ellie was particularly adept at procrastination, especially when it came to self-promotion, which was exactly what she had to do to find new clients. Selling herself was not a part of her makeup, her DNA, as someone on a television show about cops or doctors would say. Ellie had confidence in her ability to accurately and efficiently manage financial accounts; she simply had trouble telling people this, thinking it boastful and distasteful to do so. Wouldn't it be more convincing, more sincere to get promotion from others? Chris told her that no matter how good she was, her few clients had a multitude of things to think about rather than how they could help grow Ellie's bookkeeping business. He had told her so this morning, while they were eating toast with peanut butter, while he was looking at her over the top of his reading glasses. It was a look she had seen before, a look that said: *Are we really having this conversation? Again?*

Ellie was often on the receiving end of this look, whether it emanated from her husband, her father, her mother, or any combination of her six older brothers. In her excuse-making moments, Ellie blamed her large family for her inability to take charge, to do whatever she needed to do, because her brothers had, growing up, made decisions for her. If she had hesitated when asked a question, one of them had answered for her. If she had approached one of them with a choice she was facing, that one had chosen for her. And while her mother had taught Ellie to "stand on her own two feet," her brothers had, often without being asked, held her up by her elbows. Maybe this was why her *today is the day* resolutions often dissolved. Was she capable of changing her ways, of changing her life?

Ellie pushed back from the table and stood. She needed a walk to make sense of the jumble of thoughts and ideas in her head. She walked five miles a day, six days a week, often with her dog, but sometimes not. Today, she would go by herself, leaving the default two-mile loop with Buffy for Chris when he got home from school. She coated her lips for the second time that morning with the tube of balm she had in the pocket of her sweatpants and then strode to the back hall closet for sneakers, a windbreaker, and sunglasses.

She paused at the mirror hanging on the wall next to the back door and saw her mother's light green eyes looking back at her. Brigid Kilcullen hadn't hesitated one moment in her entire life—except, she liked to say at family gatherings, for a full minute after Ellie's father, Patrick, had asked her to marry him. Why couldn't Ellie be more like her mother? She took a coated elastic from her pocket and used it to put her barely long enough, wavy blond hair into a ponytail. She had been growing it since Tim left the house in an effort, and a very small one at that, at embracing change.

After a sixty-eight-minute walk, Ellie pushed through the back door. She filled a glass with water and returned to her computer. It was now close to nine. She told herself she would not get out of the chair again until she had a firm plan in place. But before she started in earnest, she decided to check the news. And as soon as she clicked on the bookmarked page for the local newspaper, she saw the headline about the shooting at the high school.

> Southwood—High school students, teachers, and administrators are reeling from the shooting at William Chester this morning that took the life of two seniors. The shooter, James Shulz, a barely known sound technician for the drama department, walked into a classroom during first period and shot Emmanuel Sanchez, a scholarly athlete, in the chest, and then turned the gun on himself. Physics teacher Bill Sanders said he led the students into the hall before returning to the classroom to check the condition of the boys.
>
> "Both of them were dead—I think instantly," Sanders said. "There was no opportunity for CPR or other life-saving measures. This is a horrible, horrible situation that took all of us by surprise."
>
> Principal Sean Greeley used the same word: *surprise*. There has been no violence at the school in his twenty-year tenure, he said. In fact, he and other administrators had recently made the decision against installing metal detectors at the main entrance or ramping up security, in spite of shooting events elsewhere in

> the country, and in spite of what happened in Newtown. Greeley said that, "Until today, danger dwelled elsewhere. We never saw this coming. We never thought this could happen in our small, coastal town in Connecticut." Greeley canceled classes for the remainder of the day—and potentially the rest of the week—and indicated counselors would be available to students upon their return.
>
> Several students interviewed who knew James Shulz were less surprised. They called him a "technical genius," but an "absolutely introverted outsider." One student described Shulz in the way other young men who commit violent acts are described: "He was always alone." Nanette Benoit, Emmanuel Sanchez's girlfriend, who was sitting next to him in class at the time of the incident, declined an interview, but did say, "I don't know why he did this. James was not a bad person."
>
> Principal Greeley, who said he was "heartbroken" over this incident, indicated he would send an e-mail to parents before the end of the day with more information.

Ellie got out of her chair and ran up the stairs to her bedroom for her cell phone, which was charging on the table next to her bed. There was a missed call from Chris and then a text message that he was on his way home. Phone in hand, Ellie ran back down the stairs and into the kitchen just as Chris was coming through the back door. "Do you know?" he said, his face bearing the creased, pained expression of someone who is digesting sadness and shock.

"Yes," she said, walking to him, tears forming in her eyes. He wrapped his long arms around her and held her tightly.

Chapter 4

Alice pulled her green Subaru Forester into the high school parking lot only to find it full. She drove up and down the rows hoping to finding a space that another driver hadn't seen, even though she already knew the futility of this exercise at an event of such magnitude. If she hadn't spent ten minutes posting pictures of her latest batch of chocolate chocolate-chip cookies to her Facebook account, she would be parked and walking toward the football field, where the candlelight vigil for Emmanuel Sanchez had just started. She drove her car back out onto the main road, where vehicles lined both sides, and managed to squeeze in between two others. After she shimmied herself out of the driver's side door, hemmed in by a large rock, she jogged toward the back of the school, now thinking it was probably too late to find a seat in the bleachers.

The field was ablaze with lights. As Alice got closer, she could hear Principal Sean Greeley's voice over the public address system. ". . . Senseless tragedy. Our presence here tonight cannot right the wrong. It cannot bring back Emmanuel Sanchez. But we can honor and cherish his memory. Our senior class has been handing out candles. If you don't yet have one, look for a student in a lime green T-shirt. These students will also light your candles. . . ." Breathing hard from running, Alice slowed her pace when she reached the fence surrounding the field. She now had visual confirmation that the bleachers, like the parking lot, were full to capacity, meaning her best option would be to stand in the end zone with the other latecomers. As soon as she settled into a space, she was handed a candle by a girl who had been crying, her tears having smeared the letters *E* and *S* grease painted onto her cheeks. Alice closed her eyes in an effort to calm her heart and mind, both racing from what had been a hectic yet unfulfilling day of errand running and domestic chores, and to focus on the ceremony. She had not taken the time that day to register its import. Just as she opened her eyes, the overhead lights were cut off, leaving the assemblage in candlelit darkness.

"Alice?"

Alice looked to her right and saw Joan Howard, Liz's mom, a fellow drama parent. Liz and Alice's daughter, Linda, had been in three productions together. And Alice and Joan had helped with fundraising, set construction, and pasta dinners before performances. "Hi, Joan," said Alice in a whisper, and then she asked the rote question that shouldn't be asked on days like this one. "How are you?"

"I've been better," said Joan, keeping her voice volume low as well. "Can you believe this? Can you believe this has really happened, and we are all standing on the artificial turf that Emmanuel should be running on this weekend?"

Alice shook her head. "No," she said. "I'm in shock, actually. I'm having trouble processing this entire situation."

"A moment of silence, please." It was Sean Greeley again, holding his candle aloft and bowing his head. Alice mimicked his stance for a moment and then opened her eyes and glanced over at Joan, who was rubbing her temple with the index and middle fingers of her left hand. Alice moved closer and put her arm around Joan's shoulder. Aside from Joan's quick intake of air, the stadium and its occupants were still; no one coughed, sneezed, spoke, moved. Alice conjured up an image of Emmanuel in her mind: a magazine cover, good looking boy, whose family had moved from Florida two or three years ago. Her daughter, Linda, had thought he was dreamy. And now he was dead. Alice didn't blame James Shulz as much as she blamed his mother, Kelly. What kind of parent doesn't lock up her guns?

Several minutes later the vigil was over. Principal Greeley asked that they all leave the field in a respectful manner and keep the Sanchez family in their prayers. Alice and Joan slowly made their way with the crowd back to the main parking lot. They stopped at Joan's car, parked in the final space in the last row.

"Putting all this aside for a moment, how are you really?" asked Alice. "How is Liz?"

Joan flashed a quick smile. "I'm good. And Liz seems to like Williams. Her roommate is from New York City, which Liz thinks is the coolest thing ever. I'm not sure she realized that some people actually grow up in Manhattan. How about Linda? Does she like UConn?"

"Loves it," said Alice. "My cell phone is uncharacteristically quiet. When she does call me, it's usually when she's walking to class and has six minutes to talk."

"Clever girl," said Joan.

"Hey, Alice. Hi, Joan." It was Ellie Fagen, Tim's mother. Tim had also been in the drama club and was friendly with Liz and Linda. Ellie, like Alice and Joan, had pitched in, with cast dinners and mural painting. Tim had played Henry Higgins in *My Fair Lady* and was now at NYU studying music and theater. The head of the Chester drama department, along with anyone who had ever heard Tim sing, thought he was bound for stardom. Ellie's Honda Fit was parked two cars away from Joan's car. Ellie walked past it to join Alice and Joan.

"Hi, Ellie," said Alice. "Tough night."

"Yeah," said Ellie. "Nice attendance, though. Sean was good."

"He was," said Joan. "He can be such a blabbermouth."

Ellie smiled. "Not tonight."

"Thank God," said Alice. "How's Tim doing?"

"Great," she said. "He absolutely loves New York."

"Good," said Joan, "because he'll be living there when he's appearing on Broadway."

"Well . . ."

"Well, nothing, Ellie," said Alice. "Your kid is talented."

"Thank you."

Joan opened her car door. "I'm going to run," she said. "What are you two up to tomorrow?"

"The usual," said Alice. "Nothing. I'm still trying to figure out this empty nest thing."

"I've got to balance some accounts in the morning," said Ellie. "And then I'm free."

"Good," said Joan. "Let's meet for lunch at noon at High Tide."

"I'm in," said Alice, backing away from Joan's car.

"Me too," said Ellie.

"See you then," said Joan. She sat down in the driver's seat and started the car. Before any of them had time to wonder about the invitation, discussed among women whose only social interactions had occurred when helping with drama productions, Joan shut the car door, pulled out of the parking space, and drove away.